In a Heartbeat

In a Heartbeat

Eric Stone

LYFORD
B o o k s

For Kate, whose love has sustained me.

Copyright © 1996 by Eric Stone

LYFORD Books
Published by Presidio Press
505 B San Marin Dr., Suite 300
Novato, CA 94945-1340

Library of Congress Cataloging-in-Publication Data

Stone, Eric.
  In a heartbeat : a thriller / by Eric Stone.
      p.   cm.
  ISBN: 0-89141-590-4
  I. Title.
  PS3569.T633315   1996
  813'.54—dc20   96-3587
                                  CIP

Printed in the United States of America

Acknowledgments

The author would like to acknowledge the many people who contributed to this book. Special thanks to former Metropolitan Police Department Chief Isaac Fulwood for giving me permission to ride with his homicide detectives; to Lt. Jim Boteler, homicide; Lt. Charles Bailey, Mobile Crime; and the many fine homicide dectives who accepted my presence and revealed something of their lives and job. These men and women consistently do excellent work under the most trying conditions.

Thanks to Barbara Haar, of the Montgomery County public libraries, for giving me a place to research and write, and to Kitty Martin, who allowed me to use her summer retreat "Ledges" to edit this book. Three fine writers—Sara King, Judy Oppenheimer, and Carolyn Thorman—taught and encouraged me. Three others—Andrea Patterson, Richard Sheres, and Jessie Thorpe—provided important feedback on my manuscript.

The belief and love of several people made this book possible. The late Sidney Wise—professor, sage, friend, and mentor to so many—told me I could do this. My wife and kids put up with many projects delayed and provided the love and moral support that fueled my efforts. My brother Mike encouraged me and provided useful comments on my manuscript. Many friends chose not to laugh at me when I said I was writing a novel. Finally, my agent Tom Epley, and editor E. J. McCarthy, had faith in me and provided valuable editorial assistance and friendship.

Book One

1

John Carnes felt good. It was a bad omen. Usually, a mood this good presaged a triple homicide, an attack on a schoolyard, or, at the very least, a presidential-assassination attempt. A small cluster of detectives from Carnes' squad sat at wood-laminate-topped metal desks under a Washington Redskins calendar.

"Weekend wasn't long enough," said Pete Rodriguez, who sat at the desk facing Carnes. Rodriguez was a middle-aged man with salt and pepper hair and the quiet dignity of a character from a Gabriel Garcia Marquez novel. Since Carnes joined homicide five years earlier, Rodriguez had been his partner.

"True. But at least I got Avery to the zoo," Carnes said.

"She have a good time?" Rodriguez' voice rose and fell with a Latin rhythm.

"Yeah." It had been one of those sparkling father-daughter days. A rarity. Usually, the ghost of Carnes' ex-wife, Caroline, haunted them. This time, a mystical combination of hot dogs, good weather, and playful primates had banished her from their thoughts. At least for a few hours. "When you're seven years old, everything's still fresh and fun," said Carnes. He wondered if it was true. "Everything's a mystery at that age."

"You understand life better now?"

"Good point." Carnes shrugged. "Sometimes it's better not to."

"That's for sure," Sergeant Bryant said, walking down the aisle toward them. He waved a slip of yellow paper. "You guys are up. Don't you have your radio on?"

Carnes shook his head. "Christ, it's early in the morning. I was in a good mood too."

"Well, here's your mood adjuster." Bryant held out the paper.

Carnes liked Bryant. He was a beefy ex-all-Met football and basketball player who grew up in Anacostia. He joined the force when he came home from Vietnam. When he started his career in a Seventh District scout car, his playground contacts were a major asset. Bryant had a sharp ear and a way with people. Over the last twenty years, those traits helped him solve more than his share of crimes. Now, his monkish fringe of kinky-black hair was flecked with snow, and he was responsible for a whole homicide squad. Although Bryant seemed easygoing, his squad cleared more cases than any of the others. Carnes thought it was a small victory for common sense and loyalty in a department of ass-covering bureaucrats.

Carnes looked at the slip of paper. He whistled. An upper Northwest D.C. address. Wisconsin Avenue. That was different. "Whatta we have?"

"Sounds bad," Bryant said. "Employer called the district—hadn't heard from the victim. Concerned. Uniform went to the apartment. Super let him in. Found the body. I talked to the guy—sounded shook. Said it was pretty nasty. Mobile crime and the medical examiner are on the way." Bryant nodded at Carnes. "Pretty boy, you're primary on this one. You guys need to get moving. I got a trial this morning. Most of the shift's already at court or at 555 Fourth Street in conferences with the U.S. Attorney." Bryant showed his teeth in a wry smile. "Hope you can handle this without us."

"Shit, Sarge," Carnes said, "don't know if we can."

Bryant gave him a fatherly pat on the shoulder. "Do your best, son." The detectives within earshot guffawed.

Carnes liked not having an entire squad and half the criminal investigation division's bosses crawling all over the scene. A typical murder drew a squad or two from homicide, detectives and uniformed officers from the local district, and technicians from mobile crime and the medical examiner's office. If a shooting involved a policeman, half the department brass also turned out. Although the manpower was useful for crowd control and witness canvasing, too often they tromped over evidence, asked distracting questions, and created confusion.

Carnes glanced at Rodriguez. "OK, lover. Let's go."

Carnes sped up Massachusetts Avenue. The warm air rushed through the windows, drowning out the rumblings from the radio as they raced through embassy row.

"What's the hurry?" asked Rodriguez.

"You heard the sarge. He said to get moving."

"She's dead," said Rodriguez. "She ain't going anywhere."

"I'm dedicated," Carnes replied.

"Speaking of dedicated, who's the lady I saw you dedicating your time to Friday night at the FOP?" Rodriguez asked.

Carnes pictured the young blond he'd met at the Fraternal Order of Police club. Sweet smile, direct eyes, long blond hair. What the hell was her name? Didn't have that much to drink. He felt depressed. He couldn't even remember her name. Concentrate. An image of W. C. Fields. My little chickadee. No, not chickadee. "Robin."

"You're robbin' the cradle with that one."

"Jealous?" Carnes was surprised by the edge in his voice.

"Hey, I'd need hormone injections to keep up with you," Rodriguez grumbled. "Couldn't have done it when I was thirty."

"Thirty-two." Carnes turned onto Wisconsin Avenue. Half a block up, he saw the pack of police vehicles. Carnes put on his flasher, made a U-turn, and parked behind the mobile crime van. The victim's apartment was in a five-story stone building across from Washington Cathedral. From the entrance, Carnes could see the gray Gothic spires of the cathedral through the trees. His watch read 9:47. A sign by the front door offered apartments for rent and proclaimed "secure building." A bank of push buttons for the apartments allowed a visitor to ring different residents until someone buzzed him or her in. "See that?"

"Yeah," Rodriguez said. "So much for truth in advertising."

The sidewalk was crowded with gawkers, blue-haired ladies, shaggy students, a pregnant woman. Murders drew people like lights drew insects. Nothing fascinated people more than proximity to a dead body. Carnes caught snippets. "What happened?" "Such a tragedy." "So young." "Who died?" A woman in curlers recorded their arrival with a video camera.

What attracted them? Curiosity about their own destiny? Carnes had seen more dead bodies than he could remember and they hadn't revealed to him any answers to the mysteries of the universe. Maybe it was simpler than that. Confronting death made people exult in their own banal lives.

Carnes examined the crowd for anyone who seemed out of place. Rodriguez moved his head slightly from side to side. No obvious mouth-foamers. They climbed the stairs. Rodriguez was puffing slightly by the time they passed a small crowd in the hall outside the victim's apartment.

"Need to start working out," said Carnes.

"Sure. I love to torture myself."

"You're a cop," Carnes reminded him.

"Good point."

A uniformed officer whose name tag read "Webster" greeted them at the apartment door. Carnes motioned to the crowd. "Get names and addresses of the rubberneckers."

"Yes, sir."

Several people were inside the apartment. "Who's here?" Carnes asked Webster.

"Crime team, new kid from the medical examiner's office. They've done the photos. Have a call in for the wagon. Detectives from the local district are canvasing the neighborhood. You're late." Webster managed a rueful grin.

"Shit," said Carnes. "Doesn't anyone in the department do anything right? Nobody's to touch anything until we get here." He rolled his eyes at Rodriguez. "Anyone follow procedures anymore?"

"Maybe they have plans for brunch," Rodriguez said.

A slaughterhouse odor overpowered the usual apartment smell of last night's cooking, disinfectant, and natural gas. The apartment was an efficiency. To their immediate left was a kitchen with pine cabinets and almond appliances. A Formica butcher-block breakfast bar with two stools divided the kitchen from the sleeping area.

A flash of light from the technician's camera drew Carnes' eyes into the sleeping area. She lay on the bed, body frozen awkwardly on her stomach, hands tied behind her, face toward what Carnes guessed was the closet door. Clothing lay around her on the bed and floor. Carnes shook his head in disgust.

Before he had left for work this morning he looked in on Avery. She lay across her bed, knee drawn up, arm flung over the stuffed dog she'd named Ro Ro when she was too young to say Rover. He had brushed back her hair and kissed her forehead. "Someone's daughter," Carnes said.

"Yeah." Rodriguez' face was grim. His own daughter was about the same age as the victim.

To the left of the bed, a door opened into a bathroom. The apartment was furnished in early careerist style: mismatched love seat, ancient stuffed chair, double bed with pink headboard and finials. A cheap Parsons table with a ceramic lamp, phone, and clock radio sat next to the bed. But for the touches Caroline had added before she left, Carnes' town house was decorated in the same style.

The sergeant in charge of the crime-scene team was an old-timer named Charlie Wingate. With quick, efficient commands, Wingate directed one of the younger officers to take photos. Carnes caught his eye. He came over.

Wingate looked like a World War II general. A bristling crew cut framed his lumpy face. He hitched up his pants over his bulging middle. "Sorry, dispatch must've fucked up. We killed half an hour and then figured we better get to work. Haven't touched anything. Just doing the photos."

"And tromping on any evidence," said Carnes.

Wingate glared. "What do you have a hard-on about? I've been doing these investigations since you were in diapers. I don't tromp on anything."

Rodriguez gave Carnes a warning look, then smiled at Wingate. "I'm sure you don't, Charlie."

"Yeah, right!" Carnes grunted. In a street shooting, the only evidence was usually the spent shell casings and bullets. In an indoor murder, they were more likely to find physical evidence and they needed to be careful to preserve it. A hair, fiber, tobacco ash, partial fingerprint, or something just slightly out of place might—if it survived—serve as a beacon illuminating the murderer.

They walked over to the bed. The naked woman had uneven, wavy brown hair. "Someone chopped off clumps of her hair," said Carnes.

"Or she needed a new hairdresser," commented Wingate.

A blouse bound her arms behind her. Bloodshot eyes stared into infinity. Something was stuffed in her mouth. A pair of pantyhose was knotted around her neck. Carnes took a closer look—a simple granny knot. In life, she must have been attractive: rounded in the right places, slim waist, good muscle tone. Now, she was a slightly spoiled piece of meat.

The investigator from the medical examiner's office hovered near the apartment door. "Come here," Carnes said to him. Carnes introduced himself and Rodriguez.

"Jim Kelly." The young man's freckled face looked pale.

"This your first one, son?" asked Rodriguez.

Kelly stuck a finger in his ear and pumped it in and out. "First woman.

Guess so. At least, without a toe tag. I've done a couple of street shootings."

"You'll get used to it," said Carnes, "—very." He pulled a pair of latex surgical gloves out of his pocket and drew them on. Then he turned toward Wingate, who was directing the photographer. "Have enough pictures?"

"Yeah."

"Let's get to work," Carnes said. Kelly and Rodriguez pulled on gloves. "Mid-twenties?" Carnes asked.

Rodriguez nodded.

Kelly picked up an arm and then a leg. "Well"—he could have been dictating into a cassette machine—"skin cool to the touch. Mild rigor. Dead one and a half, two days, I'd guess. Rigor mortis usually disappears after forty-eight hours. This place is nice and cool or it wouldn't be very pleasant."

"It's not exactly a perfumery," Carnes said.

"Of course, there's a downside," Kelly said. "Flies could have told us how long the corpse was here." His eyes lit up. "I did a study in school on generations of maggots—"

Rodriguez rolled his eyes. "Lord, spare us."

Kelly smiled sheepishly. "Sorry. Professional enthusiasm. I'll take an internal temperature. Then, if we can piece together more about her movements the last few days—"

Carnes could not hide his impatience. "We know the drill."

Kelly rubbed his hands together nervously. "Yeah, OK." He knelt beside the bed. "Cause of death probably strangulation. Notice her eyes and throat." He pointed to bruises on the neck. "The guy probably twisted the pantyhose by hand. The eyes are slightly protuberant and bloodshot. Almost certainly a strangulation."

Carnes winked at Rodriguez. "Really?"

Kelly had not seen the wink. "Yes. See the petechiae around the eyes?" He droned on, seeming to pick up confidence as he talked. "We'll have to confirm this during the autopsy, of course, but judging by these signs, she was throttled, apparently from the rear, most likely in this position, lying on her front. Maybe a knee in the back for leverage." He pointed. "Those may be abrasions from his knee."

Carnes pointed to some crusted material on her buttocks. "Look at this." He called Wingate over and pointed to her buttocks. "You guys have a UV light with you?"

"Naw."

"Take the sex kit and get samples at the medical examiner's. Got tweezers?"

Wingate strode over to an equipment case and came back with tweezers and a small evidence bag. He handed them to Carnes. Carnes picked up a single curly black hair from the corpse's buttock and deftly put it into the bag. He made a note on the outside of the bag. "I do that right?"

"If you need more overtime, I've got a job for you," Wingate said.

Carnes examined her wrists and hands. "Tied with her own blouse?"

Rodriguez nodded.

Carnes pointed to the knot. "Double granny?"

Wingate craned his neck to see. "Yeah."

"So, we cross sailors off our suspect list," Rodriguez deadpanned.

"What suspect list?" Carnes carefully examined both hands, squinting at each fingernail.

Carnes touched the clipped ends of her hair where her scalp was visible. He glanced at Rodriguez. "A frustrated barber?"

"Not a guild member."

"OK. let's roll her—gently."

Once she was turned over, Carnes ran his fingers softly over a bruise that extended from her left eye and down her cheek. "Whatta you think? A right-hander?"

"At least he bats righty," said Rodriguez.

Kelly looked disgusted. "This was a living person—"

"Spare us," said Carnes. "If you cry over everyone, you go nuts. A little graveyard humor is . . ." He turned toward Rodriguez.

"Therapeutic," said Rodriguez.

"Exactly." Carnes continued to examine the body. He pointed to the black stains on her skin. "Bite marks on the nipples. Enough to draw blood at a couple of spots." He turned to Kelly. "Done while she was still alive?"

"Hard to tell, since she's been lying on her stomach. There's a lot of lividity from the pooling blood, and there'd be seepage. If he bit her, it would've been when she was on her back. Assuming we're right that she was strangled from behind."

Carnes glared at Kelly. "So the answer is yes?"

"Yes."

"Thank you."

Bruises mottled the inside of her thighs above the knees. "He surprised her with the blow to her face, then after she was stunned he tied her hands and gagged her. Tore off her clothes." Carnes gestured to the items around the bed. "Make sense?"

They all nodded.

Carnes continued. "He wanted to humiliate her. He cut off clumps of her hair, bit her—"

"Guy never learned foreplay." Wingate chimed in.

"That bite had to hurt," continued Carnes. "Then he forced himself between her legs and raped her. Right?"

"Yeah." Rodriguez nodded like a teacher appreciating one of his promising students.

Carnes resumed his examination of the body. "Looks like dried semen on her pubic hair. This guy was a reservoir."

Wingate pursed his lips. "We'll get plenty of samples."

"So he raped her," Carnes conjectured, "then rolled her over and either buggered her or masturbated on her before or after he strangled her?" Carnes turned to Kelly.

"Sounds plausible."

Carnes imagined the killer pulling at the pantyhose, the victim's back arching as she fought for breath. He shivered as though an arctic front had just swept through the room, and he felt a tinge of nausea. This wasn't one of his street thugs, pumping drug-poisoned blood onto hot pavement. This woman had a job, a nice apartment, maybe a caring family. He took a deep breath. "OK. See what you can confirm during the autopsy. Anyone see her panties?"

"No," said Rodriguez.

Wingate and Kelly shook their heads.

"Our killer cut her hair, took it, and stole her panties. What does that say?" Carnes asked.

"A collector," said Rodriguez.

"Mommy didn't love me," Wingate whined.

"Yeah." Carnes stood. "Why don't you finish up while we look around," he told Kelly.

Next to the small lamp, phone, and clock radio on the night table, a framed picture lay facedown. Carnes picked up the picture by the corners. The victim and an older man stood arm in arm in front of a boat. They wore the aggressive vacant smiles people put on for posed snapshots. Why was the picture facedown?

A purse lay beneath the night table. Carnes opened it. While Wingate watched and took notes, Carnes pulled a license out of a red leather wallet. "D.C. license says she's Victoria Benton." He made a quick calculation. "Twenty-six." He rummaged some more. "Pay stub. Worked at Haines and Pardo."

"The big time," said Wingate.

"Yeah." Carnes continued through the wallet. "Twenty-three dollars and change, credit cards—"

"Not a robbery gone wrong," said Wingate.

"Right." Carnes pulled a burgundy checkbook out of the purse. "Wildlife pictures on the checks. Doesn't look like she ever balanced the thing. Regular entries. No checks missing." In the purse was a small olive green, faux-leather-bound book, the kind drugstores sell for a couple of dollars. "Address book." He held up a flowered rectangle. "Samantha's Gift Store calendar." He flipped through a few pages. "Nothing for the last few days. Hang on. Saturday it says 'FP-6.' Got several FPs the last few months." He paged through the address book. "Bingo." He put his finger on a name. "Fitz Pardo." He wrote the name and phone number in his notebook. "Haines and Pardo? Hmm."

Her purse contained a comb, brush, lipstick, compact, keys with an attached whistle, a felt-tipped pen. "Matchbooks from two nightspots." He wrote the names in his book before dropping the matches into an evidence bag that Wingate held.

While Carnes was examining the purse, Rodriguez studied the doorway and the kitchen. "No signs of forced entry," said Rodriguez in a loud voice so Carnes could hear. Rodriguez walked into the kitchen area. "Two glasses in the sink." Dark patches stained the refrigerator's surface. A technician was working his way across the kitchen, leaving print powder residue on countertops and cabinet doors.

"Got all your prints?" Rodriguez gestured toward the refrigerator.

"Yeah."

Rodriguez pulled open the refrigerator door and leaned inside. "Open bottle of wine. Cork's not pushed in too far." Rodriguez pulled out the vegetable drawer, then examined the items in the refrigerator door. He opened the freezer. "Carton of mint chocolate chip ice cream—unopened. Couple of ice trays, frozen peas, frozen burger, and some orange juice." He closed the door with a thunk. Rodriguez noted the contents in his notebook. "Paper bag on counter with package of Oreos and bag of chips. No receipt."

He worked his way around the kitchen, opening drawers. "Stainless steel utensils. Knives. Scissors. Maybe our friend used them to cut her hair, then put them back." Rodriguez turned to the technician. "After you get prints, collect the scissors, the wine bottle, and the glasses."

Rodriguez studied the two stools at the counter with a curious look. One stool was pulled back farther than the other. "Anyone touch these?"

Wingate looked over from the bed. "No."

"Then I'd say one of them sat on the stool. The other was probably standing. Check the seat and the underside for prints."

"Yeah." Carnes walked over. "They're having a friendly glass of wine."

"OK. Then they're done. Someone puts the glasses in the sink."

"So what happened? She shows him the door and he hits her, or were they going to do something else?" Carnes asked.

Rodriguez shrugged. "Date rape? Things got outta hand?"

"Maybe," Carnes said. "Course, there is the bag on the counter. Maybe she went out shopping and met some guy. Could've been the munchies that killed her."

"Could be. But you can see she was no housekeeper. The bag might've been sitting there for days. Besides, would she bring home some guy she'd just met shopping?" asked Rodriguez.

"Maybe." Carnes sighed. "Well, let's see what else there is." He walked into the bathroom and froze. "Hey, Pete. Come here." His voice crackled with urgency.

A large red horseshoe was drawn on the wall over the toilet in front of them. A lipstick lay on top of the white porcelain toilet, a tongue of red sticking out of the black tube.

"Must've used some of her lipstick. Not very original," said Rodriguez. He pointed to a black plastic cylinder on the floor between the toilet and the bathtub. "Maybe mobile crime can get some prints off the lipstick or the top of the tube."

Carnes sketched the horseshoe in his notepad. Rodriguez glanced over his shoulder and then back at the original on the wall. "What do you make of it?" he asked.

"Hell, maybe the guy's a horse freak or something."

"Definitely a freak." Rodriguez crossed himself.

Wingate came up behind them. "You found the artwork?"

"Yeah." Carnes studied the wall as though waiting for it to talk.

Rodriguez rubbed his cheek. "Could be an upside down U or maybe a picture or symbol of some kind."

"What?"

"Some satanic symbol?"

"Or just a horseshoe."

Carnes cleared his throat. "I have the feeling—"

"Woman's intuition?" Wingate winked at Rodriguez.

"—this guy isn't done."

"Hold on a sec. I don't follow." Rodriguez arched an eyebrow.

Carnes stared at the wall. He spoke softly but in a tone that left no room for debate. "He's killed before. He's going to kill again."

"You doing funny mushrooms or something?" Rodriguez asked. He made a face at Wingate. "I hate it when he gets like this."

"Laugh, but my hunches are usually right. Aren't they?"

"Unfortunately," Rodriguez said.

They walked around for several more minutes, making notes and pointing out evidence they wanted collected. Finally, they walked to the door. A tall, shapely black woman with a plain but pleasant face waited for them in the hall. She put out her hand. "Detective Henderson. We're working a canvas up and down Wisconsin," she said. "I've got a couple of people outside you may want to talk to. Building super, some neighbors." Brusque and efficient. She handed them each a card. "Call me for an update on the canvas." "Make sure they check all the carryouts and markets in the area," Carnes said. "She may've been shopping just before she was murdered."

Henderson made a note. "Uh-huh."

Carnes turned to Rodriguez. "How do you want to divide things up?"

"You're the primary. You want to finish the scene?"

Carnes nodded. "Yeah. And I'll talk to the witnesses."

"OK. I'll start on family and friends."

"Wanna hit the ME's for the autopsy?"

Rodriguez had a strong stomach. "Sure."

Carnes watched the medical examiner's team wrap Victoria Benton in the sheet, then slip her into the body bag. He felt he'd been here before. Was he sensing the past or the future?

2

Becky Granite stared at the computer screen. She needed a catchy phrase, a slogan. Maybe free-associating would help. She typed what came into her mind. Phones, people, talking, Alexander Graham Bell, James Earl Jones, long distance, communications, connections. She highlighted the word *connections* with the mouse. What qualities did the firm want to emphasize? Service, support, quality. That's it! Quality connections. She typed the words. It sounded good.

If Greystone & Martin got this account, it would be a significant and lucrative deal. She was still shocked they'd given her a chance to prepare the proposal. At twenty-six, Becky was still one of the youngest employees in the department. But she had worked hard, both in her student internship when she was still at Maryland, and since they'd made her a full-time member of the team. She had a progressive boss who seemed to believe in evaluating even an attractive young woman on the quality of her ideas and work, not just her clothes and appearance. If she could only get this right.

The phone rang.

"Marketing, Becky Granite speaking."

Silence.

"Hello?"

Nothing.

"Hello?" Becky heard a click and then a dial tone. Strange. She'd had several of these calls lately. No heavy breathing, but nobody answered when she said hello. Maybe someone kept misdialing her extension and was too embarrassed even to apologize. Right now she didn't want any interruptions. She looked back at the computer screen. Quality connections. She liked it.

He hung up the phone. Even when he had to be at his desk he liked to call them. Check up. It took a lot of control not to talk. He wanted to tell them: look in tomorrow's newspaper. He imagined the story. "Paralegal Found Dead."

His heart pounded. He half expected a knock on the door. We have you surrounded. Give yourself up. Give up? No way. Did he have to kill her? No choice. An unstoppable force drove him. It was outside of him and yet inside as well. Maybe that was how the born-again experience God.

But now? Now, his stomach contracted in a spasm of pain. He could barely sit upright. Try to calm down. They knew nothing. As long as he kept quiet, they'd never know. No one's crashing through the door. This was his office. He was safe.

He played back the scene like a videotape. In his car, watching her. This was the night. He'd known it would come to this for quite a while. Where and how, but not sure about when. Every muscle taut. He breathed in shallow gasps. A bus screeched to a stop and she looked toward the street. He slid back into the shadows. Not time for her to see him yet.

The streets were almost empty. Safe. Nobody would see him. Wait, be patient. The right moment would come. The pressure built inside his chest and he tried to breathe evenly. She walked into the deli a block away. Tonight.

Tonight, she'd pay for what she did, for what Fran and all the others did. They'd ridiculed him. Rejected him. Their names were branded on his brain like data on a computer chip. He couldn't delete them from his memory if he wanted to. They called to him like the sirens, tormenting him. They came to him in his sleep, just as his mother did, climbing into his bed, defiling him. He'd pushed them away before, but they always came back. Only one way to get peace. Self-defense.

Tonight's the night. Maybe he would sing a little Rod Stewart to her. She'd like that. Tonight's the night. Everything'll be all right. Oh, what a sight. He laughed. Just like the dentist says, it will only hurt a little bit. A drill bit. The laughter bubbled through his lips.

He watched the deli entrance, afraid to even blink. His eyes hurt; his head pounded along with his heart. He was ready. It had to be now or he would just burst. Or maybe spontaneously combust like that man he'd read about in the tabloid. He patted the bottle of wine. She won't know, not even suspect. You'll take me inside, my friend. We'll get comfortable. We'll drink a little of you. Yes, Vicky, I'll serve wine before your time. The end of your time.

He played it back, every second. The storyboard in his brain controlled every word, every scene. Lon Chaney—or was it Bela Lugosi?—eat your heart out. God, it all worked. He'd torqued up the charm. She ate it up. He could be so charming. The girls swooned for him. Vulnerable, needy. His approach always worked. They were all mothers at heart. He had them fooled at work. They loved him there.

He caught himself grinning—a thousand watts. He chuckled. Vicky flew to that smile like a moth to a flame. And he burned her. He burned her good.

Juan Mendez, the building superintendent, looked as small and cluttered as his office. His face reminded Carnes of an unsuccessful welterweight: scar tissue rimmed each eye, and his nose took as many turns as a mountain road. Still, the sad brown eyes saved his middle-aged brown face from ugliness.

The man's office was a tool graveyard. Although a few wrenches and screwdrivers hung on a board amidst a jungle of empty hooks, more tools rested haphazardly on the workbench and shelves next to the desk and in an obstacle course around the floor. A well-used copy of *The Handyman's Bible* sat on the side of the desk next to a pile of receipts.

Someone had tacked a calendar with a famous hardware company's name to the wall above the desk. An attractive brunette in skimpy denim overalls and nothing else posed with some of the company's latest products. The calendar still read May, although June was already more than a week old. Carnes didn't know whether this was a tribute to Miss May or another symptom of the super's sloppiness.

Normally, homicide detectives took witnesses to headquarters for formal statements, but Carnes sometimes found it useful to deviate from procedure. He leaned against the doorjamb and studied the man carefully, weighing whether he'd get more here or at homicide. He pulled out his notebook. "You're Mendez?"

The man jabbed a thumb at his own chest. "Yes. Juan Mendez." His speech was heavily layered with South American intonations. Mendez moved a wrench, a piece of pipe, and a can of pipe dope off a folding metal chair and gestured toward it with the back of his hand.

"You sit?" Carnes stood, so Mendez sat in the chair.

Carnes explained that he liked to talk to everyone near the scene of a murder as soon as possible. Any small fact or recollection might break a case wide open. He asked about the tenants.

"This nice place. We not get bad crowd here." Mendez did not pronounce the "h."

"Did you know the victim—Miss Benton?"

"No. I see, here and there. She seem nice girl."

"Have you ever spoken with her?"

"Once, maybe two, few times." Mendez stared at the ceiling for a minute as though searching for a vision of their last encounter. "I fix disposal in kitchen once but she at work."

"So when did you talk to her?"

"Maybe in hall, or in front of building. One—two times in lobby or at food store."

"About?"

"Maybe the weather, got any problem need fixed?—that talk."

"When was the last time you saw her?" Carnes asked.

Mendez shifted uncomfortably in his seat. His expression became pained. "It real bad. Me let in policeman. She first dead person me see not in—what the word?—box. At funeral?"

"A coffin?"

"Yes. Coffin. It bad. She nice lady. He loco."

Carnes leaned forward. "What 'he'?"

"I see body. Man did that. Had to be—"

"Why?"

Mendez shrugged and held out both hands, palms up. "Lady not do that."

"All right. Let's back up a minute. When did you last see her alive?"

Mendez scratched an ear as though that would help him remember. "Maybe week ago. Early week." His face brightened. "Yes. It Monday or Tuesday. We talk weekend weather."

"Didn't see her since?"

Mendez scratched his ear again and studied the ceiling. "No. That last time."

"Have you seen anyone visiting her?"

"Her man. He come."

"When?"

"Many time."

"Her man?"

"Yes. Nice dressed—expensive suits. He come, them go out many time. I see." Mendez lowered his head and his voice and leaned toward Carnes. "Sometime he stay—how you say?—at night. I see leave in morning."

"Do you know his name?"

"No."

"Can you describe him?"

Mendez scratched his ear, then pulled on his nose with his thumb and forefinger. "Ummn. He drive BMW. Tall, maybe *cuarenta*—forty. Rich face—you know, like he better than most people."

"When was the last time you saw him?"

"Ummn." Mendez pulled on his nose again. "Maybe one, two week ago."

Carnes gave Mendez his best piercing look. "When did you see Ms. Benton last?"

Mendez started to shift around in his chair uncomfortably. "Before. I tell."

"Tell again."

"Today, when open door for policeman."

"When was the last time you saw her alive?"

Mendez shifted in his chair. "I tell you that. Week ago."

Carnes' voice became soft, serious. "This is your best chance to be straight with me. I can help you if you're honest. You sure it wasn't this weekend?"

Mendez' voice rose an octave higher and he moved his hands rapidly. "No, last week."

"Did you find Ms. Benton attractive?"

Mendez cocked his head and studied Carnes with wary eyes. "What you mean?"

"Don't you understand the word 'attractive'?" Carnes groped for the Spanish. *"Bonita."*

"Si."

"Did you want to fuck her?"

"No!" Mendez moved back in his chair like a cornered rodent facing a cat.

Carnes watched the squirming man. Surely he was lying. But was he lying because he had something to hide or because of the accusation inherent in the question. "Did you fuck her this weekend?"

"No. No way. Why me do that?"

"Because she was a pretty woman. Maybe you thought she wanted it."

"No!"

"I'm a man too. I understand." Carnes held out a placating hand. "Say she came on to you. She asked you in. You could see she wanted it—"

"No!" Mendez pounded a hand on his desk. "You loco. No way. I no go near her. Marita, she rip off my *cojones*."

"Who's Marita?"

"My friend. She know me. I not that way."

Carnes stared at Mendez for a minute, gauging what tack to take next. He wondered if he'd made a mistake, questioning Mendez here in his office. Should he take him down to homicide, throw him into an interrogation room, and let him stew? But was there really any reason to suspect him? Mendez had the key to Benton's apartment. He was a man. It wasn't much.

Carnes spoke softly. "I'm trying to help—to let you explain"—he held up his hand to silence Mendez—"in your own way what happened. If you lie, it'll be worse for you, because I'll find out. Say she invited you in, led you on—"

"You loco cop."

"Where were you this weekend?"

Mendez blinked. "This weekend?"

"Yes."

Mendez smiled. "She not dead today?"

"She certainly dead today." Carnes couldn't help picking up speech patterns when he questioned someone. "But she died this weekend."

"I in New York City—the Bronx—with my Marita and some"—he played with his ear—"cousins."

"You sure?" asked Carnes. "Because if I check—"

"You check."

"Oh, I will."

In Carnes' experience, most murders were solved within the first few days or not at all. Sometimes, everything you needed was at the scene. The domestic quarrels were the easiest. A drunken husband or an angry wife driven to murder by real or imagined abuse might strike with whatever weapon was at hand and then be overcome with remorse. Carnes had investigated cases where a husband or wife stuck a kitchen knife in their spouse and then called 911, greeting the police with a tearful and heartfelt confession.

Unfortunately, most homicide investigations were not so easy. Rapid action was critical. The investigator sucked up everything like a vacuum—the overheard remark of someone at the crime scene, the unrehearsed story told right after the murder. Get it fast. Preserve it. Memories decayed almost as fast as corpses. Witnesses moved, forgot, or became frightened.

Solving the crime quickly was important for another reason. During the last few years murders deluged the D.C. homicide detectives until they were barely treading water. Since there was only so much a detective could do—even one who was particularly conscientious and needed the overtime pay—each new murder was attacked fast before it became lost in the flood of cases.

Carnes spent most of the day knocking on the doors of empty apartments or talking to tenants. Most of the people at home were older women. Some wouldn't open their doors even after he held his badge and identification to their peepholes. Several had seen Victoria Benton come and go but didn't really know her. No one seemed to have seen or heard anything even remotely helpful.

By 2:30 that afternoon, Carnes had learned only that Victoria Benton was "nice" and "friendly," and at one time or another had greeted everyone with a smile. By the time he knocked on Jessica Kramer's door, Carnes needed a break.

After a day of Sominex, Jessica Kramer was an injection of speed. Every ounce of her five-foot seven-inch frame, clad in a loose-fitting neon T-shirt and tights, burst with vitality. She looked like a video exercise instructor who had leaped out of the TV. Her face was a lively triangle with bright green eyes and a dimpled chin. Her mouth was sensuous and full lipped.

After being held at bay by suspicious matrons all day, Carnes was half grateful, half dizzy when Jessica swept him into her apartment with the easy grace of a society hostess expecting close friends for dinner. Before he knew it, he was comfortably ensconced on her couch, listening to her talk way too fast.

Jessica said she heard about Vicky's death that morning. Vicky was a "dear friend." What a tragedy! she said. What a world! And she thought this was a safe part of the city. Is there such a thing anymore? Jessica couldn't face work today. She called in sick so she could mellow out. She just couldn't believe it!

"How did you meet?" Carnes asked.

Jessica laughed. "It was very prosaic. In the laundry downstairs. Hit it off right away. We both hated doing laundry." She laughed again and squirmed in her chair. Her left eye twitched several times. She bounced up. "You sure you don't want something cold to drink?"

"OK," said Carnes. "How about ice water?" Carnes watched appreciatively as she moved across the room to the kitchen area. She swung around the counter with a fluid grace that reminded Carnes of a dancer he'd known. Carnes liked the way her nipples pushed out the fabric of her shirt and her breasts rose and fell like gentle swells as she moved. Even before he became a homicide detective, he knew how to read that clue: no bra. She must be about thirty. Hitting her prime. Carnes wondered how those long legs would feel wrapped around his waist.

He pulled his eyes away and examined the apartment. It mirrored Victoria Benton's but was decorated more lavishly in coordinated pinks and plums. A potpourri of scents—soap, flowers, spice, and something undefinably feminine—sweetened the air.

"You decorate this place yourself?" he asked.

"More or less." She turned from the refrigerator with a bottle of water in her hand.

"You should be doing this"—he swept his hand around the apartment—"for a living."

"I do, in a way. I haven't been doing very well as an actress so I make ends meet doing set design at the Arena and some of the other theaters. I guess it's similar to decorating." She poured the water into a glass and put the bottle back into the fridge. Then she glided over and handed him the glass. Carnes felt a rush of hormones as her warm scent washed over him. Did she brush his hand that way by accident?

"You move like a dancer." Carnes smiled his best smile.

"Ten years of ballet, five years of chorus parts. I guess it shows, although I haven't really danced much the last few years." She cocked her head. "Are we here to talk about me or Vicky?"

"Victoria—I mean Vicky. When was the last time you saw her?"

"About four days ago, I guess. Yeah, Thursday. She came by to shoot the bull." Jessica brushed the dark brown hair back from her eyes with a practiced movement of her right hand.

"Anything special?"

"You mean, anything related to her murder? Not that I can figure. We talked about her boyfriend, Fitz Pardo."

"F. P."

"Huh?"

"His initials. Tell me about Fitz Pardo."

"He's one of the lawyers she worked with. Fitz for Fitzhugh, I think. Big-time lawyer. Sort of a dried-up kind of person. No oomph. Honestly, I don't understand what Vicky saw in him. She was so alive—" Jessica put a hand to her mouth, blinked her eyes, and took a deep breath.

"Did you socialize with them?"

"Mostly just Vicky, but of course I'd met him several times."

"When did you see him last?"

"Oh, I think I ran into him coming or going a week or two ago. But I spoke to him this morning."

"You did?"

"Yes. He called asking for Vicky. Sounded worried. She hadn't come to work, didn't answer her phone. Very unlike her. He told me he was going to call the police."

"What did Vicky tell you about Mr. Pardo?"

"Well, just the usual kinds of things. She wondered if anything was going to happen, if he was ever going to get around to popping the question. She's twenty-six—" She covered her mouth and blinked. "There I go again. I'm sorry. She was twenty-six."

Carnes wondered how long Jessica could hold back her emotions. "It's OK. Was she a good friend?"

Jessica looked at him warily. "Yes," she said quietly.

"This must be awfully difficult for you."

"Oh . . ." She waved a hand but said nothing. She slumped slightly in her chair; her face muscles began to relax, released from her manic grin.

"Dealing with the death of a friend is difficult. I'm sure it was a shock—"

"It's so hard to believe." A single tear rolled down Jessica's cheek, and her voice sounded throatier.

Carnes went over to her. "I know." She leaned toward him, head resting against his thigh. He wrapped his hand around her shoulder. His heartbeat accelerated and he took several slow, deep breaths trying to control the other part of him that was reacting to her nearness.

"I'm sorry," she said. She gulped air like someone surfacing after too long underwater.

"She was your friend," he said. He willed himself away from her side and returned to the couch, crossing one leg uncomfortably over the other.

Jessica produced a handkerchief from her sleeve like a magician and daintily blotted her eyes. "Thanks. I'm not very good about dealing with my feelings. I needed that hug. I'm much better."

"You feel up to telling me more?"

She nodded.

"Tell me about the last time you saw Vicky. What was happening in her life? What did you talk about?"

"Well, about our goals, I guess. She wanted to start a family soon. She was trying to get Fitz to make a commitment."

"How'd he feel?"

"I think he was using her. She was attractive, convenient. It would have been OK, if it were mutual." She pursed her lips. "Don't get me wrong. If both people are thinking along the same lines . . . but Vicky wanted more."

"Did they fight?"

"Fight? No. He was just . . . I guess the right word is evasive—stalling, keeping a good thing going as long as he could without making a commitment."

"How'd she feel about that?"

"Frustrated. I know where you're heading with this. She wasn't the kind to make a scene." She smiled. "I'm the actress, remember."

"Did you counsel her to make a scene?"

Her eyes lit up with a mischievous twinkle. "No, I told her to let him know what she wanted and make it impossible for him to resist."

Carnes felt his heart starting to pound again. "What do you mean?"

"We women have our ways." She glanced at him coyly out of the corner of her eyes. "Use your imagination."

His eyes swept over her, caressing every curve, savoring everything. "I am."

Her eyes lingered on his lap. "I can tell."

The voices began a raging debate in Carnes' head. Is this girl coming on to me? All I did was give her a hug. *On duty, don't mix sex and business, big trouble.* She wants to be comforted. *Who are you kidding?* I can get more information this way. *Oh sure, tell internal affairs you sacrificed yourself for the good of the department. They'll give you a medal.* This has nothing to do with the department.

Jessica stood up and reached for his glass. "You need more ice water?"

He took her hand and pulled her down onto his lap. She laughed. "A cold shower is more like it." She started to get up.

He pulled her to him, feeling her soft, warm mouth resist, then give in to his lips. Their tongues probed and thrust. Carnes was breathless. Jessica pushed him back.

She stood before him, legs slightly apart, and studied him with sleepy eyes. "Whew."

He pulled her closer, burying his face in her warm belly.

"Don't," she said. But she didn't pull away.

He slid the hem of her shirt up slowly, kissing her tight tanned stomach, the white half-moons of her breasts, the charged nipples, the taut silky ropes of her collarbones. She made soft, throaty sounds.

"Oh, Jesus." She groaned. "It's been too long."

She straddled him, her fingers working like dancing fairies on his belt and zipper. With some sleight of hand, she had him out, warm and hard, in her fingers. "God!"

He shuddered like a teenager. She backed away slightly—probably far-sighted, Carnes realized—and examined him.

"Mmmn," she said. Then she said nothing more, her warm tongue and mouth otherwise occupied.

When Carnes could talk again, he said, "You're incredible."

She stood and slithered out of her tights like a snake shedding its skin. Her panties followed, revealing a soft black forest. "Your turn."

"Come here." He cupped his hands around her firm bottom and pulled her to him, inhaling her ripe scent. Carnes flicked a tongue at one nipple, then the other. Jessica moaned. Carnes let his tongue roam. He became the choreographer now; with a movement of his mouth or the flick of his tongue he directed her dance. He pulled back a moment to savor her. Every woman the same and yet so fabulously different.

When Carnes was a boy, his father drove to the local convenience store every Sunday morning for the newspaper. A donut shop next to the store perfumed the air and drew them in through its clanging front door. It was a tiny store without the bright colors or tables of the chain stores. A small display case separated the customer from the steel trays of rising dough and the fryers churning beneath their metal hoods. Every week Carnes' dad stopped for a bag of sweet donuts. Carnes especially loved the puffy filled donuts because each held a surprise inside; custard, creme, apple, and sometimes a fruit jelly.

Every woman was a surprise to be discovered and savored. He explored Jessica with his tongue until he found the right spot. With quick little movements, he flicked at her moist flesh until he felt her muscles tense, her back arch. "Oh—God!" Jessica screamed. Carnes clung to her bucking body until she fell back exhausted. "Jesus. You seem to've done that before."

"Never like that." Carnes meant it. He always did. They lay on the floor on their sides, kissing and exchanging soft caresses. Electricity passed from her warm, silky skin into his body.

"Is that a pistol poking me in the stomach or are you glad to see me?" Jessica did a passable Mae West.

"Guess." Carnes hunched slightly and holstered his weapon. His beeper went off in the background.

Whoever it is can wait, he thought. Then he lost all capacity for thought.

Afterward, they lay side by side, their shoulders and thighs welded together. He ran his fingers absently over her thigh, around her hip bone, over her stomach, skirting the edge of her pubic forest, then back again. An infinite sadness had descended upon him. After ascending so far up the mountain of lust, wasn't it normal to crash afterward into the valley of despair? But a new feeling seemed to settle over him more often now. The sex was still good. He sought it all the time, alert to the slightest look or body movement that indicated interest. He enjoyed the tension of the hunt and the sweet release of the act itself. But when it was over, all he felt was disgust with himself for succumbing again.

This time with a witness. They could break him down to uniform for this. And for what? For a fleeting moment of pleasure? What would he do next, start hitting on hookers for freebies? Only one thing could lift the veil of his depression. More sex. But then he'd feel awful again. Ay, there's the rub.

"It's really sobering," said Jessica.

"Post-coital depression," Carnes said.

She stared at him blankly. "Huh?"

Whoops. "What's really sobering?"

"What happened to Vicky." She looked into his eyes. "I mean, you're here, and we had sex, only because of what happened to her. *It's* terrible—not that we had sex."

"Well, I'm glad to hear that." He poked her playfully.

She giggled and tried to tickle him. They rolled around on the floor, trying to tickle each other and laughing like maniacs until they collapsed back in near exhaustion.

She propped herself on an elbow and gave him another serious look. "I don't jump into the sack with every policeman I meet."

"How many policemen have you met?"

"What I mean is, you caught me at a vulnerable moment. I needed someone to hold me."

"I understand."

They lay there quietly for a minute, lost in their own thoughts.

"Do you think Fitz Pardo did it?" she asked.

"I don't know. Do you?"

"Maybe. I hope not." She seemed thoughtful. "Are you going to catch the guy?"

Carnes rose up on an elbow and looked at her. "If he can be caught."

3

A vein pulsed in Rodriguez' forehead and his mouth barely moved as the clipped words came out. "I've been paging you half the afternoon."

It was 5:10 P.M. and they were working overtime. Carnes tossed his notepad on the desk and collapsed into his chair. "Sorry. I was doing interviews and I left my pager in the car. Since I was coming right in—"

Rodriguez raised his eyebrow skeptically. "Yeah, sure." He emphasized the second word. "What was her name?"

"What makes you think—"

"If you weren't such a good detective, I wouldn't put up with this sh— these shenanigans."

"Shenanigans?" Carnes opened his mouth in mock surprise.

Rodriguez shook his head. "I give up. Did you learn anything?"

"Victoria Benton was involved with her boss, Fitzhugh Pardo. She wanted to settle down and he didn't."

Rodriguez pulled out his notepad. "That jibes with what I got. Spent a long time on the phone with Mrs. Benton, the victim's mother. Took me half an hour to get anything out of her. Sounded real shook. Didn't like this Pardo very much. Apparently, he's about forty. Mrs. Benton thinks he was just using her daughter. Thought they were headed for a confrontation."

"That's what I learned too." Carnes pulled a box of crackers from his desk and popped one in his mouth. "Skipped lunch." He tipped the box toward Rodriguez, who shook his head. "What else you get?" Carnes asked.

"Lot of background stuff." Rodriguez read from his notebook. "Born in Westminster, Maryland. Grew up in the D.C. area. Went to college, at Maryland, College Park campus. Graduated four years ago. Majored in English lit. Law firm paid for some paralegal courses."

"Any enemies, problems, other boyfriends—things like that? I couldn't get a handle on any."

"No. Mrs. Benton thought everyone loved her Vicky. Pardo was her only problem. Mother acted as though he must be the guy who did it."

"Jessica didn't think Vicky had an enemy in the world."

Rodriguez raised an eyebrow. "Jessica?"

"Jessica Kramer. Lives in the same apartment building. She and Vicky were friends." Carnes outlined what he learned in a few terse sentences. "She took it pretty hard."

"Mother did too. A refreshing change. Sometimes, I think we care more than the victim's family." Rodriguez rubbed his eyes. "Remember the Jefferson case? The family called and wanted to come in."

"Talk about the caring family."

Rodriguez nodded ruefully. "All they wanted was the victim's address book."

"With all his customers." Carnes laughed.

Rodriguez grimaced. "Mrs. Benton cared. She wanted to know everything."

"You didn't give her any details, did you?" Carnes asked.

"Do I look like I was born yesterday?"

"No. You look like you were born when dinosaurs still roamed the earth." A minor exaggeration. Rodriguez' graying hair and bulging gut testified to the time he had spent in homicide. After all these years, Rodriguez had two ex-wives, three children he barely knew, and a generation of young cops to lecture. Carnes knew what was coming.

"You know," said Rodriguez, "you kids think that just because you made it through the academy—"

Carnes sighed. Rodriguez' venting was a natural phenomenon, almost as regular and energetic as Old Faithful. Carnes had not learned how to stop the geyser. All he could do was wait out each eruption.

Carnes had decided that nothing in a person's genetic code or upbringing prepares him or her to be a homicide detective. Nothing equips a cop for a daily diet of death, mutilation, and decay. Some cops internalize it. They become driven to solve every murder. Then, depressed over their inability to save the world, they lose interest in living. The smart ones visit a shrink or get out. Others eat their service revolvers.

The successful homicide cop—Rodriguez was a good example—puts up barriers, separates feelings from the job, copes by depersonalizing everything. An arson victim becomes a "crispy critter," a jumper "splashes down." The survivors develop a shell as thick as a turtle's. But no matter how tough the shells, most cops are not impervious to the pain they witness every day. Some pickle their livers in alcohol. Some eat to kill the dull pain in their guts. Some play around. Rodriguez had developed some sense of balance in middle age, but it was too late to salvage his marriages.

Rodriguez completed his lecture with a wave of his hand. "Got it?"

Carnes nodded profoundly, like a physics student who had just listened to Einstein lecture on the theory of relativity. "Sure." He hadn't heard a word. "So what do you think—we pay Fitzhugh Pardo a visit?"

Rodriguez squinted at him for a minute, then shrugged helplessly. "Yeah. He's our best bet so far. We don't have anyone else, and we won't have anything from forensics or the Bureau for a few days."

"More like a few months," Carnes said.

"No. They'll step it up for this one. Forensics is going to examine hair found on the body." He looked at his pad. "The preliminary tests confirm sexual assault. Semen traces in her vagina, anus, pubic hair, and buttocks. Killer probably came as he finished choking her. He's a secretor, so they could tell his blood type from his semen. But no great news. He's type O, like most of the population. Assuming there's enough material, they may be able to do a DNA analysis on the semen and hair to match a suspect."

Rodriguez stared at his pad. "Stomach contents—wine, salad, and bread. Well digested. She ate several hours before she died. That's about it. What did you get from her papers?"

"Some more names to check. Nothing leaps out. Talked to the janitor. He had the key to her apartment. Got real nervous when I questioned him, but he claims he has an alibi. Probably clean." Carnes summarized his interview of Juan Mendez.

Rodriguez made a note. "I'll check out his alibi. Anything else?"

"I found two books of matches in her purse. Looked fairly new. She doesn't seem to've smoked, so she must have collected them. Maybe they have sentimental value. Place downtown called The Comedy Alley, and a singles place, The Village. We should hit them on the way home."

Carnes flipped a page in his notebook. "Also found some pictures and an address book. If worst comes to worst, we can always call everyone in there." He made a note. "I'll check with the phone company to see if there's anything useful on her number."

Rodriguez handed back the matches. "OK. Pardo can wait until the morning. I told the medical examiner this was your case. They'll send you the report on the postmortem and anything they get in the lab." Rodriguez examined his watch. "Can't do the nightspots. I'll be late. I can't miss this church meeting."

"The hair gets gray and all of a sudden you're Mr. Pious."

"I've been going to church since before—"

"I was in diapers."

"—you were born."

"It's not going to help. When you're dead, first guy you see is going to have horns and a pointy tail."

"No way. Place is too full of your friends and relatives. I'll have a direct ticket to heaven."

Carnes sighed. "Well, I might as well hit the nightspots."

"You'll suffer."

Carnes smiled. "Someone has to do it."

"You'll get cancer. All that tobacco smoke. But it's your thing. I hear The Village is the hot new meeting place."

"As hot as the FOP?" asked Carnes.

Rodriguez guffawed. The Fraternal Order of Police club, located near the old Superior Court buildings, was one of the cops' after-work hangouts. Although a good place to chew over the day's events with people who understood, it hadn't made the *Washingtonian's* list of hot nightspots.

"Like that, huh?" asked Carnes.

"Don't get any ideas. I don't wanta hear you got up on stage at that comedy place."

4

Becky Granite shifted uncomfortably on her bar stool. "What am I doing here?"

"Being sociable," said Carol Bromley.

"I'd rather be upstairs working on the quality connections proposal for the long-distance firm. I think I've got a good—"

"You're hopeless." Carol laughed. "Now, this is the place to make some real quality connections!" Carol nudged Becky and pointed at an attractive, dark-haired young man sitting at the end of the bar. "What do you think?"

"Not bad."

"Not bad? The guy is a stone fox. Believe it or not, he works up in accounting."

"You're kidding." Becky glanced furtively down the bar. "He doesn't seem like an accountant, more like—"

"A model?"

"An actor or something."

"Exactly!" Carol put out a finger, made a hissing sound, and pulled her hand back quickly. She giggled.

"You better watch out or you're gonna get burned," Becky said.

Carol smiled and pointed to her arm. "I tan, I don't burn."

"Cute."

Becky shook her head. She couldn't think of anybody who'd started a serious relationship in a singles bar. Not like the relationship she'd had with Brett. Well, *had* was the operative word. She still felt the ache in the pit of her stomach even though it was nearly a year since Brett had announced he'd met someone else and left a gaping hole in her life. "Don't you get tired of the games?" Becky gestured toward the couples along the bar, heads bobbing, teeth gleaming, eyes batting, hands touching shoulders, swirling in an urgent mating dance.

"Why should I?"

"It's too easy to get hurt."

"You only get hurt if you're not playing too. I'm blond, fit, and single. I'm a player."

"But this isn't the kind of game you can win."

"Geez, Becky. Lighten up. You're so damn competitive, you see everything as losing or winning."

"No. It was just a figure of speech. What I mean is you'll get hurt."

"Not me." Carol smiled. "I'm the heartbreaker, not the breakee."

"I knew I should've worked later and gone straight to aerobics."

"Stop being such a party poop. There are other ways to burn calories."

"A one-track mind. All you think about—"

"Well, what do *you* think about, sitting up there in your office? New campaigns?"

"Yes. That's my job."

"I believe it. You want to be the youngest vice president ever."

"What's wrong with that?" Becky asked.

"What I meant was, don't you ever think of guys?"

"Of course," said Becky. "But not every second. Besides, there's a difference between guys and sex."

"You're missing something."

"No, I'm not. You are. What about relationships?"

Carol tore a strip out of her napkin. "Overrated. You just end up getting hurt."

It was hard to argue with that. Becky pointed at a couple leaving the bar. "They just met about three minutes ago."

Carol tore another piece of napkin. "So?"

"So? You can't tell me they got to be close friends in three minutes."

"Who said you have to be close friends to leave a bar together?" Carol smiled. "What planet are you from? Hell, you're the one who went to college at party central."

"People do more than party at Maryland."

"Yeah, right." Carol tore another piece out of her napkin.

"Picking up people in bars doesn't appeal to me. Haven't you heard of AIDS?"

"Yeah, I have a friend in that section of the State Department. They do some sort of foreign assistance work." Carol giggled.

"Very funny." Becky shook her head. "I'm trying to be serious."

"Serious? OK. Use condoms and don't make it with bisexuals or intravenous drug users."

"You know what I mean. I'm talking about serious relationships. Depth."

"You just don't have any hormones." Carol shook her head. "Now, that's serious."

"I have hormones, but I believe in romance."

Carol rolled her eyes. "Romance?"

"Yeah. Eyes-meeting, heart-pounding, soul-shattering, feel-it-in-your-gut romance. Like *Wuthering Heights*."

"Life isn't the movies, except the ones rated X."

"*Wuthering Heights* was a book. Brontë." Becky gestured toward the door. "Look, all I know is whatever that was, it wasn't romance."

"I know your dad was a priest or something—"

"A realtor." Becky blushed. "But he was a deacon in the church."

"A beacon?"

"But that has nothing to do with it."

Carol smiled slyly. "Sure."

"It doesn't."

Carol eyed her accountant. "Well, I'm all for romance, but horniness will do!" She slid what was left of her napkin—a crude depiction of a penis and testicles—over to Becky.

Becky groaned. "I give up."

"Buy him a drink."

"No way. You've tried this before," Becky said. "I'm not interested."

"Maybe, but it works for me. The guys see those blue eyes, high cheekbones, and dark hair and they're hooked. Then, when you reject them"—Carol made a quick twisting gesture with her right hand—"all I have to do is scoop them up in my net."

"Hey, it's not my job." Becky imitated one of their coworkers. "Besides, how much did you spend on that hair?"

Carol patted her blond curls. "About eighty bucks for the perm, cut, and roots."

"Well, put it to use."

Carol pouted. "You're such—such an old-fashioned"—she groped for a moment—"sourpuss."

Becky sighed. Carol's quarry still stood at the bar, shoulders back, head tipped casually so he could see them in his peripheral vision. His forearm rested on the dark wood and his fingertips caressed his drink— an actor, performing for his audience. Cute, but not destined for her stage.

"OK. I plead guilty—sourpuss in the third degree," Becky said. "This one is yours. Besides"—she looked at her watch—"I promised to meet Marcia at aerobics tonight. I'm late." Becky opened her purse.

"What a spoilsport!" Carol smiled. "It wouldn't hurt you to miss karate or aerobics once in a while."

"Sound body, sound mind."

"Oh, well. It's a tough job—" Carol caught the accountant's eye. He smiled. "But someone's got to do it!" She curled her finger and pointed to the seat next to her. He nodded and started over.

Carol turned to Becky. "Wish me luck." Her eyes focused over Becky's shoulder. "Hey, don't look now, but there's a guy near the door giving you the twice-over."

Becky slowly turned toward the door and caught a glimpse of a tan jacket as the door slammed shut.

"Must be shy. He ducked out when you started to turn around."

Carnes sat at the bar in The Comedy Alley listening to some guy— introduced by the master of ceremonies as the funniest staffer on the Senate Finance Committee—struggling with his shtick. He shouted hoarsely over the low hum of voices, clinking glasses, and shifting chairs.

"I woke up with a pimple the other day. Forty years old and I still get pimples." The comic pointed to his cheek. "Now, this thing was huge."

"How huge was it?" bellowed a drunken voice.

"It was so huge, when I walked into the supermarket, the manager told me, 'Clearasil's in aisle four.'"

Carnes joined the chorus of groans.

"Speaking about cosmetics, it really bugs me—these girls who wear these potent perfumes. You know the ones you can smell from a differ- ent time zone. Well, my girlfriend just got a new perfume—it's so strong it's only available by prescription." He pronounced it "perscription." A woman in the audience hissed.

"Listen, lady, I heard that." The comic winked at a man in the front row. "One night, I used that line in the act and a woman threw an entire bottle of Hidden Passion at me." He paused a beat. "My dog wouldn't come near me for a week." Another man in the front row chuckled weakly. The comic continued. "'What'd you do that for, Mom?' I asked." Several patrons groaned again and the comic wiped sweat from his forehead with the back of his sleeve.

"Speaking of mom . . ."

Carnes studied the crowd—mostly young, upwardly mobile, professional couples. A dark-haired man in his forties and a fresh-faced brunette who didn't look more than twenty sat at a table nearby. Maybe a boss and his secretary—or mistress.

Carnes swiveled back to the bartender—a tall, athletic man of about twenty-five wearing a blue Comedy Alley T-shirt. He sported shoulder-length curly dark hair and a perpetual smile. Carnes caught his eye.

"Need a refill, buddy?"

"No, just information." Carnes frowned. *Sound like I've been reading too many Mickey Spillane stories.*

The bartender gave him a quizzical grin.

Carnes pulled out his shield. "Detective Carnes, homicide."

The bartender stepped back and examined Carnes. He smiled. "With that suit and the styled hair, I had you pegged for a salesman." He leaned forward. "Name's Ken."

"How are you with names and faces?" Carnes asked.

"Better with faces, but I know most of the regulars."

"Know a lady named Victoria Benton?"

"No." He studied Carnes for a moment. "Should I?"

"Maybe. I think she's been in here."

The bartender smiled. "Is she the suspect or the victim?"

"Does it matter?"

Ken smiled wryly. "Does to her, I'd bet. What does she look like?"

Carnes pulled out a photo of Benton and slipped it across the bar. Ken played with the hoop earring in his left ear. "Maybe."

"Maybe?"

"Hell, lots of people come here for drinks or the show. I don't know everyone."

"Well, is it 'maybe' or just 'no'?"

The bartender rested his elbows on the bar and stared at the photo. He closed his eyes. Carnes decided Ken was a would-be actor. Ken opened his eyes and smiled. "You know, I think I've seen her a couple of times—at least someone who looked like her. Pretty gal."

"By herself?"

"Naw. Came in with a guy. A few times, I think. They came on the weekends for the name acts."

Carnes wondered what Ken considered a "name" act. "What'd the guy look like?"

"Hell, I'm not so good at remembering the guys." A man held up his empty mug. Ken nodded at him. "Hang on a sec." He twisted around, filled a mug with draft beer, and carried it down the bar. He retrieved the empty, placed it in a plastic rack, then returned to Carnes. "Where were we?"

"You were describing the guy you'd seen with this girl."

"Well, you know, just an average guy. Nothing stands out . . . " The bartender closed his eyes again. "Except he was older than she was. Yeah, I'm pretty sure. At least ten years. That's the only thing that really made an impression. Lots of gray hair."

On stage, the comedian gyrated wildly in imitation of his girlfriend doing some new dance. The audience made hostile noises. Carnes turned back to Ken. "You better get that guy off."

"Why?" asked the bartender.

"I don't have time to work another homicide."

5

Hell has nothing on a Washington, D.C., summer. Hell has searing heat. Washington has searing heat and suffocating humidity. Whoever selected Washington as the capital city must have decided the miserable weather would force the government to close down for the summer, minimizing its ability to create mischief. Right. Carnes and Rodriguez made a dash from the semi-air-conditioned car toward the office building.

The cool breeze from a nearby air-conditioner vent chilled the damp shirt plastered to Carnes' back. He pushed the up arrow embedded in the dark gray marble wall. "Does it ever bother you? Guys like Fitz Pardo sit high up in these air-conditioned towers, while we're out on the street sweating our asses off, cleaning up the garbage."

Rodriguez smiled. "Yeah, that's us, the cleanup crew." The elevator to their right dinged and the up arrow lit. "Has a certain ring to it."

Carnes groaned. "I'm not sure I want to take a chance on getting stuck in an elevator with *you*."

"Maybe we should get 'Cleanup Crew' T-shirts."

"You're a sick man."

Carnes finished updating Rodriguez on his previous night's efforts at the comedy club. "And I didn't learn anything at The Village other than that it's a good place to girl-watch."

"You just watch?"

At that moment, the elevator doors slid open, so Carnes didn't have to tell Rodriguez about the coed from Georgetown he'd met at the bar. To their left, a Greek temple facade framed the entrance to Haines & Pardo. Inside the entrance, a middle-aged woman sat behind a half circle of black marble. Bifocals rested precariously on the end of her nose.

"Detectives Carnes and Rodriguez to see Fitzhugh Pardo," Carnes announced.

The receptionist wrinkled her nose as though someone had just poured curdled cream in her coffee. "Do you have an appointment?" She put the emphasis on the last syllable.

Carnes shook his head. "But I'm sure he would want to speak with us."

The woman raised an eyebrow. "Have a seat over there." She waved them into the reception area. Maroon velvet chairs with fat cushions were arranged around a marble coffee table. A silver-haired woman was half buried in one of the chairs, reading a copy of *Mirabella*. Her feet did not touch the floor. Other magazines fanned across a corner of the table around a core of Haines & Pardo brochures.

The receptionist glared at them until they were seated. Then, watching them as though they might steal a brochure, she picked up her phone, punched a button, and whispered something.

"Miss Congeniality," murmured Rodriguez.

"The office Gorgon."

"Huh?"

"Greek mythology. Remember Medusa and Perseus?"

Rodriguez rolled his eyes. "What're you talking about?"

"Don't tell me you never studied—"

Rodriguez shook his head. "Why the department ever went out and hired all you college boys—"

Fitzhugh Pardo, Esquire, swept into the room like a Prussian prince. Pardo wore his expensive pinstripe suit and silk tie as though he'd been born in them. His features were sculptured of stone, and every gray hair on his head seemed to be cemented in position.

"Gentlemen. I must say this is a surprise. But not a pleasant one." His voice was deep and resonant. "Don't you, ahem, public servants know how to call for an appointment?"

Carnes forced a smile. "This is important or we wouldn't be here."

"Yes. Well, I'm booked solid today." Pardo glanced meaningfully at the older woman. "Isn't that right, Mrs. Novak?" He didn't wait for her reply. "Please make an appointment."

"I think now would be a good time, Counselor," Carnes said in a tight voice.

Fitzhugh Pardo's face flushed and his body trembled, but his voice remained controlled. "You can't expect me to drop everything I have to do this morning." He looked toward the receptionist as though seeking support. "I'm a *very* busy man. I always want to help in any way I can, but, regrettably"—he appeared anything but regretful—"I can't be available at your whim."

Carnes turned to Rodriguez. "I guess we'll have to get that warrant."

Rodriguez shrugged. "We have no choice."

Pardo glanced nervously at the silver-haired lady who was peering at them furtively over her magazine. "Warrant! Nonsense. You have no cause."

Carnes stood up and Rodriguez followed. "Let's go see the judge," said Carnes.

Pardo shifted from one foot to the other and looked at them. "If this is about that poor girl Ms. Benton, I know nothing. She just worked here."

"You were her lover," said Carnes.

Pardo stepped back; his eyes opened wide, as though Carnes had struck him. The old lady's eyes glowed with excitement and she cocked her head.

Rodriguez smiled benignly. "You didn't really think we wouldn't know that."

Pardo stared at them for several seconds, then turned toward the receptionist. "Maggie, we'll be in conference room two. Hold my calls. See if Mrs. Evans—I mean Mrs. Novak—would like some tea and something to nibble on." He turned to the old lady. "My apologies. This should take just a couple of minutes." He nodded at Carnes and Rodriguez. "Come along, gentlemen."

Carnes raised an eyebrow at Rodriguez and, imitating Pardo's strut, followed him down the hall. From behind, he saw that the cuffs of Pardo's pants were stained and badly in need of dry cleaning.

Dark antique woods with shiny brass hardware furnished the conference room. Expensive prints—Carnes recognized Andrew Wyeth—adorned the walls. A built-in bookcase with a large two-door cabinet in the center would have commanded attention if not for the impressive cityscape view through the windows that served as one wall of the conference room. Pardo stood in front of the glass peering out over the city, his hands clasped behind his back.

"Yes, I was dating Vicky."

"How long?" asked Rodriguez.

"For the last couple of years. She was very special to me." Pardo turned and gave each of the officers an earnest look. "I want her killer brought to justice as much as you do." His right eyelid twitched and he rubbed at his eye. A tear or dust?

"When did you see her last?" Carnes asked.

"Well, let's see. You discovered the body Monday. I guess it must have been Friday—no, Saturday night. We went out for an early dinner."

"What restaurant?"

Pardo named an expensive Italian restaurant on the Georgetown waterfront where Carnes had once been stuck with a sixty-dollar bottle of wine.

"Did you take her home?" asked Rodriguez.

"Yes, of course." Pardo stared out the window as though mesmerized by the sun glinting off the office buildings.

Rodriguez scribbled in his notepad. "What time was that?"

"Oh, nine or nine-thirty."

"Isn't that pretty early?" Carnes asked.

"I still had work to do that night. Major merger deal. I had two associates and a paralegal devoting the weekend to it."

"You saying you went back to the office?" Carnes asked.

"Well . . ." Pardo adjusted his tie.

"It should be easy for us to check."

Pardo cleared his throat. "Well, no. I did some work at home."

"Let me get this straight," said Rodriguez. "You took Vicky home at nine-thirty."

"But I didn't go inside. I just dropped her in front." The eyelid was still fluttering.

"Why?" Carnes asked. "You were sleeping together."

Pardo glared at Carnes, started to say something, then swallowed and took a couple of deep breaths. Finally, he sighed. "Well, if you must know—"

"I'd say we must."

Was Pardo's look one of anger or just pure contempt? "We had a bit of a tiff that night."

"A bit of a tiff?" Carnes couldn't keep the sarcasm out of his voice.

Pardo took a deep breath. He turned to Rodriguez, a plea for understanding on his face. "We had a discussion about our future. Victoria had become increasingly—how can I phrase it?—determined, yes, that's a good word, that I should make some formal commitment. You see, I was divorced several years ago. Although I thought the world of Vicky, I still felt a bit gun-shy about—uhm—long-term commitments. Certainly, you can understand that."

Rodriguez grunted.

"Anyway, things were a bit strained when we got to her place, so I just said I'd see her Monday and dropped her off."

"What time was that again?" Rodriguez asked.

"Nine, nine-thirty, no later than quarter to ten. I'm afraid I'm not sure. I try not to check my watch all the time when I'm not working. Stress reduction trick. Trying to get away from the pressures of billing time and all that."

"But you went home to work?" Carnes asked.

"Yes, but I don't bill every minute."

Carnes was sure he was lying about that. He probably billed every minute twice.

"Did you call or go to her apartment after that?" Rodriguez' tone was conversational, unthreatening.

"No. I was very busy on this deal. Put in most of the day Sunday." He held up a hand. "Here at the office."

"So you didn't see or hear from her?"

"No. On Monday, after she didn't show, I called. No answer. At first I thought she was angry at me, trying to punish me in some infantile way. However, upon reflecting, I became concerned. Victoria was very responsible. Even if she were still angry with me, she would have called the office. I decided it would be wise to have someone check on her."

"Didn't you have the key?" Carnes asked.

Pardo gave Carnes a look most people reserve for a dog turd on the sidewalk. "Well, yes, but I was very busy. Besides, I thought I might not be the first person she'd want to see. Even you can understand that." Pardo held his hands out to his side, palms up, and shrugged.

"I assume you can account for your whereabouts from Saturday night until Monday." Rodriguez smiled, the "good cop" to the hilt.

"Certainly not every second." Pardo stared out the window. "Let's see. After dropping her off, I went home, then to sleep around midnight, I think." He tugged at his chin. "Yes, I did some work, then sat up reading for a while. On Sunday, I did my usual things, read the *Washington Post* and *New York Times* over breakfast, then came into the office for several hours. I have the billing records. I could show you what I was doing most of the time. I'd have to check the records."

"Please," said Rodriguez.

"It will take a couple of minutes." Pardo left the room.

"A doll," said Carnes. "Slick, pompous, everything you'd want in a high-priced lawyer."

"Yeah, a real sweetheart."

"His grief is overwhelming. The mother certainly had him pegged."

"Well, maybe he's relieved he doesn't have to make a commitment. Doesn't make him a sadistic murderer," said Rodriguez.

"Yeah, but how many times do people go crazy when something goes wrong in a relationship? Even *refined* people flip out. This guy has this pompous exterior, but who knows what he's really like? All signs say the killer was someone Benton felt comfortable with. She drank wine with him."

"Maybe, but did Pardo really have a reason to kill her?"

"Reason. Who's talking reason?" Carnes said. "Let's assume he goes to the apartment. I don't believe for a minute he just dropped her off in front. They start to have a drink. Then they fight over the course of their relationship. She calls him a bad name. He loses it."

"So why wouldn't he just go storming out? Why work her over and murder her? He had too much to lose."

"Anger, revenge? Maybe she questioned his masculinity." Carnes could almost visualize the scene. "So he decides to show her what a man he is. He gets too carried away. Decides he has to kill her. Adds a few touches like the horseshoe on the bathroom wall to make it look like a random lunatic killing."

"Well, why not fake a robbery? That's what they do on TV."

"Maybe he's seen too many serial killer movies. Maybe he's just crazy. Maybe he's been waiting to explode his whole life. Who knows? He could be a first-class psycho. For all we know, this isn't his first."

Rodriguez ran his fingers through his hair. "Don't get me wrong, I ain't going to invite the man to the policeman's ball." He pursed his lips. "You notice he hasn't asked us for details—hasn't even asked if we've got a suspect. You'd think he'd be curious, at least."

"Well, he's our best bet—our only bet—for now."

6

Carnes drove down South Capitol Street toward Buzzard's Point. Some bureaucrats had decided to build government office buildings on the graveyard of trash and decay that nosed into the Anacostia River. Unfortunately, nobody wanted to work there, and for years the nearly vacant buildings stood as monuments to governmental ineptitude.

Carnes turned and pulled up beside a two-story gray and tan building that, without all the blue and white police cruisers at the curb, might have been mistaken for a warehouse. He entered through the garage. The air was thick with the odor of oil, gasoline, and solvents. Carnes tried to hold his breath as long as possible. Rows of police vehicles, Taurus and Caprice scout-cars, a beat-up old Chrysler plain-clothes vehicle, motorcycles, and a scooter sat on lifts or on the cement floor. Parts and tools littered the area. The air resonated with the angry hum of power tools. Carnes walked through the office and up the back stairs to the mobile crime unit.

Sergeant Henry James, a dour man with a droopy mustache and a shirt pocket full of pens and pencils, met Carnes and escorted him back to his lab. Every corridor, office, bull pen, and laboratory in mobile crime was robin's-egg blue. Carnes decided someone in the department must have received a great discount on that color of paint.

"How's Avery?" James asked.

"Great. Growing like a weed. She's becoming a real social butterfly." Carnes couldn't remember the names of all James' children. "How about your crew?"

"All fine. Franny's starting college in the fall. Can you believe it?"

Carnes shook his head. "No way. Seems like only yesterday she was younger than Avery."

"Yeah, I know." James looked wistful. "The time gets away from you." James used his card key to pass them into a small conference room that served as part of his lab. "Cases like this Benton thing make a dad worry."

"I know." Carnes walked carefully around the Polilight laser and the Cyvac fingerprint chamber and sat at the head of the conference table. "This place has finally joined the twentieth century."

"Almost." James sat at the side of the table next to him. "Little by little. Now, if I just had a few more technicians." He sounded weary. He opened a green file marked with the case number and the name Benton, Victoria. "We got some partials taken off the faucets and a bunch of prints on the phone near the bed and on other items. Identification says the prints belonged to the girl."

Carnes never understood why the department, in its infinite wisdom, placed the identification section, which retained fingerprint records and did comparisons, under different management than mobile crime. "Other prints?"

"Fitzhugh Pardo. Got the match using AFIS. I guess he worked for the government or was in the military at some point. At any rate, he was in the Automated Fingerprint Information System." James studied Pardo's file. "Also found prints on the door that match the ones you had taken from the maintenance guy. You said he let in the patrol officer?"

"Yeah," said Carnes. "What about the refrigerator and the glasses?"

James paged through his notes. "Only the girl's on the refrigerator. The glasses were pretty clean. Only smudges."

"Wiped clean?"

"Can't say for sure, but it's a better bet than Powerball. The wine residue in the bottom of the glasses says they hadn't been washed."

"Shit!" said Carnes. "For a nut case, this guy was cool."

Carnes sat behind a clutter of files and notes. He doodled small circles on his steno pad as he examined the PD 123 forms on which he and Rodriguez had recorded a running account of the case. It was time to take inventory, review what he knew, and revise his plan of action. Some detectives never took the time to stop, sit down, review, and plan. Carnes' willingness to do so made him one of the most effective detectives in the department.

Victoria Benton was still too flat a personality, as dimensionless as a cardboard cutout. He needed to know her better. Carnes drew a line down the middle of the page. He began to list what he knew about her on the left side: address, twenty-six years old, born Westminster, raised Silver Spring, schooled at University of Maryland, lived at home and then sorority. Judging by the address book and the photo albums he found, she had lots of friends. It would take forever to check all those names. He went back to his list. Paralegal to Haines & Pardo. More than that to Fitz Pardo. Sometimes went out with other friends. Attractive.

On the right side of the page, Carnes wrote "Suspect's characteristics" and started a shorter list: right-handed, fairly tall, mad at victim and/or women in general, victim probably knew him.

He stared at the page. Benton didn't seem to have any enemies. So who would want to hurt and humiliate her that way? Of course, those who appeared to be friends were often the most likely suspects. He turned the page and wrote "Suspects" on the top of the page. Fitz Pardo. Relationship with the victim. Maybe he wanted out? A self-centered, egotistical slimeball. Key to the victim's apartment, right-handed, and doesn't have an airtight alibi. She'd certainly let him in and drink wine with him.

The timing pointed to Pardo. She died within a few hours after their dinner together. The waiter at the restaurant confirmed roughly when they left, but there was no one who could confirm that Pardo went home at 9:30 or 10:00 P.M. Carnes wondered whether Pardo's blood was type O. He would try to find out, but the District's privacy laws made getting medical records a pain. Maybe he could get Pardo to agree to provide records or a blood test. Carnes was willing to bet that the asshole would insist on a court order. Did he have enough evidence to get a court order?

Carnes stared at the page. Did Pardo really fit? Pardo seemed the kind who would ooze his way out of a relationship. He didn't seem the physical type. If Pardo had wanted to hurt her, he'd have tried to damage her self-esteem in a thousand little ways. Sophisticated slime like Pardo hurt and destroyed subtly. Carnes had dealt with too many of them. On the other hand, there was something hidden beneath the hostility and paranoia Pardo displayed. Carnes could feel it.

The bag of groceries bothered him. Had those been sitting there for a while or did she go out after Pardo left and bring a killer home? Carnes paged through the reports from the officers who canvased the neighborhood. A supermarket and a couple of delis and carryouts within walking distance. Nobody remembered her.

He went back to his list. Juan Mendez. He had the key but claimed an airtight alibi. Would Benton have entertained him in her apartment? Carnes didn't know her well enough. Was she into slumming? Mendez was only about five foot seven and pug ugly. Probably not big or attractive enough. Mendez seemed OK. Of course, Carnes was no human lie detector. Sometimes, the most sincere face masked guilt. He made a note to see if Rodriguez had talked to Marita.

So who was left? Someone she met in a bar? Some psycho off the streets? There were enough around. But why would she let him in? She seemed to be a relationship person, not the kind who picked up guys in bars or on the street. On the other hand, if she had just fought with Pardo . . . No great leads at either The Comedy Alley or The Village. She didn't seem to be a regular at the bars. Still, it could be some bar lizard. It could also be someone from her past, someone she dated, someone who'd lusted after her from a distance. The possibilities were mind-numbing.

The killer could have posed as a repairman, a postman, or even a cop to get into her apartment. If the guy was someone she didn't know, he might have set up the wineglasses and the stools like props in a play, to mislead the police. But at that hour? Carnes rubbed his temples. He was getting a headache. Everything seemed possible.

What about other motives? Maybe the murder had another angle. Did anyone benefit financially from Vicky Benton's death? Better check any financial angles. Maybe she was involved in something or had information about someone who was dangerous. Carnes slapped the pen down on his desk. This speculation wasn't getting him anywhere. He needed to do more interviews, dig up her roots. He took a deep breath and picked up the phone. This was the part he hated.

7

Carnes drove north on Georgia Avenue—past the palm readers, pizza parlors, laundromats, carryouts, bars, and discount furniture stores, past the Fourth District police station, past the old neighborhoods decaying without grace—into the suburbs. The new high-rises of Silver Spring towered around him. He turned onto Colesville Road and glanced at the map on the seat next to him. After a mile or two, he turned left and then right. Despite a wrong turn, which caused considerable cursing, he soon pulled up in front of a wood and glass contemporary on a Silver Spring cul-de-sac. He checked the number against the address he'd scribbled on the corner of the map.

The woman who answered the door seemed deflated like an old balloon. Her eyes were a foggy gray shrouded in a netting of red veins. Disarrayed blond hair crowned a lined face. She wore a simple white blouse, loose-fitting black pants, and fuzzy pink slippers. Fifty going on seventy.

"Ms. Benton?"

She nodded her head slightly, as though with great effort. "Yes, Monica Benton." She held out her hand. It was as cold and lifeless as her daughter. "You must be the detective who called."

"Carnes." He showed his shield.

"Come in." She shuffled back and led him into the house, slippers shoosh-shooshing across the floor. The foyer was open, light, and airy. A ficus tree loomed to his right and a garden of tropical plants filled the corner to his left. Several bouquets of flowers, probably sent by well-wishers, sat atop an oriental chest.

"This way."

Carnes' heels clunked hollowly on the slate floor as he followed Ms. Benton past the ficus tree into a large room. Wide glass windows along two walls looked over the tree-lined yard. To his right, a brick wall with a massive fireplace anchored the end of the room. Beside the fireplace hung a painted bamboo screen: oriental figures kneeling on mats before a low table, eating a meal.

"The screen tells a story," Monica Benton said. Carnes looked surprised. "Everyone asks about it. That scene is of a child who is about to leave the protection of his family and go out into the world for the first time." Her voice caught and a cloud passed across her face. She placed her hand over her mouth and turned away from Carnes toward the window.

Carnes studied the room. The furniture was contemporary, but oriental artifacts and knickknacks were mixed in. Despite the eclectic nature of the collection, everything seemed to fit. A carved brass lamp belonged behind a stuffed recliner, a jeweled screen looked perfect on the side table. Carnes couldn't begin to decorate a room, but he knew when things worked. This room, with its odd blend of modern American pieces and Eastern antiques, worked.

Monica Benton spoke again. "After his time in Vietnam, Jim, my ex, was stationed in Japan. We traveled a bit and collected some of these odds and ends." She swept her hand around the room.

"Do you read minds? If so, I have a job for you."

Monica forced a polite laugh. "No. I saw you looking at things and I know from experience what questions people ask. I've lived here for over twenty-five years, since Vicky was a baby—" She stopped again, blinking eyes wide with pain. She shook her head. "Sorry. Have a seat. Can I get you something to drink?"

"No, thank you." Carnes sat down on a chair, and Ms. Benton settled into the couch. "I know this is very difficult for you. I really hate to bother you at a time like this, but I need your help if I'm to make any sense of this—to find Vicky's killer." The words sounded hollow in the large room, maybe because he had said such words hundreds of times. Sometimes, he felt like a vacuum cleaner salesman making his pitch, but this time he really meant it.

"Yes, I know. You explained on the phone. I'm still not sure there's anything I can tell you that I didn't already tell that other detective with the Spanish name."

"Rodriguez."

She must have been attractive once. With a little exercise, sleep, a few meals, some makeup, and a different outlook, she might still be attractive. Right now, her blond hair looked dull with gray and was pulled back haphazardly. Wrinkles cut into the skin beside her eyes and mouth. Still, except for a small sag of flesh beneath her chin, her face was tight around the bones.

Carnes wondered what forces had eroded her looks and caused her to implode. Certainly, Vicky's death accounted for some of the signs— the bags beneath the eyes, the carelessness about her makeup. But he sensed there was more. A deeper unhappiness haunted her.

Carnes pulled out his notebook. "I needed to see where Vicky lived, to learn more about her. Usually, we learn more in person than on the phone."

She nodded.

"Tell me about Vicky."

"What do you mean? I mean, where do you want me to start?"

"Wherever you feel comfortable. Was she a happy child?"

"A happy child?" Monica Benton's face crinkled into something resembling a smile. "Yes. She was smart, happy, playful. I know I'm prejudiced—what mother isn't?—but she was truly a delight. Our problems didn't really affect her too much."

"Your problems?"

"Yes. My ex left when she was a teenager. After the war, he used his contacts in the Orient to start an export-import business. He had a woman"—she looked pained—"or girl in every port. One morning, he ate his eggs and toast and announced he was moving to Hong Kong. Just like that." She snapped her fingers. "Vicky and I weren't going." She stared out the window.

"He promised to bring us over when the time was right. That was almost eight years ago." She cleared her throat. "I guess the time hasn't been right."

"I'm sorry."

She waved her hand. "Oh, you don't need to be. I mean, it was long ago." Her voice faded on the last words, and Carnes strained to hear her.

"How did this affect Vicky?"

"Not at all. Well, not really. I mean, she was happy and well-adjusted, a good student, a cheerleader in high school. She did very well at Maryland. She graduated with a degree in English. A 3.5 grade point average! Dean's list." She allowed herself a proud smile.

Carnes understood. His throat still constricted with pride at each of Avery's accomplishments. "I have a daughter."

Monica smiled sadly. "Then you forgive this mother's immodesty." Carnes smiled. "Of course. Tell me more."

"Well, Vicky was very popular in college—an officer in her sorority. She made friends easily. A nice bunch of kids." She stared out the window.

Carnes hated to interrupt her reverie. "What did she do after college?"

"Well, she went to work for that law firm." She said the words as though they tasted bad. "Picked up a paralegal certification from University College soon after she began working there."

"How long did she work at Haines and Pardo?"

"Well, she's worked for them the last few years. She seemed happy and everything, but I wasn't really wild about the situation."

"Fitz Pardo?"

"Yes. He was too old for her and he's a user." She smiled wistfully. "I should know."

"Did they seem happy?"

"Well, happy is relative. He wasn't exactly rushing to marry her."

"Was that an issue?" asked Carnes.

"It was for me. I mean, we'd talked about it a few times. Vicky was beginning to agree with me. When we talked last Friday, she told me she was going to press him about, you know, making a real commitment." Monica looked slightly lost for a second. "But I guess that doesn't make him a murderer, does it?"

"What do you think?"

"Well, Detective, I think he's a cold, ruthless bastard. You know how these lawyers are, smiling at you as though they're your best friend while they're slipping a knife right between your ribs." A shocked expression appeared on her face and she covered her mouth with her hand. "I'm sorry. That sounded so—bad. I mean, he couldn't. I shouldn't—I guess it's just that he's so much like my ex." She pulled a frilly handkerchief from her sleeve and wiped at the corners of her eyes. "But it's really too hard to believe. I mean, who would do such a thing to my baby?"

She sobbed quietly and Carnes looked away. He could look at a naked body or search through the most intimate effects of a victim without feeling as though he had intruded, but Monica Benton's grief was making him uncomfortable. Her pain was so deep, so complete, he didn't know how to comfort her. He studied the fireplace.

When she seemed to be in control again, he continued. "Please don't take these questions wrong, but I have to know more about Vicky, about her habits. Did she go out with other men?"

"Not really."

"Did she ever go to bars—"

"My daughter was not that type of girl."

"It's possible her killer was someone she met on the street or in a fairly casual encounter in a bar or store."

"Impossible."

"How do you know?"

"I know my daughter. I taught her values. We confided in each other like—like close friends. She couldn't have done such things. It's not the way she is—was." Monica looked out the window. A tear rolled down her cheek and dripped off her jaw, leaving a dark stain on her pants.

"I'm sorry, but I have to ask more questions. Did your daughter have any enemies, you know, anyone she fought with or anyone who bothered her?" His voice was gentle.

"No. I mean, everyone liked her."

"Was there anyone she'd dated who continued to call her? Maybe someone who liked her too much—wouldn't give up? Did she ever complain about anything like that?"

"No."

"Anyone from college who called her after they graduated?"

"No." Monica Benton's eyes roamed the room. They rested on the bar for a minute, growing wide. "I guess there was some guy from college she'd dated a few times. He called her after she went to work for the law firm. She told him she wasn't interested but she let him down easily. It was her way. They may still keep in touch." Her face twinged with pain.

"What was his name?"

"Bar-something. I met him once. He seemed like a nice boy. Head over heels for her. Sophomore or junior year. An accounting major or something like that. Let me think. Barlow, Barnot, Bardash. Yes, that's it: Bardash! James Bardash."

"Do you have any idea where this James Bardash is?"

"No. I mean, this was several years ago. If I remember the boy, he was sort of quiet and, well, I guess the word they use now is 'nerdy.' I think he helped her with a course or two. Nice, studious boy but not her type."

Carnes jotted some notes. "Can I see her room?"

Monica Benton's face displayed a kaleidoscope of emotions—pain and grief but also determination. "Yes."

Victoria Benton's room still said high school. A picture on the wall displayed a smiling group of high school cheerleaders next to a school banner. Across from the bed was a poster of a greased John Travolta hanging over a bookshelf. A small Maryland Terrapin paperweight and some other collectibles were neatly arrayed on the desk. Frilly pink and white curtains and bedspread completed the decor.

"Did she keep anything here?" Carnes asked.

"What do you mean?"

"Well, personal things, clothes, papers, books?"

"Not really. Wait! There's a box of papers and things from college in the closet, and some books and stuff"—she pointed toward the bookcase under John Travolta,—"but not much else. She really hasn't lived here since high school, except, I guess, for weekends home from school."

"Can I have a few minutes to look around?" Carnes asked.

For a moment, Monica looked as though she might argue, but she finally conceded. "Go ahead." Carnes listened to the soft shuffle of her feet receding down the hall.

He sifted through the contents of Vicky's desk: old papers, drawings, notebooks. Another drawer held pens, pencils, dried old erasers, paper clips, stapler, stubby scissors. Nothing of interest. He tried the bookshelves. An assortment of children's books sat on the top shelf. These must have been favorites she kept. Paperbacks and textbooks filled the other shelves.

He remembered going through the boxes of things he'd left at his father's house. His mother didn't come for the funeral. When Carnes called, she told him in a slurred voice—this was before she joined AA—that she hadn't seen the "old bastard" in years and couldn't cope with funerals. Carnes' older sister, Margaret, and her husband and children came and sat dry-eyed through the service. Later, he and Margaret cleaned out their father's apartment, dividing up the few items of interest and giving away or trashing the rest. Carnes had been surprised to find his baseball cards, old books and records, the collection of *Playboy* magazines he'd hidden under the mattress and examined almost every night with a flashlight—things he couldn't throw away but never bothered to retrieve before his father died.

Carnes shook off the memory and focused on Vicky Benton's bookcase. On the bottom shelf he saw a University of Maryland yearbook. He paged through it and found a younger long-haired Victoria Benton staring back at him, the corners of her mouth turned up in a friendly smile.

He examined the blurb next to her picture. Major, English; sorority, Alpha Omega; interests, boys, basketball, and Bon Jovi. He placed the yearbook on the desk and started for the closet.

On the closet shelf Carnes found a large photocopier paper box. He pulled it down and placed it on the floor with a soft thud. When he removed the lid, dust, mold, and the odor of stale paper assaulted him. He sneezed once, twice, and waited for the third sneeze. Nothing. The box's contents were unremarkable: papers, pens, and other odds and ends.

Carnes picked up the yearbook and headed downstairs. Monica Benton paced in the front hall. He held up the yearbook. "Can I borrow this?"

"Why?"

"I'd like to have pictures of some of her friends. I may need them."

"You'll take care of it?" Monica pleaded.

"Of course."

Carnes craned his head to see Avery around the bouquet of flowers Carmella had placed on the small butcher-block kitchen table. He smiled and Avery made a funny face. Carnes parted the flowers and peered through, a big-game hunter studying his quarry. Avery laughed. "You'll wreck Carmella's flowers, Daddy."

"We wouldn't want to do that." Carnes pulled the flowers over toward him, growled, and opened his mouth wide as though he intended to eat all of them in one bite.

"No!" Avery dissolved into laughter. "Carmella would die."

"We wouldn't want that." That was for sure. What would they do without Carmella? When Caroline left, Carnes panicked. Would Caroline change her mind and try to take Avery? But after a day or two it began to dawn on him, Caroline didn't want Avery. Then the problem became how could he keep her? After all, he was a homicide detective. His schedule was erratic and not entirely within his control. How could he care for a four-year-old daughter?

Pete Rodriguez solved his problem by bringing him Carmella, a Salvadoran refugee whom Rodriguez' church was helping. Carmella, a slightly rotund, fast-talking woman with a sparkle of fun in her eyes, needed work and a place to live. After five minutes of watching her play with Avery, Carnes knew that Rodriguez had discovered a Spanish-speaking Mary Poppins.

"So how was school?" Carnes asked.

"OK, I guess. Do you know what a dummy Jimmy Harris is? He kept making funny noises today at recess. Every time I tried to play with Jenny and Kerry, he'd come up behind me and make a noise." She pinched her face in a look of disgust. Carnes knew that expression. In their final months, Caroline's normally attractive face seemed to be perpetually twisted into that look.

"Maybe he just likes you."

Avery grimaced. "No. He's just a pain." She picked up a french fry, dipped it in the glob of ketchup, and bit off the end. Since it was Carmella's night off, Carnes had stopped at McDonald's for burgers and fries on his way home. Nothing like a Happy Meal to create instant bonding.

"What else did you do in school?" Carnes asked. Under the table, Duke, their German shepherd, rested his head on Carnes' foot with a grunt.

"Nothin' much. School's almost over. They just let us watch movies and stuff." Avery chewed for a minute, then her eyes lit up. "Did I tell you about Kerry's new Rollerblade skates? She's got the Lightnings. They're just awesome, Dad. You've got to get me some."

"What happened to your other roller skates?"

"Those dumb old Barbie skates?" Avery gave him the look of patient exasperation kids reserve for impossibly un-hip parents. "Dad, those are lame. I mean Barbie? I'm going to be in third grade!"

"Please don't whine."

"I'm not whining," she whined.

"Well, your Barbie skates work perfectly fine and they still fit, don't they?"

"But Daaaad . . ."

"Look sweetheart, Christmas is coming—"

"Christmas is months away. I can't wear those dumb ol' Barbie skates all summer." She studied him for a moment. "Never mind, I'll ask Mom."

Carnes grimaced. They had played this game before. The counselor said it was normal for a child to play one parent against the other, particularly in these kinds of situations.

What got him into "these kinds of situations"? He and Caroline married mostly because she got pregnant. Of course, she'd sworn she was on the pill. Even though they'd convinced themselves that getting married was the thing to do, distrust had been the unspoken subtext to their marriage.

For a while, Avery anchored their lives. As a baby, she demanded their attention. Every conversation centered around her; every plan they made for her benefit. Avery connected them. Unfortunately, she seemed to be their only connection. Carnes was ambitious, and ambition equaled overtime. Carnes brought home stories about police work, and Caroline discoursed on the latest doings on Donahue or Oprah. Neither cared much about what was important to the other. Carnes wondered if they ever had.

Carnes moved into the room next to Avery's and began having affairs. He thought he was discreet. Caroline began working part-time as a travel agent. At first, Carnes thought it might be a good sign. She might develop her own career, her own interests, maybe something they could share. But before Carnes knew it, she was leaving for long weekends to visit resorts with her boss. She worked late several nights a week. She left clues. Carnes decided she wasn't careless; she was rubbing his nose in it.

Carnes even read one of those self-help books about relationships. It said a good marriage must be built on a foundation of mutual sexual attraction, trust, and friendship. By that time, they were aught for three. Even so, Carnes was surprised the night he came home and found Caroline pacing the apartment, suitcase packed and at the door.

"What about the Rollerblades?"

Avery's sensitive seven-year-old face, crowned by its mop of brown curls, caused a tightening in his chest. It was the same feeling he got every time he looked in on her sleeping, her arm curled around Ro Ro. He imagined her skating with her friends, armored in fluorescent pads, a transcendent smile on her face. "I'll see what I can do, sweetheart."

8

Carnes stared at the green screen and sipped his morning coffee. His watch read 9:10. He put the cup down carefully. Recently, after several officers shorted out their keyboards with spilled beverages, the chief sent out a tersely worded memo warning about bringing food or drink anywhere near the terminals. A copy of the missive, stained by various beverages, hung above the terminal. No cop was going to sacrifice his caffeine to protect a computer.

Carnes pushed another key. According to the Washington Area Law Enforcement System database, known as WALES, James A. Bardash drove a silver Lexus and lived in Potomac, Maryland.

Carnes picked up the telephone, dialed 9-411, and asked for a business listing for Bardash, James A. He dialed the number he was given.

The large gold letters on the wooden door read Cummings, Braintree & Bardash. Carnes smelled the faintly sweet odor of brass polish. He turned the shiny knob and heard a tinny chirp as the door opened. The pert receptionist directed him to an overstuffed armchair and scurried out the door behind her desk. While he waited, Carnes tried to calculate how much of his life he spent sitting and waiting in someone's outer office, at the counter of some dingy diner, in the hall of an apartment building, in the witness rooms at court, or in one of the unmarked cars. On balance, the District of Columbia paid him a large portion of his salary to sit and wait.

"Detective Carnes?" asked a pleasant tenor voice. A thin, bespectacled young man, several years younger than Carnes, stood in the door. He wore paisley suspenders and matching tie over a stiff white shirt. Carnes appreciated quality clothing, and he knew that the man's suit had cost him dearly.

"Yeah."

The man strode over as Carnes stood up. A firm handshake. "James Bardash. Nice to meet you. Come with me—we'll use my office." His tone implied this was an unusual privilege. Carnes followed him down an off-white corridor, past etchings of sailing ships, to a comfortable modern office. Two well-padded, maroon leather chairs were arranged before a large oak desk. A high-backed black leather chair sat behind the desk. There was a computer terminal of the matching oak built-in behind the desk. Beside it were several boxes of manuals for accounting, tax, and word processing programs. Bookshelves above the computer were filled with law books, accounting texts, and volumes of IRS opinions. Bardash waved Carnes to one of the maroon chairs.

By any measure, the office was impressive. The window to their right offered a view of the Potomac River and the Rosslyn skyline. The wall to their left was papered with an array of certificates: a bachelor's degree cum laude from the University of Maryland, a license as a certified public accountant, and certificates attesting that Bardash was a member in good standing of various business and accounting organizations. Several pictures adorned the wall closer to Bardash's desk: Bardash with the mayor, Bardash and an older gentleman on a golf course with the last vice president, Bardash on a dock holding up a large bluefish, and a studio shot of Bardash, a young woman, and a child, faces frozen in porcelain smiles.

The desk was empty except for two files on the right side. Not a file cabinet in sight. What would it be like to work in an office like this instead of the noisy and cluttered squad room? Carnes couldn't imagine it. He felt an instinctive, irrational resentment of Bardash.

"Would you like coffee? Soda?"

"No thanks. I don't drink on the job," Carnes said.

Bardash smiled. "Well then, what can I do for you?"

"As I told you on the phone, I'm the detective who's investigating the murder of Victoria Benton."

"A terrible business. Vicky didn't deserve that."

"Nobody does," Carnes said. "Right now, I'm searching for background information about her, trying to fill in the gaps in our knowledge. Routine."

Bardash leaned forward, elbows on the desk, his fingertips pressing together in an **A**. "Well, I for one am glad you're being so thorough. It's really a tragedy. I'm relieved that the police department is taking this so seriously."

"We always take murder seriously." Carnes couldn't keep the sarcasm out of his voice.

Bardash waved his hands in a "no foul" sign. "I didn't mean that as a dig, Detective. I just meant, well, you see on the news all the time about the murder rate in the city, and I know how the department must be over-worked." He tried an ingratiating smile. "I just meant to compliment you on your thoroughness. After all, I haven't seen Victoria in"—he paused and looked at the family picture on the wall—"at least three years or so. You must be doing a thorough investigation if you're tracking down her old friends."

"No offense taken." Carnes made his voice friendly and professional. "Tell me about the last time you saw Victoria Benton."

"Let's see—" Bardash paused dramatically. Carnes was always fasci-nated by how people became actors in his presence. "Ran into her on the Metro. We had a nice chat."

"About what?"

"Oh, jobs, family. I dated Vicky a little in school. Hadn't seen her in a year or two at the time." He smiled. "But you probably already knew that. Hadn't seen her since I got married or had Brendan, so I had lots to share." He pointed at the studio picture in explanation. "She was work-ing at some downtown law firm and—if memory serves—dating one of the partners." He shook his head. "Just like Vicky."

"What do you mean by that?"

"Well, she had a thing for older, mature men. I always thought she went out with me in school only because I was a little more mature than some of her classmates. I was a couple of years older and pretty serious I guess. Besides, I helped her with all her math and accounting classes." He chuckled.

"How well did you know Vicky?"

"Pretty well, but we didn't sleep together, if that's what you meant."

"Were you confidants?" Carnes asked.

"Well, she told me a little about her family life. Her father was always traveling. He left when she was a teenager. I think she was maybe look-ing for someone like—well, a father figure."

"You sound like a psychologist, not an accountant."

"Well, it's something that took me a while to understand. I used to go for counseling myself. I was sort of a nerd in college. I didn't have much self-confidence. After all, I'm no Robert Redford. But there was more inside me than I knew." Bardash reminded Carnes of a puffer fish that inflates itself to intimidate potential predators.

"Counseling has also given me perspective on other people."

"Vicky?"

"Sure."

"Her mother told me you called and asked Vicky out a few times after college."

"Yeah. I had just graduated and was struggling to make an impression in the firm. I didn't have many male friends, and Vicky was a friend more than anything else." He looked sheepish. "I guess I bugged her for a while."

"What happened?" Carnes asked.

"Well, we went out a couple of times, but mostly she put me off with excuses. It finally got through my thick skull"—he tapped his head with his knuckles—"that she wasn't interested. I didn't want to be a jerk, so I stopped calling."

"Getting the brush-off didn't bother you?"

"No." Bardash held up a hand. "Don't get me wrong, it hurt a little at first. It made me feel more unattractive. But I worked it all out with my counselor. Besides, I started to make myself a success here"—his glance took in the office—"and I met Joanne." He nodded at the family portrait.

"How long ago was that?"

"What? That I met Joanne?"

Carnes nodded.

"Gee, four, almost five years ago." Bardash studied the portrait for a moment. "Your life really changes when you have a family. Are you married, Detective?"

"Used to be."

"Oh. Gee, I'm sorry."

Carnes waved his hand. "No need to be." He leaned forward, engaging Bardash's eyes. "Can you remember anyone who was mad at Vicky? Had it in for her? Anyone who was obsessed with her? Anyone who was just weird?"

"Well, if we're talking weird, I think that probably covers half the people we went to college with." Bardash smiled. "But seriously, I've been

searching my brain ever since I heard the news, trying to think of anyone who could have done this. Any reason. It just doesn't make sense.
Vicky was a sweet, sensitive person. She didn't put on airs, even though
she was a pretty girl—I mean woman. Some of the girls in her sorority
were real pigs. But Vicky wasn't like that." He shook his head. "No. I'm
convinced her killer couldn't have been anyone who knew her."

"To know her was to love her?"

"Something like that."

9

It was hard to sit at his desk and smile at people. Sure, he could do it. He was smart, well educated, some thought charming. A professional. But it was hard staying there. His mind kept straying. He'd be sitting across the desk from someone, nodding his head as though he cared about his or her problems. His mind would drift off, into the past or maybe the future. Reliving or anticipating. That was what made him whole. In between was misery.

People wanted what he knew, what he could do for them. They didn't want him. Not even those who had been close to him. They'd all deserted him. His father had tried to get as far away as possible. California. Even his mother— had she really loved him or had she only used him for her own pleasure? Sure she said she loved him. She'd paid for his education. In her own way, she'd provided. But what about later? He'd still needed her. Bitch. She'd left him too.

A jolt of cold terror hit him. He took a deep breath. Collected himself. Now, he knew what to do. They wouldn't laugh at him again. No. They wouldn't desert him either. He made the decisions now.

Carnes had gone through the phone book and dialed all the female Pardos. No luck. Finally, he walked over to the domestic relations office at Superior Court. After an hour, he had what he needed.

Now, Carnes sat on a plush couch in an office with a view of Farragut Square. Renata Wilson, formerly Pardo, sat before him. She was smartly dressed in a pinstripe suit. Her brown hair, short and businesslike, framed an angular face. Crow's-feet around her eyes and creases near her mouth gave clues to her age. Carnes guessed she was closing in on forty. Although she was not pretty, she had taken pains with her appearance: her clothes fit well, her scent was expensive, and she conveyed an air of femininity. Some might call her handsome.

Her office was sparsely decorated in light woods and pastels. Even the computer terminal on the credenza behind her desk seemed to blend in with the decor. The diplomas on the wall revealed a bachelor's degree from Vassar and a juris doctorate from Georgetown. A variety of bar associations claimed her as a member. Judging by the size of the office and the view outside the window, she was a partner in the firm.

"I divorced Fitz about ten years ago. I remarried within a year—a physician I met at a party. We have two school-age children."

"When did you see Pardo last?"

She thought for a minute. "Two years ago at some bar function."

"I know this is personal, but it might help," Carnes started. "Why did you get divorced?"

Wilson sat back and studied Carnes, an amused smile on her face. "What do you expect me to say, that I thought he was a closet murderer?" She chuckled. "Why does anyone get divorced? I guess the cliche is 'we grew apart.'" She placed her hands in front of her and pulled them apart. The dynamics no longer worked.

"When we met, we were both law students. He was very smart and accepted me as an equal. He needed a woman. I needed a man. We became pretty good friends and everything else followed. After we graduated and started working, things got—well I guess 'different.'" She made quotation marks in the air. "We didn't work in the same firm. Both of us were doing associate's hours—sixty to seventy hours per week. He got all wrapped up in the idea of success and somewhere along the way began competing with me. If I went in on Saturday, he'd go in Saturday and Sunday. If I worked late four nights, he'd work late five."

She smiled like a polite hostess at a cocktail party. "Can I have my secretary get you coffee or something?"

"No, thanks." Carnes shook his head. "You were telling me you were competing?"

"Oh, yes. I guess there's really not much to tell. Our sex life went to hell. Frankly, I began to wonder if he was having an affair. He got so distant. When he was around, it was as though he existed only in a physical sense. Whatever it was he wanted I couldn't give him. Hell, I didn't know what he wanted. He had nothing to give me."

Carnes nodded. He understood too well. "What kind of person is Pardo?"

"That's not easy to answer." She stared at her desk for a moment. "He's very complex, very bright, but he's also socially retarded. He works so hard at being on top—in charge. I think he's pretty insecure. He's self-centered. I don't think he's capable of a giving relationship—at least he wouldn't give much. Of course, it's always possible he's changed." Her expression said she didn't think it was likely.

"Did he have a temper? Ever see him out of control, break things, hit someone?"

Wilson gave Carnes an appraising look. The corner of her mouth twitched slightly. "Everyone has a temper."

"For example?"

A genuine smile transformed Wilson's face. Carnes decided she was indeed handsome.

"Well, once when we were still in our first apartment, Fitz was trying to hang a picture—he was really a klutz at that sort of thing—and he hammered his finger. You should have seen it. He dropped the hammer on his foot. Then he hopped around on the other foot, holding his hand and howling like an injured moose. It was like one of those Three Stooges' movies." She chuckled—a rich, throaty sound. "I'm not sure how I managed not to fall on the floor, I laughed so hard. Well, the next thing you know he started kicking and hitting the wall. Must have put three or four good-sized holes in the drywall before he broke his hand." She chuckled again, and Carnes couldn't help but join in.

"He ended up with several fingers splinted together and about a hundred dollars in drywall repairs. We laughed about it for a year or two."

"I can imagine." Carnes got serious. "Did he ever hit you?"

She stared at him for a long minute, the corner of her mouth twitching again. "No."

"You're sure?"

"That's a very stupid question," she said. Her voice had grown sharp.

"I just thought I detected—"

"Well, you're mistaken," she said. Her eyes narrowed. She tapped her fingers on the desk.

"OK. Did he ever hit anyone else?"

Wilson met his eyes with exaggerated sincerity. "Look. Fitz could be a bastard—snippy and sarcastic. As I told you, he's something of a klutz. I think he's a coward."

"Cowards can be bullies."

She looked as though she might say something. Then she shook her head almost imperceptibly and compressed her lips.

"Did he have any—uh—sexual"—Carnes thought for a moment—"peculiarities?"

"Like did he dress up as a walrus or something?"

Carnes kept a straight face. "The old walrus routine. Haven't run into that one in a while."

Wilson raised an eyebrow, but a smile tugged at the corners of her mouth.

"Seriously, I know this is personal. But I have to ask. Was he into bondage, S and M?"

She studied her hands for a moment, then barely shook her head. "Only emotionally."

"Earlier, you said he might have had an affair."

She met Carnes' eyes again. "Possible. A feeling."

"So he may have had"—Carnes struggled for the right words—"a secret life?"

"Well, I'm no psychologist. I suspect most of us harbor some secrets."

"And Pardo?"

"Maybe more than most."

10

The department hierarchy considered Capt. James Malcolm Fletcher a rising star. Personable, bright, a tireless self-promoter, he had been a childhood friend of the new chief of police. With the murder rate averaging more than one per day, the chief needed someone in homicide who could glibly answer questions from the press. Personal loyalty was also a plus. Fletcher was the chief's first choice.

Fletcher was a large man, but he had the grace of an ex-athlete. He'd been a star tight end at Howard. Although he was an imposing man, his smile made the first impression. Fletcher could light up an entire room with his smile. He was equally adept at focusing it on an individual. Under the beam of that smile, a person felt like one of the chosen. But Carnes disliked and distrusted him.

Behind an expansive desk, Captain Fletcher sat on a raised chair towering over Carnes, Rodriguez, Lieutenant Rogers, and Sergeant Bryant. He liked to keep his men after their shift ended for these little heart-to-heart talks, something he'd probably picked up in one of those management courses the department gave its supervisors.

Fletcher tapped the eraser of a pencil on his desk. "The brass've been all over me with this Benton thing. They want an arrest yesterday. The media is like flies on shit. We're not talking drug dealers or domestic beefs in the projects. We're talking uptown—white woman, prestigious law firm, sex crime. Sex sells advertising. Press eats up this shit." He flipped the pencil and caught it with a quick flick of his hand. "One of those investigative reporter types over at channel four wants to run a story with details of the autopsy. Some asshole over at the ME's office is leaking again. Think I convinced the reporter to cool it for a few days, but who knows?" He shrugged. "Gentlemen, the heat is on."

"We're doing the best we can, sir," said Sergeant Bryant.

Fletcher leaned forward, elbows on his desk. "Yes. That's my point. Got to do better. We're a team. Say the word. What can I do? More personnel? Cooperation from other offices? Anything?"

"No, sir," Carnes replied. "Right now, we're following all the leads. As you know, there's a point of diminishing returns. We've used patrol personnel and other detectives to sweep the neighborhood—didn't find anything—but there's not too much more to do except follow the few leads we have and wait for the lab work."

Fletcher leaned forward again and pointed his pencil at them. "You know, I have the utmost faith in you men, but I need to know we're doing everything possible. Gotta answer to the higher-ups. Well"—Fletcher tapped his pencil again—"give me an update."

Carnes summarized their investigation quickly and efficiently. "We really don't need more investigators at this point. Patrol is searching for cars the neighbors didn't recognize. The lab and forensics have everything more or less on track, but lab work takes time. If you want this case to get priority treatment, I guess you could put in a word there."

Carnes regretted his words as soon they slipped out. The lab guys were overworked and constantly under pressure from the U.S. Attorney's office to finish work in time to comply with the speedy trial laws. The last thing Carnes needed was to piss them off. "Um, if it was clear it was coming from up above, you know. We're not complaining."

Fletcher patted the air with a well-manicured hand. "Sure, Detective. I understand. Remember, I used to sit on that side of the desk." Carnes and Rodriguez glanced at each other but kept their faces impassive. The captain was known more for his political savvy and ability to promote himself than for his accomplishments as a detective. "Lieutenant, you sure you don't need more people on this?"

"Not yet, sir," said Rogers. Carnes, Rodriguez, and Bryant nodded.

Fletcher sighed and tapped his pencil. "So what about your suspects?"

"Rodriguez checked out the maintenance man's alibi. His girlfriend and several friends swear they were all in New York."

Rodriguez took over the story from Carnes. "Alibi checked out pretty good. Even had a credit card receipt from one of the gas stations on the New Jersey Turnpike last Friday. Unless they're all lying, he's clean."

Carnes continued. "Pardo's still our best bet. The line between love and hate is thin. He's the last one we can place her with, and he can't prove an alibi."

"Ah, yes. Mr. Pardo. Wanted to mention that. A man with some connections. Councilman Radcliffe already called—Pardo must be a campaign contributor. Radcliffe was inquiring about—uh—'disturbing reports' that we were 'harassing' the man."

"That's ridiculous," Carnes said. "We just—"

Fletcher raised his hand. "I know. I assumed we were clean. I only want you to understand the heat I'm getting. From all sides. Be sensitive, gentlemen."

"Sensitive?" Carnes said. Rodriguez placed his hand on Carnes' arm.

Fletcher smiled. "What other leads do you have?"

"Other than Pardo?" Carnes asked.

Fletcher nodded.

Carnes explained about the matchbooks. "I checked out the bars—"

"I bet you did." Fletcher liked to be one of the guys.

"I didn't come up with much. Sex crimes is looking for suspects from the neighborhood who fit the profile. I've started interviewing old friends of the victim."

"Well, then. I'll try to hold the wolves at bay for a while. I can't work miracles." The captain smiled benevolently and stood. "Let me know the moment anything develops." He looked at Rogers. "I want daily updates at least."

"Yes, sir."

"We've really got nothing but dead ends." Rodriguez tapped the papers on his desk. "Is Pardo one of those secret crazies?"

"Maybe. His ex was definitely holding something back," said Carnes.

"Mendez' alibi seems pretty secure. Unless we get real lucky on the latents or a car seen in the neighborhood, we got nothin'."

"Yeah, tell me something I don't know. What galls me is it just doesn't fit together. We've got a victim everyone says was Snow White, perfect in every way. Everyone liked her; no one had a grudge against her. Even Pardo, prick that he is, doesn't really seem to fit. What does that tell you?"

"She picked up some nut in a bar?" asked Rodriguez.

"It's happened before. There doesn't seem to be a financial angle. No drug connection. Other than the jilted lover theory, we don't have shit."

"So whatta we do?"

"Yank on Pardo's chain a little."

"Fletcher won't be happy."

"Neither will Councilman Radcliffe."

Rodriguez smiled ruefully. "I guess I already have enough years in for my pension."

Carnes and Rodriguez caught up with Fitz Pardo at his club. They'd needed their credentials and some fast talk to get past the snooty desk man. Then they'd nearly overdosed on dark woods, etched glass, and brass before they found the exercise center. TV monitors and gleaming chrome equipment filled a room walled on one side with a full-length mirror.

Pardo rode an exercise bike, his eyes locked on the digital readout before him. Dressed in a "Lawyers Do It in Their Briefs" T-shirt, shorts, and scuffed exercise shoes, his hair matted at the temples, Pardo seemed smaller than he did in his office.

"Counselor?" Carnes said.

Pardo started. "What the fuck are you—" His patrician face momentarily contorted into something between a grimace and a snarl. Then he regained the superior expression they'd seen in the office. With exaggerated calm, he climbed off the bike and picked up a towel from a nearby stool. He buried his face in the towel for a moment. Carnes could almost feel him counting to ten. Pardo draped the towel around his neck. "Gentlemen. This is a surprise." He did not smile. "What are you doing here?" Pardo pulled up the waistband of his shorts.

"We just needed to ask you something, and your office said we could find you here," Rodriguez said.

Pardo sighed. "Gentlemen, how can I help you?" His tone sounded somewhat less than polite.

"Well, you may have heard of DNA testing." Carnes kept his voice flat and professional. "Experts can match bodily fluids or tissue found at a scene to a suspect's."

Although Pardo's face was expressionless, his eyes glared. "So?" He raised his eyebrows in mock curiosity.

"So, we were wondering if you'd consent to giving some samples of blood, hair—that sort of thing," Carnes said. "Assuming you have nothing to hide . . ." He let his voice trail off.

Pardo pointed his finger at Carnes as though it were a pistol. "Detective, I would do anything to help you find Victoria's killer. However, it's troubling to hear what you're saying. You think I am a suspect. That's ridiculous."

"Then you should have no problem—"

Pardo smiled bitterly. "You're daring me, as though this were some playground game. I am not a child. It's because I have every interest in your finding Vicky's killer that I find your request so troubling. I had nothing to do with Vicky's death, so I must conclude that your request means you have nothing. You gentlemen are stumbling around in a fog. Very troubling."

"Look," Carnes said quietly. "We thought we'd give you a chance to do this voluntarily. If you have nothing to fear, it shouldn't be a big deal."

"You obviously don't have a thing on who killed Victoria. You're wasting time and taxpayer money with your incompetence. You know I was sleeping with Victoria. I would certainly expect you'd find some traces of me in her apartment."

"These samples could clear you and allow us to focus on other subjects." Rodriguez' tone was reasonable, but a vein pulsed in his temple.

"If I did give you samples, I'd want my own expert testing them as well. We wouldn't want any mistakes."

Carnes glared at Pardo and took a step toward him. "Are you suggesting—"

Pardo stepped back a bit uncertainly, holding up his hands. "Detective, you misunderstand. Mistakes can happen with the best motivations. I'm a lawyer. I don't take chances." Pardo spoke in the well-modulated tones he'd used in his office. "Although this is an unwarranted—and, I assure you, unfounded—intrusion on my privacy, I have nothing to hide. However, I know mistakes happen." His smile was tight, controlled. "But I'll tell you what. I'll talk to John Brennan, a criminal lawyer friend of mine, about whether I should agree to this and how it should be done. I'll get back to you."

"Is that a yes or a no?" asked Carnes.

"We'll consider your request." Pardo's face was a mask.

"We'll consider your request," Carnes mimicked as they walked out the front door. "Isn't that lawyerese for 'fuck you'?"

"Yeah, that's usually what it means," said Rodriguez. "But the guy's right. We don't have squat."

"No." Carnes sighed. "I guess we don't—not yet anyway."

Rodriguez saluted the desk man, who nodded stiffly at them as they left.

"The thing is, if he were innocent, wouldn't he just consent? If it's not his semen, the DNA test would clear him," said Carnes.

"True. But he is a lawyer," said Rodriguez.

"Meaning?"

"Everything by the book."

Carnes nodded. He looked at his watch. "I guess I better go pound the pavement some more. The bars should be opening. I'll work on the random pickup theory."

"You mean you'll work on a pickup."

"Funny."

11

Carnes had visited seven of the city's hottest nightspots and come up empty-handed. He'd found no information about Vicky Benton and, even worse, been turned down by an attractive redhead. Now, he pulled up a bar stool at The Choice, a dark cave with recessed lighting, soft jazzy music. The bar was known for its rowdy happy hour which owed its popularity to its two-for-one drinks and gargantuan hors d'oeuvres buffet. At this late hour, the place was quiet. A television hung in each corner of the bar, lending a muted bluish tinge to the few upturned faces. Carnes scanned the sets. One showed the Orioles game; the other had summer reruns of a sitcom. The clientele was young, mostly couples. Silver foxes not welcome.

"Can I help you?" the voice purred, smooth as a fine brandy. A leggy blond who filled out tight blue shorts and a white "The Choice" T-shirt smiled at him over the bar. Choice is right. USDA Grade A. A square white patch of apron covered the juncture between her legs like a loincloth. Even in the dim light, her teeth shone in a bright Pepsodent smile. Her face and arms were tanned a rich brown. Carnes took in her Caribbean blue eyes and pretty face and decided she was only a small bump in the ridge of her nose away from perfection. Darryl Hannah before a nose job. Carnes instantly created a biography: college student, would-be actress, making ends meet tending bar during the summer.

Carnes flashed his friendliest smile. "I hope so."

Her laughter was full bodied but with a little roughness at the edges. "What're you drinking?"

"Nothing yet." Carnes indicated the empty expanse of glossy wood in front of him.

She folded her arms beneath her breasts, the tight material displaying erect nipples. "True. What can I get you?"

"Two things. Your name, and a Beck's dark."

"Marlene," she said. She pronounced the second "e" as though it were an "a." "One Beck's dark coming right up." She moved off down the bar with a grace that made Carnes revise his biography to include ballet or figure skating. She pulled a bottle out of the stainless steel refrigerator, removed the cap with an efficient flick of her wrist, and poured the dark liquid down the inside rim of a tipped mug. No foam. She floated back and put the mug on the counter with an affirmative clunk. She dried her hands on the small white apron at her waist. "Haven't seen you here before."

"No," Carnes said. "I haven't been here in a while. You weren't here. I would have noticed."

She squinted at him. "Pretty lame." She grinned to show she wasn't angry. "I just started here a month ago."

"Let me guess—graduate student in law at Georgetown but also an aspiring dancer and fashion model?" Carnes liked to let women know he appreciated their brains as well as their looks.

Marlene laughed. "Law student? Haven't heard that one before. Why not astronaut or physician?"

"OK. Psychologist?"

She shook her head.

"Botanist?"

She shook her head again.

"Agronomist?"

"What's that?"

"You're asking me?" Carnes smacked his hand down on the bar. "I know—you're some kind of physicist. Nuclear, particle, whatever."

"Not even close. I'm a teacher—kindergarten."

"What's a kindergarten teacher doing—"

"I love bars. Besides, I've gotta make money during the summers. Work here in the evening, tan during the day. How 'bout you?"

"Guess."

"Let's see, brain surgeon, astronaut—no, existential philosopher." She showed off the perfect white teeth.

"On the money. Police detective." Carnes held out his hand. "John Carnes."

"Most of the guys who want to impress me"—she squinted at him again—"claim they work for 'the company.' Can't remember any who said they're cops."

Carnes smiled. "Well, I really am a cop. Homicide." Carnes pulled out his shield and flopped it open on the bar.

Marlene examined it. "Looks real."

He flipped it back and put it into his pocket. "It is." He pulled out the picture of Victoria Benton. "Actually, I came in hoping to find out if this girl has been in here before."

Marlene examined the picture carefully. "Maybe. Probably once or twice—can't be sure. Lots of people come in once or twice." She nodded down the bar. "Course, some're here so often they have their own stools."

"Remember when she was here last?"

"Maybe a week or so ago."

"What day?"

"Not sure, but I think it was a weekend." She put her hand over her eyes. "Could've been a Friday or Saturday."

"She with anyone?"

"Let me think." She chewed for a moment on her lower lip. "Yeah, I think she met some guy. Came in alone, but I saw a guy with her later."

"Can you describe him?"

"Haven't a clue really. Might recognize a picture."

Carnes pulled out a driver's license photograph of Fitz Pardo. "This the guy?"

"No, don't think so. Pretty sure it was a younger man."

"Can you describe anything about him?"

"Not really. I mean, we get lots of people in here and—especially if they don't sit at the bar—I can't remember everyone."

"Not even the charming CIA agents?"

"I especially try to forget them."

"How about cops?" Carnes tried his best smile.

"I'll be off in an hour. Why don't you hang around and find out?"

12

Wiley sat on the edge of his chair and laughed at Carnes. "You are one hurtin' dude. Thought I was fucked up in the mornin'." Although Carnes was nearly six feet tall, Wiley hulked over him like a large black bear. Wiley's white shirt strained against every button. The legs of Wiley's desk bowed slightly under his weight.

"You trying to surplus that desk, Wes?" asked Carnes. A picture of Wes Unseld, the former Washington Bullets' star, a dead ringer for Wiley, adorned the wall beside his desk.

Carnes walked back to the coffeemaker. Four more hours of sleep, five more cups of coffee, a blood transfusion, and he'd feel just fine. He looked into the mirror some sadist put up next to the coffeemaker. Even the bags under his bloodshot eyes had bags. He tried to remember how much sleep he'd had. His memory of the night was a vague fantasy of tangled limbs, Amaretto licked off hot flesh, catlike noises, and—way too late—the sleep of the dead. Only a crushing exhaustion remained. He'd hurried home, barely having time to shower, dress, and look in on Avery, before he came to work.

Seeing Avery, spread across her bed in innocent sleep, he'd felt a deep stab of guilt. Once again, he'd missed homework and dinner, wasn't around to read her a story or tuck her in. Instead, he was with Marlene, already a fading pastiche of memory.

He felt miserable. Avery kept him anchored. His feelings for her were genuine and unselfish. They transcended all other emotions. Yet, in the presence of a Marlene, he'd lose his compass and drift off, neglecting Avery. How much could she endure? When did the bond between father and daughter fray to the breaking point? It was bad enough when his job pulled him away, but *this* he could—he should—be able to control. Carnes stared into the tired eyes in the mirror.

"So what's got your butt in an uproar? You sit on a letter opener or something?" Carnes asked Wiley.

"No," said Rodriguez. "He's just a bit distressed."

"Distressed?" Wiley opened his eyes wide in mock horror. "Distressed?"

"About the memo in our boxes," Rodriguez said. "Chief's lamenting our statistics again this month." Rodriguez ran his fingers through his hair.

Wiley tapped his temple. "Lamenting? What are you, a fuckin' talking dictionary?"

Rodriguez smiled a slight Mona Lisa smile. "Gotta keep up with these college kids." He hooked a thumb at Carnes.

Wiley waved his hands. "Now, the captain's on our asses. Mandatory overtime until we clear another five to ten percent of these fuckin' cases. If you ask me, we need more cops, not more quotas."

"What're you bitchin' about? You need the OT to make the payments on your Caddy," said Carnes. "With all the tight budget talk, we gotta take advantage of OT when we can get it. You wouldn't be happy in a whorehouse."

"Try me." Wiley cast an apologetic glance at the picture of his wife and kids.

Rodriguez watched the byplay like a spectator at a tennis match. He hitched up his suspenders and winked at Carnes.

Carnes lifted the memo from the stack in his in box. He glanced at it, then slid it over the side of the desk into the circular file. "What else is new?"

"It's bullshit," Wiley said. "Murder rate's up again. You see any more fuckin' detectives in here?" He spewed powdered sugar and bits of donut. "And mobile crime's worse. Other night, the same two techs worked three different scenes. Now, tell me how long they can keep that pace before they start fuckin' up."

Rodriguez grinned. "Why doesn't the chief simply ask the youngsters to stop blowin' each other away?"

"Now, that's an idea. Maybe a fuckin' public service announcement on the morning cartoons?" Wiley slapped his hand on his thigh and showed a mouthful of shining teeth and one gold crown in a broad smile. "I like it. 'Hi kids. As chief of police, I'm concerned about the number of youngsters who are dying on the streets of the nation's capital.'" His imitation of the chief was perfect. "'This unfortunate trend has led to many personal tragedies for citizens and substantial additional work for my department.'"

"Live at five," said Carnes. They laughed.

After Wiley quieted down, Carnes paged through Victoria Benton's address book. There were at least forty names and addresses. Some were obviously relatives. He would pass on those for now. He decided to focus on the names in the metropolitan area. After a moment's thought, he listed in his notebook the names and numbers of all the people who lived or worked within a half-hour radius of Victoria Benton's apartment. That reduced the number to be contacted to thirteen.

Forty minutes later, Carnes had crossed three names off the list because the phones were disconnected. Two more did not answer. Others, such as Mark Fremont, a gruff-voiced older man who employed the victim as a secretary during school vacations, had been "out of touch."

Carnes rubbed his eyes, got up, and stretched. Rodriguez was reviewing files of known sex criminals who lived within several blocks of Benton's apartment. Rodriguez caught Carnes' eye. "Learn anything yet?" he asked.

"Yeah, this is a transient city." Carnes' knees creaked as he walked over to the coffeepot and refilled his cup. He took a sip. Potent stuff. "Who made the witches' brew today, Breech?" Breech was notorious for his strong coffee.

"Grows hair on your tongue, huh?" Rodriguez peered at his cup as though it were filled with poison. "Or eats a hole in your gut."

"Yeah. Next time Breech goes near the coffeemaker, let's shoot the sorry motherfucker," Wiley chimed in from his desk, even though he appeared to be in the middle of a phone conversation. Carnes had never figured out how Wiley listened to two things at once.

"Just what I need." Carnes took a gulp and made a face. With a sigh, he slid his cup onto his desk and sank back into his chair. The next name in the book was Becky Granite. He picked up the phone and punched in the number.

A bright voice answered the phone. "Marketing, Becky Granite speaking."

Carnes introduced himself.

"Homicide?" Becky's voice sounded uncertain.

"Yes. I'm investigating a murder and found your name in the victim's address book."

Carnes waited several seconds. *She's sitting there trying to figure out who I'm talking about, preparing herself for bad news.*

"Who? I mean, who was murdered?"

"I'd rather not discuss this on the phone. Can we meet somewhere, maybe after work?"

"No. I mean, yes we can meet, but I need to know who. I can't sit around wondering all day."

"I understand." Carnes took a deep breath. "The victim's name is Victoria Benton."

"Oh my God!" Becky's voice broke. "Vicky?"

"Yes, I'm sorry." He heard a muffled sound. "I'm sorry I had to tell you this way. It happened Monday."

"God, it's Thursday already."

"Well, it was in the papers and on TV."

"I never pay much attention—God. Vicky!"

"Is there someplace we can meet and talk?"

"Um, hang on a second." Becky's voice cracked. Carnes heard a rattle as though she had put down the phone, then a distant honking sound. The phone rattled again. "I'm not thinking too clearly." A pause. "I was going to do karate tonight. Let me think." Another pause. "How about the bar downstairs? Barnstormers. You can see it from the street."

"What time?"

"I get off at five." Becky paused. "Can you meet me then?"

"Sure," said Carnes.

"How will I know you? Are you in uniform or do you wear a trench coat or something?"

"In this heat?" According to the forecaster on the morning news, the high would be eighty-nine degrees with 80 percent humidity. "How 'bout if I find you? What do you look like—what're you wearing?"

"Long dark hair, blue eyes, about five-six. I'm wearing a flowered blouse and blue skirt."

"OK. I'll see you later."

The weatherman had lied. The thermometer had crept past ninety and the air was as thick as soup. Luckily, Carnes' air conditioner was working for a change, so the temperature in his car was a relatively moderate eighty. Carnes parked in front of Barnstormers and left his "police business" card on the dashboard. Once past the heavy wooden door, he let the cool air chill him as his eyes adjusted to the dimness.

To the right of the door stretched the bar, fifteen feet of dark wood and polished brass. Over it, shimmering glasses hung from wooden racks. A young man who bore an uncanny resemblance to the Woody character on *Cheers* stood behind the bar shaking a drink. Several rows of bottles rose on stepped shelves behind him. To Carnes' left, dark wooden tables and chairs were grouped in an informal L around the bar. Booths lined the far wall. Air-show posters and pictures of biplanes, the Wright brothers, Lucky Lindy, and other airmen and women adorned the walls. Models of old planes hung from the ceiling. Not a fern or philodendron in sight. Soft jazz provided a backdrop for the hum of conversation. A very comfortable place.

At the bar sat a weathered blond woman and balding man. Several feet down, a morose young man stared into his beer. Two stools away, two young women leaned toward each other giggling. A couple of middle-aged men in suits sat at a table already filled with empty glasses. They laughed too loudly. Salesmen. In one of the booths at the back, a solitary man checked his watch and then the door every few seconds. Two men sat at a table filled with papers and talked animatedly, pointing to the papers every few seconds.

Warm air washed over Carnes' back and light flooded into the bar. "Sorry I'm late. You're the detective?"

Carnes turned. Becky was framed by a halo of light from the door. She had the strong, high cheekbones of a model but smiling blue eyes that telegraphed a frank, uncomplicated friendliness. She blinked, adjusting to the dimness. She offered her hand. Although her fingers were long and slim, her grip was firm and competent. Carnes introduced himself and led her toward a booth in the back.

An eager waiter trotted over. He smiled in recognition at Becky, frowned slightly at Carnes, and took their drink orders. After several minutes of small talk about the heat and humidity, Carnes plunged in.

"I'm sorry I dropped this on you by telephone, but there were a lot of names in Victoria's address book. I had to use the phone to—"

"I understand. It was just a shock." Becky shook her head. "You don't expect—"

"I know."

"When did it happen?"

"This past weekend. As I told you on the phone, it was on the news Monday and in the *Post* and *Times* Tuesday."

"Oh? I guess I don't really pay attention to the hatch, match, and dispatch."

"Huh?"

"That's what my mom used to call the announcements of births, weddings, and the obits." Her grin was simple and disarming. Her face became serious. "Besides, it's like overload or something. There are so many murders here. But I guess I don't have to—"

"Tell me? No."

Her face was strained and serious, her voice low. "What happened?"

"Well, I can't give you too many details." He studied his hands. "You wouldn't want too many details. Leave it at this: she was sexually assaulted and killed."

"Oh." She stared into her drink. Her upper lip trembled slightly and her eyes glittered, but she maintained her composure. Carnes caught himself staring at her and forced himself to look around the bar.

Becky took a deep breath and sipped her drink. "So what can I do— I mean, what do you want to know?"

"Tell me about the victi—about Vicky. How did you meet her? How long did you know her? When did you see her last?"

"Gosh." Her eyes swept absently toward the entrance to the bar as a noisy group entered. "I'm not sure where to start." She studied her hands for a moment. "Let's see. I met Vicky in college—at Maryland. She was in my pledge class freshman year."

"Sorority?"

"Yes. Alpha Omega." She took another sip of her drink. "We lived in the house our junior and senior years. Did lots of things together. I haven't seen her too much lately, maybe at an occasional party or sorority event. You know how you sort of lose track of people?"

Carnes nodded.

"Well, I think I saw her last year. Must have been the Duke game. Football. We lost, as usual."

"Was that the last time you saw her?"

"I think so. She wasn't my best friend or anything." Becky's eyes seemed to fog again. "We had fun though."

"Did you know anything about what she was doing?"

"Doing? Like where she worked, that sort of thing?"

"Yeah."

"Well"—she nibbled her lower lip—"I think she worked for some law firm. A paralegal. Not too far from here. The name and number are on my Rolodex."

"That's OK. I have it."

The waiter appeared. "Can I get you something to eat? An appetizer?" Carnes raised an eyebrow.

An expression of uncertainty passed across Becky's face and then she smiled. "Yes, I guess so. The potato skins are good and they have a great sauce for the fried zucchini."

"So much for a low-fat diet," Carnes said. He turned to the waiter. "OK. I'll just have to run an extra mile."

The waiter smiled as though he'd heard that line a thousand times, then departed.

"You run?" Becky asked.

"Have to. Otherwise I'd probably weigh three hundred pounds and have an ulcer besides."

Becky smiled. "I try to work out too."

"Oh?"

"Yeah. I was sort of a jock in school. My mom said I was the local tomboy—"

"There's nothing boy about you."

Even in the dim light, Carnes could see Becky's face darkening. When was the last time he'd seen a woman blush at such a simple compliment?

Becky hurried on. "I still do aerobics and karate and play tennis a little."

"I haven't played tennis in years. Do you want—" Carnes stopped himself. "Sorry. Getting a little off track. What kind of woman was Vicky?"

"How do you mean?"

"Personal habits, interests—that sort of thing."

"That's tough. In college she was fun, liked to party. Don't get me wrong, she was a good enough student. She dressed well. Wasn't the neatest housekeeper." She laughed. "We had to bug her to do her share of the cleaning. I guess some things were more important to her than others."

"Guys?"

"Sure."

"Tell me about them."

"What do you mean?" Becky shifted in her seat. "Do you want to know who she dated, or what they were like?"

"Both."

Becky sipped her drink and stared over Carnes' head. The waiter bustled over with the appetizers, inquired about whether he could get them anything else, and rushed off to another table. Barnstormers was packed now. Carnes realized he'd been straining to hear Becky over the sounds of voices, clinking glasses, scraping chairs, and music.

"Well, I didn't really care for the guys she dated. Most were self-important—you know, the kind who think you're lucky they'll go out with you. Lots of upperclassmen. One guy was different—bookish, but a nice guy."

"James Bardash?"

"Yes. That's it. She liked him, but I think she only went out with him so he'd help her in school." She put her hand to her mouth. "Gosh, I know that makes her sound awful. She really wasn't. She was sweet and kind—"

"Good to animals?" Carnes smiled.

Becky colored again. "OK, I'm overdoing it. But she really was a good person. Just had bad taste in guys. You know what I mean?"

"Actually, I haven't had that problem."

Becky rewarded him with a soft chuckle from low in her throat. Her eyes twinkled again. Carnes liked making her smile.

They discussed the boys and men in Vicky's life: athletes, rich kids, graduate students, even a professor. Carnes liked the way the corner of Becky's mouth twisted and her nose wrinkled when she described a distasteful characteristic, the unself-conscious way she laughed at a particular mishap. Several times he lost himself in the musical sound of her voice and had to mentally kick himself.

Something about the way she talked was particularly appealing. Perhaps it was her directness. She described people and their behavior with a sharp eye for their flaws, but at the same time she was not judgmental. Her outlook was positive. She saw the humor in life. Carnes took notes and asked occasional questions until he thought he knew everything he cared to learn about Vicky's old boyfriends.

"So what about Fitz Pardo?"

"A user."

"Why?"

"Too full of himself. He thought of Vicky as a pretty accessory. She was like a piece of jewelry or a nice suit he wore to enhance his own appearance."

"That's pretty tough."

"I saw them together. He didn't look at her the way a man looks at a woman when he loves her. No real feeling or connection there."

"Did she know?"

"Maybe." Becky shook her head sadly. "This is something she did. It was a pattern. She always attracted guys like that."

"And you?" Carnes' eyes locked into hers.

"Is your interest professional?" She raised an eyebrow.

"And personal."

"I'm not sure I want to be personal with a policeman."

"Why not?"

"You know, you hear all sorts of stories."

"Stories?"

"Yeah, you know, like some woman gets stopped for speeding and the police officer hits on her."

"You been speeding?"

Becky chuckled. "I take the fifth."

"So what kind of guys do you date?"

Becky munched on a potato skin. "Why did you become a detective?"

Carnes' face windowed his surprise. "Huh?"

"I asked you a simple question."

"Who's the detective here?" He tried a Jack Webb growl.

"So," Becky teased, "you feel uncomfortable when the tables are turned?"

Carnes held his hands out before him in surrender. "I confess. What am I confessing to?"

"Why you became a detective."

"Heavy question. I probably wanted to solve mysteries, seek the truth."

"Psych 101!" Becky mocked. "OK, I deserved that. But don't we all seek our own truths?"

"You a philosophy major?"

"No. Marketing. I'm just curious about people. Why do you think you're different?"

"Different? Who knows? All I know is that many people—probably most—spend their lives running away from the truth. The truth can be hard and painful. It can be ugly. Whoever said 'the truth shall set you free' certainly wasn't a cop."

"What's it like?"

"Being a cop?"

"Yes."

"What's it like being a marketing manager?"

"Hey, I'm asking the questions now," said Becky. "You vill answer my questions. Ve have vays of making you talk."

Carnes laughed. "You've watched too many late, late, late, late shows."
He cocked his head. "Did I get the right number of lates?"

"Close. But you still haven't answered my question."

"Geez. You're relentless. Can I bring you in as a consultant for the
tough interrogations?"

Becky stared at him, unsmiling.

"OK, you win. Being a policeman is a lot of things. Sometimes it's boring. Regardless of what you see on TV, there's little glamor in being a
cop," said Carnes.

Becky leaned toward him, eyes sharp with interest.

"There's bureaucratic stupidity that makes you want to tear out your
hair—or someone else's. Politics and PR. The average cop sometimes
feels like he's part of an occupying army, patrolling enemy territory. That
often means headache-inducing frustration and sometimes self-loathing.
The difference is we're undermanned and outgunned.

"Then there's our fine citizenry. You'd expect people to want to help
make a case against someone who murdered a close relative or neighbor. Most of the time, you get Sergeant Schultz on *Hogan's Heroes:* 'I know
nossing.'"

Becky smiled.

"So far, I've had few car chases and fewer gun battles, and the drug
lords aren't inviting me to party on their private yachts. It's nothing like
TV, especially for the beat cop. It's mostly mind-numbing boredom, bad
food, pathetic people. For a homicide cop there's less boredom, more
gore."

"So why do you do it?"

Carnes grinned. "I told you, I'm a seeker of truth, a righter of wrongs."

Becky grinned back at him. "You sound like a recruiting commercial.
Be all you can be, join the Metropolitan PD!"

Carnes smiled ironically. "Catchy. Yeah, I could be the Metropolitan
PD poster boy." He tried an announcer's tone. "Learn to treat gunshot
wounds while waiting an hour for the ambulance—"

"Learn free enterprise in our new street drug markets."

"Travel northeast to southeast, from Capitol Hill to Foggy Bottom."
Carnes winked. "This has potential."

13

As he pulled the comforter over Avery's shoulders, Carnes smelled the fresh scent of shampoo. He tucked Ro Ro in beside her and kissed her forehead. "Love you," he whispered.

Avery grunted something undecipherable and rolled onto her side, resting the crook of her arm over the stuffed dog. Carnes smiled. In the morning she wouldn't remember he came in. Yet this was part of their bonding ritual, a moment of contact on some elemental level that transcended consciousness. The bonds between Avery and himself were profound and spiritual.

Carnes had never felt that way about Caroline, even early in their marriage. At their best, they were acquaintances who did things together, had sex, made a baby. Carnes leaned against the doorjamb, aware he'd acquired a stupid grin watching Avery sleep. Nothing like that happened with Caroline. He remembered the nights he came home late, slid naked between the sheets, glided over toward her warmth, and kissed her on the neck. Usually, she grunted and pulled away, presenting her bony back in silent reproach. When did he stop going through the motions? When did he start seeking comfort in other women's beds?

Avery's shoulder rose and fell in time to the gentle song of her breathing. Maybe for Avery's sake Carnes could feel some guilt about his contributions to the breakup of his marriage. But you can't damage a marriage that exists only on paper.

What a contrast Becky provided. Where Caroline was blond and regal, Becky was dark and natural. She was so direct and open. And they'd had fun just talking. It was the first time in a while that he'd really enjoyed just talking with a woman. Usually, his conversations with women were merely part of a presex or aftersex ritual. What was different? Maybe Becky was the kind of woman who could be a friend. Or more.

Carnes watched Avery's chest move in a peaceful rhythm. At least one good thing had come from his marriage. "Good night, sweetheart," he whispered.

14

The anticipation was exquisite. Exquisite anticipation. It had a certain ring to it. He glanced at his watch. How long did he have to wait? Not long now. Sometimes he couldn't get out of the office this early. Today he couldn't sit still. The restless creature inside him wouldn't succumb to discipline.

It was time to do some planning. He was good at planning. He savored each detail. In a psych course, he'd learned some people were process oriented. He loved the process. At times, he could plan every moment. But sometimes, his ideas refused to submit to structure. Then things would come to him in an explosion of inspiration.

Every time he saw her, the itch grew stronger. He knew only one way to scratch that itch.

Enough sitting. Did he dare get out of his car? If he went closer, she might recognize him. So what? She'd never put it together. His excitement rose. No. Keep your distance. Not time yet.

Still, he wanted to see her. She wouldn't suspect a thing. It's OK. Get out. He climbed out of his car.

"And turn, and one, two, three, four, right foot now . . ." Katie, the nuclear-fueled aerobics instructor, bellowed over the pulsing sound of the dance music. She moved to the music, her ponytail bouncing off her back while the rest of the class struggled to keep up. She doesn't even have the decency to break a sweat, Becky thought. Becky gritted her teeth into an expression between admiration and pure loathing, the way millions of young soldiers glared at their drill instructors.

The sweat ran down Becky's sides in rivulets, soaking into her leotard at her ribs and waist. Dark blotches appeared at her breasts, on her stomach. She wiped the sweat off her forehead, then scratched a spot on her head with a quick movement of her hand. She was paying her dues for the dinner and drinks last night. Her breath came in tight rasps as her body cried out for oxygen. Move to the music, move to the music, left, right, left, right, up, down, up, down. The music switched to a salsa number and Becky's breathing settled into a rhythmic pant. Maybe she wouldn't die after all.

Around her, several women were slowing down or taking a rest. She smiled. She'd always been stronger, more athletic than most of her friends. As a girl she'd climbed trees, played ball, run races, trying to keep up with her older brothers and their friends. Although she was usually one of the last kids picked for the ball games behind the school, the boys treated her as an equal. Constant effort and determination allowed her to hold her own. She thrived in the competitive atmosphere. The rough-and-tumble ways of boys appealed to her.

The way the boys treated her changed though. Almost overnight, her arms and legs sprouted like magic beanstalks. Her face tightened over both cheekbones and jaw, and her breasts pushed out and waist pulled in as though invisible hands were remodeling her body. Seemingly caught up in a hormonal rhythm of their own, her hips began to sway slightly as she walked. Quite suddenly, boys who had treated her like an equal became awkward and tongue-tied in her presence. The next thing she knew, they were offering to carry her books or give her rides. Nothing was so simple again.

Not that Becky stopped being a "jock." In school, she played field hockey, tennis, volleyball, and lacrosse. Now, she took regular karate and aerobics classes to stay in shape. Not only did Becky enjoy being fit, she also liked the unity of purpose she found in team play and, now, in her classes.

They were into their cooldown program of slower, stretching movements. Becky was bent over, hands on the floor, legs stretched out in a V beneath her when she felt a chill at the base of her neck. She looked up quickly and caught a shadow of movement beyond the long windows beside the classroom door.

Pretty typical. Becky and some of the other women often joked after class about the men who peeked through the window to watch the

women bounce through their routines. When they came out and dis-
persed toward their cars, men lounged in the halls pretending to be deep
in conversation or absorbed with the bulletin boards. Their eyes followed
the women. Once, a paunchy, balding man wearing a thick gold wedding
ring tried to strike up a conversation with Becky about whether aerobics
would be good for him. He stared hungrily at her breasts. "Why don't
you take aerobics with your wife?" she had cooed softly.

"Stretch two, three, four." Katie's voice blared. Becky felt the muscles
behind her legs protest as she touched the floor. The chill returned at
the back of her neck. *Oh hell. Let him watch.*

She wondered if John Carnes would peek in the window at her. She
could tell he was attracted to her. They'd talked and laughed until way
too late. It had been a while since she'd had such a good time with a man.
She felt a pang of guilt. After all, she wouldn't have been sitting there
having dinner with him except for Vicky Benton's death.

Carnes was hard to read. He made her laugh but he seemed serious
too. He listened carefully when she talked, but how much of that was cop
technique? When his eyes locked into hers, her heart began to palpitate.
She usually wasn't attracted to an experienced ladies' man, and she could
tell he was one. He seemed to genuinely like her, but how much was real
and how much was a put-on? Still, there was something in his dark-brown
eyes beyond lustful thoughts. She sensed a veiled pain, a vulnerability.
That was part of what drew her to him.

"That's it for today, ladies." Katie hopped down off the platform and
punched the button to end the hissing of the boom box. Sounds of relief filled the room: pained sighs, grunts, a high-pitched laugh, the mut-
ter of voices.

"You wanna go get something?" Marcia asked.

Becky wiped her face with the towel she pulled out of her gym bag.
"Yeah, a transfusion."

Marcia laughed. "Hell, you're in better shape than most of us. God
knows how you find the time to be so damned healthy." She swept her
hand around in a large arc that included red-faced, panting women of
all shapes and sizes, slumped against the wall, hunched over, sucking on
bottles of liquid, or wiping their faces with towels. "Why the hell do we
go through this? I could be home eating a gallon of ice cream. Hell,
maybe I'd even give Brad a workout."

Marcia launched into a lengthy comic monologue about Boring Brad,
the guy she lived with. It seemed he couldn't do anything right: he left

the toilet seat up, threaded the toilet paper roll so the paper pulled out
from underneath the roll, put red shirts into the laundry with the whites,
squeezed his toothpaste from the middle of the tube, and sat like a zom-
bie in front of the TV for virtually any sporting event.

"Half the time, I have to take his pulse to make sure he's not dead."
Marcia laughed. "The other night I danced in front of the TV and did a
striptease. He was watching some Australian rugby match. Australian
rugby! He doesn't even understand the game! Know what he said?"

"Move over?"

"Close. 'Wait until the half'—or whatever they call it—'is over.'"

Marcia had repeated variations on this theme after every class. It was
part of their personal cooldown ritual. Becky wondered what they'd talk
about if Marcia didn't have Boring Brad to kick around.

"So why do you stay with the guy?"

"Once you get his attention, he has his uses." Marcia grinned, revealing impossibly perfect white teeth. For emphasis she bit her towel and
shook it. "He must be related to Warren Beatty. Know what I mean?"

"Really?" Becky had heard this all before, but she feigned surprise.

"Wouldn't you like to know?" Marcia crowed. "C'mon, let's get a snack."

Becky and Marcia sat at a small, red Formica table in the back of the
Fernwood Deli. The place was virtually empty. The wire metal racks with
the salt, pepper, ketchup, mustard, and the cone-shaped sugar dispenser
rose from each table like city skylines. Becky sipped at her lemonade. The
tables were arranged in an L around a refrigerator case of bottled drinks.
Posters advertising cream soda and "genuine draft beer in bottles" decorated the walls. A long refrigerator case of meats, cheeses, and salads
ran back toward their table from the front entrance. The air, thick
with the aromas of spicy meats, garlic, and vinegar, made Becky's tongue
tingle.

Becky listened to the quiet hum of the refrigerator compressors, the
higher-pitched whir of the meat slicer, and the soft murmur of the light-
rock station. She realized Marcia was saying something. "Huh?"

"Becky Granite, space queen." Marcia laughed.

"I'm sorry, I just—"

"I know, you were lost in some fantasy about some hunky guy."

"Not really. I guess I'm just tired," Becky said.

"You said you had dinner with a cop last night?"

"It was mostly business. He was investigating a murder."

"A murder?"

"Did you ever meet Vicky Benton?"

"No, you asked me on the phone. You really are spacy today." Marcia sipped her beer and gave Becky a sympathetic look. "She a close friend?"

"Well, she used to be. I haven't seen her much the last year or two." Becky's voice was heavy with regret. "But we were really close in college. She was my roommate in the sorority."

"Damn. Do they know who did it?"

"Not yet. John—"

"John?" Marcia raised an eyebrow.

"The detective handling her case—he gave the impression they're checking on everyone who knew her."

"It's a crazy world. Could be some loonytoon she met in a bar." Marcia nibbled at her sandwich, then took another sip of beer. "It's kind of weird, you know. I've got a great-grandmother in her nineties and my folks are still alive and yet here's someone our age who's dead. Yeah, pretty damn weird."

"I don't know if 'weird' is the word," said Becky "but I know what you mean. Do you think about dying?"

"Well, there are these moments with Brad when I wonder if I'm going to have a heart attack or something." Marcia smiled. "But so far, so good. Anyway, what a way to go."

Becky sipped her lemonade. "You're as bad as Carol. A one-track mind."

"Hey, at least I'm on the right track."

Becky smiled. "I'm being serious. I mean, you only think about older people or drug dealers when you think about dying. It's not that—in the back of your mind—you don't know the possibility exists. You could get hit by a speeding bus. But death seems so remote. You don't expect it to touch you. Now, I don't know."

"Yeah." Marcia sipped her beer, a thoughtful expression on her face. "See what you mean. Sorta makes you think, refocus priorities. When you get older, dying becomes more real."

"That's why they get kids to serve in the army," Becky said. "When you get older, life becomes more precious and death becomes more"—Becky searched for the right word—"inevitable."

"True. That's why my parents are always asking"—Marcia switched into an older voice with a New York accent—"'Who are you dating? Is it serious?'"

"'Settle down, have a family.'" Becky mimicked. "'Joannie's daughter just had a baby—'"

"Border collie." They collapsed into giggles.

"So, did I tell you about this detective I had dinner with last night?"

"Speaking of Border collies?"

"No, speaking of guys."

Marcia leaned forward. "Speak!"

"Well, there's something about this guy that's just so—"

"Sexy?"

"No—well, yeah. I guess he is a hunk, but that's not the word I was looking for." Becky stared over Marcia's head for a moment. "Appealing. I guess that's the word. He comes across real sophisticated, but there's still something a little . . ." Her voice trailed off for a moment. "I guess it's . . . well, he seems . . . vulnerable. He's also got a great sense of humor."

"Must be married," Marcia said. "Whenever I meet one like that, he's married."

"Well, not married. Divorced."

"Even worse," Marcia said.

Becky ignored her. "He has a daughter who's seven or eight."

Marcia's voice was suddenly serious. "Heavy." Then she smiled impishly. "So, how is he?"

"How is he?"

"Yeah. Don't play dumb with me. How is he?" Marcia emphasized the "is."

Becky shook her head. So much for Marcia's serious side. "I told you. Nothing happened."

"What's wrong with him?" Marcia grinned. "Or you?"

"Or you?" Becky snapped. "Sorry. Maybe I'm a little old-fashioned," she wrinkled her nose, "but I figure anyone worth sleeping with can wait. It's not that he wasn't interested. Me too. But I don't jump into bed with every guy I'm attracted to. Some things—relationships—can age a little bit, like fine wine."

Marcia nodded. "That's fine, but fine wines turn to vinegar. Remember Brett?"

"Low blow." Becky felt a jolt of pain. "But I'm serious. Any guy worth caring about can wait a while."

"We're not talking lifelong celibacy here, are we?" Marcia gave Becky a look of mock horror. "I mean, I know you're a little retarded in the guy department, but I didn't think it was anything serious. I didn't think you were a prude."

"I'm not a prude. It's just that I exercise some self-control. If I jumped into bed with everyone the first time they asked—"

"At least they ask. I should have that problem."

15

Carnes had learned nothing at this bar. He was bored and slightly depressed. He looked around. Couples everywhere. Slim pickings. Anyway, he really wasn't in the mood. He wondered what Becky was doing. The place had a pay phone in the back. To his amazement all the parts were present and the phone actually worked.

Becky Granite answered on the third ring. "Hello."

"Hi, John Carnes here."

"Detective John Carnes?"

"One and the same."

"Aren't you supposed to be out catching criminals or something?"

"I am, but I have a few hours and I wondered—"

"If I have a few hours?" she concluded.

"Yeah, I guess so."

"What do you have in mind?"

"Have you had dinner?"

"Aerobics, drink, and dinner."

"How about dessert?"

"Where?"

"I know this place in Georgetown. They bake the greatest tarts and pastries right on the premises."

"I'll be ready in fifteen"—Becky looked at herself in the glass front of her oven—"make that twenty-five minutes."

"See you then," Carnes said.

Carnes tried to remember when he last felt this way. His heart pounded and his stomach was tight with a nervous excitement. He'd felt like this when he took Melanie Trenton to his junior prom. What had happened to her anyway? Probably a mother of four. He certainly hadn't felt this way with Caroline. Even in the beginning.

Carnes watched Becky devour the Napoleon with an animal ferocity. She caught him staring and turned bright red. "This is really good."

Carnes raised an eyebrow. "I see." He pointed to the corner of his mouth. "You have a little cream right here."

Her pink tongue slashed out and zapped the little white speck. "Mmmn." She smiled at Carnes with an innocent enthusiasm. Carnes felt a flutter in his chest.

"God, I love sweets." Becky sipped her tea. "Tomorrow, I'll have to work out longer."

Carnes smiled. "You sound like me. Every time I overindulge, I say, 'Well, I've got to run an extra mile tomorrow.'"

"Do you?"

"Most of the time."

"And Shakespeare said, 'Vanity thy name is woman,'" Becky snorted.

"Guilty as charged." Carnes smiled.

"Speaking of 'guilty as charged,' have you made any progress—is that the way you say it?—on Vicky's murder?"

"Some suspects. Can't really give you many details." Carnes took a bite of his hazelnut torte. "Not bad." He gestured toward it with his fork. "Want a taste?"

"Sure."

He stuck his fork into the torte and with a twist of his wrist broke loose a bite-sized portion. "Now open the hangar." He began making airplane noises and Becky laughed. He flew the piece into her open mouth. "It still works on Avery too."

"Your daughter?"

Carnes nodded.

"Tell me about her."

Carnes did. "There's just nothing like the feeling you have for your kid," he concluded.

"What about your wife?"

"Very different."

"Why?"

"Not much to tell. It's been a couple of years."

"What was she like?"

Carnes thought for a minute. "Well, she was pretty, but it was that unapproachable, patrician kind of beauty. She's like those women you see at cocktail parties who look great in their cocktail dress, perfectly put together and made up, a glass held casually in their hand, a tight little smile pasted on their face. You think they're afraid if they really smiled their face would break. That's Caroline."

"You make her sound cold."

"Cold?" Carnes wrinkled his nose. "We're talking ice age."

"Kaboom."

Carnes grinned. "She may have had emotions, some feelings below that ice-cube exterior, but she didn't choose to share them with me."

"Oh." For a minute, Becky was seven again. Her mother was in what her dad called her blue period, walking around frozen-faced, always on the verge of tears. It wasn't until several years after the thaw that Becky learned from a friend what everyone else in town knew—her father had been having an affair. She told Carnes the story.

"No, Caroline is just cold. In the last two years, she's made almost no effort to see Avery. Not the way I was brought up," said Carnes. "In my family, everyone is emotional. We cry at weddings and movies, even reading books. When we celebrate, look out world!"

Once he began to talk, Carnes picked up momentum like a train on a downgrade, rolling on and on, almost breathless, through the story of his childhood, school, Avery, Caroline, the divorce. He found himself telling Becky more than he intended. "I certainly can't claim I was blameless. After a while, I just gave up. I looked for love and companionship in other places."

Carnes drank some coffee and tried to control his breathing. He hazarded a fearful glance at Becky. How would she react? He'd let his guard down and said too much. Would that scare her off? Why did he care? He didn't know, but he did. He felt like he'd swallowed something too big and it was stuck somewhere in his throat.

He tried to remember the last time he'd opened up like this to a woman. Certainly not to Caroline. Most of the time, his conversations with women were carefully orchestrated waltzes around, and ultimately leading to, one subject: sex. Carnes was expert at masking his flaws behind a veil of words. If he revealed part of himself, it was usually done strategically, part of the seduction. Why should he open up to Becky?

Maybe the steam had built up inside of him until it had to be released. She hadn't really probed. Maybe it was her simple gestures: a nod of encouragement, a small smile, a sympathetic turn of the mouth, the sincerity in her eyes. Or maybe it was something more profound, happening at the subterranean level where the streams of souls run into each other. Why analyze it? He felt comfortable talking to her.

He cleared his throat. "Not exactly an uplifting tale . . ." His voice trailed off.

"It's OK," Becky said. A slight smile kissed the corners of her mouth and eyes.

"I'm not usually such a motormouth," Carnes explained.

"It isn't easy to tell—to really share—serious things with somebody else. I know. Sometimes I act like my mom—keep things bottled up inside for a long time. But finally—boom—I just blow."

"Sounds dangerous." Carnes grinned.

"Not really. It's more dangerous to keep it all in. My parents were wonderful people, but sharing emotions was something we didn't do too often." Becky studied her hands. "When I was seven, my grandmother died. Everyone tiptoed around me. No one told me what it meant, what they felt. I had to keep the pain inside. My grandmother was—" Her voice caught in her throat. She breathed deeply for a few moments. "Much later, I realized they were afraid of being overwhelmed by their feelings. So they didn't acknowledge them."

Becky told him more, told him about Brett, about the pain she still felt. "I guess, if I analyzed it, I've focused more on my career and exercise routine to fill this emotional chasm."

"Makes sense," said Carnes.

"I feel exhausted."

"Me too."

"But good." She smiled.

"Me too."

"Can I take you home?"

Becky looked at him appraisingly. "Can you just take me home?"

"It wouldn't be as much fun." Carnes paused. "But, yes, I could."

Carnes drove Becky home, the radio playing light rock, the warm air washing through the open windows. They rode, mostly without talking, up Wisconsin, over Macomb to Connecticut, listening to the music and the song of the wind. Carnes, who usually needed to fill any conversational gaps, felt at peace tapping the beat on the steering wheel.

"Up there." Becky pointed to the right and Carnes turned.

He pulled up in front of a small brick apartment building. "Would you like—"

"I really had a great time." She planted a quick kiss on his right cheek and was gone. Carnes felt the soft touch of her lips on his cheek long after she had skipped along the sidewalk and vanished into her apartment.

Book Two

1

"You ain't hardly shit for flies, man." Slick McNeil held his Beretta automatic under Chito's chin. He smelled the sharp stench of urine and looked down at the wet spot spreading between Chito's legs. "You're a fuckin' pig—man, you know what I'm sayin'? Peed in your pants like a baby. You don't deserve to live." Slick looked at Mason and Smallfry, who held Chito's arms. "Should I waste him?"

Mason was older than Slick but slow-witted and mean. "Do the fuckin' hound. He dissed you. Do him." Mason's teeth glowed in the dim light from the streetlight at the corner. "People'll know better than to fuck with Slick McNeil." Mason twisted Chito's arm. Chito moaned.

Slick heard the distant sound of tinkling glass. He held a finger to his lips and peered out of their alley between the check cashing place and the liquor store. The sputtering light of the street lamp disclosed someone weaving up the sidewalk across the street. The man meandered past their alley and up the street forty more feet. He stumbled up the steps and into a brownstone apartment building. "Damn drunk." Slick turned back. "Smallfry?"

Like McNeil, Smallfry was twenty-eight. Unlike McNeil, who was a solid six-footer, Smallfry was five-six in lifts and looked like he'd benefit from a few good meals. Despite Smallfry's size, McNeil listened to him. Smallfry figured the angles.

Smallfry examined Chito as though he were a specimen pinned to the table in biology lab. Chito gurgled, too scared to even plead for his life. "This pissant ain't worth no bullet. Don't need to worry 'bout no pissant spic. He won't come back here, no ways." Smallfry shook Chito's arm. "Will you?"

Chito stammered out the words. "N-no m-man. No way."

"Louder!" Smallfry growled.

"Man, I promise. I didn't know this was your turf, man. I didn't mean to diss you. I didn't know. I new in town." Chito forced his lips open in a rigid smile. He had a gold crown on one of his front teeth.

McNeil locked into Chito with a blood-freezing glare, his eyes conveying a promise of violence. Chito dropped his eyes toward the ground. "Oh shit, man. Don't kill me, I'll do anything—"

"Anything?" McNeil's voice rose with the question. "OK. Blow me."

"You kiddin', man?" Chito's eyes widened, more with surprise now than with fear.

"Blow me, fucker." McNeil shoved the muzzle of the semiautomatic harder into the soft tissue of Chito's neck.

"OK. Whatever, man," Chito stuttered.

McNeil stepped back and Chito dropped to his knees as Mason and Smallfry pushed him down. "You kiddin' me, man, right?" Chito's face twisted into a grin that displayed a glimmer of gold.

"Now, fucker." McNeil pointed the Beretta at a spot between Chito's eyes. Chito reached with a shaking hand toward McNeil's zipper.

"What a fuckin' pervert." McNeil kicked Chito hard in the stomach and stepped back. Chito pretzeled forward, covering his head with his arms. Mason kicked him hard in the ribs and Slick heard bones crack. Chito moaned. Mason kicked him again.

For a moment, Slick was a small boy, scrunched up in a ball in the corner of his kitchen. His father, in one of his drunken stupors, kicked him, screaming, "You little shit, you're worthless." He kicked and kicked until he lost interest, then staggered off to collapse across the sagging bed.

McNeil put a hand on Mason's arm. "Enough, Mase." McNeil opened his zipper and peed. Chito squirmed miserably on the hot concrete. Sirens wailed in the distance, coming closer. The flow stopped as though a faucet had been twisted shut. Slick spit on Chito. "This time you got off easy. You ever show in my 'hood again—you dead."

2

The flashing lights defined an eerie scene. Police and bystanders moved in palsied, silent-movie motion in the strobing light from the parked cruisers. Carnes screeched the Caprice to a stop behind a blue and white police cruiser. He tore his sweaty body away from the seat. His clothing was a swamp of perspiration. Carnes cursed. If he ever got his hands on the bureaucratic bastard who failed to schedule his air-conditioner maintenance . . . For good measure, he cursed the sergeant who called him out of his cool bedroom to this godforsaken part of the Sixth District.

"Detective Carnes?"

"Yeah, I think so."

"Funny. Sorry I had to wake you, but a call came in. Dead girl in an alley. Naked. Beat up. Del Clinton's on the scene. He thought you'd want in on this one."

Carnes tried to get his mind working. Delbert Clinton was one of the newer detectives in homicide and he wasn't in Carnes' squad. Tall, thin, always dapper in a suit and hat, Clinton walked with a bounce that hollered "I love it!" A rich cocoa, Clinton sported a pencil-thin mustache and wore his hair short. He was handsome in a Billy Dee Williams kind of way.

Carnes had heard the scuttlebutt on Clinton. He joined homicide during the hiring boom that trailed the explosion in the murder rate. Unlike most of the homicide detectives, Clinton came directly from patrol. At first, his primary qualification seemed to be an uncle in the deputy chief's office, but Clinton had developed a decent reputation. "Clinton wears out a lot of shoe leather" was the way Wiley put it. Clinton knew the streets and people in the rougher parts of the city. He worked hard.

Carnes' watch read 1:15. A typical June night in the nation's capital—

sweaty people pressing too close together on a warm sidewalk trying to catch a glimpse of a body simmering on the asphalt. The yellow tape, emblazoned every few feet with the words "POLICE LINE DO NOT CROSS," formed a tenuous border between the sidewalk and the crowd gathered in the street. A number of officers stood along the tape, watching but mostly pretending to ignore the people. This was the rite known in department manuals as "crowd control." An Action News team took shots of the milling police and citizens for the morning broadcast.

Del Clinton and two uniformed policemen stood in front of a dry cleaners making a show of talking casually but watching Carnes approach with their peripheral vision. Several detectives from Clinton's squad and the Sixth District were working the crowd and fanning out into the neighborhood.

Retail property lined this part of the street: a dry cleaners, a carryout, a small grocery, a wig shop. Side streets started perpendicular but then curved away into working-class neighborhoods: small brick, single-family houses with trim yards. On the other side of the street, however, streets wound into a maze of identical apartment buildings. Carnes had been inside them too often, searching for a suspect, a witness, or the family of a victim. He'd chased dealers through the dark corridors alive with cockroaches and rats and perfumed by the stench of despair.

Carnes had studied anthropology in college. When he visited the projects, he tried to maintain an anthropologist's detachment. Maintaining detachment was easier when you returned to your cloistered office to write what you saw in impersonal academic terminology. The Metropolitan Police Department had its own terms for these neighborhoods: "high drug area" or "street market."

Like many MPD members, Carnes had earned overtime in drug enforcement efforts in this neighborhood. These operations went by catchy names such as Operation Clean Sweep. The technique was simple. Police blitzed like an invading army into an area known for its drug activity, sometimes from two directions. Drug dealers and buyers dropped whatever contraband they carried and ran. Police arrested everyone they could catch and confiscated the drugs. The cops groused but collected their overtime. The mayor and chief of police declared victory after victory in the war on drugs. All knew that the dealers were only inconvenienced. These sweep operations didn't shut down the drug trade, they merely forced the dealers to move a block or two away. When the heat moved to another block, they'd be back. Law enforcement for sound bites.

An alley separated the dry cleaners from the oriental carryout. Both had been closed for hours. The sidewalk was littered with cigarette butts, blown newspaper, and grime. In the crowd that had gathered were addicts, sellers, and their neighbors getting a good adrenaline rush from death in the morning. The faces were distinct but blended together: a fat woman dressed in an Omar the tentmaker housecoat, a sticklike young woman with hollow eyes, a young girl clutching her hem. A young man in a T-shirt touting a hot local singer and Reebok basketball shoes, light glinting off his gold jewelry, was as much in uniform as if he wore a tag that read "John Doe, Sales Manager, Drugs 'R' Us."

All would say they had not seen or heard anything useful. That was the way now. People were afraid to see things. Even so-called normal, law-abiding citizens feared retaliation if they came forward, and not without reason. Only last week, the defendant in a drug-related murder was released after his brother "offed" the only eyewitness. The message on the streets was clear: helping the cops could be hazardous to your health. Besides, even if some public-spirited citizen came forward, terrified or hostile jurors might let the defendant off.

Carnes strode toward the officers. As he ducked under the tape, he heard the muted half whispers. "Whozit?" "Dude's a detective." "Yeah, looks like one." "I seen that one before."

"Del." Carnes offered his hand. "What's the story?"

"You look like shit." Clinton smiled broadly. "Sorry to ruin your beauty sleep. Met Willie Sloan?" He gestured to a stocky patrolman with an imposing square mustache. "And this is Skel James." He nodded at his other companion, a tall, thin officer with sunken cheekbones and deep-set eyes.

Carnes grunted at each in turn.

"Thought this looked enough like that apartment sex-murder case you caught a couple of weeks ago that I should get you out here," Clinton said.

"Good move." Carnes nodded. "Where's mobile crime?"

"On the way"—Clinton snorted—"for the last hour."

"Well, you know how things are. Department still doesn't have enough crime-scene techs."

"Yeah," Clinton said. "Last we heard, they were finishing a drive-by over on Rhode Island."

"Only one?" Carnes raised an eyebrow. "Slow night." He changed gears. "So what happened here?"

Clinton turned to the uniformed officers. "Sloan?"

"Well, we were on patrol. James was operating the spot. We've had several break-ins recently, so we go by real slow and sweep the area with the spot."

Carnes nodded. There was a time when officers patrolled on foot, checking each doorknob by hand. Cops really knew their territory then. However, there wasn't much nostalgia for those days. Cops felt the hostility of these neighborhoods. On foot you were exposed, vulnerable. A car offered a modicum of protection. Fear had converted even the oldest patrol officers to the department's religion of mobility.

"Anyway," James interrupted, "I thought I saw something in the alley. It didn't look right, so I told Willie"—he nodded at Officer Sloan—"to back up. At first, it looked like a wino or something. When I got there and checked—well, we called it in."

"Touch anything?"

"Her neck—for a pulse. Stone cold dead." James shook his head.

Carnes turned to Clinton. "Find anything on the scene?"

"Some clothes, trash in the alley. Haven't touched anything. Left it for mobile crime and the medical examiner."

"Show me," Carnes said.

They approached the alley. Sloan held one of the department's bulky rechargeable spotlights. It held back the dark brick buildings on either side of the narrow alley. A very confident driver might push the speedometer up to six or seven miles per hour in this one, Carnes thought. The carryout had a steel side door with enough locks to provide the profit margin for some locksmith. All the hardware might frustrate a real burglar for about one minute. Fragments of a bulb hung from the light fixture above the door.

The body lay a few feet beyond the door. Her head faced toward the middle of the alley. The lower part of her body was unnaturally turned in the other direction, so her toes touched the wall. Her left arm was twisted back under her body. Women's clothing had been dumped on top of the body, and pantyhose were visible around her neck. Carnes couldn't see any panties, but he decided not to move anything.

Her face was not pretty. Dark circles surrounded eyes that bugged out of a bruised round face. Dried blood crusted the nose, upper lip, and chin. "Mid-twenties?" asked Carnes.

"Yeah," said James. He sucked in a few shallow breaths and glanced away.

She was slightly heavy. Carnes fought an urge to cover her sagging nakedness. He examined the stocking. "Granny knot?"

"Looks like it," Clinton agreed.

A bloody stump of flesh tipped her heavy breast. "Like the other. Nipple bitten."

"Jesus," said Sloan.

"He didn't have anything to do with this," said Carnes.

"Wait till you see this." Clinton moved around to her feet and pointed. A bloodied wooden rod protruded between her buttocks. "A piece of broom or mop handle or something."

The patrol officers seemed green in the pale light. "Why don't you guys go find out what's keeping the medical examiner and mobile crime while Del and I finish up here." Carnes gestured toward the patrol cars. "Let me have the light."

Carnes pointed the light at her buttock. A dark shadow took on definition. "What do you make of that?"

"The blood smear?"

"Yeah."

"Like someone drew something," said Clinton.

"Yeah," Carnes agreed. "What?"

Clinton smoothed his fingers over his mustache. "A horseshoe, I guess."

LaVonna Roberts slept, her two-year-old body balled up against the peeling wall. Slick McNeil smiled down at her and touched the tight little cornrows of hair. He wondered how any child, especially his child, could be so beautiful. For a moment, anchored in his domestic harbor, he felt happy. He covered her carefully with a blanket and tiptoed out into the living room.

"Get me some food, babe. I'm hungry."

Doris Roberts struggled up from the couch, the weight of her full belly wobbling her knees. Although rounded by the hormones of pregnancy, her eighteen-year-old face was pretty, and she took care with her hair and makeup. "Bad night?" she asked as she flipped on the kitchen light. Roaches scrambled from counters and floors for the safety of dark crevices. Sometimes, Doris would reach around the corner and flip on the light, then count to ten before she went in.

"Yeah," said McNeil. "Some dumb spic named Chito dissed me, selling on my corner. You believe it? I had to teach him a lesson."

"You didn't kill him, did you?" Her voice was tight.

"No, baby." He spoke softly and touched her cheek. "Just scared him." McNeil sat at the table and watched as she made a sandwich with quick, economical movements. He marveled at her competence. There must be a thirty-year-old woman in that young body. "I think Mase broke a couple of his ribs though."

"Oh." She kept her eyes on her work, but she had that wounded-bird look.

"Babe, you know I gotta protect my turf or I'm a dead man. I ain't killed nobody."

"I know, but—"

"I work hard to feed you and the baby."

"I know." She looked at him this time. "I don't want you to get hurt."

McNeil waved his hand in dismissal. "Nobody can touch me."

"Sure." After three years of sharing his bed, she knew. She'd seen him awaken from his nightmares. They'd become her own.

"Really."

"Yeah, that's what Johnny Lamb said." They'd had this discussion before. Slick knew what to say next.

"Johnny wasn't careful. I'm careful."

McNeil had been less than a block away when he heard the pop, pop, pop, pop of automatic weapon fire. He saw Johnny fall and watched the BMW speed away. It had been almost comical. The BMW looked like a porcupine with all those guns sticking out its windows. As he stood over Johnny and watched his life spurt out onto the sidewalk, Slick knew fear for the first time. Johnny was another murder statistic, another folder on the desk of some cop who didn't give a shit. And Slick was afraid.

Before Johnny's death, Slick felt invulnerable. He was faster and smarter than everyone else. He was nice to the right people, avoided the wrong ones. Now, terror seized him like something malevolent and alive every night he went out. He'd suck in a few breaths and fight down the nausea. He'd tell himself, it's not fear. No. He was a family man now. LaVonna and Doris depended on him. They cared about him. If he went out and did something foolish like getting himself shot, well, he'd be letting them down. That was all it was. He'd be careful.

Doris stood with hands on hips. "Momma says they need some people over at Agriculture."

"What? Another mail-room job?"

"It wouldn't be bad."

McNeil snorted. "I make good money on the streets. Can't make shit in no mail room."

"But you'd be alive for your family."

"I'll be alive on the street."

"You don't have to be out there every night. You got choices."

"Yeah, lotsa choices. I can get a job at some fast-food joint, or tote furniture, or work in the mail room for three dollars an hour. Then I can watch my family starve. Lotsa choices."

"You're smart—"

"I'm not book smart and that's all that counts. I don't know no one offering top-paying jobs to dumb niggers."

"You could go to school. UDC would—"

He held up his hand. "I don't know nothing 'bout math or science, or punching no clock."

"Course you do. You know how to cut a key, how much it should cost, how to test it. You know math and science."

McNeil studied her suspiciously. "You been going to church again?"

"Besides, you could learn."

Slick shook his head. "I told you this before. I don't need no schooling. I ain't no honky 'xecutive. It ain't me. The street's my business. On the streets I'm like Quincy Jones. I know the players. I feel the rhythm. I remember the words. I can sing the tune. In the rest of the world, I'm just a half count off. Shit. Life don't offer any real choices. Not to people like us."

Doris turned away. She was making those quiet snuffling sounds he heard more frequently now. It would be better after she had the baby. He got up and put his hands on her shoulders and pulled her back into him. "No need, babe. I'm OK. Everything's OK."

"I heard sirens tonight. Police. Fire truck. Ambulance. I sat here wondering if it was you." She tried to pull away. "So, today you're OK. What about tomorrow?" Her voice rose. "What about next week?"

For a moment, McNeil felt terror creep out from behind the wall he'd built in his mind. He pushed back the terror and concentrated on calming her. "Hey, baby, don't worry yourself." He sounded good. His hands slid down to her breasts and began twiddling her nipples the way she liked. "I've got a family to take care of. I'll be fine."

She grabbed his hands. "Stop it," she whispered.

He continued to move his fingers. "I can't, babe. I can't."

Carnes sat behind his cluttered desk sipping a cup of bitter coffee. After three hours at the crime scene with Clinton and the mobile-crime team searching every inch of the alley, checking the ground for tire tread

marks, the wall for flakes of paint, he felt light-headed. The ME investigator and attendants arrived halfway through the search. They estimated
the time of death as within the last eight to sixteen hours. Then, to preserve any trace evidence, they bagged the victim's hands, zipped her into
a body bag, and carted her away.

While Carnes was still under the influence of the adrenaline, he had
put aside the idea of going home to bed and headed for the office. Now,
the adrenaline was gone and his body was crashing.

"Anna Durant." Rodriguez put down the papers. "Anna Durant," he
muttered to himself. "Think it's the same guy?"

Carnes nodded.

Rodriguez shook his head. "This one seems even more violent. Some
new twists. The broom handle. The body dumped. Nastier. Doesn't really fit."

"Yeah, but it's the same guy. I feel it." Carnes held up a hand and began ticking off the points on his fingers. "She's about the same age, white,
definitely not from that neighborhood. The nipples and the strangling
are the same. Then we got the horseshoe. None of that stuff made the
news, so it's not a copycat."

"Yeah, but this ain't the first freak who's bitten someone's nipples or
strangled them to death. Besides, Del said the horseshoe thing could be
a blood smear, like the guy wiped his hand on her."

"Too much of a coincidence. Look at the pictures. It's the same guy,"
Carnes said firmly. "He did her somewhere else, maybe his place or somewhere he could tie to him, so he dumped the body."

"Why *that* alley?" Rodriguez asked.

"Maybe he drove around until he found a nice quiet place where he
would have a minute—"

"Or maybe he knows the neighborhood. Say he lives or works near
there. It's not one of those areas you're likely to take a spin."

"Well, she doesn't seem to belong in that neighborhood. Del's working that angle—checking out the possibility either she or the killer was
connected to the neighborhood—but I think it's like the alley: a dead
end," Carnes said.

"Maybe. Course, Saint E's is nearby," Rodriguez said. "You've driven
guys in for evaluation or detox?"

"Sure. You thinking a former mental patient or maybe some kind of
outpatient?" Carnes knit his brows. "Certainly worth a try. Course, it's also
near 295 and not too far from 395. Could be the guy was on the way out
to Prince George's County or down toward Virginia."

"You spoken to her family yet?"

"No, this is Del's case. You and I are along for the ride. Del's partner is on administrative leave."

"Branton?" asked Rodriguez.

"Yeah, Branton. So P. J. Roper, who's Del's sergeant, assigned Action Jackson to handle the family and the ID. Saw him before he went off duty."

"And?"

"Not much. Talked to the mother and father around five this morning. They were in shock. Didn't say much. Father's a senior VP for one of the Beltway bandits—management consulting firm. Mother and victim worked for the firm. Firm's in one of those high-rises across from White Flint in Bethesda, Rockville, or wherever it is. Family home is in Potomac. Victim lived in Rockville in a garden apartment. Montgomery County's checking the apartment."

"Why'd he have to dump the body here?" Rodriguez rubbed his eyes. "Coulda been Montgomery County's headache."

Carnes smiled. "If he'd dumped the body in Montgomery County, we might not even know it happened. We certainly wouldn't have enough details to connect it to the Benton case."

"Assuming it is connected."

"Humor me."

"Story of my life," Rodriguez said.

"I'm serious. We've been working the Benton case as an isolated thing. Now, we've got to look at it differently. Hell, if Del Clinton hadn't overheard some bullshitting about the Benton thing, we might never've heard about this case. We'd still be running around with our heads up our asses."

"You keep assuming there's a connection," Rodriguez said. "Let's not jump the gun."

Carnes couldn't hide his exasperation. "I keep telling you, this is the same killer. Virtually the same MO, same vibrations—"

Rodriguez raised an eyebrow. "Vibrations? Don't start getting mystical on me."

"Joke all you want, but don't lose sight of the facts. These cases have too much in common for coincidence. We may have a serial killer on our hands."

"Oh, pleeease." Rodriguez glanced around quickly to see who was within earshot. "Don't say those words to anyone." Rodriguez spoke in a low, urgent voice. "We already have every tie in this place on our rear ends over the Benton case. Can you imagine what would happen if the press started screaming 'serial killer'? We'll have reporters following us into the bathroom." He shook his head. "No more serial killer talk."

"Pete, we've gotta consider the possibility. Even the captain's gonna see the similarities." Carnes held up his hand and started ticking off points. "Two white girls. About the same age. Beaten and bitten and worked over sexually. The horseshoe shit, same knot on the panty-hose—"

"Everyone in the world knows a granny knot—"

"The panties taken."

"Yeah, but this ain't our case."

"Del caught this case, but if it's tied to Benton, we gotta make the connection and work with Del."

Rodriguez shook his head forlornly and muttered to himself in Spanish. "I've been through this kind of thing before."

"Yeah, I know. Back in the good old days." Carnes waved his hand. "It's the same guy. I know it. The perverted bastard did everything but sign his name. Besides, even if I'm wrong—and I'm not—we've got to explore the possibility."

"You already said that." Rodriguez' face softened. "I'm not saying you're wrong. You may be right. But you've been up all night. Why don't you go sleep on it for a couple of hours?"

Carnes shook his head. "Not now. Can't afford the time. Another coffee and I'll be fine."

"You're stubborn as a mule." Rodriguez sounded like a proud father. "OK. We'll cover all the angles. But take it from experience, you don't want to stir up this hornet's nest"—Rodriguez hooked a thumb toward the captain's office—"with serial killer talk. We'll check it out, we'll check everything out, but we'll keep our mouths shut. If anyone asks, we play down the possibility that the cases are linked.

"Besides, the body being dumped is different, the broom handle is different. This one's fat and not too attractive. The other one was thin, like a model. And we can't rule out Pardo in the Benton case."

"Hell, Pardo could've killed both of them." said Carnes. "But if it's some crazy guy, the link may not be obvious. He may pick them up in bars, meet them out jogging—who knows?"

"What're you planning?"

"Check files, talk to the staff quack—see if maybe he can give us a profile. Check with the FBI. They might be able to match our guy to other killings."

"OK, but—"

"Don't worry. I'll play down the serial killer angle. But I don't want to look like an idiot."

Rodriguez held out his hands in a gesture of surrender. "Did Jackson learn anything else?"

"Durant grew up in this area, went to Catholic schools. Graduated from Georgetown three years ago—business management degree. Working for the father's firm since. Close to her family." Carnes sipped his coffee and studied his notes. "Left work at five last night. Parents didn't think she had a date or anything. Montgomery County's trying to backtrack her movements."

"Not much to work with."

"No."

3

Carnes shivered. In contrast to the steam bath outside, it was cold in the morgue. He shivered again. Maybe it was the unpleasant chemical odors, the cool tile walls, or some aura from the bodies in the drawers. Carnes imagined he could feel their presence, so near yet so far away. "So what do you think, Stretch?" he asked.

Dr. Alvin "Stretch" Jefferson stared at the body of Anna Durant on the examining table. Stretch was a tall, balding black man known equally for his laconic manner and his hook shot. Most of his friends at Howard Medical School were shocked when he decided to go into pathology. How could such a nice guy spend all his time with stiffs? Jefferson had started out as a surgical resident but decided the one thing he disliked about being a physician was causing pain. "Dead people don't feel pain," he insisted. Now the D.C. medical examiner's office had the tallest pathologist on the East Coast.

Stretch did a thorough, competent autopsy. He was pretty good company as well. "I'd say you're right. Judging by the contusions, the victim was beaten while she was still alive. Facial bruises consistent with a blow." He pointed a gloved finger at a bruised spot under the ribs. "See this?"

Carnes saw a large bruise.

"I'd guess he grabbed her and twisted. See these pinch marks around the thighs?"

Carnes nodded.

"This guy was into causing pain. You saw the bite marks on the breasts and buttocks."

Carnes nodded again.

"Bruising of the vulva. Before you came, I did vaginal and anal swabs for semen. The ultraviolet light showed semen traces on the pubic hair. We combed for hairs.

"Positive for semen in the vagina. He's a secretor. Type O, same as in the Benton case. I preserved a semen sample. If we're lucky it's enough for DNA analysis. Did scrapings, but nothing under her nails. If I were to guess, I'd say the guy caught her by surprise and subdued her without much of a fight."

"Yeah." Carnes had already come to the same conclusion.

"See these bruises on the wrists?"

"Yeah."

"Tied her up. I read Ed Barclay's report on the Benton girl. There are some things that are different, but it's very similar."

"What about the broom handle?"

"Probably find some vaginal tearing. From the volume of blood loss, he did it while she was still alive. Maybe he worked it with his knee while he was throttling her. She did not die peacefully," he said in an apologetic tone. "Frankly, I've seen some pretty awful things. This is right up there." Stretch looked sheepish. "No pun intended."

Carnes groaned. "Morgue humor."

Stretch's face grew serious. "This one's bad. Ranks with some of the child abuse cases I've seen."

Carnes knew what he meant. Carnes was a rookie on patrol when he got the radio run. Dispatch reported a neighbor called 911 complaining, "She's killing her baby." Carnes raced to the scene, heart thumping, stomach clenching, blood pounding in his ears. He ran up the dark stairs through the stink of urine and stale cooking odors, past sounds of blaring TVs and crying babies to a filthy apartment.

A heavyset woman leaned out a door. "She's in there. I think she's killin' that chil'."

Carnes knocked. "Police. Open up."

He heard a baby wailing and tried the door. Unlocked. A distraught sixteen-year-old girl paced among the trash and fraying furniture. She pulled at her nappy hair and wailed. Farther back in the apartment, the baby cried. He grabbed the girl by her shoulders. "What happened?"

She blubbered nonsense. He pushed her away and followed the sounds through the clutter. The baby lay in a puddle of water on the floor of the kitchen. Probably Avery's age, but it looked like an alien creature, its skin red and blistered, face and body contorted. It screamed with its whole body, legs drawn up to its chin, fists clenched, tiny eyes pinched shut. Sink full of water. He stuck a finger in and pulled back at the stab of hot pain.

Carnes clenched his fists hard at his hips, fighting the nausea. He breathed deeply and tried to remember the lecture on child abuse he'd heard at Children's Hospital. The girl watched from the doorway, face puffy, eyes almost invisible.

"What happened to the baby?" Carnes demanded. She stared at his clenched fists. He willed them to open. He tried to use a calmer tone. "What happened?"

"She wouldn't be still. I tried." The girl blubbered. "I really tried. She wouldn't be quiet. I changed her. She kept crying. I was heating a bottle and she kept crying. I couldn't take it no more." A saucepan sat on the stove; a bottle lay on the counter, milk pooled beneath the nipple.

Just a few hours earlier Carnes had been in his own kitchen watching Avery crawl across the floor, his throat choked with love and pride.

The baby screamed until it exhausted the air in its lungs. It gasped, sucked in more air, and wailed again. Carnes vomited into the sink.

Carnes shook off the memory. "What about fibers, hairs—anything else?"

"Some. Picked up all kinds of shit when we scanned her with the ultraviolet and laser, but the lab guys are going to have a hard time figuring what came from the alley and what came from a car or somewhere else," said Jefferson

"Do me a favor?" Carnes asked.

Stretch cocked his head.

"Keep any connection between these cases under your hat."

Stretch's face radiated blissful ignorance. "What connection?" Stretch reached for the saw. "You going to stay around for the postmortem?" He pressed a switch and a high whine filled the room like a scream of pain.

"No. I've gotta go see some people."

"OK, man. Later."

"Sure." Carnes heard the high-pitched cry of the saw as he went through the door.

4

He'd awakened depressed, almost hungover. It seemed like a dream now. The night had blurred into fragments. Meeting her. She went with him. No problem. But she got suspicious. She fought. He'd hurt her more for that. Anna begging. More like it. He'd felt good. Anna moaning against her gag. He'd thought her eyes might pop out of her head. Over too fast. Driving. Searching for a place. He'd been afraid. You could get killed in this neighborhood. He rolled her out of the car. Her body thunked against the pavement like a sack of melons.

Did he make any mistakes? He couldn't remember anything. The paper had very little. Nothing about a link to the others. They didn't seem to know about the others. They still didn't know about the first one. Where it started. A year ago.

His mom had deserted him. The doctors claimed she had no choice. Cancer. He knew better. She'd left him by himself. He'd almost ended it there and then, sitting in the garage with the car running. It would have been painless. Easy. They said, "Take some time off, you need a break. Get some sun." He drove to the beach. Ocean City was in high season. Clusters of vacationers packed the beach—old people here, teenagers there, young families, gays. All working on their tans.

The boardwalk was packed with fat mamas sagging out of their suits. Many dragged sniveling children who left a wake of food in their paths. Giggling girls sashayed by, flashing provocative expanses of firm flesh. He decided to get social.

He'd met her at a popular beach bar. At first, he hadn't recognized her. She was only a cute cocktail waitress. When she brought his second drink, she stared at him for a long moment.

"What?" he asked.

"Don't I know you?"

He studied her. Attractive, well built. Very familiar. Then he remembered. "Sure." He smiled broadly and introduced himself.

"I thought so." They chatted idly. Very friendly. He bought her a drink. She sipped it covertly each time she came over. He was surprised to find he was having a good time. Another drink. More talk. They made a date. He left before the bar closed and waited for her in the parking lot.

She took him home. Her apartment was small and not very tidy. "Rum and coke?"

"Sure."

She made the drinks and brought them to the couch. A small stereo system sat on a shelf—a board resting on two milk crates. She turned on soft music and came back to the couch. There was something raw about every movement. Sensual yet simple and direct. Sensitive pout to the lip. He liked sensitive. He told her about his mother.

"God," she said. Then she held him, his chin resting on her shoulder. Who started the kiss? He didn't remember. At first, she was sweet, kissing him soulfully, eyes closed. Her face grew hot. He felt her moving against him. Hot and restless. His excitement rose in response. He fondled her breasts through the shirt, then slipped his hands underneath, raising it. She lifted her arms over her head. The bra unhooked in front. Her body was golden except for white triangles around her nipples.

"Don't move," he said. Her breasts were firm, soft curves with pointing nipples. She smiled. He teased her nipples with his tongue until they stood out.

"Oh, that's good," she groaned. "But my arms are getting tired."

"OK."

She lowered her arms. "You don't have to stop."

"Take off your shorts."

She stood up and opened the button, then pulled down the zipper. Slowly. It was a show. She slid her shorts and panties down her long brown legs, then stepped out of them—one foot, then the other. She kicked them to the side with her foot.

"Lie down," he said.

She did. He licked her nipples again until she began to moan. His hand found her wet opening. She arched up against his hand. Panting hard.

"Now it's my turn," he said. He stood up and slowly raised his shirt over his head. He knew his muscles were good but not overdeveloped. He worked at it. She seemed impressed. He began to dance slightly, pulling off his shorts.

She giggled. "Now, I remember." She caught her breath. "You."
"Stop laughing!"
She didn't stop. Shame ignited rage. Rage spread through him like a fire blown by strong winds. He was shaking with it. As though it had a will of its own, his hand struck her hard across the face.
"Hey." Her eyes widened with fear. "You didn't have to do that."
"You laughed at me." His voice trembled.
"I just remembered—" She began to lose it again, giggling at the memory.
"Shut up." He pounced on her, his hands around her neck.
It really hadn't been his fault. Things just got out of hand. He hurt her. At first, he didn't mean to. But he enjoyed it. He didn't rush. It was like the time when he was a kid—he'd caught a frog down at the pond. With his jackknife he'd cut off its legs and watched them twitch on the ground. She was not as silent as the frog. When it was done, she lay there dead. A still life of death.
The cops had no clue. They were stupid. He could out-think, out-maneuver any cop. He folded the newspaper and glanced at his calendar. It would be a busy day. He felt strong again. Time to put on his work face.

Carnes made several phone calls to bored Montgomery County bureaucrats before he reached the detective assigned to the Durant case. After getting permission to talk, Detective Fox called him back. "Sorry. Can't take a shit around here without permission."

"I know what you mean," said Carnes.

Fox's voice rumbled pleasantly—a warm, full-bodied baritone. Carnes thought of a DJ he listened to as a kid. They discussed bureaucracy, the recent heat, and the fortunes of the Orioles for a couple of minutes. The detectives' bonding ritual.

"So what did you find?" Carnes asked.

"Her apartment was clean. We talked to the neighbors and they hadn't seen or heard her since yesterday morning. A little old lady lives downstairs. Says she heard Ms. Durant go to work at her normal time."

"Anything in Durant's apartment indicate she had a date yesterday?"

"No. She had one of those calendars with the funny cat drawings. Nothing for yesterday. I've got a request in for phone records. No reason to expect anything."

"Any way I can check out her place?" Carnes asked.

"There was no sign of a struggle or anything."

"Well, I'm still interested. Maybe I'd spot something useful."

"I'll have to clear that." Fox's voice was suddenly formal. "I hate to have to do this—"

"Sure. I understand." Carnes tried to hide his frustration. Coopera-tion between police jurisdictions was often limited. No cop wanted someone else, especially someone from another department, running around their crime scenes, making suggestions and second-guessing their work. Besides, unless you knew the person you were working with quite well, you could find that cooperation worked in only one direction. Especially with the feds.

"I appreciate your help," Carnes said.

Dr. Victor Crenshaw looked like a refugee from the *Late Late Show*. The psychiatrist was short and round. Carnes guessed he wasn't much more than five feet tall but must weigh close to two hundred pounds. He wore a checked shirt, dark tie, and suspenders. His pants were an inch too short and his collar constricted bulging jowls. The right side of his face twitched periodically as Carnes told him the story. Crenshaw cleared his throat several times a minute and scratched the back of his hand so vig-orously that Carnes expected him to draw blood.

"Very interesting," Crenshaw interrupted at intervals. "F-fascinating." His voice sounded like a soprano sax, occasionally cracking on the high notes. Crenshaw leaned forward. "So you think one killer did both these crimes?"

"Don't you?" Carnes tried to keep his voice level. "You're the expert."

"Yes, yes." Crenshaw smiled absentmindedly and cleared his throat. "Yes."

"Was that 'yes, I'm the expert' or 'yes, it's one killer'?"

"Hmmn." Crenshaw got up and paced around his office as though he had not heard. "You know that Douglas and the behavioral sciences peo-ple over at the Bureau have done some remarkable work. We know so much more about serial killers than we did before."

"So you're saying this is the work of a serial killer?"

"M-maybe, maybe." Crenshaw cleared his throat. "Yes, it's fascinating stuff." He stared at his bookshelf. "Have I told you about Dietz and his work—"

"Please, Doctor. I'm not interested in the history of psychology." A hurt look clouded Crenshaw's face.

"Sorry," said Carnes. "I just want to know what I'm dealing with." He took a deep breath. "They told me you're as good as any of the Bureau's profilers. Tell me about this killer."

Crenshaw smiled sadly at Carnes and shook his head like a disap-pointed father. "I w-was"—he cleared his throat—"trying to be helpful."

Crenshaw plopped down into his desk chair. The diplomas on the wall rattled. Then, slowly, with a theatrical air, he leaned forward. He formed his hands into a pyramid. "Human beings are like an iceberg. You see so little on the surface." He lowered his hands until only the tips of his fingers were visible above the edge of the desk.

"On the surface, a serial killer looks like a very normal person. He may be the soft-spoken, friendly neighbor you treasure. Remember that nice boy who charmed all those young men and boys into his house? The police found he killed them, had sex with them, and stored and occasionally consumed certain, ah, body parts. Then there was Ted Bundy. He w-was a charmer. Charmed all those girls into his car. Everyone thought he was wonderful. He even went to law school. Tells you something about the legal profession, doesn't it?" Crenshaw grinned. "Cheap shot. I testify a lot in insanity-plea cases. Spend too much time fending off obnoxious defense attorneys."

"I know what you mean."

"Certainly you do." Crenshaw continued. "Anyway, where w-was I? Oh, yes. Typically, beneath this nice, quiet, normal exterior is an inadequate child." For the moment, all of Crenshaw's twitches subsided. "Unfortunately, we don't understand all the mechanisms. Some inadequate people become alcoholics; some become addicts. The serial killer becomes addicted to killing. Sometimes, they've suffered some severe accident or head trauma. Often, they've been sexually or mentally abused as a child."

Abused as a child. Abused as a child. The words echoed inside Carnes' skull. A memory began to emerge, dark ink from the past blotting out the present. Carnes vaguely heard the doctor's voice droning in the background. *Abused as a child.*

That cool fall day came back to him now, through an eleven-year-old's eyes, full of terror and excitement, repulsion and curiosity. His mother was going somewhere. She was leaving him with Aunt Mary. Mary was a busty, darkly-attractive woman who approached the world with fierce enthusiasm. As a girl, she had been a beauty, much sought after. She acted in all the local productions, dominating the stage with the presence of an opera singer. She had a sweeping style and emotional range that seemed to exceed ordinary human capabilities. This style carried over into everyday life. Whether Aunt Mary praised the newest TV show, debated the latest fashions, attacked a politician, or upbraided Uncle Frank, she did it on a Wagnerian scale. She was the sun, and everyone revolved around her and basked in her radiance. Her only son, Richard, fled to a monastery as a teenager.

Carnes walked quickly up the walkway to the house. The air was crisp with a pleasant leafy scent. He turned and waved at his mother, sitting behind the wheel of the old Ford. He pushed the doorbell and heard distant chiming. He hopped up and down to stay warm and wondered miserably what he would do all day at Aunt Mary's. The door opened. Mary stood in the doorway, wrapped in a pink robe with a collar as white and fluffy as the clouds that danced across the fall sky.

"Come in." She waved at his mother and he watched with foreboding as the Ford pulled away from the curb and disappeared up the street.

"Hurry. It's cold out there," Mary commanded. He stepped inside. The warm air wrapped him in unknown perfumes and suffocated him. He shivered and tried to catch his breath. Mary grabbed a hunk of his cheek between her knuckles and twisted until he winced.

"Look at those rosy cheeks." Her laughter rose in waves from the deep chasm between her breasts. "You look like you got into your Moma's blush." She released his cheek, oblivious to the tears in his eyes, and patted his face hard enough to make his teeth hurt. "So adorable." She engulfed him in a hug. He struggled for breath in the hot, perfumed embrace. She held him out at arm's length.

"Take off your coat. Warm up." Mary almost pulled his arms off with the coat. He checked to make sure all body parts were intact as she hung his coat in the closet. The thickly padded carpet gave the floor a swampy feel.

Mary gathered the robe around her dark cleavage. "I'm just putting my face on. Come. Keep me company," she commanded.

Mary floated up the stairs like a hot-air balloon. He followed uncertainly. At the top of the stairs, he made the left turn toward the bedroom in time to see the tail of her robe and a flash of pink calf disappearing through the door.

He stood in the doorway for a minute. Mary was not in sight, but a rumbling that he thought might be humming came through the bathroom door. The bedroom was a dark floral cave. Flowers he could not identify adorned the wallpaper in a surreal jungle of tangled stems. Heavy curtains with a floral motif shut out all daylight except for a slash of brightness that cut between one pair. The large bed was a rumpled garden of flowers. A floral perfume combined with a foreign scent made him dizzy.

"Have a seat on the bed, Johnny," Mary called. He hated to be called Johnny. He took a step to where he could see her sleeve flapping like a fettered bird as she combed her hair.

Cautiously, he sat on the edge of the bed, holding onto a carved wooden finial.

"Dear, bring in the clothes on the chair." Mary pointed to a chair beside the bed.

He pulled himself off the bed. A thin, lacy-black brassiere and lacy-black panties lay on the chair. He was thrilled but also repulsed. He wondered what they felt like but did not want to touch them.

"Come on Johnny, pick them up," Mary spoke from the doorway. "I don't have all day." Her voice conveyed that tone of impatience adults were so good at.

She stuck her head through the doorway, and her face twisted into an amused smile as she saw his discomfort. "Go on. They won't bite you. Really."

He felt fire rush into his cheeks as he picked them up between the tip of his forefinger and thumb. The silk was soft, hard to grasp.

"Come on." Mary spoke in a tone that conveyed both amusement and exasperation. He walked over to the bathroom and stood tentatively in the doorway. Mary shook off her robe and stood naked, her large breasts tipped by imposing red nipples pointing at him. Her white belly curved down into a dark delta of hair between her thighs. He began to back out of the bathroom, stammering apologies, but he couldn't tear his eyes away.

"It's all right. There's nothing to be afraid of." She grasped his wrist and drew him back through the door. He staggered in like a pliant drunk.

Mary smiled at him. "Haven't you seen a naked woman before?"

"Nuuuhn," he replied. His mother never walked around the house naked. He pulled his eyes away from her hairy center and glanced at the floor.

"I won't bite."

He held her clothes out toward her and let go. They floated to the floor.

"Now look what you've done," said Mary sternly. "Pick them up."

He felt the blood rush to his face again. Conflicting feelings of embarrassment, shame, and a strange stirring of excitement made his head pound. He reached down to pick up the clothes and saw her feet step closer. He stood up quickly and found her breasts hovering at eye level, her nipples staring into his eyes. Grunting an apology, he started to step back, but she grabbed his wrist again.

Mary spoke in a husky contralto. "Don't be afraid."

She touched his hand to her nipple and then to the smooth flesh of her breast. "Soft," she said.

A shock ran through him. He held his breath. She ran his hand down the warm silk of her body and then back to her nipple and smiled, her eyes half closed. "Very soft." Her heat seemed to flow through his fingertips to the rest of his body.

"See?" She smiled. "I don't bite."

His heart pounded. His mouth felt dry. She pulled his head into the hot cleft between her breasts. He felt overwhelmed by her heat and perfume. She pushed him back a step and smiled. "There's really nothing to be frightened about. Women aren't something to be feared. We're just built differently than men." She touched his hands to her nipples again. "See how my nipples get bigger and harder if you touch them?" She moved his fingers. Her face was pink and full, her eyes lidded. "Yes, like that." Her voice seemed huskier now. "That's not the only thing that's different." She took his hand and directed it down to the forest between her legs. Wiry hair pricked his fingers. He tried to pull his hand away.

"Feels like steel wool?" She laughed. "Don't be afraid. There's something smooth and wet inside."

"Detective? Detective?" asked Crenshaw. "Are you listening?"

Carnes felt disoriented. "Uhm, sure." Carnes nodded. "Go on."

Crenshaw stared at him curiously, then shrugged and resumed his lecturer's pose.

"Why do serial killers kill?" Crenshaw raised his hand to show his question was rhetorical. "Well, to the extent we understand, we think he's overcoming his sense of inadequacy by exercising ultimate power—the power to take life. The serial killer gets a thrill from this power, this control he exercises over someone else. It's almost sexual." A beatific smile spread over Crenshaw's face. Clearly he was a man who loved his work.

"Serial killers may begin killing by accident. They kill once, perhaps out of passion, perhaps by plan, maybe almost by mistake, and they develop a—I guess the word is 'taste'—for it. They find out how much they like it. Then," he paused dramatically, "you have a real problem. Before you know it they're fantasizing about the next victim. Who will they kill?

How will they do it?

"They enjoy the planning, the hunting. Perhaps you've seen one of those nature shows with a tiger sneaking up on some unsuspecting beast." He smiled. "A good image. The serial killer feels the power of the tiger. He gets almost as much of a thrill from stalking as killing. Maybe you've had a little bit of that feeling when you plan a special date?"

Carnes knew what he meant. He'd had the feeling hundreds of times. He saw a woman. It could be anywhere: in a bar, crossing the street, on the job. It usually didn't matter whether he knew or even liked her. He'd fantasize an approach, an encounter, sometimes the sex act itself. Sometimes these fantasies popped up at very inconvenient times, and although Carnes would try to quell them, they would spring back into his conscious mind.

"I can see you know what I mean." Crenshaw grinned. "Of course, it's a lot more complex in the dysfunctional mind. After a while, the serial killer develops a ritual. Most serial killers evolve a careful killing ritual. It becomes"—Crenshaw paused, then snapped his fingers—"almost a signature. After the killing there's a letdown. Maybe the killer experiences some remorse or decides to stop. But soon he feels the need again and starts to plan his next killing."

"So we *are* dealing with a serial killer?"

"Probably. You're dealing with one man. He doesn't like women. I'd guess he comes from a split family or was abused by his mother or some other woman. He's been humiliated and rejected by women—at least that's the way he feels. He's learned how to get his revenge. There's probably some commonality between the women he's killing and the woman or women who he feels victimized him.

"Your killer feels a need to punish women, to get his revenge, to dominate them totally. He spends a lot of time fantasizing about killing. I'd say he's very intelligent. He might stalk them for months, maybe befriend them, lure them into a false sense of security. It would heighten his feeling of power."

"So he could've been close to one or more of the victims?"

"It's possible."

Carnes thought about Pardo. Could he really be so crazy?

"I'd say he's evolving a ritual, although it's still not very elaborate. He may be fairly new at this." Crenshaw picked up the files Carnes had brought and paged through the photos of the victims. The twitches and tics returned to his face. "I could tell you the obvious things. Most serial killers are in their twenties to forties. This one obviously has some sort of transportation. Often they work jobs that aren't too demanding, or don't work at all, but some lead what appear to be normal working lives."

Crenshaw pulled together the papers in front of him. "Let me keep these files for a day or two, Detective. I want to get a better feel for our man."

5

"What a day!" Carnes took a long pull on his beer. He looked around the FOP. It was packed with cops, uniform cops, detectives, and lab men. He smiled at Robin.

"I'm glad you came." Robin wrapped a long tress of blond hair around two fingers and rolled her fingers as though she was curling her hair. "Haven't seen you in days." Her eyes were soft. "I hoped that after the other night, I mean it was special and—" She looked lost. "I know I'm not saying this right."

"It's OK," said Carnes. "I understand." And he did, too well. He knew what was coming. She wanted more than just sex, she wanted a piece of his soul. Some women were like that: they sleep with you and instantly see the two of you at eighty sitting in matching rocking chairs by a fire enjoying pictures of the grandchildren. Carnes wondered why he had called her back. He didn't share her fantasy. If he admitted it to himself, he didn't even like her too much. Not the way he liked Becky. Talking with Robin was merely prolonged foreplay, charged with excitement to be sure, but ultimately nothing more than the mating ritual. He explained how busy he'd been.

Carnes liked women who wanted from him no more than what he wanted from them. What did he want? Was it just sex? He hadn't had sex with Becky and yet they connected at some meaningful level. They could talk—not flirt but really communicate. Even though he'd spent only a few hours with her and she politely turned him away at her door, he felt much closer to her then he did to Robin. Carnes couldn't understand it.

Robin touched his arm. "Can we go somewhere quieter?"

He didn't want to mislead her. But she wasn't asking for a commitment, was she? He felt a twinge of shame. It would be taking advantage. He imagined the feathery touch of her long hair on his stomach and thighs, her small breasts moving as she rode him, her face dissolving into bliss. He remembered the little cries that escaped from her throat as she shuddered to her climax. He knew why he'd called her. "Sure."

An hour later, Carnes lay on his back with Robin on top of him, his penis softening inside her. She tightened her muscles. "I think I may keep it," she said.

"I may need it."

Robin pushed up on her elbows and gazed at him with an I-want-to-have-your-children look. "Have you ever thought about getting—I mean not now, just in general—remarried?"

Carnes closed his eyes and snored loudly. Robin lowered herself until the tips of her nipples brushed his chest. She moved her hips in a slow circle, pulling at him with her muscles on each rotation. His body responded as it always did. He reached for her hips. She laughed and rolled off. "Not so fast. Answer my question."

Carnes sat up. "Did you say something?"

Robin rolled onto her side and gave him a soulful look. "Have you ever thought about—"

"Tickling you?" Carnes' hand shot out. He tickled her, his fingers dancing over all the sensitive spots, until she was breathless with laughter. Then he kissed his way around her body, enjoying the differences in texture and taste. He found the spot that made her lose control. When her trembling subsided, he took her from behind, his fingers busy in her soft fur, until they dissolved into a limp, warm lethargy. They fell asleep without talking.

The windshield displayed a blurred kinescope of overlapping images. Carnes ducked his head and squinted, trying to distinguish real objects from the ghosts that flashed by. A cluster of vehicles with strobing red, white, and blue lights painted buildings and people onto the dark canvas several blocks ahead. *That must be the place.* Carnes surveyed the scene. Two patrol cars, an ambulance, and a fire truck blocked the right side of the street. Dark figures scurried about on the sidewalk in front of a sandstone-colored apartment that seemed oddly familiar.

Carnes hopped out of the car. A small cluster of uniforms knelt or stood near the side of the building. Hovering around the edges of the light were phantoms, their faces etched with gay excitement—not tension or pain. "Police, homicide," said Carnes as he brushed through the circle.

A pair of feet that lay toe up on the concrete were visible between the uniforms. It was a man. Something about those feet tightened his stomach. Only part of the body was visible through the crowd. A medic in dark uniform kneeled before Carnes, a tank of oxygen by his side. A second uniformed man worked over the body. His hands were ghostlike in surgical gloves—a prophylactic against AIDS, not an effort to keep the wound clean. The medic tried to hold a bundle of gauze over the victim's chest where a small red geyser pumped into the air with every heartbeat. *Still alive. Maybe no business tonight.*

The other medic started an IV. "Shit! This guy doesn't need us, he needs Red Adair." Several of the bystanders understood the reference to the famous capper of oil wells and cackled with approval.

Carnes turned to the uniform beside him and asked, "What happened?"

"Dumb sonuvabitch was dippin' into some neighbor lady. Wife came home. Took a kitchen knife to him. A big 'un."

"Where's the wife?"

"Upstairs. Yelling her head off 'bout what a no-good hound he is. Couldn't shut the bitch up."

Carnes watched one of the medics trying to slide a pressure suit over the man's legs. He heard the thunk, thunk, thunk, thunk of a chopper's wings beating the air. "Is this guy going to make it 'til the chopper gets here?" he asked a medic.

The medic looked at him with a twisted grin. Carnes felt his heart thumping in rhythm to the geyser from the man's chest. The thunk, thunk, thunk was getting louder. In the distance a siren moaned a lament. A strange perfume filled Carnes' nostrils. Across the crowd he saw his mother, staring at the body and shaking her head sadly. *What the fuck is going on here?*

Something drew his gaze upward toward the window of an apartment. It was his old apartment. His ex-wife, Caroline, looked down at the body. A smug look of satisfaction on her face. *Shit! This is getting too fucking weird.*

"We're losing him," yelled the medic. The geyser weakened into a drool as Carnes watched. Carnes' own heart thumped weakly. His knees sagged. Everything began to dim around him except the thunk, thunk, thunk, and the wails of the sirens.

Carnes jerked awake. His heart pounded against his chest like a black-smith's mallet hitting an anvil. He took several deep breaths. He looked around, trying to reorient himself. *Shit! That was too real.* He pushed back the dream and concentrated on his surroundings. He settled onto the pillow and took more slow, deep breaths, hands behind his head. Light from passing cars danced across the ceiling. The fan turned slowly, thunk, thunk, thunk. A siren moaned past. Carnes recognized the tune: a scout car.

Carnes rolled over on his side, and the smells of perfume mixed with the funky odors of sweat and sex got stronger. He was filled with despair. He'd had the dream before. Each time it seemed more vivid. In the dark-ness of the morning, he wondered whether sometime he'd die in his dream. He had to leave. He reached over with his hand, running his fin-gers lightly over the soft skin of her shoulder. Wake her gently. No fights.

"Ummn," Robin grunted and rolled over onto her back.

"Gotta go."

6

Carnes sipped his coffee through the triangle he had torn in the lid of the 7-Eleven cup. Raccoon eyes peered back at him from the rearview mirror. God. Tonight he was going to go home, put Avery to bed at 8:30, and then hit the sack himself. Guilt shot through him like a physical pain. He'd awakened in Robin's bed too late in the morning to go home. Later, he'd call Avery and promise to bring pizza home tonight. Meatballs and extra cheese, her favorite. It might make her feel a little better. Him too.

Carnes sucked in more coffee. The caffeine and sugar were starting to kick his system into a higher gear. As he crawled along sandwiched between a silver Honda and a cream-colored Toyota, he finished planning his day. He had called Del Clinton from the 7-Eleven. Clinton and several Sixth District officers had canvased the neighborhood where Anna Durant was found. Nothing. Carnes was not surprised. Most citizens cultivated ignorance like gardens of flowers. Clinton was back in the neighborhood, trying again.

Carnes was still waiting for lab work in the Benton case, and he hadn't heard back from Fox yet but there was no reason to think Montgomery County would have missed anything. He'd exhausted Benton's address book and known friends. That left several things to do. Sex crimes was compiling a list of perverts and sex criminals who might have been released from St. Elizabeth's or be from Prince Georges County in Maryland. *Can't wait to cull through that list.* Carnes snorted. He made a mental note to check on sex criminals who lived anywhere near Vicky Benton or Anna Durant. First, he'd have to spend part of the day in court on a liquor store robbery that had turned into murder. He wondered how Del was doing in the neighborhood.

Clinton hadn't been back to the neighborhood much since he and Frances bought the small town house in Prince Georges County. Memories of the old neighborhood made Del Clinton feel queasy. The school where he was tormented by classmates as "teacher's pet," the alleys where he'd encountered scurrying rats and dazed addicts, the corner dry cleaners where his mother labored for years inhaling the pungent chemicals that eroded her lungs, the crumbling apartment where his father beat him on the rare nights he came home. Del's father had disappeared forever when Del was eight.

Not all of Clinton's memories were unpleasant. He remembered hours of frenzied excitement on the playground near his apartment. He saw children on the swings and still felt the exhilaration of his own soaring rides—leaning back, pulling at the chains, trying to swing all the way to the sky. When he was older, he played basketball on that old cracked blacktop, trying to soar like Dr. J.

Clinton could still taste the free ice cream with the crunchy ice crystals he got from Mr. Williams whenever the freezer went haywire in his little market up the street. Two years ago Mr. Williams sold the place to a Korean family who huddled in their store unable or afraid to be so generous.

Clinton passed the small, square brick house. He needed to stop in soon and see Mrs. Bailey, the third-grade teacher who had always provided him with a refuge when he needed it.

Contributing to his queasiness was what he'd seen of the neighborhood as a cop: two teenagers shattered by a hail of bullets in their car in front of the dry cleaners, the Jamaican lying in a pool of blood on the old basketball court, the young man and woman he'd known in school and their two year old, splattered against the walls of their apartment. Now, sight of the neighborhood caused a Pavlovian response: instant nausea.

Del parked at the curb and walked down the cigarette-butt-strewn pathway through the brown brick buildings. He tried to ignore the trash in the weeds and the occasional scurrying sounds in the hedges. When he got to the building he sought, he opened the squealing door and stepped into the dark hallway. He stood still for a moment to let his eyes adjust until he could see the crumbling paint, the sockets without light-bulbs, the scraps of trash. The air smelled of stale food, mildew, and urine. Clinton vaguely remembered when the building was new, a monument to the "Great Society." There were lightbulbs in the ceiling then, and the only smell was of fresh paint.

Clinton found the correct door and knocked. He heard a child cry and a woman's muffled voice say "Coming." Footsteps approached, the peephole darkened, then the chain rattled and the locks clicked. The door swung open. Doris Roberts stood staring at him, her face a mask of alarm.

"Oh, God, what's he done?" she asked. She held LaVonna on her hip. The child stared at him with wide, curious eyes.

"Nothing." Del smiled, embarrassed. "At least nothing I know about."

Last time he'd seen Slick McNeil, Slick was standing on the sidewalk in front of the project talking animatedly with several black men in warmup suits and expensive jogging shoes. When Clinton's department-issue Caprice rolled up the street, they'd all watched with exaggerated nonchalance until he turned the corner.

Doris smiled faintly. "I'm sorry. I guess it's—I mean we ain't seen you in a while. I didn't expect a social call."

"Well, it isn't really." Her eyes become alert and wary. "I just want to see if he can help me with something. He might have some information—"

"You ain't going to get him in no trouble, are you?" she pleaded.

"Not if I can help it." Del raised his hand and touched her on the shoulder. "You know, Slick is like family."

Del Clinton's friendship with Slick McNeil started on the neighborhood basketball court; it became closer when they discovered they both had abusive alcoholic fathers. They'd fought wars on the court. Del smiled slightly as he replayed some of Slick's favorite moves: the quick fake jumper followed by the lowered shoulder and bulldozer drive to the basket, the quick step, then the pull-up to pop the twenty-footer. Del liked to take Slick in low, working with his back to the basket. He'd fake one way and then pop a turnaround, or he would use a head fake, and when Slick anticipated the turnaround, he'd roll in for the layup. Slick would yap at him every time he made a shot. Of course, Del had held his own.

"Family? OK." She looked apologetic. "You're a cop and I got a baby coming." She patted her stomach. "We don't need no trouble."

"Don't worry," said Del.

Doris backed into the apartment. The living room was sparsely furnished. A tattered plaid couch and chair sat across from a large-screen television and a black rack-stereo system. The carpet was stained and threadbare in places, but the room was neat. Doris was a good housekeeper.

Del looked past the kitchen down the short hall that led to the bedrooms. "Slick sleeping?"

"Yeah," said Doris. "I'll get him."

She waddled down the hall in that loose-hipped way common to pregnant women. She went into the bedroom, leaving the door slightly open. Del looked around. He wondered if the TV and stereo were hot. He heard the muttering of voices, the movement of furniture. A toilet flushed, water splashed. Finally, Slick McNeil sauntered down the hall rubbing his eyes and yawning. Even half asleep he could still strut like a rooster.

"Rough night in the old 'hood." Slick smiled and slapped Del's hand. "What brings you to my crib at this hour, bro?" He eyed Del suspiciously.

"It's ten-fifteen, you lazy bum." Del smiled broadly. "I thought even you would be up by now."

"Hey, give me a break. Bad night." Slick gestured at the couch. "Take a load off."

Slick flopped down loosely into the chair. "Want something to drink? A smoke?" Without waiting for an answer, he turned to Doris, who stood close to the wall by the kitchen. "Hey, babe, get us coffee." His tone turned the command into a request.

For a while, they talked about how long it had been. They traded sanitized accounts of what they'd been doing. Doris brought a pot of coffee in from the kitchen and put it down on a copy of a tabloid on the coffee table. LaVonna tottered along behind.

"You're getting big." Clinton picked her up above his head. She gurgled happily. He made airplane noises as he swung her around and then put her down in a perfect two-point landing.

"Come here," said Doris. "Let them talk." LaVonna toddled away.

Slick poured the coffee and turned spoon after spoon of sugar into the cup. Slick hadn't lost his sweet tooth. After he finished, he said to Doris, "Why don't you take LaVonna out to play, babe."

For a moment it seemed she might protest, but then she gathered up LaVonna. "You goin' to be here long, Del?" she asked.

"Not too long," he said.

"Then I probably won't see you."

"No."

After Doris left, they shared news of old friends and razzed each other about old battles on the basketball court. "Play much now?" asked Slick.

"No time," said Del. "Homicide is a fifteen-hour-a-day job."

For a minute, they sipped coffee and studied each other.

"Well, you didn't come by to chat about old games."

"No." Del's voice changed to the professional tone he used in the office. "I came to ask a favor."

Slick raised his eyebrows and opened his mouth in mock surprise. "A favor?" Amusement bubbled in his voice.

"Yeah," said Clinton. "I'm looking for some information."

Slick's face clouded. "You know I ain't no snitch."

Del raised his hand in a placating gesture. "Hey, I know that. It's not like that." He explained about the body found in the alley.

"Yeah, I heard the sirens and some talk," Slick said. "White girl?"

"Yeah," said Clinton. "And we think the guy who dumped her was white."

"So what do you want from me?"

Del sipped the coffee. "Keep your ears open for anything about the guy, the car—that sort of thing. Someone must have seen or heard something."

"Say I were to hear somethin'—"

"What do you get?"

"Yeah." Slick grinned.

"The satisfaction of knowing you did the right thing."

Slick made a sour face.

"That you helped me out," Del said.

"Hey, man. I can't afford no reputation as a snitch. People get paid to take risks. What they call it? Hazardous-duty pay? I wanna help you, but doin' the right thing don't pay doctor bills. It don't put food in our mouths. Know what I mean?"

"It don't buy crack," Del said sharply.

Slick sat forward in his chair and pointed a finger at Del. "Don't start with me again. You don't live here no more. You ain't got the right."

"I grew up here same as you."

"So what?"

"So, I haven't given up."

"I ain't given up."

"Bullshit!" said Clinton.

"I shoulda become a cop?" Slick asked.

"That supposed to be an insult? I'm proud of what I do. But that's not the point. You're just as smart as I am. There's no reason you can't do better—"

"Sure," Slick said, "I can get a good job. Think they'll overlook the arrests for possession? Maybe they won't care that I got no college." Glaring, he stood up and paced angrily back and forth. "You know, you been outta touch too long. What you think I'm gonna do? I can get a job for a few dollars an hour doin' day labor or loadin' groceries at the Giant, but I can't hardly feed my family on that." He swept his hand around at the stereo equipment. "And I got expensive taste."

Clinton was standing too. "Expensive taste and no sense. Owning things won't do you any good if you get yourself killed out there," said Del, gesturing toward the door.

"I'm not goin' to—"

"You're kidding yourself. I know, I clean up the messes, remember?" Clinton shook his head. "I thought you were smart. Only smart thing you've done is hook up with Doris."

McNeil's face softened. "Yeah, she's somethin'." He smiled wryly. "Always give me the same lecture." For a while he stared out the window watching LaVonna and Doris play. "Man, I'd do somethin' else if I knew what to do. Sometimes I feel like I'm in prison, like I'm caught and I can't escape. But mostly I don't want to. They know me on the streets. I know the 'hood like a singer knows the words to a song. In your police department you're somebody. In the 'hood . . ."

"In your 'hood, you could be dead for good," said Del.

"Funny man." Slick continued to stare out the window. "Sometimes I'm scared. Not for me—for LaVonna and Doris, and the baby. They depend on me."

"Why don't you give yourself a chance? Move out of this neighborhood. Start again somewhere else—"

"Del, you're wastin' your breath. Doris and I been through this all before." Slick's voice was resigned rather than angry. "This is me."

Clinton knew he was getting nowhere. "OK, it's your life. Keep your ears open?"

"Sure. I beat your ass so many times I guess I owe it to you." He smiled. "But if I come up with anything good, you gotta come up with some cash. The department must have bread for stuff like that. It's not for me, it's for them." He pointed out the window.

"I'll see what I can do," said Clinton.

7

Carnes tried to focus on the bearded young attorney fencing with him. He fought his frustration. Playing word games with attorneys was a necessary evil. Sometimes—when you scored points with the jury—it was satisfying. But Carnes needed to be out on the streets searching for Vicky Benton and Anna Durant's killer; it was only a matter of time before he killed again. Carnes felt it was a sure thing, like the air-conditioning in his car failing on the hottest day of the year.

"So, you said there were two other folks who carried guns into the liquor store?" The attorney smirked for the jury.

"Yeah," said Carnes. Even if the defendant hadn't fired the shot that killed the liquor store owner, participating in the robbery made the defendant guilty of felony murder. The ballistics tests and a closed-circuit camera established that the defendant was the shooter. His fingerprints were all over the semiautomatic that was used, and he had powder traces on his hands when he was arrested. The attorney knew that. He didn't have any real defense, so he was trying to blow smoke at the jury. Carnes wasn't worried.

Carnes caught the eye of the court clerk, a pretty black woman named Karen who bubbled with energy. Well, at least if he was going to spend time in court, he had someone to look at. He answered a question, then glanced sideways at the clerk. For a moment he forgot he had promised Avery he'd get pizza tonight. Was that a wink? It could be an interesting evening.

Del met his wife, Frances, for lunch at the Department of Labor, where she was an administrative officer. It was one of their occasional treats when he worked days. Homicide was a few blocks from the Labor Department. When he was down, Frances could lift him up, make him see everything in perspective. Usually, the sight of her pretty oval face was enough to turn a bad day around.

They went through the line in the cafeteria and sat by the windows facing the Mall. Del liked the view. It was a different Washington than the one he knew: the Capitol, museums, government buildings—monuments of power and money. It was the tourists' Washington, not the Washington a homicide cop inhabited.

"Food gets lousier every day," Del grumbled.

"But the price is right," Frances said.

"They should throw in antacids and free medical care."

"It's not that bad."

Clinton made a face. "That's a matter of opinion."

Frances raised an eyebrow. "What?"

"What do you mean 'what'?"

Frances reached forward and took Del's hand. "Honey, it's me you're talking to. You're so obvious. Something's bugging you, and it's not the food."

Del grinned sheepishly. "I guess it's Slick. He's so damn self-destructive." Del told Frances about his encounter with Slick McNeil.

Quietly she asked questions. Del knew she was struggling to understand. Frances grew up in a small town in the South. She'd come from a close-knit family; her father was a minister and her mother was an elementary schoolteacher. The Washington that Slick and Del grew up in was as alien to her as Paris, France.

"What really burns me is he's given up."

"You didn't give up."

"No."

"Why didn't you?" she asked. "What made you different from Slick?"

"I don't know. We both came from similar family backgrounds, grew up in the same shithole." He looked sheepish. "Sorry. Maybe I learned from my mom, or maybe it's my genes—"

"Or maybe all those talks with Mrs. Bailey when you were having problems."

"Yeah, it could be some or all of those things. I don't really know. But it's scary—and painful. Too many of my old friends are like Slick. They're doing drugs, selling their bodies, killing each other. Most don't believe there's anything better for them."

"They're adults now. You can't change them." Frances put her hand on his. "At least you believed in yourself. It's not something to feel guilty about. You made your choice. They made theirs."

"Was it a choice? I guess that's what bugs me. I have no idea why I went in one direction and Slick the other."

"Does it matter?"

"If I understood more, maybe I could help."

Frances smiled. "That's why I love you."

Del squeezed her hand.

Frances quickly turned serious again. "You know, if we have a family, you'll be too busy to save other people's kids . . . " Her voice trailed off.

Del and Frances had been trying to start a family for the last six months. Nothing had happened since Frances stopped using the pill. Of course, with his crazy work hours Del hadn't been home much when she was ovulating.

"You going to get home at a decent hour tonight?" she asked mischievously.

"I have a feeling I'd better try."

Slick McNeil stood at his corner talking to Mason. He'd been out since 9:30 that night and he'd made a few deals. His stash sat several feet away behind the stone wall. It was never safe to have it on you. He'd learned his lesson the hard way when he was arrested for possession.

"These guys are hot." Mason was talking about a go-go group he'd seen in a club. "You gotta see 'em."

"Doris would kill me."

"Take her."

"She'd probably go right into labor."

A short man Slick knew as "Shifty" was working his way over. Shifty scurried along, slightly hunched, moving almost sideways like the crabs Slick saw during a trip over to the Eastern Shore. Shifty looked up and down the block in quick, furtive motions as he came. Slick nodded at Mason, who went over to the wall and sat near the stash.

Shifty was one of the most paranoid men Slick had ever met. If you asked Shifty, the entire Metropolitan Police Department, FBI, Drug Enforcement Administration and probably the CIA had only one mission: to bust him. Shifty stopped beside Slick. He spoke rapidly, his eyes in continuous motion, scanning first one side of the street and then the other. "What's happening?"

"Not much. You?"

"Nothing, man," said Shifty. "Been around. Know what I mean?"

Slick nodded.

"How's the product?"

"Grade A."

"Yeah, sure." Shifty glanced around again. "Coupla rocks?"

"No problem." Slick held up two fingers. Mason dipped a hand behind the wall and in a moment came over. They checked to see if any cops were around, then Shifty gave Mason some money and Mason shook his hand, slipping him two small glassine bags. Mason wandered back to the wall as Shifty casually slipped his hand into his pocket.

"Later."

"Yeah, sure." Slick smiled. Then he remembered. "Say, you hear 'bout the white girl got snuffed a few blocks from here the other night?" He'd asked the same question in a casual way about twenty times in the last few hours.

Shifty glanced up and down the street, then over at Mason. He shuffled up the sidewalk a few feet. Slick followed. Shifty leaned toward Slick. "I saw the guy who dumped the body," he whispered.

"What?"

"You deaf?" asked Shifty. "I saw the guy."

Slick whistled a single drawn-out note of surprise. What a world. He almost hadn't said anything, thinking he'd be wasting his time asking a crazy nobody like Shifty about the girl. Life was pretty strange.

"What's so funny?" Shifty sounded offended.

"The world's pretty funny. Some guy dumps a body thinkin' he's found a nice quiet place where nobody's goin' to see him, and you do."

"Yeah," said Shifty, somewhat mollified. "It was dumb luck anyways. I was walking back from a party and I sees this car go past. Then, as I get near the alley where they found that girl, the same car's backin' out the alley."

"What kind of car?"

"Some sorta little boxy thing. Japanese or German, who knows?" Shifty chewed his lower lip and studied his oversized feet. Then he brightened. "But I remember it had Maryland plates and a U Maryland sticker on the back window. White guy 'hind the wheel."

Slick was impressed. "Man, you really notice stuff."

"Yeah. Well, it was sorta weird—a white guy 'round there at that hour, in the alley and all. So I guess I noticed. Then when I heard 'bout the body, I figgered it all fit."

"You tell the cops?"

Shifty stared at Slick as though doubting his sanity.

"Stupid question. Get a good look at the guy?"

"No. Streetlights reflected off the windows. But I know a honky when I see one."

They chuckled.

"Which way he go?"

"Out Minnesota. Figger he musta been headin' for 295."

"Prob'ly," Slick agreed. "You gonna tell anyone?"

"Hell, no." Shifty looked around nervously. "Don't want nothin' to do with no cops."

"Well, they'd be happy to get the information. Prob'ly do you a favor some day." Slick smiled. "Shit! Might even be a reward."

"Yeah, sure. More likely they start askin' questions 'bout the party I went to, what I was doin' at that hour. Next thing I know, they be sayin' I did it."

"Yeah, maybe," Slick said. "Bastards."

Shifty glanced up and down the street again. "Gotta go. See ya."

"Sure," said Slick.

Carnes listened to Karen's quiet hiss of breath in his ear. Her scent was pleasant, her body warm and soft against his side. Her body was even better than he'd imagined—firm in all the right places. She'd been a good partner. But now that the sex was over, he felt down. Guilt tugged at him like an anchor. He'd lied to Avery on the phone, telling her he had to work late. The disappointment in her voice had almost changed his mind, but at that moment Karen had walked into the room wearing only a thin T-shirt.

Lately, he seemed to be letting Avery down a lot. He'd let Rodriguez down. He'd let Becky down. Now where did that come from? He decided he'd better go home and see Avery.

Del Clinton was enjoying his dream. He was twelve, watching the circus in the D.C. Armory with his class. The clowns were playing out a street drama, chasing each other around, waving guns and shooting them off—pop, pop, pop. One of the clowns fell down and held his chest. Suddenly a bell rang and an ambulance full of clowns came roaring across the ring. The ringing continued. Gradually Del realized it was the phone.

He pushed himself up on one elbow and reached across Frances. "Yeah, I mean—hello."

"Del? It's Slick."

The clock radio read 1:30. Clinton grunted. "You have any idea what time it is?" he demanded in a harsh whisper.

"Sure." Slick sounded too happy.

He must be high, Del thought.

"I found out some info 'bout your guy."

Del sat up. "What?"

"Hey, don't be inna hurry. I think you owe me somethin', and breakfast would be nice."

Del groaned. He'd be too wound up to go back to sleep. If he left now, he'd have to take money out of his own account with his ATM card and get the department to reimburse him out of the snitch fund. Where could they get breakfast at one or two in the morning? "OK. You got wheels?"

"Sure, man."

The bastard's probably going to steal a car, Del thought. "All right. You know the pancake place where we used to meet—the one out by the PG County line?"

"Sure."

"Give me an hour," said Del.

Frances stirred beside him and muttered "whozat?" in a hoarse whisper.

"Slick," Del said.

"Huh?" asked McNeil.

"Talking to Frances. One hour."

"Make it an hour and a half. I got somethin' to take care of first," said Slick.

The bastard is going to steal a car. "OK," Del grunted, and he set the phone back into its cradle.

The pancake place was almost as ugly in the dark as it was in the daylight. A garish neon sign tinted the small parking lot pink. A pickup, an ancient Caddy, and a late-model Japanese sports car sat in random array in the potholed parking lot. Clinton scanned the area around the lot. Nobody in sight. He pulled in next to the front door and killed the engine.

When Del went in, he saw Slick McNeil sitting in a plastic-coated booth in a dim corner. Slick displayed his teeth in a broad smile. Del lifted his eyebrows and nodded slightly, then glanced around the rest of the room. Nobody suspicious or out of the ordinary. He walked over and slid into the booth.

"Hey, bro," said Slick. "What's happenin'?"

"What's happening is I'm not home in bed sleeping with my wife. I'm having breakfast at some fucking ungodly hour of the morning."

"Like old times." Slick grinned.

Del couldn't help himself.

"Remember the time we did that party over at old—what's his name?" Slick scratched his head.—"Andy—"

"Andy Linwood?"

"Yeah, that was it. He had that party. It got real noisy and the police came—"

"And we dove out the back window," Del said.

"And ran for 'bout a mile like two chumps. Left our coats, our money, and all our ID." Slick laughed. "How long'd we wait out there in the cold for the cops to leave?"

"An hour, at least."

"Came here for breakfast after we got our shit. Cops fucked up that party." Slick chuckled. "And there hardly was anythin' there. A little grass, a few beers."

"Yeah." Del hadn't thought about those days lately. Back then he'd had the indefatigable energy of youth. He pulled himself back to the present. "What'd you find out?"

At that moment the waitress, a slow moving battleship of a woman who reminded Del of his grandmother, cruised over with a pot of coffee. She flipped the cup at Del's place and poured. "Freshen yours?"

Slick nodded. She filled the cup. "You boys want something to eat?"

"Sure." They ordered and watched her navigate toward the kitchen.

Del turned back to Slick. "So, what you got?"

Slick cleared his throat. "Don't want to make a big deal 'bout this, but did you—"

"Yes, I brought money." Del tried to hide his exasperation, but it crept into his voice. "I even brought a little extra in case this is really good."

"Well, it's good. The guy you're lookin' for is white, drives a boxy car with Maryland plates. Might go to, or went to, the University of Maryland. Car has a Maryland sticker in the back window."

Del whistled. "Where'd you get this?"

"Contact of mine."

"Does this contact have a name?" Del arched his eyebrows.

"I ain't at liberty to disclose my sources." Slick used an establishment voice.

"Is this source reliable?"

"Yeah."

Del considered. He'd better not push now. "Tell me what your 'reliable source' had to say, as close as possible."

"Not much. Saw the car pull out of the alley. Thought seein' a honky there at that hour was unusual, so he noticed things."

"He see which way the car went?"

"Yeah, out Minnesota toward 295. Figures he was headin' back to Maryland." Slick grinned slyly. "Pretty good guess, wouldn't you say?"

"He get a plate number, car dealer name, anything else?"

"You think this guy's sittin' out there with a notebook writin' everythin' down?" Slick shook his head as if to say you can't please some people.

"Can I talk to this guy?" Del asked.

"No way."

"But he may have more details."

Slick shook his head. "Ain't no way this guy'll talk to a cop. He's 'bout the most paranoid guy I know. No way. Besides, I got it all."

"Well, I may need a witness—" Del started.

"Man, you forgotten what the word 'no' means? Nada, no way, it ain't goin' to happen. Forget about it."

Del sighed and leaned back. From long experience, he knew how stubborn Slick could be. He wasn't likely to change his mind.

"Well, did this guy tell you anything else?"

McNeil shook his head.

"Just to be sure, let's go over it again."

They did.

"If you happen to see this guy again—"

"Yeah, yeah," said Slick. "I know what to ask."

8

John Carnes picked through the files on his desk. "You got court today," Del said flatly, without question. Homicide detectives, cops in general, spent most of their days either in court, in witness conferences, or on call for court.

"Yeah," said Carnes. "This asshole is still cross-examining me. He's gotten me to repeat the story so many times the jury has it memorized. The jerk is frying his client."

"Love that kind," Del said.

"Yeah, well, he's wasting my time." Carnes studied Del. Del's eyes crinkled and the corners of his mouth twitched. Carnes had seen him come in, almost bouncing. "All right, tell me about the canary you swallowed."

"Huh?"

"You know, the cat who swallowed the canary?"

"Huh?"

"Let me guess, something on the Durant girl's murder?"

"You got it. One of my informants talked to a guy who saw the car that probably dumped her."

"And?"

"And the guy was white. Drove a little boxy car—Maryland plates."

Carnes raised his eyebrow. "Don't tell me the guy got his plate number."

"No," Del said wistfully. "But he didn't do too bad. Said the guy we're looking for has got a University of Maryland sticker in his back window."

"He reliable?"

"Well, I'm not sure. It's a friend of my source. He won't ID the guy."

"Great. Let me guess, you paid him for the info."

"Yeah, but I've known this guy a long time." Clinton's tone was defensive. "It's legit."

"Pardo drives a BMW. Could look like any other boxy car in the dark," Carnes mused. "Course, Pardo wouldn't have Maryland plates, and I don't think he has a Maryland sticker unless he got one from Benton. You sure your guy was right about the Maryland plates?"

"That's what his source told him."

"Any way we can talk to the guy?"

"Don't think so," said Del. "I can work on Slick—that's the name of my contact—but he's a stubborn SOB."

Carnes rubbed his chin and thought. University of Maryland. Victoria Benton was from Maryland. "Wasn't your girl—"

"Anna Durant."

"Yeah, Anna Durant," Carnes said impatiently. "Wasn't she from some other school?"

"She graduated from Georgetown," Del said. "But you're wondering if she has ties to Maryland?"

"Yeah," said Carnes. "Maybe an old boyfriend; there might be something."

"Worth checking." Del pulled out a notebook and scribbled. "Where do things stand with your case?"

"Nowhere. Thought I had a good lead, but it didn't play out. I'm gonna try to check out the Maryland angle a bit more too, soon as I get done with court, anyway." Carnes shrugged. "When you don't have anything, you gotta clutch at straws."

Carnes sat in the witness room waiting for the judge to deal with some preliminary matters. Where did Clinton's information fit in? Was it legit? The information didn't seem to fit Pardo. What about Bardash? He was a Maryland guy. His car was a Lexus. Possible.

Carnes still didn't have a favorite suspect. He had no doubt the same perp was involved in the two cases. So what was his link to the girls? Was he one of these Ted Bundy types who cruised around for likely victims, charmed them into his car, then turned nasty? Or was there some link between the victims and the killer?

This seemed to be the classic serial killer who randomly selected his victims. If so, Carnes would need luck to narrow down a potential universe of suspects. Maybe he could bug the Bureau to see if they'd identified any serial killers with the same MO. He thought about all the paperwork and groaned.

In most murders, there was some obvious tie between victims. If Del's stoolie was correct, Anna Durant's killer had a University of Maryland sticker on his car. Vicky Benton went to Maryland. Was it a coincidence? They'd have to work both approaches: check out the serial sex-criminal angle and the Maryland connection. He almost longed for a simple drug killing.

What about Pardo? Did Pardo know Durant? He could have met her through Benton. If so, none of the people Carnes interviewed had been able to establish it. Of course, Carnes didn't ask about Durant when he'd talked to most of them. He'd have to reinterview some of them.

By lunch, Carnes had finished with court and was calling back through his list of Benton acquaintances.

"How's it going, Carnes?" The booming baritone voice of Lieutenant Rogers commanded attention. Rogers was a tall black man with a relaxed manner and a fine sense of humor. People instinctively liked him. When he wanted to, however, he could draw himself up to his full height and use his voice as a weapon. Carnes had seen perps confess to Rogers as though he was their priest, or maybe the Lord himself.

"Just fine, Lieu. Trying to find a lead on our women killer."

The lieutenant raised his eyebrows. "Women killer? Interesting you said that. Got a press call on the cases this morning, Carnes—that young woman from the *Post* asking if there was a connection between the Benton and Durant cases. You saying there is?"

"For the *Post,* no. To be honest, I'm in a minority on this one. I think it's a strong possibility. You've seen the paperwork. If you were betting, where'd you put your money?"

"I think we have a problem."

"Yeah," Carnes agreed.

"Keep your opinion to yourself. We've been getting calls from the families, and the cases have gotten enough attention. Channel nine has done a couple of pieces. Fletcher's antsy enough. We don't want to give them some crazed-killer angle."

"No problem."

"Good." Rogers walked away.

How long before the brass really put the pressure on? One big story and they'd lose control. Carnes sighed. Rodriguez was right. No reason to get everyone excited. Carnes was about to pick up the phone when he saw Del Clinton coming in.

"What's got you grinning like the Cheshire cat?"

"Anna Durant."

"Anna Durant?" Carnes shook his head. "You always grin about dead girls?"

"Only when I find out they went to the University of Maryland."

"No shit? I thought she went to Georgetown."

"She graduated from Georgetown." Del grinned.

"But—let me guess—she transferred?"

Del nodded. "After her sophomore year. Apparently, she fell out with a boyfriend. Wanted to start fresh. Her parents were pretty vague about the reasons, and I couldn't get much out of them."

"Any name for this boyfriend?"

"No." Del's face contorted into a look of mild disgust. "They couldn't remember. Said they'd look around and if they found anything or remembered, they'd call."

"Guess it's time for me to visit Maryland."

It had been some time since John Carnes had been on the Maryland campus. When Lefty Driesell was still the coach he'd gone to basketball games at Cole Field House. He and Caroline used to go to the university's dairy store for the best ice cream he'd ever tasted. He pictured her with a mustache of cream on her upper lip and a white tip on her nose. Then Len Bias died, Lefty departed, and Caroline left. It had been a while.

Carnes saw the spire of the chapel in the distance and moved to the left lane. He turned off Route 1 into the main entrance. A bunch of kids—now he thought of them as kids—played touch football on the long expanse of grass to his left. He wondered how many were in summer school. When he came to the circle, he went three-quarters of the way around and exited toward the red brick administrative building. The building's facade reminded him of a Greek temple. He pulled into the small lot between the administration building and the armory and walked around to the front.

At the information counter a pale girl with bad skin, wire-rimmed glasses, and stringy brown hair directed him to the registrar's office. He worked his way back through an obstacle course of desks to the registrar's. A well-built young man with curly hair and a thin mustache was seated behind a desk typing something into a computer terminal. When

Carnes cleared his throat, the man, clearly annoyed at being distracted, looked up. "Yes?"

Carnes pulled out his badge and identified himself.

The man stood up and smiled. "Jim Grayson." His handshake was firm. "Sorry. This report is late, and no one's supposed to be back here now."

"No problem." Carnes appraised the man. Grayson didn't fit his stereotype of a registrar. He vibrated with an athlete's energy. His face was square and he had a strong chin and a small mouth that disclosed an even set of white teeth when he smiled. Carnes decided Grayson was about twenty-five.

"You're outside your jurisdiction, aren't you?" Grayson seemed proud of his knowledge.

Carnes nodded.

"I was a criminology major. Used to work for the campus police, but"— he smiled slightly—"the university pays better over here. I'm still interested in police work though," he added. "I've got applications in with the Maryland State Police and PG County. Took the tests. Should be hearing something soon. What can I do for you?" Grayson tipped his head to the side the way Duke, Carnes' German shepherd, did.

"I'm investigating the murders of a couple of former Maryland students, Vicky Benton and Anna Durant. You may've read about them in the paper or seen something on TV."

Grayson nodded gravely. "I saw the stories on TV. Real tragedy. I was a student here a few years ago myself. I think I had a class with Vicky Benton or met her somewhere. Her picture looked familiar anyway." He shook his head. "Anything I can do?"

Carnes was pleased. Not everyone liked police officers. Although Maryland wasn't exactly a hotbed of student radicalism, Carnes had been concerned about what reaction he'd get. Grayson seemed to be one of those people who enjoyed the excitement of a murder investigation. Such people usually were eager to get involved, to provide assistance. The trick for the investigator was to sift reliable information from well-intentioned misinformation. After all the drug-related murders where no one, not even the family of the victim, wanted to cooperate with the police, it was a pleasure to discover someone willing to help.

"Any idea where you met her?"

"Maybe a class or a frat party or something. Pretty girl. You know, it's hard to believe." Disgust swept over Grayson's face.

Carnes nodded.

"So what happened?"

"Can't give you too many details," said Carnes. "But I know that both Durant and Benton went to Maryland. I'm trying to get some information about their backgrounds here, something that might be helpful." He paused to let his statement sink in. "If I could see their records. . . ."

Grayson chewed his lower lip. "Well, you know, I don't think I'm allowed to give those out. Besides, if these girls graduated more than a year ago I don't think I'd have much beyond date of graduation and major."

"Durant never graduated. Our information indicates she transferred out," Carnes said. "Don't you have any paper files?"

"Well, yeah, but it would take a while to pull them from storage and, as I said, I'm not sure I can do that. You know, Mrs. Sanders, my supervisor . . . She isn't even here today—went to the beach." Grayson chewed his lip again. "Shit, I'd like to assist in any way I can."

Carnes gritted his teeth. "It would be a big help. You might be saving someone's life."

"Well-l." Grayson looked past Carnes for several seconds. He glanced at his computer screen. Finally, he seemed to reach a decision. "What the hell, I'm not going to be a glorified file clerk all my life. Rules are made to be broken. Give me ten minutes." He started to get up but stopped, his face displaying momentary indecision. "But I could get fired. You can't make copies or take anything . . ." His voice trailed off.

"OK," Carnes said. "It's a deal."

Carnes drove around the Beltway. He had finally charmed Grayson into letting him make photocopies of the Benton and Durant files. Although these papers sat in manila folders on the seat next to him, they did not explain the grim set to the corners of his mouth. That resulted from the conversation he had with Grayson as they walked out of the building.

As they hit the outside steps, Grayson cautiously glanced from side to side and then, in a low voice, said, "I know this may not be anything, but it seems to me another girl died under suspicious circumstances. I think she went to school here around the same time as the other two."

Carnes stopped in his tracks and stared with his mouth wide open. "What—I mean who?"

"Well," Grayson said. "It was almost a year ago. I think I saw something in the alumni paper." He stared off into the distance. "She was living down in Ocean City or Fenwick and working"—he closed his eyes in thought—"as a waitress or something."

"What was her name?"

Grayson closed his eyes in concentration. Finally, he opened his eyes, face filled with dismay. "Shit, I can't remember."

"Remember how she died?"

"Not really. It sticks in my mind that it wasn't a natural death."

9

Carnes stopped on Route 1 to call Rodriguez. After only a couple of minutes, Rodriguez called back, his voice higher than normal with excitement. "You got something, partner!" It had taken Rodriguez only two calls to find the investigating officer, a Sergeant Broderick of the Ocean City Police Department. "Her name was Francine Lynch and he wouldn't talk about it over the phone. He'll talk to you if you'll go out there. He said he'd stay around until six."

"Good work. Do me a favor and call Carmella. I'm heading right to Ocean City. Should take me three, three and a half hours," Carnes said. "Tell her I'll sleep over if we're done late."

"I'll bet," said Rodriguez. "See if you can stop by and see Broderick before you start partying." There was an unusually hard edge to Rodriguez' voice.

Carnes kept a bantering tone. "You're just jealous, you old buzzard."

Carnes eased his car off the Beltway to the right, following the signs to Route 50, Annapolis. What was bugging Rodriguez? Carnes tried to recollect the last few weeks. Rodriguez had seemed pissed off the time Carnes spent the afternoon with Jessica Kramer and didn't answer his beeper. But it couldn't be that alone.

Carmella! Carmella and Rodriguez must have talked. Carmella probably complained about the late nights. Shit! What about loyalty? He paid her salary and expenses. Hell, he was a single guy. He had a right to go out and have a good time. At least he came home at night—or early in the morning. He thought of Avery. Well, maybe he should spend more time with her.

* * *

Sergeant James Broderick was a beefy man with the bulk of an ex-football player gone to seed. His face was weathered by a lifetime of sun and salt and was as craggy as a piece of driftwood. His crew cut bristled like a hairbrush. Broderick's voice was a low growl, but his smile was direct and friendly. His Eastern Shore drawl was contagious, and Carnes knew he'd start to sound like Broderick after a few hours with the man.

Broderick scanned the file he'd pulled from a battered file cabinet and spread it out on the desk in front of him. "Yep, her name was Francine Lynch all right, though I guess all her friends called her Fran or Frannie. The dates fit. She woulda been a classmate of your Vicky Benton." Broderick tapped on the file. "I've worked this case a full year, every spare minute I've had."

He started taking photos out of the file. The first shot was a posed photo of Francine Lynch in tight shorts and a knotted white blouse that showed off a firm, tanned middle. Her long brown hair cascaded over her shoulders like a waterfall, framing a face with high cheekbones. Sexy smile. "Yeah, she was a looker," Broderick growled. "Hard to tell when we found her."

He flipped to the crime-scene photos. "This was her apartment. As you can see, we found her body on the floor. No sign of forced entry." He pointed to a picture. "That's the way we found her, with her naked bottom up in the air, arms tied behind her with some of her clothes. You can barely make out the gag. Turned out, those were her socks in her mouth and that there's her pantyhose knotted around her throat. Medical examiner said it was a strangulation. Hell, you didn't have to go to medical school to see that."

"What kind of knot?" Carnes asked.

Broderick grinned in appreciation of the question. "An old granny knot, nothing really fancy; this wasn't no Boy Scout or sailor knot."

Broderick flipped through the pictures, narrating as he went. "Bruising on the face . . . bite marks on the breasts and abdomen . . . bruises on her thighs. Look at this one—some of her hair was chopped off. Didn't find it. For that matter, didn't find her panties." He put down the photos and pulled out some reports. "Semen found in the vagina and in the pubic hair. More semen in the anus. Semen on the face and hair. The guy definitely could get it off." Broderick's smile was tight and didn't extend to his eyes.

"Could they determine his blood type from his semen?"

"State lab said Type O. Pretty common—seventy percent?"

Carnes paged through the photos. One had particularly caught his eye. It was a black and white picture of a wall with a large upside-down U. "What's this?"

"Oh, yeah, that's a real puzzler. It was next to the bathroom wall. A big horseshoe. Found out the girl used to ride. We checked to see whether she rode anywhere around here. Nothing. Then we looked for jockeys or other horse people in town at the time. Nobody we could tie to her. Maybe it's some sort of satanic symbol." He shook his head in puzzlement.

Carnes nodded. "Yeah, I know." He explained about the similar drawings in the Benton and Durant cases.

Broderick whistled. "Pretty strange."

"What else've you learned?"

"Her boss saw her last at one in the morning when the place closed. It's one of those bar-restaurants that does a big summer business and barely makes it through the winter. We checked on all her boyfriends—she had a bunch. No reason to think it wasn't one of them, but no reason to think it was. All had weak alibis. No one admitted to any jealousy, but clearly she got around. I look at this"—he held up a picture of the victim—"and think someone was real angry at her. Couldn't find no other motives. No signs of forced entry, so I assumed it was someone she knew. I've been pursuing every angle on every suspect. So far, no luck."

"Who are they?" Carnes asked.

Broderick dragged out a piece of paper headed "Possible suspects." Half of the names were crossed out. None were familiar.

"Mind if I copy the names?" Carnes asked. He saw Broderick's face tense. "In case I come across them in my investigation. I'll call you, of course."

Broderick handed over the sheet with a flourish. "Be my guest."

While Carnes wrote, Broderick continued his narrative. "Ain't had any other cases like this, so I didn't really give much thought to the sex-pervert weirdo angle. Not that we don't get rapes around here. Sex goes with sun, bathing suits, and partying, and those are the prime industries. We get all types—straights, gays. Hell, we spend half our time chasing the male prostitutes out of the men's rooms along the beach." His face turned serious. "But we don't get many murders. Nothing like this. This ain't Washington."

Carnes nodded. During his student days at Salisbury State he had spent many weekends in Ocean City, living in overcrowded rental houses or fleabag hotels and cruising in an old Mustang convertible. It was a care-free, friendly atmosphere where booze and drugs enhanced the party-ing. Willing sex partners were as available as the sand. The only violence he'd seen was a drunken brawl.

"Well, anyway, I couldn't find any sex pervert angle, so I've concen-trated on the guys in her life." Broderick continued. "I even checked out her boss and all the guys she worked with, just in case, and every guy who lived in her building. I've tried every snitch I know. There's nothing on the streets. That's real unusual. Though we get lots of tourists and sum-mer folks, this is really a small town at heart."

"You must've gotten a lot of pressure on this one from the local pols. Bad for the tourist trade?"

"Actually, we were able to keep it real quiet. One of the advantages of a small town. Nobody wants to scare off the tourists. Kept all the details under wraps."

"Were there other clues, anything unusual about this case?"

"Nothing. No one saw or heard anything."

"If I gave you a name of someone, could you find out if he was in town at the time of the murder?"

"Well, it depends. There's people who own condos or houses, tons of rentals, all kinds of hotels. Some are real nice, but some are fleabags." He smiled. "But, hell, give me the name and I'll see what I can do."

Carnes scrawled two names on a piece of paper and handed them to Broderick.

"James Bardash? Fitz Pardo? That wouldn't be the lawyer Pardo."

"Yeah." Carnes leaned forward. "You know him?"

"Sure do. He's got a condo down here. Had some sort of prob-lem . . . let me think." Broderick stared at the ceiling fan spinning around and drummed his fingers on the table. "Hmmn." He drummed some more.

Carnes fought an urge to shake him.

"Yeah. There was some sorta complaints about break-ins in the con-dos. He was on the condo association board. Nice place. Upscale, up-town. My recollection—it was just kids looking for a place to crash. But Pardo's an obnoxious fucker. Drove us crazy for a while until we con-vinced the condo association to hire their own security."

* * *

Carnes sat at the bar in the Big Pecker and mulled things over. The place was popular with the younger set. For a tidy sum, tourists could purchase T-shirts with a caricature of a large bird, "Big Pecker." Carnes still had one somewhere. A real conversation starter.

Carnes eyed a couple of girls in tight shorts—a blond and a brunette. Frank Perdue didn't have the only fresh birds on the Eastern Shore. Sisters? College girls? Carnes sipped his beer and caught the blond's eye. He tipped his head in an almost imperceptible nod. She smiled back. Good sign.

"Bartender," Carnes said. A young man with a good tan and long brown hair wandered over.

"Yeah."

"See those two young ladies?" Carnes indicated the girls. "Refills, my tab." The bartender gave him a conspiratorial wink. "Sure, bud." He wandered away. Carnes watched as he prepared the drinks and took them over. The girls asked a question, and the bartender hooked a thumb toward Carnes. They giggled and talked to each other for a minute, then started over.

Carnes liked the way they moved. Their bodies had the firmness of youth, but they walked with the sinuous grace of mature women. *Very nice.*

"Thanks for the drinks," said the blond, who looked slightly older. "My name's Cindy." With a slight movement of her head she indicated the brunette. "My sister Mandy."

Mandy nodded. "Hi!"

"Care to join me?" Carnes asked.

They exchanged glances, then seemed to reach a nonverbal agreement.

"Sure," said Cindy.

Carnes had a feeling it was going to be an interesting night.

Becky Granite and Carol Bromley munched chicken wings and swayed to the music that could barely be heard over the roar of voices, the clinking of glasses, and the scraping of furniture. The song was one of Becky's favorites from her aerobics class, and her body wanted to do its routine.

"What happened to that detective you like?" asked Carol.

"Oh, he's fine. Been real busy lately. I haven't seen him in a few days." Becky tried to keep her voice casual. She'd been wondering why Carnes hadn't called her.

Carol squinted her eyes and leaned forward. "Slept with him yet?"

"What kind of question is that?" Becky couldn't quite manage shocked outrage. It was hard to be mad with Carol.

"A good one," Carol said, eyes full of mischief. "But I know the answer."

"You do?"

"Of course." Carol paused dramatically. "You haven't slept with him. Therefore, you haven't heard from him."

Becky's composure crumbled slightly. "Now that's not true."

"You have slept with him?" Carol's sounded skeptical. "Then it must have been lousy sex."

"Sex, sex, sex. Is that all you have on your mind?" Becky shook her head with disgust. "You always act like you're in heat."

"You act like someone who isn't getting any."

Becky paused and studied Carol for a moment. She sighed. "OK, I give. You're right. I haven't slept with him. I wanted to make sure—well—that everything was right, first."

"And you haven't heard from him?"

"No," Becky said.

"Bad sign."

"Maybe. But it's not like we didn't hit it off. We had fun together. Great talks. Real personal stuff. The kind of things you don't talk about with most guys. I think he's just real busy working these murders." She wished she was as sure as she sounded.

"Bad move," said Carol. "You gotta keep secrets. Mystery is what keeps guys interested." She licked up one side of the straw from her drink and down the other. "At least, that's part of what keeps guys interested."

Becky laughed. "You are so—bad."

"That's not what the guys say."

Carol was a case. Of course, she might be partly right. Becky wasn't against sex. She just thought sex should be part of an intimate relationship. She'd had a great sex life with Brett. At least she'd thought so. It wasn't that she was afraid to have sex with Carnes. But why rush it? He'd made hints, but he'd seemed OK about taking their time. Was she misreading him?

"Speaking of guys, remember the shy one I saw watching you a couple of weeks ago?"

Becky nodded.

"Well, don't look now, but he's back."

"You sure?"

"Yeah, it's him."

Becky began to turn.

"No, don't. Oh shoot. He ducked out again."

Becky turned in time to see the front door swing closed.

10

Carnes saw the exit for the Pottery Factory, an outlet mall with pastel-colored stores. For a moment, he wondered if he needed any clothes or anything. No. He just needed some sleep and a massive infusion of energy. He tried to remember when he and the sisters finally fell asleep. His memories of the night were a tangle of thrashing limbs, moans, shuddering explosions, and exhausted unconsciousness.

This might have been the best, the wildest night of sex ever. So why did he feel like shit? He was thirty-two years old. A father. Mature. Supposedly responsible. He'd just spent the night with two women nearly half his age. It was unlikely he'd ever see them again. As the old Peggy Lee song went, "Is that all there is?"

He pulled into the right lane and turned into the shopping center. After passing a cluster of designer stores, he spotted a phone. He parked.

Rodriguez was in court, but he caught Del Clinton at his desk. "Your ass is grass," said Del.

"Whatta ya mean?"

"Captain called a meeting this morning. *Post* did a speculative piece about a possible serial killer. Quoted department sources. Had pictures of Benton and Durant. Captain chewed our asses. Wanted to know where you were. He had someone call Ocean City PD. They said they hadn't seen you since last evening. Captain was raving. Rodriguez covered for you with some bullshit about interviewing witnesses. Bryant didn't buy it. He pulled us aside afterward. Asked if you were doing your share in this investigation or if you were too, um, distracted."

"What did you say?"

"We lied. Said you knew what you were doing." At least Del sounded playful.

"Thanks a lot. With friends like you guys—"

"I'd lie low if I were you."

"OK."

"To satisfy my curiosity, where were you?"

"Private business."

The line was silent. "Hey, I barely know you, but if I were you—"

"I don't need advice," Carnes barked.

The line was silent.

"Sorry. I'm just tired." Carnes filled Del in on what he'd learned from Broderick.

Del whistled quietly. "Should we get a warrant for Pardo's house and car?"

"Too early," said Carnes. "Pass it by the lieu. It'd probably help if we could show that Pardo was in Ocean City the night of the killing."

"Hell, I haven't even pinned down where he was the night Anna Durant was killed. You think he met her through Vicky Benton?"

"Possible," Carnes muttered. A truck rumbled by on Route 50 drowning out Del's voice. "What was that?"

"I said I'd check on it with Anna's family and friends."

Carnes waited while a woman and young girl with bulging shopping bags walked past him, then said, "This guy is one sick puppy. There's too much here for coincidence. He's got some link to these girls. Pardo could be our man. No reason a prominent lawyer can't be a killer. He's been ducking our request for blood and hair samples for DNA testing. Why not a lawyer? Hell, we've had university presidents who make obscene phone calls."

"Yeah. Every arrow points to Pardo except the Maryland plates on the car my source reported."

"But that's not the most reliable tip I've ever heard."

"True," said Del. "Wasn't that notorious serial killer Ted Bundy a law student?"

"Yeah. Think it's something they teach in law school?"

Clinton guffawed.

"Can you do me a favor?" Carnes said. "Call the department's consulting psychologist, Crenshaw, and set up an appointment for me. Maybe he'll see something we're missing. I've gotta be at the U.S. Attorney's this afternoon for a witness conference. Make the appointment for tomorrow."

As Carnes walked back to the car he passed the discount bookstore where he and Avery stopped last year and bought every Disney book in sight. Avery! Shit! He had promised to visit her class today to talk about what it was like being a policeman. He checked his watch. Damn, he'd never make it in time. He swung back to the phone booth and called the school to tell them he wouldn't be there. Afterwards, he purchased a hair ribbon. Maybe this would buy him some forgiveness.

A pile of messages greeted Carnes. One read: "Becky called." There was another from last night and one from this morning. He dialed her number.

"Marketing, Becky Granite speaking."

"Hi, John Carnes."

"Where've you been? You're harder to reach than the mayor."

"Working." He glanced around the squad room. No one seemed to be listening. "Following a lead on the murder of those girls."

"Oh." Becky sounded as though she was straining to keep her tone light. "I wanted to see if you'd slipped off the edge of the earth or something."

He thought about his night with the sisters. "No, although I feel like I did."

"Oh." She seemed disappointed.

It was almost as if she knew. Damn her. She had no right. "Did you call for a specific reason?" His voice was sharp.

"Uh, just to see if you'd learned anything about Vicky." Strain was evident in her voice.

"Nothing I can tell you." *Why was he acting this way?*

"Oh. Well, I guess I'd better let you get back to work. Sorry to bother you."

"No, wait!" The line had already gone dead. He cursed at the phone and slammed it down. He heard a chuckle and saw Wiley staring at him across the room.

"Girl trouble?" Wiley smirked.

"Fuck you." Carnes grabbed his coffee mug. A layer of scum coated the surface of yesterday's brew. He carried the floating biology experiment down the hall to the men's room, dumped the sludge into the sink, and scrubbed the cup with the soap from the dispenser and a paper towel.

He pictured Becky sitting at her desk, staring at her phone, face full of pain, wondering why he was pushing her away. Also, he'd let down

Avery again. The captain was after his ass. Even Rodriguez was disgusted with him. What a fuckup! That was it exactly. His life was fucked up because he couldn't pass up an opportunity—any opportunity—to jump into bed with a woman. Hell. Sex was fun. It made him feel good. But the pleasure was transitory; it passed as quickly as a cloud scudding across the sky.

Carnes put down the mug and washed his face vigorously with the strong soap and hot water. The paper towels felt like sandpaper on his skin. He still didn't feel clean. He wanted to go home and sleep for a year. His watch said otherwise. *C'mon. Shake it off. You've got a witness conference.*

Avery pushed at her food with her fork.

"Want something else, sweetheart?" Carnes struggled to maintain a smile. Avery didn't look up or respond. Carmella and Avery had both given him a cold shoulder when he surprised them by coming home early. He'd shoved a twenty-dollar bill into Carmella's hand and sent her off to "have a good time" for the evening. She'd acknowledged his generosity with sad, almost pitying eyes.

The hair ribbon had elicited only an "I don't like it." Avery dropped it on the table as though it were contaminated. She went into the family room and turned on the TV.

Carnes cooked two of Avery's favorite foods, macaroni and cheese and hot dogs, while she sat in front of the TV playing with her dolls. He even pretended to be a waiter, grandly placing the food in front of her, but his playacting had earned only a weak smile. He doubted even the cupcakes he'd picked up at the Giant would break her mood.

Avery barely spoke, face set in a pout. After dealing all day with liars and hypocrites, Carnes usually enjoyed the openness of her face. Tonight, it was a hot sword thrust into his heart.

"Sweetheart"—Carnes heard the plea in his voice—"I said I was sorry. Sometimes I have to work."

Avery looked up, eyes welling with tears. "Yeah, that's what you always say: 'I have to work.' You always have to work."

"But it's true," he pleaded. But it wasn't true. He sensed that she knew he was lying. How could she? She was a little girl. The idea of her father frolicking with two girls in Ocean City was beyond her experience. It sounded ridiculous even to him. She couldn't know. On the other hand, children were very good at sensing falsehood. How many times had he lied to her over the years? How many times had he given her reason to doubt his love? He felt a sick pain in his stomach.

Why should she trust him? Could he trust himself? After all, though he felt something special for Becky, the feeling hadn't stopped him from hopping straight into bed with strangers for whom he felt no more than momentary lust. He'd bedded women he didn't care about and treated Becky like shit. What was wrong with him?

Avery was staring at her food, refusing to meet his eye. He pushed back his chair and went to her. He tried to pull her toward him. She pulled away and grunted angrily. He almost smiled but it hurt too much. He pulled back her chair and picked her up. "No!" She pushed him with her little hands.

He settled with her into the rocker-recliner where he'd read to her since she was a baby. Her small body strained away from him. Carnes rocked back and forth, humming Brahms' lullaby softly to the creak, creak, creak of the chair's movement. He inhaled the aroma of the baby shampoo she still used, and his thoughts retreated back in time. Avery was the one he loved, the one he held onto when his life with Caroline was unraveling. Avery had been his anchor. Yet his compulsion—what else could he call it?—threatened to break the links that connected them.

Carnes stopped humming. He smoothed her hair and whispered "I'm sorry" and "I love you" over and over until the tension eased out of her and her body began to conform to his. "Sometimes," he said, "mommies and daddies do stupid things. We take things for granted—forget what's most important to us." The tightness in his throat made it difficult to talk. "You're the most important person in my life." He stroked her face and felt the wetness of a tear running down her cheek. His own eyes responded.

"You have a right to be mad at your daddy. He got so wrapped up in what he was doing"—he struggled to find the right words—"he forgot what was really important."

"It was terrible, Daddy," Avery sniffed. "I told everyone you were coming and the teacher didn't know where you were and I didn't know where you were—" Her voice broke.

"I know." And it was worse than she thought.

"And you promised."

"You're right, sweetie." He tried to think what promises he could make, what promises he could keep. "I'll try to do better, sweetheart. I really will." He wiped a tear away from his cheek. "I love you so much. The first time I sat in this chair with you, you were barely this big." He pointed to the area from the tips of his fingers to his elbow and saw her mouth turn up into the beginnings of a smile. This was an old routine.

"Oh, Daddy. You always say that." She giggled.

"But it's true." Carnes smiled back. "And I loved you then more than anything or anybody in the whole world. I can't even come up with words to describe—"

"And you still do," she finished.

"That's right. I still do."

"I love you too, Daddy."

11

Dr. Crenshaw ushered Carnes into his office. "So, Detective, w-what can—what can I do for you today?"

"Well, remember the case of the two girls I talked to you about before?"

Crenshaw nodded and rubbed his hands together nervously.

"Well, it's now three."

Crenshaw cleared his throat in short staccato bursts. "Another killing? I didn't see anything—"

"This one happened a year ago. It didn't make the papers." He told Crenshaw about his visit to the University of Maryland and his subsequent trip to Ocean City.

"Curious, very curious," Crenshaw muttered, as though to himself. "What triggered him to kill like this—a year apart? Or are there other victims in between? Very strange."

"I was hoping you could tell me," said Carnes.

Crenshaw smiled enigmatically. "I'm a psychologist, not a mystic. I can give you some theories, make educated guesses, maybe tell you how advanced your killer is in his ritual, but I don't have all the answers."

Carnes could see that Crenshaw liked to be seduced. "Nobody has your expertise. I need your insights."

Crenshaw sat back in his chair and put his hands behind his head. He closed his eyes for a minute. "Yes, yes. Something triggers him, sets him off. Maybe some personal failure, a breakup with a girlfriend, troubles at his job, a death in his family. He kills to regain power, control."

Carnes scribbled in his notebook.

"There's some link between these girls and your killer. Your killer is killing University of Maryland girls of a certain age. Psychologists don't believe in coincidence. This Maryland thing doesn't quite f-fit the typical serial killer. I've heard of serial killers who kill a particular type of person—body type or profession or something—but girls from the same school? No. That's different." He rubbed his hand, and his lips contorted into a blissful smile. "No, he either knows them or he has something, real or imagined, against them."

"What?" asked Carnes.

"Maybe he's a Duke fan."

"A Duke fan?"

"Just joking." Crenshaw grinned. "I do have a sense of humor, you know."

"Oh." Carnes felt stupid. "Then what's his motivation?"

"That—as they used to say—is the $64,000 question."

Carnes gritted his teeth. "Isn't there anything else you can tell me? I mean, is Pardo my man? Does he fit?"

"M-maybe."

Carnes fought an urge to stutter. "Maybe?"

Crenshaw smiled. "I'm sorry, Detective. All I can say for sure is 'maybe.' It would help to know more about this fellow." Crenshaw held up a finger. "Like his family history, whether he has lots of friends, how successful he is, things that give a clue to his self-image." He had added a finger for each point.

"Great!" Carnes couldn't hide his frustration. "So if I find out everything that makes him tick, you might know if he could be our killer?"

Crenshaw smiled sadly. "You know, Detective, this is, uh, as upsetting for me as it is for you. It's a professional challenge. But you have to understand, psychology is like detective work. We learn basic principles of human behavior as you learn how to investigate crimes, how people commit them. But we have to fit together our observations and the clues to a personality the way you assemble the clues to a crime. Sometimes, we don't have enough clues to put the puzzle together"—he smiled shyly—"to mix metaphors somewhat."

Carnes decided he liked Crenshaw. "Can you tell anything more about the killer's personality?"

"Not really." Crenshaw shook his head. "He's someone who doesn't like himself too much. He gets off on the power and control that goes with these ritualized killings. It seems there might be an element of—I can only call it revenge. Remember the case in Virginia of the guy who was killing prostitutes who looked like his ex-girlfriend?"

Carnes nodded. He had helped question hookers for possible witnesses. The guy had been caught because he left a credit card receipt in the plastic bag he'd placed over the head of one of his victims.

"Is there anything else you can tell me about him?" Carnes asked.

"No." Crenshaw shook his head sadly, then smiled. "Well, there is one thing that might help."

"What?"

"He knows some Greek."

"Greek?" Carnes was a silent movie actor's pantomime of astonishment.

"Yes."

"How on earth do you know that?"

"Why, uh, the omegas at the crime scenes," said Crenshaw.

"Omegas?"

"Detective, I could understand that maybe, uh, you didn't study Greek, but didn't you have fraternities or sororities wherever you went to school?"

"Fraternities or sororities?"

"What you've been calling a horseshoe is the Greek letter omega. Fraternities and sororities are often called Greeks because their names are Greek letters. Some universities even call their fraternal organizations 'Hellenic societies.' You know, fraternities are called things like Phi Kappa Tau, Chi Phi, Gamma Delta Iota. That one's my favorite."

It flooded back. "Gamma Delta Iotas—goddamned independents, right?"

"Now you're cooking with gas."

"Holy shit." Carnes stared at Crenshaw, his eyes suddenly wide with excitement. He jumped up and grabbed Crenshaw's hand and shook it vigorously, causing the man to bounce around in his chair. "Greeks, omegas. What a motherfucking great clue."

Now it was Crenshaw's chance to look nonplussed. "I'm sorry, I don't follow."

"All the girls went to the University of Maryland, and the killer leaves omegas at two of the sites, so what do we conclude?"

"It has some connection to a fraternity or sorority. Yes, Detective. Bravo!"

They muttered congratulations back and forth for several moments. "I'd better get moving on this. Best clue I've had in a while," said Carnes. "Thanks."

"N-no problem. Anything I can do to help." Crenshaw beamed.

Carnes paused at the door. "Well, if it isn't imposing. I have an unrelated question for you."

"Fire away."

"Well, I have a friend . . ."

Crenshaw nodded. "A f-friend. Ahh. What's troubling your friend?"

"This friend was wondering if there's such a thing as too much sex drive. This friend has sort of been running around screwing, I mean having intercourse—"

"I think I understand the term 'screw,' Detective."

"Well, anyway, this friend has been screwing every woman—well, almost every woman—in sight. It's gotten to the point where it gets in the way of things. Now, he's got his part–uhm—he's in trouble at work, his family's mad at him, and he has this girl he's been seeing."

"And do—how does your friend feel about this? Is he enjoying himself or does he feel shame and remorse?"

"Both. He enjoys it, he loves sex and women and all, but he feels bad afterward—you know, postcoital depression, that sort of thing."

"Oh?"

"And, of course, he's not wild about how this problem—"

"D-did you say problem?" Crenshaw asked.

"No." Carnes displayed an embarrassed smile. "Well, maybe I did."

"Well, how does your f-friend feel about himself?"

"OK, I guess—well, sometimes pretty lousy."

"Would you say your friend has a compulsion to have sex?"

"Yeah."

"Does he have any complete love relationships? Sex and love together?"

"Not really. He's found someone he's interested in, but nothing's happened yet. It hasn't stopped him from sleeping around."

"Hmmn." Crenshaw made a tent with his fingers and stared at it for a moment. "You know, there is a disease—at least some psychologists consider it a disease—called sex addiction. It's similar to alcoholism. People habitually engage in these quick sexual encounters instead of real relationships. You've probably seen something about it on Donahue."

"Never watch it."

"Does that description sound like your friend?"

"A little."

"Typically, the sex addict has very low self-esteem, as do other addicts. Usually, we learn that the sex addict was victimized as a child—abused sexually, mentally, or physically. Often sex addicts grew up with parents who were alcoholics or some other kind of addict. Does that sound like it fits y—your friend?"

Carnes stared out the window and swallowed. "My friend was sexually abused as a child. But he repressed it for many years. There may have been some family history of addictions."

Crenshaw nodded. "Yes, that fits. Sometimes, an abused youngster feels responsible for the abuse. There are all kinds of complex feelings involved—arousal, shame. The sex addict confuses sex with real interaction. Usually, the addict has a compulsive desire for sex and can't form real relationships. Does your friend feel more comfortable relating at a sexual level rather than a more intimate, emotional level?"

"I think so. But he wants to have a real relationship."

"Does he feel ashamed about his sexual encounters?"

"Recently. At least, he didn't think about it much until recently."

"Well, it sounds like sex addiction. Sex addicts make themselves feel better with more sex, which in turn makes them feel worse, and the cycle repeats. Breaking the cycle is crucial."

"You mean abstinence?"

"It's often the first necessary step, after admitting there's a problem, of course."

"Oh."

Crenshaw looked at his watch. "It's a very complex area and I have a patient waiting, but I'd be happy to make a referral for your friend. I know someone at Hopkins. They have a program there that might help." He paged through his Rolodex. "There's also a group called SAA, Sex Addicts Anonymous. Sort of like Alcoholics Anonymous." He tore a piece of lined yellow paper off a small notepad and wrote down an address and phone number. "You might give this to your f-friend."

"Thanks, Doc."

"No problem." Crenshaw cleared his throat. "Good luck."

12

Carnes, Rodriguez, and Clinton sat in a Long John Silver's restaurant on Rhode Island Avenue. Carnes chewed on a crunchy fillet doused with vinegar while Rodriguez grumbled about how the grease would give him a massive dose of heartburn. Carnes finished his fillet and wiped his fingers on a paper napkin. He'd been telling them about his meeting with Crenshaw. "I know this fraternity-sorority idea sounds far-fetched," Carnes concluded, "but somehow it fits."

"You know," Clinton ventured quietly, "it's not that crazy. Remember, my informant mentioned a car with a University of Maryland sticker seen near the Durant girl's body, and it was near 295. Route 295 hits the Beltway an exit or two from College Park, a perfect place for someone associated with the university to be living. The girls all went to Maryland."

Carnes nodded his head. "And we haven't found anything to lead us elsewhere."

"That's right, no obvious suspects at St. E's—inpatient or out—or anywhere else. And the tie-in to the other girls is strong."

"But"—Rodriguez scowled—"none of that points to a fraternity or a sorority link for the girls or our killer."

"Vicky Benton was in some sorority," said Carnes. "I know that somebody told me that."

"Well, a white guy on Minnesota Avenue isn't automatically a killer. Del's informant could have just seen some poor guy going home from the Fort Dupont ice rink. Isn't that right down there near where the Durant girl's body was found?" asked Rodriguez.

Clinton nodded.

"See what I mean?" Rodriguez looked at Carnes. "We could be on the ultimate wild-goose chase. This horseshoe thing is as likely to be the darned Arc de Triomphe as an omega."

Carnes and Clinton laughed. "Yeah," said Carnes. "Let's go check out the Paris angle first. I can see it: 'Sarge, Pete here thinks our killer is from Paris. We need travel authorization for two'"—he looked at Del Clinton—"'three enterprising homicide detectives to Paris, France.'" His voice got serious. "Come on, Pete, be real. You've got three victims connected with Maryland and not much else."

"We've still got Pardo."

"Yeah, but we have nothing to tie him in. Maybe he has something to do with a sorority or fraternity. It certainly doesn't hurt to check it out. We've been spinning our wheels for a couple of weeks. So far, all we've got is more victims. What do we have to lose?" Carnes held out his hands, palms up—the universal cop gesture.

"Nothing," Rodriguez admitted. "But I'd sure like to take another crack at Fitz Pardo. *He* has a link to Maryland and to at least two of the victims. Heck, he might have been a fraternity brother himself."

"Hey, I don't like the fucker any better than you do. Maybe he is our man. But you've got to admit having a place in Ocean City doesn't prove he was there or that he murdered Fran Lynch," Carnes said. "But I agree we gotta check it out."

Clinton nodded. "Why don't you let me take a crack at that? Pardo doesn't know me, and I might find a fresh approach. Maybe I'll learn if he was ever in a fraternity."

Rodriguez turned up his hands. "Why not?" He sounded resigned rather than enthusiastic. "And we need to check out each of the girls for sorority memberships."

"Right," Carnes agreed. "Does your nefarious network of Salvadorans and illegal aliens reach as far as Maryland?" Carnes asked.

"Sure," said Rodriguez. "But who are we looking for—some guy who has a hard-on for some sorority, a frat man, or some idiot with the names and addresses of ex-sorority sisters? Did our killer go to Maryland or some other school? Was he rejected by some sorority chick? Heck, maybe his mother was a member of the sorority. Now, that one sounds real deep psychologically. I bet Crenshaw could get into it." Rodriguez snorted. "What kind of link are we searching for?"

"That"—Carnes mimicked the high-pitched tone of Dr. Victor Crenshaw—"is the $64,000 question." Carnes laughed. Rodriguez and Clinton exchanged a raised-eyebrow look.

"I think he's lost it, Del," said Rodriguez.

Clinton nodded. "Definitely."

"It's something Crenshaw says," explained Carnes.

"Sure," Clinton and Rodriguez agreed in unison.

Becky Granite stared at the work on her desk. She was not focusing. Every time she stopped concentrating she found herself thinking about John Carnes. She felt stupid. Sure, he was fun and they'd had some good talks. Still, she should have recognized the signs. Carnes was divorced. People get divorced for a reason. It's never as one-sided as they say. She should have seen all this coming. Anyway, she had no claim on him. They hadn't even slept together. So why was she so hurt?

What attracted her to him? Certainly, part of it was physical. He was the kind of man she found attractive. But there was more. He was interesting. Was she a police groupie? No. It was something deeper, more complex: his sense of humor, the vulnerability she sensed in his eyes. Something in their personalities meshed. Their conversations were lively and honest. They'd exchanged much and, at some level, understood each other. At least she'd thought so.

Maybe it was all ego. She responded to him because she thought he felt something for her. Was that all love was, an ego responding to attention? Now her ego was hurt. Maybe Carol was right and they should have slept together. Maybe that's what his ego needed.

Becky sighed. Maybe she was overanalyzing. Why not just accept that they'd clicked? She and Brett had clicked. Then they'd clacked. So where had she gone wrong? She tried to concentrate on the papers in front of her. It was futile. She sighed.

Becky picked up the phone and dialed quickly. A familiar voice answered.

"Carol Bromley."

"Becky."

"What's up?"

"How about Barnstormers, dinner?"

"Well," Carol's voice sounded almost bubbly, "believe it or not I've got a date."

"Oh."

Carol must have detected the disappointment in Becky's tone. "Hey, but tell you what. I'll meet you for a drink. My date can pick me up there."

"Oh, it's OK." Becky tried to sound convincing. "I don't want to wreck your plans."

"No problemo. This guy's a real hunk. I'm dying to show him off."

"OK. Five?"

"Sounds good."

Carnes and Rodriguez stopped at the registrar's office. Jim Grayson was working at his computer terminal. When he saw them, he smiled broadly. Carnes made introductions.

"Any luck, Detectives?"

"Yeah, your poop on the girl in Ocean City was good. Could be the same killer," Carnes said.

"Glad to help." Grayson appeared pleased. He seemed to be getting quite a rush playing the insider's role.

Carnes decided to take advantage of the situation. "Can I trust you to keep a secret?"

Grayson nodded eagerly.

Carnes glanced at Rodriguez, who raised an eyebrow, then back at Grayson. "I mean it. I don't want to read this tomorrow in the *Post*."

Grayson seemed hurt. "You can trust me, sir."

Carnes told him about the symbols left on the wall. "Since there seems to be a tie-in to Maryland, I thought I'd check out the possibility there's some connection to the frats or sororities here."

"That's a great idea." Grayson looked thoughtful. "Course, that's a pretty tall order. There are probably about thirty frats and maybe twenty or more sororities at Maryland. I don't know how many of them have omega in their name. Besides, it could be something else."

"Not an omega?" Rodriguez asked.

"No, assuming it's an omega, it may not be a sorority or fraternity." Grayson smoothed his mustache with his forefinger. "For example, there are all kinds of honor societies on campus."

"Any with omega in the name?" asked Carnes.

"Let's see." Grayson stared at the ceiling. "There's an Omega Chi Epsilon—that's the engineering honor society—and Omega Rho, for business and management students. Heck, there may be others. I know those two off the top of my head."

Carnes scribbled the names in his notebook. "So you don't think the sorority and fraternity angle is a good one?"

"Heck, it's a great idea." Grayson smiled. "It's brilliant, especially for someone outside the university setting. I just wanted you to know about the other possibilities."

"I appreciate it. Do you have a list of sororities, fraternities, and these societies?"

"No, but I bet you could get one at the student program office over in the Stamp—that's the student union building. It's maybe five minutes, across the quad."

"Thanks."

"Of course, the killer might not even be from a sorority or fraternity. It might be some sort of a dodge. I mean, why would the killer leave you an obvious clue? It's sort of like signing his name."

"Maybe he's fencing with us." Carnes remembered some of the things Crenshaw had said. "Gets off on the thrill."

Rodriguez nodded. "Yeah. He thinks he's a lot smarter than the police, or he wants to show us up."

Grayson looked dubious. "Well, I'm no expert. I'll leave that sorta thing to you guys. Anything else I can help you with?"

"No," said Carnes, "unless something else occurs to you. I gave you my card, didn't I?"

"Sure."

Carnes and Rodriguez stood on the administration building's broad steps. "Let's walk over to the Stamp building," suggested Carnes. "Grayson said it was less than five minutes. It's a nice day."

"If you're in something air-conditioned," Rodriguez said. He wiped his forehead with his sleeve.

Carnes glanced sideways at Rodriguez' spreading midsection. "You need the exercise, partner."

"Yeah, I'm sure that's why we're walking." Rodriguez snorted. "I know you. You want to walk so you can scout the coeds at closer range." Although Rodriguez smiled, his voice was hard.

"A man needs hobbies."

"Hobbies, not obsessions."

Carnes turned on his partner. "What's this moralistic bullshit? It's not like you're a goddamned virgin or something." Carnes waved a hand. "Geez! I'm partnered with Jimmy Swaggart!"

Rodriguez gave Carnes a patronizing glance. "Nobody's suggesting you be a virgin, but you're totally woman crazy. You live and breathe it. Half the time you're not thinking about your work. Your gonads control your brain. All you seem to think about is getting women into bed."

"And you don't think about the same thing?"

"Not all the time. There's such a thing as too much of a good thing."

"Maybe for an old man like you." Carnes began walking again.

"No, John. You're kidding yourself."

"Hey, I appreciate your concern, but I've got things under control."

Rodriguez looked serious. "No. You've been *out* of control, letting this stuff get in the way of your work, your family—"

Carnes swung around. "What the hell do you know about my family?" Carnes' face was dark with rage. "I'll fire that bitch. What kind of bullshit's Carmella been feeding you?"

Rodriguez' eyes showed concern and sadness, not anger. He planted his feet. "This has nothing to do with her."

"No?" Carnes realized some students were staring at them. He began walking again.

Rodriguez joined him. They walked side by side, feet rasping along the sidewalk in an angry duet.

Finally Rodriguez spoke. "This job can crush you. It brings out the worst in all of us. I used to bring the job home. A few before-dinner drinks, a few after-dinner drinks. Didn't get smart until after my family left. Still took a push or two to get me into counseling. That's between you and me; no one on the force knows. Worst times were at night, when I wasn't working. I'd sit in my apartment wondering about what my wife and kids were doing. I mean, when they're there you can't stand the bickering, but when they're not . . ." His voice trailed off. "One night, I almost ate my service revolver."

Carnes could not conceal his surprise. "I'm sorry, I didn't know."

"Hell, this was before you. But you know what? I had a partner who tried to straighten me out. Saw what was going on. I told him *he* was wrong, *he* was an asshole, that he should mind his own business. One morning he drove me over to the church. Boy was I mad." Rodriguez chuckled. "I used to cuss then. I teed off. Used every cussword I knew— Spanish and English—then I made up a few." Rodriguez smiled at Carnes. "So now you know why I can't keep my two cents to myself."

Carnes kept his eyes on the sidewalk. Finally, he said, "You're right. I've been learning about it lately. Sex is sorta what makes me feel good. But I've been overdoing it and I feel miserable anyway."

"I should keep my mouth shut," said Rodriguez.

"No, you're right. I've been out of control. Maybe it's partly the stress of being a cop. But there are other things too. Someday we'll have a beer and talk it through."

* * *

The Stamp was a red-brick building with impressive white columns in the front. Carnes and Rodriguez climbed the steps. A cute brunette managed an information counter in the lobby.

"Do you have lists of campus groups like sororities and fraternities?" Carnes asked.

"Through the lobby," she pointed, "to the student program office."

"Thanks."

"Is there anything else you need, sir?"

For a second, Carnes thought she was flirting. Then it struck him. *She called me "sir," like I'm some old fossil.* Carnes laughed. The girl and Rodriguez looked at him as though he'd grown a second head. "No, I think not."

The student program office was a long hall with small office cubicles on either side. A vaguely Middle-Eastern girl sat at a desk at the entrance. She ignored them and talked in an intimate tone on the phone. Carnes tapped his toe and studied a poster until she finished.

"Yes, sir?"

Carnes felt older by the minute. "Do you have a list of fraternities and sororities?"

"In the rack over there above that table." She pointed to the wall.

Carnes found a list titled "Registered Student Organizations, Phone Directory." As Rodriguez watched over his shoulder, Carnes looked through its ten pages. The listing included several sororities, fraternities, and honor societies with omega in their name.

"Do you have addresses?"

"Yes, sir, but we don't give out that information."

Carnes started to explain they were policemen. The phone buzzed again. The girl held up her hand. Carnes stood shifting his weight from one foot to the other for a minute or two while she spoke into the phone in a low voice, giggling occasionally. Carnes turned to Rodriguez. "Let's go."

They went downstairs and past some eateries until they found pay phones. They split the list in half and began calling houses trying to talk to an officer. Soon, they realized these officers had been around only a few years and didn't have much information that would help. Carnes watched the coeds going by, their hips moving in that innocent but sexy way that marks the transition from girlhood to womanhood. He realized that, for him, changing would not be easy.

Carnes reached into his pocket for another quarter and found the folded piece of yellow notepaper that Crenshaw had given him. He stared at it for a moment, started to put it back, then put a quarter in the phone and dialed the number. He listened to the recorded message and noted a time and location on the yellow paper. He shoved it back in his pocket and returned to his list.

About halfway through the list, Carnes' beeper went off. He pressed the button. Del Clinton's number. Rodriguez was still on the phone. Carnes dialed and Del answered on the first ring.

"What's going on?" Carnes asked.

"We plain fuckin' missed it." Clinton chortled. "Of course, we weren't really looking at the time."

"Excuse me," Carnes said. "What the hell're you talking about?"

"Vicky Benton. She was a member of Alpha Omega sorority."

"She was?"

"Damned right. It's in your running resume. Figured it was worth a trip over to her apartment. Guess what I found in a box of shit in her closet?"

Carnes remembered going through a box of memorabilia and college papers. Suddenly, it struck him. He'd seen a group picture of a younger Vicky Benton and a bunch of other girls. "Her sorority picture?"

"You got it. The greek letters Alpha Omega were right in the fuckin' middle."

"Great." Carnes' mind raced. "We probably should talk to the families of the other girls—"

"Done." Del sounded proud. "I may be new in homicide, but I ain't no rookie."

Carnes smiled.

"Get this: Anna Durant—before she left Maryland—and Francine Lynch were both members of Alpha Omega at the same time as Vicky Benton. I'm pretty sure they're both in the photo too."

"Any chance our killer saw the photo at one girl's place and decided to kill all the girls?" Even as the words came out, Carnes decided it was unlikely.

"Naw, though if it were Pardo, this could be some sort of sick thing—killing all of Benton's close friends."

"But neither Durant's name nor Lynch's were in Benton's address book. I doubt they were close. Besides, Lynch died last summer." Carnes smiled ruefully. "That I do know."

"Well, I've been nosing around Pardo. He has no real alibi for the night Anna Durant was killed. Says he was home watching TV, but no one can confirm it. And get this, he was in Ocean City when Lynch was killed."

"You *have* been busy. That's too many coincidences to ignore," Carnes said. "Can we get a warrant for his place?"

"I'm working on it with the sarge."

"All right." Carnes thought quickly. "Can you feed this to the FBI and see what they come up with?"

"Sure," said Clinton. "But you know it'll take at least a few days."

"If we're lucky." Carnes glanced at his watch. "I need to get moving. We've got to hit the sorority, and I've got a meeting I need to go to tonight on the way home. It's real important. Can the warrant wait until morning?"

"That'll be better. I doubt I'll have it done this afternoon. Besides, Pardo'll be at work during the day. I'll see who the night judge is."

13

She was in Barnstormers again. That seemed to be her place. The blond sat next to her. She was a hunter too. He wondered whether they'd leave together. Not if that blond had her choice. At least the damn cop wasn't with her again. These cops thought they were so fucking smart, but they didn't have a clue. He could take her out right under their noses. The idea made him shiver, and he stifled a nervous giggle.

It wouldn't be long now. Everything in its turn. Last time, it was the fat one's turn. Be patient. Your time is coming.

She wouldn't expect him. Maybe she'd be walking to her car or opening the door to her apartment. He'd be low-key. Maybe ask for her help. She'd want to help. The thrill of anticipation coursed through his system. It always felt good.

She was pretty. Nice smile. She had no right to smile. He imagined her smile turning into a mask of terror, then pain. Heat pulsed in his groin. She would be fun. He'd plan some special twists—good pun—for her. Oh, they'd have fun!

She would beg, make excuses like the others. It wouldn't matter. His mother used to tell him she believed in fate. When your time comes, there's nothing you can do about it. Maybe she'd be a fatalist. Maybe she'd show some dignity. It would be more of a challenge. The last one started begging right away. It almost ruined his fun. Maybe this one would be different. It wouldn't be long now.

The room felt hot and steamy despite the labored whine of the window air conditioner. Someone had arranged gray folding metal chairs in a crescent moon around a rickety podium. Twenty people sat in the chairs. They represented a cross section of that part of the city—some young, some old, mostly men, mostly white. They all cocked their heads toward the woman who was speaking, struggling to hear her over the noise of the air conditioner.

The woman had identified herself as Rita. "It was too late when I realized he was an undercover cop. Boy was I furious"—her face contorted and her voice choked in her throat—"and ashamed." She swallowed a couple of times to reestablish her composure. "They treated me like a common prostitute. I mean I was out there charging for it, but it wasn't that I needed the money." She laughed, and her audience joined in a nervous chorus.

"During that night in jail—isn't it amazing? It took a night in jail—I decided to get help. I'm staying away from sex now, trying to get to know—really connect with—people. I've been sober now for four months." Her voice ended on a note of triumph. She sat down.

A thin, bespectacled young man named Pete sat in the front row. "Thank you for sharing that with us, Rita," he said. Several other voices chimed in, "Thank you, Rita."

Pete looked around. "Is there anyone else who wants to share?"

Carnes felt the tension in his chest. His stomach tightened again, the way it had when he pulled his car up in front of the church for the meeting. For an hour, they had told their stories. At first, he eyed the exit. But their stories kept him in his seat. The stories were at turns pathetic, comic, even ridiculous, yet he found he identified with something in each one.

One woman told how, when she was ten, her grandfather put his hand between her legs, then sniffed it. "You stink," he'd said. She'd suppressed the memory for years but hadn't been able to suppress the feelings of inadequacy and shame. A gay man talked about his hundreds of impersonal encounters with strangers at bookstores and cruising areas. Eventually, fear of AIDS caused him to seek help. The stories were all different from his own but frighteningly familiar. Some of these people lost family or jobs in their single-minded pursuit of sex. Few had experienced complete relationships. Carnes could see the parallels to his own life. What would happen to Avery if he got AIDS? It made him feel sick.

Pete's eyes passed over the room, acknowledging, making contact. "For anyone who's new and came in late, we use the AA twelve-step approach here at SAA. We don't use full names. After all, who wants to be anonymous more than sex addicts?

"It's important that we recognize our powerlessness over our addiction and seek support from a higher power. The first part of that process involves coming to terms with who we are. We are sex addicts." Several people grunted and nodded their heads. "Some of us are also love addicts, or codependents. Others are alcoholics or drug addicts as well."

He scanned the group. "We're here to support each other. Is there anyone new here, anyone who wants to introduce himself?" Pete's eyes lingered on Carnes for the briefest moment. "We've all been there. We know it's hard, but if you're here, you must have reached the point where"—he paused thoughtfully—"where we've all been."

The tension squeezed at Carnes' insides like a tightening knot. The nausea rose in his throat. He breathed deeply and studied his feet, as he'd done when he didn't want the teacher to call on him in school.

Barnstormers seemed busier than usual. The place reverberated with activity: glasses clinked, the music thumped at a rapid tempo. While Carol rattled on about her new beau, Becky sighed. She felt as out of place as a nun at a revival meeting. She couldn't catch the spirit. Becky had wanted to talk to Carol about what happened with John and how she felt, but that seemed impossible. Carol was flying in a different, decidedly more upbeat galaxy. Coming tonight was a mistake.

Carol's voice faded back into Becky's consciousness. "And get this, the guy lives in my apartment building. I mean, he only moved in a few weeks ago. Just think, if I hadn't gone over to the laundromat . . ."

Becky smiled stupidly. She needed to escape. Soon.

"Look!" Carol Bromley's voice changed. Urgent.

"What?" Becky asked.

"Over there." Carol glanced toward Becky's left. "That man's been smiling at you every few minutes. Are you blind or something?"

Becky casually turned to look. She saw an attractive man with prematurely gray hair, probably about forty. His fashionable pinstripe suit reeked of class and money. He caught her eye and smiled. She returned the smile. Something about him was familiar. He walked over.

"Hi." He held out his hand. "This could be very embarrassing. I hope I'm not making a total fool of myself." He smiled shyly. "You looked familiar. Didn't you come to a party Vicky Benton and I had last year? My name's Fitz Pardo."

Becky remembered the lavish party, rooms filled with food, tuxedoed help, lawyers, clients. She'd felt out of place. Only a few of her contemporaries—Vicky's friends—were there. "Oh, yes, I remember." She took his hand. "Becky Granite."

"I, uh, saw you sitting here and recognized you. This isn't one of the places I usually come, but I was"—his eyes dropped and his voice got so quiet it was almost inaudible in the din of the bar—"sort of feeling lonely." He met her eyes. "I assume you heard about Vicky."

She nodded.

"It's been tough." His voice sounded raspy.

"She was a good friend." Becky searched for words. "It was quite a shock. I'm sure it's been difficult."

"Yes, an incredible ordeal. Between her death and the police nosing around . . ."

Becky thought she knew who he meant. She felt herself tense. "But isn't that their job?"

"Oh, of course, but they tromp around treating everyone as though they're guilty."

"They didn't treat me like I was guilty." It slipped out before Becky could stop herself. She saw that Carol was locked in on them as though they were players in a daytime soap.

Pardo's eyes studied the floor as though he was afraid to look at her.

"I'm sorry, I don't know why I said that."

"Can I buy you a drink?" Pardo offered. "I don't think I've gotten off on the right foot here."

"No, thanks, not this time. I don't think I'm very good company tonight. Besides,"—she looked to Carol for support—"my friend and I are waiting for someone."

"Oh?" Pardo raised an eyebrow. "Sorry. Maybe some other time?"

"Sure, some other time."

14

Carnes dialed the number for the third time that night. No answer. He hung up on her answering machine. No sense making her think he was desperate. His watch read 9:00. Where was she? He'd tried her before the meeting and twice since he'd come over to the diner with Kim and Pete. Becky was probably out with her girlfriends. Then again, it would serve him right if she was having a good time with some other man. He stalked back to the table.

"Anything wrong?" Kim's eyes showed concern.

"Just trying to call . . . a friend." He'd almost said "girlfriend." How could he call her that? Did a few laughs give him a right to make that claim? She didn't seem so enchanted with him last time they talked. "She doesn't seem to be home."

Pete nodded his head and with a forefinger pushed his glasses up the bridge of his nose. "You must feel rotten."

The obvious concern on Kim and Pete's faces annoyed him. Who had appointed them as his guardians? Carnes imagined tearing off Pete's glasses and stomping on them. Now that would be therapeutic! He settled on a slightly more moderate course. "Yeah, I feel like shit. Subhuman." He stood up. "Look, if I drink any more decaf my bladder will explode. I'm going home. I'm going to go kill myself, so don't worry if I miss the next meeting."

"Are you OK?" asked Kim.

Carnes felt his face turning red. "Of course I'm not OK. There's a murderer running around the city mutilating women and I can't catch him. My family life is shit, a girl I was really starting to like is probably fucking some guy, and I'm sitting drinking this swill and playing group therapy with a bunch of amateurs."

"I've been where you are, John." Pete's voice was firm but warm. "I understand your anger. It's your stress and frustration over your addiction talking." Kim nodded her head in agreement.

Carnes bit back a very therapeutic reply.

The harsh shrilling of the phone dragged Del Clinton out of the blissful nothingness of sleep. He glanced at the clock radio: 1:00 A.M.

"Clinton." He sat up, facing away from the bed, but he felt Frances' eyes on his back.

"Detective. Sorry to disturb you at home." Del recognized the voice of Sgt. Dickie Watson.

"Right," Del said. He hoped his voice sounded impassive.

"Look, we've got a multiple shooting off Minnesota Avenue in the 6th District. Two DOAs. Officer on the scene said the third victim was asking for you."

Del felt sick. "What's his name, Dickie?"

"McNeil. Ya know him?"

Del's stomach churned. "Yes. He still alive?"

"So far. Took him over to shock-trauma at the Hospital Center. Didn't look good. Said he's got something else for you. Sounded like he was talking 'bout 'the girls.' Make any sense?"

"Yeah. Need me on the scene?"

"No, I've got everyone on midnight shift out there. 6D is taking the family to the hospital. I've sent Grissom over there. You want to help with the family?"

"OK." Del hung up and dressed in a casual shirt and jeans rather than his usual uniform of suit, white shirt, and bright tie. He wanted Doris to feel he was off duty.

"What?" Frances' voice was muffled by sleep. She pushed herself up onto one elbow. Her hair stuck out like a fright wig and her eyes were more closed than open.

Clinton felt a surge of affection. He sat down beside her on the bed and brushed the hair back from her cheek. "Slick McNeil. He got shot. I'm going over to shock-trauma."

"Want me to come?"

Del smiled and patted her softly. He knew Frances didn't like Slick. But her offer was genuine. He reached over and hugged her.

"No, sweetheart. This is really police business. I'll be OK. There's not much you can do"—he smiled—"other than what you've already done. You might as well get some sleep." He kissed her on the forehead. "Thanks. Love you."

Doris Roberts jumped out of her chair when Del came through the door. "Oh, Jesus." She threw her arms around his neck and sobbed into his shoulder for several minutes. Del imagined—could it have been his imagination?—that he felt the baby kicking through her taut belly. Finally, she pulled back. He handed her a handkerchief and she dabbed at her eyes.

"I'm sorry," she whispered.

"That's what I'm here for. Any word?"

"No. I haven't seen him or any doctors yet. Some nurse came by a few minutes ago. Said he's being operated on. Said they're doing everything they can." She wiped at her eyes again. "I've been telling him this was going to happen, asking him to get off the street. Does he listen? Now look what's happened. What am I going to do if he dies? What about LaVonna and the baby?"

Del felt uncomfortable. He reverted to his policeman role. "Do you have any idea who could've done this?"

"It coulda been almost anybody." Her eyes were slightly out of focus behind the sheen of tears. She started to cry again. Del squeezed her shoulder. He'd dealt with grieving family members and others who didn't give a damn. Some affected him, but this was a real kick in the ass. But for the grace of God, he might have been the one lying in there with strangers poking instruments into his gut.

"Usually, it's about territory," he spoke softly. "He tell you about anything like that? Any disputes recently?"

"No. Well, maybe. There was some guy—Chito. Don't know his real name. Had to scare him off one night. I think it got kinda rough."

"We'll check it out." Clinton scribbled in his pocket notebook. "Anything else?"

"No. Nothing I can think of. He don't tell me much. You could ask Mase or Smallfry." Doris' face contorted and the tears began again. "I forgot. They got them too." She cried into the handkerchief for several minutes. "Damn him! He promised he'd be OK."

"Did he say anything to you about the girls? The murders?"

"No. Well, just that he was going to talk with a guy who may 'a' seen a car or something. He's been out on the street all night." Doris started sobbing again. "Damn him."

15

Carnes found several notes from Del Clinton on his desk. He sorted through. Mostly, they were details of Clinton's efforts of the previous day. Rodriguez came over and placed a cup of coffee on his desk. *"Que pasa?"*

"Huh?" Carnes looked up. "Oh, it's you."

"Who'd you expect, the fuckin' tooth fairy?" Wiley chortled from across the aisle.

"Don't you have anything to do?" Carnes asked.

"My, we are sensitive today." Wiley raised an eyebrow and made tut-tutting sounds.

Carnes turned to Rodriguez. "I'm going through Del's notes. From his comments, he picked up the picture from the apartment."

Rodriguez scanned the desk. "It's not here?"

"No. He must have it with him," Carnes said.

"Where is he?"

"Over at Washington Hospital Center shock-trauma last I heard," said Wiley. "Some guy from his old neighborhood got shot early this morning. He's waiting with the widow-to-be and helping the detectives from midnight who caught it."

"Just what we need, another one." Rodriguez groused. "What's that make it?"

"Three hundred and six, I think," said Wiley.

"I thought we were only at three-oh-three or three-oh-four," said Carnes.

"Well, apparently the guy who shot Del's buddy took out two—uh—

business associates of his at the same time. Drive-by. Bunch of guys in the car and they all were shooting. Shells from several nines. Witnesses said it sounded like a war zone."

"Where have I heard that before?" commented Rodriguez.

"Yeah, that's how Harris described it. He was just heading out. They already found the car—"

"And it was stolen," Carnes guessed.

"Give that man a fuckin' cigar," Wiley said. "But they got some prints off the car, and Del got a name from his buddy's wife. These guys weren't too bright. ID already matched two guys to the prints. This one'll be closed."

"Well, at least that should free up Del," said Carnes.

Rodriguez raised an eyebrow.

"Hey, I don't mean to be insensitive. But there's no reason to think our killer is taking a vacation. We've got some good leads. We can't afford to lose a member of the team at this point."

"I'd be happy to help," Wiley said.

"You mean you can lift that fat ass out of your chair?" Carnes looked at him in mock wonder.

"Fuck you!"

"That's what I like about you, Wes, your witty repartee."

"Repar-who?"

Rodriguez signaled a time-out. "You'd be a big help, Wes." He turned to Carnes. "We can swing by the hospital and pick up the picture. I assume you want to start tracking the girls, find out what they know."

"Sounds good to me," said Carnes. "We also need to get that warrant for Pardo's place." Carnes looked at Clinton's notes. "Looks like the lieu has the draft. Can you take it over to court?"

"No problem."

"I'll line up some crime-scene techs to join us." Carnes looked at his pad where he'd started a To Do list. "You were also going to check your Latino network for anyone who might've worked at the sorority."

"Right."

"I'm going to work on the computer. Maybe we can come up with a correlation between the University of Maryland and known perverts."

Carnes' heart raced while the phone rang. He'd felt the same thrill of terror when he called girls in high school.

"Marketing Department, Becky Granite speaking."

Carnes deepened his voice. "I have a friend who's done something real foolish and he needs some marketing advice."

"John?" To Carnes, Becky's laughter was as welcome as holiday bells. "Is that you?"

Carnes switched to his normal voice. "I guess Rich Little has nothing to worry about."

"Hardly."

"Look, I've been a jerk—"

"I know."

"And I want to know whether you could find it in your charitable, warm, all-American heart, whether you could see your way clear to, well, giving me another chance."

"A chance to do what?"

Carnes' mind chugged. "A chance to sweep you away on wings of love, to win your heart, to capture—oh shit, poetry is definitely not my thing."

Becky's laughter rang over the phone. "Definitely."

"But I'm sincere about wanting to do this—to try—"

"Are you asking me out?"

"Yes."

"Give me one reason I should agree."

"Because I'm adorable, funny, I can cook—a little—and I'm crazy about you," Carnes said. "Besides, where else can you get a personal police escort?"

"Very convincing arguments. You should've been a lawyer rather than a policeman." Becky laughed again. "But, you know, I'm being madly pursued by another man."

"Oh." Carnes' chest tightened.

"Yes, this charming man came up to me in a bar last night and introduced himself." Her voice sounded light and Carnes realized she was teasing. "A friend of Vicky's, as a matter of fact."

Carnes felt a cold chill. "Who?"

"No need to shout. I blew him off." Her voice got quiet. "I'd like to give you another chance. Maybe we should have dinner or something—"

"What friend of Vicky's?"

"I told you it was nothing. He just came up to me in Barnstormers. Don't worry. I'm not going out with him."

Carnes couldn't hide the exasperation in his voice. "Who, goddamnit? Who'd you brush off?"

"What's the matter?" Becky asked.

Carnes tried to calm down. "Who?"

"It was Vicky's old flame Fitz Pardo."

The name exploded in his ear. What was Pardo up to? This was too much of a coincidence. Becky was in Vicky Benton's sorority. She was an Alpha Omega. "Now, listen to me. I don't want to be melodramatic, but I'm serious about this." Carnes drew a couple of deep breaths to calm his speeding heart. "Do not, I repeat, do not under any circumstance go near Fitz Pardo. If you see him anywhere, call me immediately. If I don't answer my beeper right away, call 911. Do not let him near you."

"What are you talking about?" Becky sounded puzzled.

"I can't tell you." He looked around. No one was within earshot. "Look, he's a suspect in these murders. He may be just a jerk or he could be a perverted, psychopathic killer. I don't want you to take any chances."

"OK," Becky said, "but I really can't imagine—"

"Don't imagine. Please, do what I asked. Don't trust him." Carnes thought through his schedule. "Listen, I'll pick you up at work and take you to dinner."

"I can't do it tonight. I've got karate class and I promised Carol I'd go to a movie with her." She sighed. "Timing. I guess I could blow off my class and call her to cancel."

Carnes thought about it. If Pardo were the killer, was Becky slated to be his next victim? If Carnes hung around her, would he catch Pardo, or would Pardo be spooked? Maybe it would be better to keep an eye on Pardo.

"Listen," said Carnes, "go do your thing tonight. You should be fine. Stay in public areas and don't go anywhere alone. We'll do dinner to-morrow, OK?"

"Sure. Fine."

Pardo lived in a two-story, brick row house in Georgetown. This tony section of the city featured small historical homes on tiny lots at premium prices. It was a refuge for legislators, cabinet members, and successful urban professionals. Pardo's house sat in the middle of a row of almost identical red-brick houses with gray steps and porches. An alley ran be-hind the houses, and tiny rectangles surrounded by various kinds of fences served as backyards. Several of the houses also displayed ground-level doors leading to basement apartments. Students from the local colleges often lived in these basements, along with an assortment of wanna-bes. Carnes stationed a patrol officer in the alley and returned to the front of the house.

"OK. Everyone know their positions?" Carnes looked at each of the officers in turn—Rodriguez, Wiley, a mobile-crime technician named Milford, and the uniformed officers with the ram that would be used to force the door. They all nodded.

A curious neighbor watched from her front porch across the street. She was about to get quite a show. Carnes rang the bell. "Police. Open up." He counted to twenty. Enough time for someone to answer the door. He turned to the uniformed officers. "Take it down."

The officers surged forward with the ram, hitting the door. It burst open with a loud cracking noise as the locks tore through the wooden door frame. The door bounced off an interior wall, crumbling plaster. Carnes led the group in.

Just inside the door to their right, a set of stairs rose to the second floor. A living room opened to the left. On the other side of the living room was a dining area with a large oak breakfront and an antique oak table.

"All right," Carnes said. "Rodriguez and Wiley, check out the bed-rooms." He turned to Milford. "You and I'll hit this floor and the base-ment." He glanced from one to another. "Remember, we're looking for anything that could tie him to any of the victims or the scenes. The Durant girl could have been killed here. We're going to do a walk-through first. Let's be real careful not to touch anything. Milford's go-ing to take prints from anywhere the girl might've touched and take fiber samples from everything. Let's hope his cleaning lady isn't too efficient. Any questions?"

Everybody shook their heads. "Let's do it," Carnes said.

The living room felt warm and masculine. Carnes liked natural wood, and the golden hardwood floors, thick oriental rug, and large leather sofa and chairs appealed to him. He wondered how long he'd have to save before he could afford them. Carnes smiled. Pardo may be a crazed killer, but he had a good decorator.

They moved through the dining room and turned right into the kitchen. It was a narrow room with white cabinets, a gas stove, and a new refrigerator. A white plastic trash can stood in the corner. Carnes poked through it. Coffee grounds, a can, junk mail.

He continued his search. A calendar adorned the wall near the phone. Holding the edges with his fingertips, he flipped the pages. A few appointments and dates. The name Vic on several days.

He started opening cabinets. Plates, glasses.

"Detective." Milford stood several cabinets over with the door open. "Look at this."

Amid an assortment of spice jars, stood a jar of green weedy matter and a small medicine bottle with white powder. Unlike the other containers, neither of these jars was labeled.

"Wonder what that is." Carnes grinned.

"I got a field test kit in the van," Milford said. "Should I test the stuff?"

"Absolutely."

In a few minutes, Milford was back. "Field tests are positive. Marijuana and cocaine."

"Asshole," muttered Carnes.

"Huh?" Milford looked hurt.

Carnes laughed. "Not you. Pardo."

"Oh."

"Bastard gave us something to work with."

Rodriguez and Wiley tromped in. Carnes showed them the stash.

"We may have one less smartass lawyer to deal with." Wiley rubbed his hands together.

"Maybe. What'd you guys find upstairs?"

"An assortment of videos, some pornographic. Mainstream stuff," said Rodriguez. "Didn't see any about bondage or anything else exotic. Course one isn't labeled."

"Guess we should screen it to make sure," Wiley suggested eagerly.

After Milford left, they called Fitz Pardo at his office. He must have run a few red lights because in less than fifteen minutes his car screeched to a stop in front of the house. Pardo raced up the steps two at a time.

"What the fuck—the hell—what're you doing?" Pardo strutted like an angry cock. He glanced around. "What've you done to my fucking door? Where's your damn warrant?"

Carnes handed him the warrant. Pardo's mouth dropped open and he flushed. An angry blood vessel in his temple pulsed and his body gathered into a steely coil. Carnes expected him to have a stroke at any second.

Pardo struggled for control. "You're out of your fucking minds! I'm going to sue you for every fucking penny you have. Then I'll sue the city, I'll . . ." Pardo seemed nonplussed for a moment.

Carnes saw Wiley struggling to suppress a smile. "We collected some evidence," said Carnes. "You may want to check our inventory."

Pardo stomped through the house hurling expletives nonstop until he came to the kitchen. Carnes noticed he made a particular show of opening every drawer and cabinet and looking inside before he ever so casually looked into the cabinet where they'd found the drugs. Pardo stole a quick glance out of the corner of his eye at Carnes.

Carnes grinned. "Sorry."

"You think you're so fucking smart!" Pardo shrieked. His red face contorted in an ugly grimace of rage. "You'll pay for this, I guarantee it."

"We'll see." Carnes stared into Pardo's eyes and saw insane hate. How insane? "This is a good time to advise you of your rights. You have the right to remain silent . . ."

16

Del Clinton looked terrible. His eyes were puffy from lack of sleep and his clothes were wrinkled as though he had slept in them. It was hard to believe he was one of the nattiest dressers in homicide. He seemed deflated, as though grief had pricked him like a pin. Sitting in a hospital waiting room would do that to anyone. Carnes remembered those long days of waiting in the small hospital room, his nostrils full of the odors of disinfectant, waiting for his father to die.

"How's he doing?"

"Not good. They operated for about three hours. He lost a lot of blood. Took bullets in the lung and liver. One nicked his spine. Chances are he won't make it more than another hour or two." Del sighed. "But he wouldn't want to live as a cripple." For a moment, Del's mind drifted back to the playground, to Slick's hard-driving, body-banging style of play. "He couldn't live like that."

"Sorry." Carnes gripped Clinton's shoulder.

"Hey—" Clinton shrugged and turned his palms to heaven.

"The family?"

"She's in there right now, holding his hand. God knows what she'll do . . ." Clinton's voice trailed off.

"This guy must've been a good friend."

"He's an asshole."

"An asshole?"

"A drug-dealing asshole."

"Oh?" Carnes raised an eyebrow. "You've known him a long time?"

Del nodded. "Both of us were wild kids."

"Yeah?"

"Used to kick his butt on the basketball court."

"But you made it out."

"Yeah. Somehow, I got myself straight and became a cop." Del shook his head. "Slick never got it together."

"You must've been stronger—"

"But why? Doesn't make a whole lot of sense."

"You've been a cop for how long?"

Clinton stared blankly at Carnes.

"You expect life to make sense?" Carnes said.

"Good point." Del smiled wanly. "Thanks."

Carnes waved his hand. "I read your notes. You have the picture?"

"In the car," said Del. "Walk out with me."

The heat and humidity, so oppressive to Carnes, seemed to invigorate Del. He took a deep breath of the foul air. "I was turning into a mushroom in there." As they walked, Carnes filled him in on their search of Pardo's house.

Del smiled. "Boy, I would've paid to see Pardo's face."

"He's planning to make us all pay."

"Sounds like he doesn't have a leg to stand on."

"When has that ever stopped any lawyer you know?"

"True." Clinton laughed. "What next?"

"Soon as he gets released we're going to sit on him."

Del smiled again. "Sounds good to me." His face clouded. "I need to stay a few more hours with Doris. Maybe Slick'll be able to talk. Told the cops on the scene he had to talk with me about the girls. Doris said he was going to talk with some guy about the car."

Carnes whistled. "Any chance he'll be able to—"

Del shrugged. "Right now he's in a coma. But I'll wait. Besides, Doris is going to need some support. And if Slick comes to, I'll need to get a statement. He'll talk to me."

"I heard they already got the guys," said Carnes.

"Yeah, Chito something. Harris told me they picked him up. Said something about Slick dissing him." Del rubbed his eyes. "Shit. Where does it end?"

"Answer that and we're out of business," Carnes said.

"Wouldn't that be nice?" Del opened the trunk of his car and pulled out a large envelope. "This is the stuff from the girl's apartment and some notes." His face took on a bulldog look. "Let's get this guy."

* * *

When Captain Fletcher summoned, you came. Carnes and Rodriguez paused outside his door and took deep breaths. Then Carnes knocked on the molding beside the door.

"Come in, come in, Detectives," Fletcher said, turning on the charm. "Glad to see you." He turned to Carnes. "How's Avery?"

Carnes knew that Fletcher kept file cards on each of his men in his desk drawer so he could pretend to be knowledgeable about their families. "Just fine, sir." Sergeant Bryant and Lieutenant Rogers sat uneasily on the couch.

The captain asked Rodriguez a question in rapid Spanish that Carnes did not catch, although he heard the word *"ninos."* Rodriguez' *"ninos"* were grown up now. *"Bueno,"* said Rodriguez.

"Have a seat, gentlemen." The captain gestured at the two armchairs in front of his desk. Carnes and Rodriguez sat down in the hot seats. "Like a Coke? Coffee?"

Cigarette? Blindfold? "No, thanks," Carnes said. In the six months since Fletcher had come to homicide, he had never invited Carnes into his office to socialize. Somehow, Carnes did not think he wanted to socialize now.

Carnes watched Fletcher perform. He really had nothing against the man. Fletcher was no worse than the dozens of other politician cops he'd worked for over the years. Fletcher's approach to management was typical: cajole his men, make it clear that if they didn't get results soon, he might not be able to protect them from the consequences. As Wiley pointed out after his first meeting with Fletcher, the detectives had the captain's full, unqualified support "until the shit hits the fan."

"Well, gentlemen. I'm glad you could join me." The social event of the season. "Sure you don't want a Coke or anything? No?" Fletcher picked up his pencil and underlined something on his legal pad. Then he leaned forward, resting his massive arms on the desk. "You gentlemen stirred up a hornet's nest today." He displayed a tight smile that said he wasn't amused. "The mayor and two city councilmen have already called about your little raid on Fitzhugh Pardo's residence. You know that the chief"—he raised his eyes, as though tolerant of his supervisor's foibles—"doesn't like getting such phone calls."

Carnes felt his neck and face growing hot. "But, Captain, I thought the chief wanted us to break this case. At least that's what you've been telling us almost every day." He ignored Bryant's warning look. "We have two brutally murdered women. The media is all over us. Pardo is a real suspect and—"

The captain held up his hand. "Detective!" His voice sounded like the crack of a bullwhip. He smiled and continued more benignly. "I explained that to the chief, but *you* have to understand. This man Pardo has friends in the Democratic Party hierarchy. They've supported the mayor and several of the council members—very generously, I should add. Don't act ignorant. You know how it works."

Carnes kept his reply to himself. No, *you* know how it works.

"I'm trying to buy you some time." Fletcher picked up his pencil and tapped it thoughtfully. "But we better show results. What'd you get from the warrant?"

Rodriguez cleared his throat. "Fiber samples for the Bureau, fingerprints, a couple of pictures of Pardo and Vicky Benton, some records that may help prove that Pardo was in Ocean City at the time of the Lynch killing," Rodriguez paused, "and enough marijuana and coke for a very nice party. Detective Carnes and the mobile-crime guy found it among his spices in the kitchen. We field-tested it—positive—and sent it over to DEA."

The captain smiled broadly. Fletcher disliked affluent whites who used drugs. "Well, well, well. Pardo seems to've left that part out of the account he gave his political friends. That should buy us some peace. Nobody mentioned *that* to the chief. Have we charged him?"

"He's being held, but not for long," said Carnes. "We were about to take the case to papering so the U.S. Attorney can review the charges. If it were some kid off the street they'd charge him with possession with intent to distribute marijuana and coke, but they'll probably charge him with misdemeanor possession of the coke and let the marijuana ride. He'll be out by midafternoon."

"Can you use the drug charges as leverage?" Fletcher asked.

"You mean, promise to drop the drug charges in return for a plea to murder one?" Carnes couldn't keep the sarcasm out of his voice. Sergeant Bryant winced.

"No, Detective." Fletcher leaned forward. His voice became an angry growl. "You might use them to drag some information out of him. Let him set himself up. A little cleverness—directed at the perps for a change—might work wonders."

"I think that's what Detective Carnes meant." Sergeant Bryant gave Carnes a hard look. "Isn't that what you meant, Detective?"

Carnes nodded. "Of course."

"Well, then." Captain Fletcher settled back slightly in his seat. He tapped his pencil impatiently. "What's next?"

Carnes explained what they had in mind.

Fletcher nodded. "The drugs may buy us some time with the chief, but don't give him any reasons to hang you guys out to dry. Be careful."

Carnes pictured Fletcher preparing a noose in size 15½. "We will."

"Into interrogation!" Bryant commanded. He had followed them into the bull pen. "Now!" He sounded like the drill sergeant he'd once been. Carnes and Rodriguez exchanged glances. They passed their desks and continued down the aisle to the interrogation room. "In there," Bryant said. He closed the door and turned on Carnes. "What the fuck were you doing in there? Fletcher can cut off your balls and feed 'em to you." He waved his hands in exasperation. "And don't think he wouldn't have a good time doing it."

"The man's a—"

"Don't even *think* it, Detective. The man can chew you up and spit you out without even getting indigestion. One phone call—just one—and you'll be working at Shannon Place, making entries in property logbooks for the rest of your career. And that's assuming he's in a good mood." Bryant glared. "After that Ocean City bit, I'd think you'd have the sense to keep on his good side. You out of your mind?"

"I guess I shouldn't've skipped that training seminar on how to kiss up to your boss no matter what kind of idiot he may be," said Carnes.

Bryant wrinkled his face in disgust and turned to Rodriguez. "Pete, you gotta talk to him. I can't afford to lose any detectives." Bryant smiled slightly. "Particularly those whose opinions I value."

"No problem. I'll box his ears before the next meeting with the brass."

"All right." Bryant turned back to Carnes. "How many people do you need to keep an eye on Pardo?"

"A couple of teams. Can we pull any folks from the district to back us up?"

"Think so."

"OK. Rodriguez and I'll watch him tonight. That all right with you, partner?"

"It's a date," Rodriguez agreed.

17

Carnes drew greedily on the cigarette. Normally, he didn't smoke, but boredom is the biggest enemy on surveillance. Smoking helps kill the time. Pardo's office light was still on. Every once in a while, Carnes would catch a glimpse of Pardo's outline in the window. He wondered what was going through Pardo's mind.

"The bastard may be plotting his next murder," Carnes muttered.

"Huh?" Rodriguez had drifted off for a second.

"Just wondering what Pardo's thinking."

"Who knows? Who cares?" Rodriguez was cranky when he awakened.

"Next time I do surveillance, I'll bring someone who's more fun to be with."

"Ditto." Rodriguez rubbed his eyes and sat up. "Give me one of those cancer sticks."

Carnes handed him the pack. Rodriguez lit up and drew the smoke deep into his lungs. He started coughing and Carnes laughed. "Oh, shut up," Rodriguez groaned.

They sat in silence for several moments. Rodriguez rolled the window down further. The outside air closed around them—heavy, unmoving, and humid. "Not even a breeze," Rodriguez grumbled.

"No," Carnes muttered. "How much vacation time you got coming?"

"'Bout three weeks."

"Plans?"

"No. I may save it till winter and go south, see some of the family." Rodriguez drew on the cigarette more moderately. This time he didn't cough. "You?"

"Don't know. Maybe when this case is over, I'll take Avery to the beach or something. Maybe I can get Becky to go."

"Becky?"

"This woman I met. The one who's a friend—was a friend—of the Benton girl."

"Oh." Rodriguez nodded, a knowing expression on his face.

"Hey, quit busting my chops," said Carnes.

"'Bout what?"

"Don't give me that shit!" Carnes heard the anger in his voice.

"When the shoe fits . . . You are the most pussy hungry"—Rodriguez groped for a word—"fucker, yeah that's right, fucker, I've ever seen."

Carnes smiled despite himself. He couldn't remember the last time Rodriguez used the "f" word. "You're right. But Becky is different."

"Different?"

"Yeah, there's something about her—I'm not sure I can explain it." Carnes watched the garage. "I haven't even slept with her."

"Oh? It's probably the hunting instinct."

"The hunting instinct?"

"Yeah. I was reading somewhere—"

"You read?"

"Real funny." Rodriguez gave Carnes a mock sneer. "I read that men get off on hunting women. You know, the ones who play hard to get are the ones we want the most."

"Is that what our killer is up to?"

"Well, he's definitely a hunter."

They sat quietly for a minute.

"So are you a hunter?"

"Yeah," said Carnes. "I took your advice and went to this group."

"Oh?" Rodriguez raised an eyebrow. "A twelve-step thing?"

"Yeah."

"They have an AA for hounds?"

Carnes studied Rodriguez for a second and decided he was joking. "Yeah. These people all have a thing about sex. They had sex all the time but weren't happy anyway."

"Too much of a good thing?" Rodriguez' eyes twinkled.

"Sort of. Sex screwed up their relationships and stuff."

"Their?"

"I'm not as bad."

"Oh?" Rodriguez raised his eyebrow again.

"Well, maybe I'm overdoing it a little. Sometimes I forget about Avery or other things. But some of these people were *really* out of control."

"Building relationships takes a lot of work," said Rodriguez. "I know. I've screwed up most of mine." He smiled sadly. "Sounds like you're doing the right thing."

Carnes shrugged.

"So tell me, what's different about this Becky?"

"I don't know. I have a good time with her, even without sleeping with her." Carnes smiled. "We have laughs. She's easy to talk to. She's pretty but unassuming, almost awkward, like a newborn foal still getting her legs under her. But she's a thoroughbred all the way."

Rodriguez puffed on the cigarette. "So how do you handle this sex stuff?"

"Well, they suggest you try celibacy for a while."

"Celibacy. You?"

"I'm still deciding."

"Right," Rodriguez said. "In the words of the immortal Buddy Holly, 'that'll be the day'!"

Carnes tossed the cigarette butt out into the street. "Ever think about getting remarried?"

"Sure," Rodriguez said. "But then I get my sense back."

They laughed.

"No, I'm serious."

"So am I."

They laughed again.

"Who knows? Maybe. Maybe in a couple of years when I retire. I figure I'll leave the city and move out to West Virginia or something."

"I can't see you as an ol' country boy"—Carnes tried a West Virginia accent—"twangin' 'way on an ol' banjo, sippin' moonshine, a yard full o' shoeless children."

Rodriguez guffawed. "Hey, cut me a break. West Virginia is an hour away. It's got the same programs on TV." He got serious. "But it doesn't have the crime, the crowding"—he glanced outside—"the humidity. Heck, I can have a garden full of vegetables, go fishing every day, hunt when I want to. What's wrong with that?"

"Nothing. I didn't realize that's what you wanted." Carnes sang a couple of lines from a John Denver song that ended, "Thank God I'm a country boy."

"Give me a freakin'—" Suddenly, Rodriguez sat forward, face serious. He pointed to the garage entrance. "Isn't that Pardo's car pulling out?"

Carnes turned on the ignition. "Yeah. Let the guys know we're on the move."

Rodriguez pulled the walkie-talkie out of the holder between them and spoke into it. "Three-ten?"

"Yeah." Jenkins and Madison, detectives from one of the squads doing the 3-to-11 shift, were in car 310.

Carnes waited for Pardo to clear the block, then started to pull out.

"Subject turning onto K Street going uptown." They followed. "Turning up Nineteenth."

"We're behind you."

Carnes saw the headlights in his rearview mirror. "Pulling over to park between L and M," said Rodriguez. "We're going up to M. We'll turn and circle around." They drove past Pardo's car. "You have him?"

The radio squawked. "Got him. We're sitting down between K and L." Several seconds went by. "He's out. On foot. Walking back between buildings. I think the alley goes back toward a little restaurant. One of the radio stations I listen to broadcasts from there sometimes."

"OK. I know the one," Rodriguez said. "Wait a few minutes. Then one of you go in and sit at the bar. He doesn't know you. Be careful. We'll be ready to back you up if he moves too fast."

"Got it," said Madison.

Carnes checked his watch for the twentieth time. Five minutes had gone by since one of the detectives in car 310 got out and went into the bar. It was 9:55 P.M. "This is the part I hate. I hate waiting."

"I've noticed," Rodriguez said. "You're making me nervous. Stop looking at your watch."

"I know," said Carnes. "A watched pot won't boil."

"Right."

Carnes strained to see up the street. They had parked north of K Street on 19th. Car 310 was half a block up. Suddenly, Madison ran out of the alley and down the sidewalk toward 310.

"I don't like the looks of that," said Rodriguez.

The radio squawked. "Three-ten, Madison here. He's gone."

Carnes grabbed the radio. "What do you mean he's gone?"

"I went into the place. Tried to be casual about it but couldn't see him anywhere. Checked the bathroom. He wasn't there. Bartender and bouncer hadn't seen him come in."

"Shit." Carnes pounded the steering wheel. "Where'd he go?"

"Well, the alley goes through to Eighteenth. Maybe he walked through. There are a couple of bars there and some more up at M and on Connecticut."

Carnes turned to Rodriguez. "What do you think?" If he and Rodriguez started walking into bars and Pardo saw them, he'd probably file a harassment complaint. They didn't need that.

Rodriguez must have come to the same conclusion. "Why don't we sit here and watch his car? Let Madison and Jenkins walk to Eighteenth and hit all the places within a three-block radius. If they miss Pardo and he doubles back to his car, at least we'll be in position."

"OK," said Carnes. Rodriguez relayed the instructions.

"Damnit," Carnes muttered. "Must've known he was being followed."

"He could've just been looking for a parking place and planned to hit a bar a block over," Rodriguez suggested.

Carnes checked his watch. "We'll see."

An hour later, it was clear that Pardo hadn't visited any other bars or restaurants in the neighborhood. He'd given them the slip. Carnes, Rodriguez, Jenkins, and Madison stood around car 310 cursing themselves and Pardo. "I bet the fucker doesn't even come back for his car," Madison said.

"Probably right," Carnes said. "And he's parked legally. We can't even tow the fucker."

"Does he have other transport?" Madison asked. "Maybe he's going after some other girl."

Carnes felt a cold chill. Pardo was hunting. He'd found his quarry at Barnstormers. Becky. Carnes turned to Rodriguez. "Can you ride with these guys? I need the car."

"Huh?"

"Becky. Pardo approached her in a bar the other day. She was in Benton's sorority. She'd met him before."

Rodriguez' eyes got wider. "I'll go with you."

"No, if everything's OK I don't want to spook her. Start checking with cab companies, Farragut North Metro, anywhere else Pardo might've gotten transportation."

"OK," Rodriguez said. "But if you need backup—"

"I know." Carnes ran for the car.

He pulled out into traffic. Where would Becky be? It was almost 11:00. She'd probably be home by now. He shot up 19th and turned onto Connecticut. He rushed from traffic light to traffic light. The speedometer said he was going fifteen miles per hour above the speed limit. Lucky it was a weeknight and traffic wasn't bad. Carnes weaved to avoid a car. He glanced quickly at his watch. Another five minutes at most.

His heart pounded as he pressed the accelerator. His entire body tingled like a massive electrical grid. Damnit! He cursed himself and Pardo alternately and pounded on the wheel in frustration each time he had to slow down. They'd wasted an hour looking for Pardo. How stupid could he be? The trip was taking forever. Four minutes later he pulled up in front of a fire hydrant near the three-level apartment where Becky lived.

He hopped out and ran to the door. Her apartment was on the second floor and faced to the back. He pulled the Glock out of his shoulder holster, then shoved it back in. Up the stairs, two at a time. Panting hard. Becky's door. He held his breath feeling as though his chest would burst as he pressed his ear to the door. No sound. He stepped back and pounded on the door.

Carnes shifted from one foot to the other and felt under his jacket for his gun. He pounded on the door again. He stepped back and examined the steel door. Would he be able to kick it open? He was ready to launch himself at the door when a glint of light appeared through the peephole. He paused, fighting the adrenaline. The peephole darkened. With an angry creak, the door swung open.

"John." Becky's sleepy eyes were rounded with surprise. She held a pink terrycloth robe together with her left hand. Her hair was slightly tangled. She wasn't wearing any makeup. She looked like a goddess. Carnes felt an overwhelming urge to hold her. He reached out and pulled her to him.

After a few seconds she pushed him back. "Are you drunk or something?"

"No."

"What time is it?" Becky squinted her eyes.

"Almost eleven-thirty."

"I thought we decided on tomorrow?"

"It's almost tomorrow now."

She gave him a quirky look. "You're not drunk?"

"No." His face grew serious. "I was worried about you."

Becky tilted her head with surprise. "Worried?"

Carnes didn't want to scare her, but his resolve broke. He told her about their surveillance of Pardo, how they had lost him.

"I don't get it." She held up her hand. "Look, why don't you come in. Otherwise, we'll wake all the neighbors." She stood aside and closed the door behind him.

"You want something to drink or eat?" she asked.

Carnes realized he hadn't eaten for hours. "A glass of water and anything you have—a sandwich or something—would be fine."

Becky moved with great economy, pulling lettuce, Dijon mustard, cheese, and smoked turkey out of the refrigerator. With the quick, efficient movements of a card sharp, she dealt the ingredients onto the counter and assembled them into a sandwich. She poured a glass of water from a bottle in the refrigerator. He sat at the table in the ell that served as a dining room. While he wolfed down the sandwich, she put away the ingredients and wiped the counter.

Between bites, Carnes told her about Pardo and his ties to the victims. "When you said he approached you in the bar, it crossed my mind that if he was the killer, you might be a potential victim. But, I didn't want you to worry. Besides, we don't have enough on him. So I decided to watch him. But what happens? He gets away from us."

Becky's face combined disbelief and concern. "Why me? I mean, I've barely met the man."

"I'm not sure. I think it has something to do with the University of Maryland and a fraternity or sorority."

"Alpha Omega?" Becky's voice cracked slightly.

"Yes."

Carnes started to explain. "You've lost three sorority sisters—that we know about—in the last year."

"Three?" She pulled the robe around her despite the nearly eighty-degree temperature.

"Yes. Vicky, Anna Durant, and Francine Lynch. You know them?"

"Jesus. I hadn't—I had no idea. I can't believe I didn't hear anything. I mean, I wasn't close to them or anything, but you'd think I would have heard something." Becky gave Carnes a searching look. "Why? I mean, it's so crazy. Why would Pardo—why would anyone—want to knock off my sorority sisters?"

"That's what I'm trying to find out. How well did you know Durant and Lynch?"

"A little. Anna was a class behind us. She transferred somewhere her junior year."

"Georgetown."

"Yeah, I guess so." Becky pushed a tendril of hair back from her eyes. "Franny was in our class. Nice girl. A little boy crazy. Not much of a student." Her hand fluttered to her mouth. "I don't mean to speak poorly of the—you know what I mean."

"Yeah. But I need to know everything—whatever you can tell me about them."

"Gee, let me think." Becky rested her chin on her hands.

"It's been years since I saw either of them. I think I saw Franny"—she seemed deep in thought—"maybe two years ago. A party in Ocean City, I think. Bunch of kids from various sororities and frats, brother and sister houses, got together." She saw the question in Carnes' eyes. "Yes, Vicky was there, too. Maybe twenty to thirty others."

"Pardo?"

"Could be, but I don't remember him. Anyway, Franny was working as a waitress or something. Seemed happy. She was still looking for Mr. Right."

"Any particular boyfriends?"

"Can't remember any names. I think she went through half the wrestling team in college. She was—uhmm—pretty active. Some of her boyfriends treated her like dirt. She used to get up in the morning when they slept over and cook them breakfast, you know, like she had married them or something. It was really sad."

"Any of these guys stick out in your mind?"

"Not really."

"What about Anna?" Carnes asked.

"Anna." Becky stared off into space. "Anna. I don't think I've seen her for maybe five, six years at least."

"What was she like?"

"Well, close to her family. She wanted to go into the family business. For the life of me I can't remember what they did."

"What kind of person was she?"

"A little sarcastic and snide. The kind of girl who would always let you know when she didn't like what you were doing. She'd say 'thank you'"—Becky imitated a snobbish intonation—"to let you know she was displeased."

"Sounds pleasant."

"It was just her way."

"How active was she in the sorority?"

"She joined in when we did things but she wasn't an organizer. Fran was the same way. They were sorority members but not that into it. I got along with Anna OK, but we definitely weren't close."

"Do you remember whether Anna dated any boys?"

"No. She was fairly, well, chunky, and she didn't make an effort to look good. I don't think she had much interest in boys."

Carnes raised an eyebrow.

"I don't mean that," said Becky. "Well, who knows. Anyway, I certainly don't remember a lot of guys who seemed interested. Nobody she dated."

"Anything else?"

"That's about all I know. I mean, I knew Vicky and some others much better."

"Do you have a list of who was in the sorority with you?"

"Sure. I have a picture, too." Carnes watched as she swept over to a bookcase, where she began to sort through a small pile of yearbooks and other memorabilia. Carnes suddenly remembered the picture and other things he got from Del. With all that had been going on, he'd forgotten it in his trunk. Must be losing it.

"Here." She held up a picture. She sat down next to Carnes. "Can you guess which one is me?"

Carnes smiled at the carefree young faces. Had he ever felt so free and comfortable with life? Although her hair was longer then, Becky was very easy to pick out. "There," he said, pointing to a girl with curly red hair who was about forty pounds overweight.

"No!" She punched him in the arm and laughed. "You did that on purpose."

"How about this one?" He pointed to a short blond-haired girl.

"Yeah, that's me before I colored my hair and grew a foot taller." Becky grinned.

Carnes liked that grin. Without thinking, he pointed to another unlikely candidate. "Her."

"No." Becky's voice was suddenly somber. "That's Franny."

"Sorry." Carnes studied the picture more closely. This time he played it straight. "This is you."

She nodded.

"And this is Vicky."

She nodded again.

"Is Anna in this picture?"

"No. That was senior year. She was gone by then." She flipped over the picture to look at the typed list of names she had taped to the back. "Just in case I forget—when the old gray cells start getting mushy."

"Other than Anna, are there any others who were in your sorority who aren't in this picture?"

"Sure. Upperclassmates who graduated before me, a few who dropped out or transferred." Becky shook her head. "It's sad. I hate to let people go. You have all these great memories, great moments with people, and then they just slide out of your life. Sometimes I wish I could keep them all, or bring them back."

Carnes' best friend in college had been a fiery, long-haired lunatic: Boz. They'd played ball together, partied, and argued about what was reality. Boz had introduced Carnes to Hesse, Ionesco, Kafka, and a bunch of other writers whom Carnes never felt he understood. Then he'd met Caroline. She had built barriers around the two of them. By the time Carnes realized what she had done, all that was left of his ties to Boz was a thread of regret.

"Yeah, I know what you mean," Carnes said. "Are there any things or people you'd rather not remember?"

"Not really." For a moment, Becky's eyes seemed to reveal some ancient pain.

"You can talk to Uncle John." Carnes tone was light and playful.

Becky's lips turned up into a wry smile. "There was just this guy." She blushed. "I got caught up in this perfect relationship. I thought I was going to marry him and we would live happily ever after. Then I found out he was dating a girl up in Towson. Well, you know, it was sort of a shock." Becky studied her hands.

Carnes reached across the table and grasped them.

He stared up at the apartment window. The damn cop beat him there. Did they really suspect? No. The cop had the hots for this girl. And why not, she was the prettiest of them all. Oh, she was. He could see her and the cop in bed, their bodies writhing around in the agony of ecstasy. He felt himself growing hard. Maybe he could kill them both while they slept in their postcoital daze. No. Too dangerous. The cop was too big.

Patience. It's just a matter of time. The cops are stupid. He could run them around in circles until they were so dizzy they collapsed. Maybe he'd create a phantom for the cops to chase. Somewhere far away. He imagined Keystone Kops running around aimlessly in silent-movie rhythm. He chuckled.

His turn was coming. He'd lull her into it like a hypnotist. Just when she was relaxed, when she thought he was as harmless as a puppy, he'd become a pit bull. He had some special tricks saved for her. Then the best part.

He visualized the cop staring down at her torn and lifeless body. Oh God. It would be perfect. There was nothing they could do.

Book Three

1

Rodriguez smiled when Carnes walked in, a bag of pastries in his hand. "Everything OK?"

"Yeah. Whatever Pardo was up to had nothing to do with Becky," Carnes said.

Rodriguez raised his eyebrows. "So?"

"So?"

"So you arrive on horseback—or car—her knight in shining armor, and . . . ?"

"And what?"

"You know, and . . . ?" Rodriguez held his hands in front of him and motioned toward himself. "Don't hold out on me."

"You have a dirty mind. Nothing happened."

"It's not my dirty mind."

"Fuck you."

Rodriguez made a tut-tut sound. "Such language." He became serious again. "Sounds like this sorority angle is the key. The question is why? Who has it in for this sorority? It's crazy."

"Yeah, crazy is the word. Nobody has any idea. Think about it. How many reasons can you come up with?" Carnes said. "We're not talking panty raids here, we're talking really twisted."

"Some guy who was jilted by an Alpha Omega girl?"

"Or some weirdo fixated on the sorority for no rational reason," Carnes said. "Once you get into the realm of the twisted, virtually anything is possible. Hell, it could be some guy who has decided the sorority is a coven of witches."

"Witches? I think I know those girls," Wiley chimed in.

"I'm sure you do." Rodriguez turned to Carnes. "So we track down everyone from the sorority we can find—"

"And see what quirky possibilities we come up with."

"I'm working on my network of domestics."

"Sounds good," Carnes said. "Maybe Wes can help contact the girls."

"You want me to spend my day talking to a bunch of fuckin' coeds? What makes you think I'd want to do that?" Wiley smiled like a kid who had just been offered unlimited desserts.

"Yeah, should be real tough," Rodriguez said. "Don't make us beg."

"I'd also like to check with the Bureau to see if they pulled up anything on sex criminals and the University of Maryland," said Carnes. "That is, if Del got a chance to run the request."

"Sure did." Del Clinton stood behind Carnes. Del's eyes were bloodshot and stained with weariness, but he was wearing a snappy suit with a rainbow-striped tie.

"Hey, I didn't know you were in," Carnes said. "How's your friend?"

Del grimaced. "Passed on last night."

"Sorry," Carnes said. "He talk?"

"No. Never came out of his coma."

"Damn. I wonder if he had anything new."

"Maybe. Or maybe he was just trying to get something the night he got killed and it was on his mind." Del shrugged. "Doesn't matter too much to his family."

"What a fuckin' world," Wiley said. "You OK?"

"Well, I have this feeling that maybe there was something more I could've done." Del flopped into the seat at the next desk.

"Don't be an asshole," said Wiley. "People make their own fuckin' mistakes. It's hard enough to look out for your own wife and family these days. Ain't no way you can protect everyone."

"Wes is right," said Carnes.

"I know—in my head. Now I have to convince my heart."

"At least we got the fuckers who did it," said Wiley.

"Yeah. Another drug-related murder solved. Should help the monthly numbers." Del's face twisted into a half grin. "The ironic thing is, Slick had tried to scare this guy off his turf, but he didn't take him out. There's a lesson of some sort in that. Show a little bit of humanity, a tiny bit of respect for life, and die for it."

"Another lesson from the fuckin' street," said Wiley.

"Yeah." For an instant, Rodriguez' face showed twenty years of pent-up cynicism and disgust.

Clinton nodded. "So what's happening in our case?"

Carnes and Rodriguez filled him in as Wiley listened.

"It's fuckin' bizarre, if you ask me," Wiley said. "This guy's MO for sure."

"Yeah, but mentally off or not these kinda guys are always the nice, quiet neighbor, the perfect coworker. Sorta like you, Wes." Rodriguez glanced at Wiley out of the corner of his eye.

"Fuck you."

"Pete's right." said Carnes. "Everybody's always shocked when they find out about one of these guys. You hear people say, 'He was such a nice, quiet boy. I just can't believe he filled a refrigerator full of body parts,'" Carnes mimicked in a falsetto. "'I thought all those young men he invited in were leaving through the back door.'"

"So what you're saying is that instead of looking for some guy who's fuckin' crazy, we got to look for someone who's about as fuckin' normal as they come," Wiley said.

"That's about it," replied Carnes. "We may be talking about some nice quiet computer programmer or some pillar-of-the-community attorney."

"Well, then we're doing this backward," said Wiley. "If you ask me, we should knock the fuckin' insane people off our list."

"That eliminates all the cops," Clinton said.

Wiley ignored the gibe. "And be suspicious of anyone who seems too fuckin' sane."

As they sat around chuckling, Sergeant Bryant appeared. "Nice to see you guys having such a good time."

Carnes filled him in on the joke.

Bryant rolled his eyes. "I pulled a few strings with a buddy in narcotics. The DEA lab expedited those drug samples from Pardo's. Field tests were confirmed. White powder was positive for coke and the other stuff was definitely marijuana."

"So what do we do?" Carnes asked. "We got some kinky movies and some drugs. He won't do any time."

"I don't know if we can keep the fucker from walking, but maybe this'll take the starch out of his shorts for a while." Bryant sighed.

"Most of the judges see drugs as a social problem," Carnes said. "He'll walk for sure."

"Maybe not," said Bryant. "Some judges would say 'wealthy white guy—he doesn't have an excuse.'"

"You *know* Carnes is right," said Wiley. "We got addicts out there who commit hundreds, more likely thousands of crimes to support their habits. Most of the time, they get away with it. Everyone pays but the fuckin' criminal. Higher prices for goods is the pain of being a victim. Then there's always the possibility they're going to shoot somebody— just to keep us employed. Once in a while we get lucky and catch the fucker, and what happens?"

"Some bleeding-heart judge gives the guy probation conditioned on some sort of drug treatment," said Carnes.

"Right. Six months or a year later, the guy's committed another thousand crimes. We catch him again and what do you think happens?"

"He gets a few months or a ticket to another treatment program," said Rodriguez.

"Right again. Our fuckin' motto shouldn't be 'protect and serve,' it should be 'arrest and release,'" Wiley said.

"Once," said Carnes, "when I was working burglary, I had this guy who'd committed hundreds of commercial burglaries. A crack addict. Think he had about twenty-two priors. When I caught him, he was on probation for two previous convictions." Carnes shook his head in disgust. "At his probation revocation hearing, the defense attorney requested 'one last chance' at a live-in drug rehab program, and the judge continued his probation."

"Well," Bryant said, "Pardo may walk on the drug charges, but he won't walk for murder." He waved his hands. "So stop bullshitting and get to work."

"Twenty-five calls," said Pete Rodriguez, "and I located only three sorority sisters. My stomach's grumbling and I haven't learned a thing." He peered over at Wiley and watched him working his phone. Wiley saw him and rolled his eyes.

"Yes, ma'am. Thank you, ma'am." Wiley put down the phone. "Shit. Can't even find half of them. Fuckin' Maryland girls all seem to be from New York or Jersey. They're scattered all over the fuckin' place. And of course none of them have the same names anymore. I think they all married doctors or lawyers." He rubbed his eyes with the back of his knuckles. "There's got to be a better way to do this."

"Maybe we can get an up-to-date listing from the alumni office at Maryland," Rodriguez said.

"Can't hurt," Wiley growled. He grabbed his coffee cup and headed back toward the pot.

Rodriguez picked up the phone and dialed information. "College

Park, University of Maryland, alumni office, please." He jotted down the number. It took several calls.

"Yes, Ms. Ashburton . . . I understand it's university policy . . . It really is important. This is a homicide investigation, ma'am . . . No exceptions? OK." He hung up.

"Sounds like a tough one," said Carnes.

"Yeah. Darn intransigent bureaucrats."

"Intransigent?" Wiley shook his head. "Take away his fuckin' dictionary."

"What did she say?" asked Carnes.

"She explained how university policy—she made it sound like a biblical reference—did not allow her to give out information over the telephone. Sounded like one of those prim matrons with steely gray hair and wire-rimmed glasses. A gem.

"I tried to explain there were already three dead girls." Rodriguez glanced from Carnes to Wiley. "Know what she said?"

"I don't have a clue."

"'And you could be the killer looking for more victims.'"

"Spunky." Carnes grinned at Wiley.

"I'm not in the mood for spunk." Rodriguez sighed and turned to Wiley. "Wanna take a trip to the country?" Wiley shrugged.

"The alumni office closes at four-thirty. We'd better get moving."

Carnes examined the list the Bureau had faxed over. The FBI's computer gurus had cross-checked sex offenders with any known connection to the University of Maryland or any address within five miles. Ten years of data filled nearly twenty pages: a virtual who's who of rapists, pederasts, pornographers, Peeping Toms, and exhibitionists. The university's employees, neighbors, and present and former students were surprisingly imaginative. None of this information was in any of the glossy admissions booklets. What would the parents of a prospective coed say if they saw this list?

Carnes scanned the names, arrests and convictions, searching for a name that meant something to him. It appeared halfway down the second page. "Holy shit!"

Del Clinton looked up from the pile of papers on his desk. "What?"

"Listen to this: 'Bardash, James, probation without verdict.'"

"Who's that?"

"The accountant who dated Benton."

Clinton nodded.

"Well, Bardash has a conviction as a Peeping Tom!"

"You're kidding."

"No." Carnes kept his voice calm despite the wave of excitement that had swept over him. "The conviction is in College Park. Take a ride?"

"OK."

"Try to raise Rodriguez and Wiley on the radio. We can meet them at the College Park PD." Carnes picked up the phone.

Ellen Ashburton was a pleasant surprise. Rodriguez expected a pale, pinched, elderly bureaucrat. Instead, he found a handsome woman of about forty-five with short dark hair. Her eyes and mouth were surrounded by the light wrinkles of one who spends a lot of time smiling. Her skin glowed with a warm tan.

Ashburton's clothing was feminine but professional. She wore a frilly white blouse and a knee-length navy skirt that set off a narrow waist and revealed shapely legs. Her body looked firm and trim. Rodriguez decided she worked out. Her perfume was alluring but subtle. A good sign. Rodriguez couldn't stand women who smelled like flower shops.

They'd been exchanging pleasant small talk about working for bureaucracies for several minutes when Rodriguez noticed Wiley giving him funny looks. Wiley coughed. "Can we see those alumni lists?" he asked.

Ashburton brought them the lists, then led them to an empty desk several feet away. "You can work here."

Several minutes later, Ashburton walked over. "How're you coming with that?" She leaned over Rodriguez to glance at his list. He felt the firm pressure of her breast against his shoulder. Was this what he thought? This kind of thing happened only to Carnes.

"Just about done," he said. "Found addresses for all but these last three." He looked over at Wiley. "How about you, Wes?"

Wiley stretched his arms and grunted. "I'm all done. Need to stretch and get a smoke." He'd seen the "NO SMOKING" sign on the wall. "Sorry, ma'am, we stopped at the Long John Silver's on the way out of Rhode Island." He smiled broadly. "If I don't stretch, I'll be asleep across this desk. Is there a place I can smoke?"

"Sure, Detective." She pointed toward the door. "Down the stairs and to the right. You can smoke out there."

"I'm glad it ain't raining," Wiley rumbled. "Be back in fifteen." He winked at Rodriguez and gave him a surreptitious thumbs-up.

* * *

"It warn't no big thing." Sergeant Tom Davis leaned back in his chair. Davis was a thin man with a narrow nose, bushy mustache, and prominent jaw. His hair was blond with silvery streaks of gray. "Just one of them college kids who'd read too many *Penthouse* letters." He winked at Carnes. "Gotta tell you, I feel sorry for them. These kids read these letters where people write in about how they looked in the window at some babe undressing and the next thing you know she's dragging them in through the window and tearing their clothes off. They think every babe is out there waiting to screw them blind. Then when they try it, the girl calls the cops and they get arrested." He snorted like a hog. "Yeah, we get lots of those calls. The guys are in shock that it didn't work for them."

"What about Bardash?" Clinton asked.

Davis turned toward Carnes as though he had asked the question. "Well, from the file it looks like he fits the pattern. He lived around the corner from this girl in garden apartments where lots of coeds live. He apparently knew the girl and had seen her boyfriend come over. They seem to have made a habit of leaving the curtains open a-ways. You gotta wonder what they were expecting. This kid Bardash, he was peeping in through a ground-floor window watching them getting it on and beating off. Some girl who lived in them apartments came home at just the right time—or maybe the wrong time depending on your perspective— and spotted him. Caught red handed, you might say." He snorted and smacked the desk with a large fleshy palm. "Poor kid pled out and got probation without verdict."

"Do you know the name of the people he was watching through the window?" asked Carnes.

"Sure, it's in here somewhere. Here it is." He handed across a page of the report.

"How'd they take it?" Carnes asked.

"Well, they made a big show of being upset, but you tell me, if you don't want people to peep, do you leave the curtains open? They were pretty happy he pled out. Didn't want to testify or anything."

"Do any of the witnesses have any link to the Alpha Omega sorority?" Carnes asked.

"Not that I know of. Y'all don't know the area, but this is way off campus. Ain't no frats or sororities nearby."

"Did Bardash indicate whether he'd ever done this before?"

"Well, yeah. When he got caught he blubbered like his life was over.

Says here in the report he admitted he'd done it before. The kid prowled the place at night and knew every chick who left her curtains open. This couple's window was a regular stop. Always put on a good show. I suspect Bardash could have sold tickets to half the guys—no, make that most of the guys—at the university."

"Any psych evaluation done?" asked Clinton.

"Let's see." Davis paged through his file. "Oh, yeah, for sentencing. Basically, it says he was a healthy young boy with a sex drive." The sergeant rubbed his nose with his fingertips and winked at Carnes. "Who can argue with that?"

"How'd it go?" Carnes asked Rodriguez and Wiley as they sat at a dark wooden table at Bentleys, a dimly lit bar and restaurant on Route 1 near the campus.

"We got all the addresses," Rodriguez said.

Wiley leered. "And he's not just talkin' about them girls. This Ms. Ashburton turned out to be a prime piece of ass. Your partner got hisself a date."

Rodriguez turned beet red. "Damnit, Wiley. Can't you keep your big mouth shut?"

"You old dog." Carnes smiled. "You going after the witnesses now?"

"Ellen isn't a witness," Rodriguez insisted. "She just gave us the damn list."

"Ellen?" Carnes and Wiley exchanged meaningful glances.

"So what did you learn from College Park's finest?" Rodriguez asked.

"Changing the subject?" Carnes wasn't going to let Rodriguez off the hook that easily.

"All right, I asked her out. She said yes." Rodriguez struggled to regain his dignity.

Del turned to Carnes. "I think we busted his balls enough. Tell them about Bardash."

"You should have seen this sergeant. Acted like Del was some sort of alien." Carnes grinned at Del. "Must be the threads."

"Threads? Sure," said Clinton. "He looked at me as though I were a drug dealer."

"Fuckin' rednecks." Wiley took a pull on his beer. "Fuckin' goddamned rednecks."

Carnes knew that when Wiley started with the Metropolitan Police

Department, the nation's capital was still a sleepy southern town run by whites. The plantation mentality still ruled, opportunities for a bright young black man in the police department were limited. Of course, D.C. was a virtual model of racial opportunity compared to the Virginia and Maryland suburbs. Blacks, even D.C. police officers, were likely to be harassed and sometimes beaten merely for driving through Prince Georges County. The same thing still happened, although much less frequently since the state's attorney and a significant portion of the PG County police department were now black.

Carnes gave Rodriguez and Wiley a terse account of their conversation with Sergeant Davis. "So, are we looking at a normal bit of adolescent behavior, as the sergeant suggested?"

"Doesn't sound like much," said Wiley.

"Yeah, but who's to say it wasn't the first step," suggested Carnes. "Maybe he gets more and more wrapped up in sex fantasies. He starts peeping and pretending. After a while that's not enough and he gets into something more serious." Carnes shook his head; he knew a little about this. "Maybe he decided the girls he watched were evil perverts and he's God's avenging angel."

"Partner, you been watching too many movies," Rodriguez said. "There's nothing here at all. Bardash was some oversexed teenager jerking off. It's the national sport."

"Not everyone jerks off watching someone else making it."

"No. Now they rent X-rated videos. Maybe he didn't own a VCR," Rodriguez commented.

"I think Pete's probably right," Clinton said.

Wiley chimed in. "From what I've seen, I'd put money on this fuckin' Pardo. The guy knew the girls, he was in the wrong place at the right time—"

"Or the right place at the wrong time," said Clinton.

Wiley ignored him. "He gave you guys the slip the other night. What's that mean?"

"Who knows? Maybe he didn't realize we were cops. Thought we were muggers," said Carnes. "Would you stick around when someone's following you through D.C. in the dark?"

"Naw. He knew we were cops," said Rodriguez. "But he'd do that kind of thing just to prove he's smarter."

"He dissed you," said Wiley.

They laughed.

Carnes looked around the table. "Well, we're not going to learn anything sitting here." He swallowed the remainder of his beer. "Let's divide these names and get to work. Maybe we'll find out more."

"We going to confront Bardash?" asked Rodriguez.

"Let's see what else we learn first."

2

Avery played with her peas, pushing them around with the end of her fork, creating an elaborate green tubular-shaped design. She began to fold some of the mashed potatoes into the peas. "How's the meat loaf?" Carnes asked.

"Good." Avery showed off the gaps next to her front teeth. The tooth fairy had been busy lately.

"What're you making?"

"Nothin'." She pushed a couple more peas into position, then looked up at him slyly. "Guess?"

"A crescent moon?"

She shook her head from side to side, a silly grin breaking out at the corners of her mouth.

"A banana?"

She giggled and shook her head again.

"A croissant?"

She peered at him. "A what?"

"It's a crescent—a roll that looks like that." He pointed. "It's French."

"No, silly," she said.

"All right. I give up. What is it?" he asked.

"It's a pea-nis." She giggled.

Carnes struggled to keep a straight face. "It's not spelled the same way."

"I *know* that," she said in a mildly exasperated voice. She stared at him from under half-closed lids, her head tilted to one side, as though she really didn't understand him.

Carnes decided it was time for a change in subject. "How was day care today?"

She'd seen this ploy before. She gave him a bored look. "OK. How was work?"

She was too smart for seven. "Very busy. I'm going to meet with a witness tonight. Someone who knows things about one of my cases. She might be able to help me find the bad guy."

"She? A lady?" Avery teased.

"A lady," he said.

"Is she a mommy?"

"No, she's not married."

"Do you want to marry her?"

Carnes was flustered. "Well, I'd say it's pretty early to start talking about marrying anyone." What am I saying? he wondered. She's just asking a simple, little-girl question. "Your daddy meets lots of women in his job. Don't assume they're all marriage prospects."

"What's a marriage prospect?"

"It's someone you look at and think you might want to marry."

"Oh." Avery nodded her head in a very adult way. "Is this lady a marriage prospect?"

Carnes thought about that. He was tempted to brush off the question with a joke. No. He was trying to be more honest with Avery.

"Well, sweetie, she's a very nice woman, and I guess I like her, but I've just known her for a short time. It's a little early to talk about marriage."

"Oh." Avery looked thoughtful. "Mommy said you're going to get married again."

"Maybe. I haven't given it much thought. I think it's probably something that happens. You meet someone you like and you want to get married. I guess someday I might decide to get remarried." He looked at her. "How do you feel about that?"

"It's OK if she's nice."

"So you don't want me to bring home the wicked witch of the East?"

"Nooo, Daddy!" Avery laughed. "That would be gross."

"I'm glad to hear I don't remind you of the wicked witch of the East," Becky said archly.

"Well, maybe the West," Carnes said.

She punched him lightly in the shoulder. "Real nice."

"Always a romantic at heart." Carnes took a small bow.

"Yeah, right." She gave him a more serious look. "Don't you think it's a little early to be mentioning me to your daughter? I mean, we haven't even—"

"Relax. I had to explain where I was going. I described you as a 'friend of the victim,' 'a witness.' I have no intention of proposing—until after dinner." He smiled. "Speaking of which, I'm starving. I had to watch Avery eat and I've been dying."

"We can't have that." Becky gave him a sly look. "It would deprive all the criminals of the pleasure of ending your life themselves."

Carnes' facial muscles tensed. "You've been watching too much TV. Most of the criminals want nothing to do with cops. I can't even think of a revenge shooting—"

"Hey. Lighten up. I was joking." Becky wondered at his defensive tone. Maybe she sounded a little like a police wife. Had Carnes' ex-wife nagged him? Becky imagined a pinched, frantic woman, nagging John about why he wasn't home more, why he took risks. She shook off the image. She was imagining the wicked witch. From what John had said, it didn't really fit.

"Well," Carnes said, "I have reservations at this little Italian place that nobody has really discovered yet."

"Good. I *love* Italian food."

If nobody had discovered this restaurant yet, Becky would hate to see one that had been discovered. La Trattoria Firenze was packed. Its stucco walls were adorned with paintings of sunlit buildings, bridges, and rivers. Teardrop-shaped red candles flickered atop crowded wooden tables, lending a rosy tint to the room. Becky couldn't see a vacant table. The room resonated with the sounds of raucous conversation punctuated by the clinking of silverware.

They sat in the bar while they waited for a table. The air was so thick with the aromas of garlic, cheeses, onions, peppers, and tomatoes that Becky was convinced she'd meet all her minimum daily requirements just breathing the atmosphere for a few minutes. Instead, she became ravenously hungry. By the time they sat at their table, she felt as though she could eat everything on the menu in a single sitting.

Carnes smiled at her over a glass of Chianti as she devoured the hot antipasto. "Well, what do you think?"

Becky held up a finger, finished chewing, then sipped the wine. "Fantastico." Her laughter bubbled like a sparkling wine. "Is that Italian?"

"You're asking an Irish boy about Italian? Only Italian words I know are 'pizza' and 'pasta.'" Carnes smiled. "I hoped you'd like it." He sipped the wine. "The owner is an ex-cop I know from patrol. The chef is from somewhere in southern Italy—barely speaks any English. So far, the place hasn't been reviewed by the *Post* or anything, but he has a good business. And he does pretty fair with carryout too. That's why he has the other entrance."

Becky remembered the carryout sign on their way in. She had seen several people through the glass door lined up at a counter or pulling sodas out of a large glass-fronted refrigerator. She nodded. "Even we civilians aren't totally unobservant." She laughed. "Do you bring all your women here?"

"Only the ones I'm really trying to impress." He grinned and she mirrored it. "Sort of the quickest way to a woman's heart is through her stomach."

"I thought that was the way to a man's heart."

"Hey, it usually works." Carnes smiled.

"It does?" Becky snorted. "You're an incurable optimist."

"I'd prefer to think of myself as an incurable romantic." He waved his hand around. "Candlelight, good food, wine, and thou."

"And thou?" She laughed. "God. Where did you pick that up?"

"You inspire me," Carnes said. "You saying that I'm not sweeping you off your feet with my romantic sensibility?"

"Non-sense-ability is more like it." Becky smiled. "But I'm a sucker for men who have a sense of nonsense."

"I may hold you to that."

"Do I detect some foul double meaning?" Becky turned a shade darker in the candlelight.

"You would make a great detective," Carnes said.

The waiter arrived with their entrees. Becky dove into the veal *pizzaiola* while Carnes worked on a plate of lasagna big enough to feed his entire squad—if Wiley wasn't there. Becky took a sip of the Chianti. "Are you ever serious?" she asked.

"Serious in what sense? Seriously ill, seriously deranged? Or are you asking if I'm one of the clouds?"

"That's 'cirrus.' C-i-r-r-u-s. Not 'serious.'" She laughed. "I mean it. Are you ever serious?"

"I'm serious now." Carnes sucked in his cheeks and made a dour face.

Becky rewarded his performance with a chuckle. "You're incorrigible."

"No. John Carnes." He maintained the dour look as he held out his hand. "Pleased to meet you."

"God, that's sick."

Carnes did his best Groucho imitation, waving an imaginary cigar in the air. "I was hoping you'd say that." He raised and lowered his eyebrows.

"You are so bad."

Carnes tried Mae West. "When I'm good, I'm very, very good, but when I'm bad I'm better."

Becky dropped her playful tone. "What are you, homicide's answer to Rich Little?"

"No." Carnes looked stricken. He stared at the table. He smiled half-heartedly. "This usually works. Get them laughing and charm their pants right off."

"I'm just curious why you can't be serious."

He cleared his throat. "Sometimes humor is a good defense."

"Do you need to defend yourself against me?"

"You? No. Well, maybe. I don't know." He turned his hands palms up. "It's a habit. I guess I like to keep things light. Keep the other person at bay. Don't reveal too much. Don't open too many doors."

"Oh." Becky's eyes focused on his. He looked down at his food. They picked at their food for several minutes without speaking.

Finally, Carnes wiped his mouth with his napkin and sat back slightly in his chair. "Actually, I'm serious about a lot of things. I still think what I'm doing is important. I believe passionately"—he winced at the word—"in the concept of justice. I get seriously disappointed when the system screws up. I'm very serious about my daughter. Her well-being is the most important thing in my life. The feelings I have for her are"—Carnes coughed slightly—"indescribable." He took a sip of wine. "Is that what you mean by serious?"

"It's a good start," Becky said.

"I'm serious about getting my own act together. I've bounced around the last few years since my divorce—since before then—avoiding any real commitments, any real pleasure, any real pain. I'd like to get to the point where I can have a real relationship." Carnes felt his face grow hot. "I must sound like a guest on Oprah."

"If I eat more, I'll look like Oprah—before her diet."

Carnes stared into her warm blue eyes. "What are you serious about?"

He pounded on his steering wheel in frustration. Was this cop going to spend every minute with her? Did the cop suspect anything? No, he was just a horny bastard. Hadn't a clue. He looked at his watch. 9:27. They would still be eating for a while. Then what? The slut was probably going to take him home. He looked at his hands. They trembled with rage that threatened to burst out through his skin like the creature in the movie Alien.

The psychologist had told him not to be depressed. Don't turn your rage inward. Express it. You'll feel better. He had no fucking idea! Psychology was one of the helping professions. Sure helped him. Now, he didn't hold things in. He didn't get depressed, he got even. What would the psychologist say today?

He'd waited so long to make them pay. He felt a thrill of triumph. The police were helpless sheep. He could lead them wherever he wanted them to go. He checked his watch again. It would have to be another night. He started the car.

Carnes pulled up in front of her apartment.

"Would you like to come up?" Becky smiled shyly.

Carnes looked into her eyes. He was tempted. Abstinence was for the birds. People who cared for each other could sleep together, couldn't they? Still, something special was happening. He didn't want to mess it up. "I'm not sure I'm ready."

Carnes read the quizzical expression in her eyes. Could he tell her about his visit to the sex addicts anonymous meeting? Tell her he was trying celibacy for a while, trying to go slow? Would she understand? Maybe. Still, he didn't want to scare her off. He couldn't chance it.

"I want to be sure it's the right thing and I'm doing it for the right reason."

Carnes saw the confused hurt in her eyes. "Don't get me wrong. I want to. It's just"—he looked out the windshield, his hands gripping the steering wheel—"not time."

Becky placed her hand on his arm. "This is a new one for me." She smiled. "Most of the time, I'm fighting off some guy who's letting his gonads rule his brain. I guess the tables are reversed."

"It's not really like that. My gonads and brain are fighting World War Three. I'd better get out of here before my gonads win."

"OK." She pecked him on the cheek and hopped out of the car. "I *did* have a good time." She slammed the door before he replied and hurried toward her apartment. Her back concealed her face, but Carnes could read the slump of her shoulders. *Shit!* He pulled away.

As he drove he hashed it out. Maybe he was doing this wrong. Should he go back? Should he tell her or should he just sleep with her? She wouldn't reject him then. Of course, that must be the addict side talking. He thought about hitting a bar. There were a few good ones down here off Connecticut. Some female companionship would work wonders. *Who are you kidding? You'll feel like shit again afterward.* But now? Now I'll feel good. One more time wouldn't hurt. *Stop kidding yourself.* A phone booth materialized on his right and he pulled over.

The card was in his wallet. He dialed the number. It rang once, twice, three times. "Hello."

"Hello, Pete?"

"Yes."

"My name is John. I don't know if—" *This is crazy. I don't need—*

"From the SAA meeting the other night?"

"Yes."

"Looking for more decaf?"

Carnes grimaced. "God, no!"

"You want to talk?"

"No." *Then what are you doing on the phone?* "Well, maybe."

"I'm glad you called."

3

James Bardash stood in the doorway of the brick colonial in his T-shirt and jeans. His face was haggard and unshaven, his eyes puffy with sleep. "What can I do for you gentlemen?" he croaked.

"We tried the office and they said you were home sick. May we come in?" Carnes gestured with his hand to include Rodriguez.

"I—I guess so." Bardash stepped back into the doorway to let them enter.

The entrance to the house was impressive: a large, marble-tiled foyer. Planters filled with exotic tropical plants stood guard on either side. An oak stairway started ten feet in front of them and snaked up to the second floor. Carnes looked up toward the balcony that lined the open second floor hall. Sunlight from the window above their heads shone onto a large chandelier of brass and glass that shattered the tight beam of light into thousands of colored fragments that splattered the white walls. The effect reminded Carnes of the view through the cardboard kaleidoscope he got for his fourth birthday.

"Why don't you follow me, gentlemen?" Bardash opened the French doors to their right and walked into a well-lit, oak-paneled room with a desk and a couple of maroon leather chairs. Pale oak cabinets were built into the wall behind the oak desk. Books on accounting and economics created a serious, almost severe atmosphere. Except for a personal computer and telephone, the desk was an empty plane of highly polished wood. Bardash gestured to the padded leather chairs.

"Can I get you anything?"

Carnes and Rodriguez shook their heads.

"Then what can I do for you?" Before they could respond he began to chatter nervously. "I mean, I know it must be something about Victoria. What a tragedy. I still can't understand how anyone—" He pulled out a drawer in his desk and with a flourish produced a tissue. He blew his nose with a trumpeting sound. "Have you officers—" He glanced at Rodriguez. "I assume you're a police officer too?"

"Detective Rodriguez." Rodriguez started to reach out to shake hands, then, seeing the tissue, withdrew his hand rather daintily.

"S—sorry, Detective." Bardash managed an abashed grin. "Summer colds are the absolute worst. Can't remember the last time I had one this bad. Must be from going into air-conditioned buildings—they really keep them too cold—then back out into the heat and humidity. Anyway," he turned toward Carnes, "have you made any progress?"

"A little." Carnes looked for a reaction. There was nothing he could detect. "We're still digging into her past."

Bardash nodded as though he were aware this was standard police procedure. Carnes knew that everyone who watched TV thought they knew police procedure, especially with all the new "true" police shows. Although some of the shows used actual footage, they were far from true. They tended to focus on the rare excitement rather than the mind-numbing routine. TV was interested in the glamor and excitement of the job, not the paperwork, boredom, and frustrations.

"Was Vicky in a sorority?" Carnes asked.

Bardash took off his glasses and pushed his forefingers up the sides of his nose into the corners of his eyes. "Darn sinuses. I took two Sinutab pills just half an hour ago. You ever have one of these sinus things where it hurts so much your teeth ache? God!" He put his glasses back on. "I'm sorry. What was it you were asking?"

"Was Vicky in a sorority?"

"Oh, yeah. Sure. Let me think." He pushed at his glasses. "Yeah, let's see. Of course. Alpha Omega." He glanced at Carnes like a pupil awaiting praise from his teacher. Carnes nodded slightly in encouragement. "Yes, Alpha Omega," Bardash repeated.

"Did you ever go to the sorority, see her there, that sort of thing?"

"Well, I helped her with homework and went to some of their parties."

"What kind of house was it?"

"The house, or the girls?" Bardash's tone was light. He saw that Rodriguez and Carnes were not smiling. "Just a little jest—minuscule actually." He smiled to show he wasn't insulted by their failure to dissolve into hysterics. "The girls were mostly OK. I mean, in any house there are bound to be a few who are stuck-up and won't give you the time of day unless your name is Rockefeller. But all in all, not a bad group."

"So your memories of the sorority are good?" Rodriguez smiled his encouraging, Uncle Pete smile.

"Sure, they were fine." Bardash studied his hand for a moment.

"But?" Carnes asked.

"Well, nothing about the girls, I guess, but I have to say I wasn't too wild about their brother house."

"Brother house?"

"Yes. It's not unusual for a fraternity to be paired with a sorority. They do it for various reasons. Often, they do social stuff together, sometimes charitable works, floats—that kind of thing."

"And you didn't like their brother frat?" Carnes asked.

"'Didn't like' is probably too strong a phrase. It's just that the guys in the house weren't much like me. I mean, I'm not the sort of guy who frats recruited. I'm certainly not a jock—a 'manly man.'" Bardash managed a rather good impression of one of the bodybuilder characters from *Saturday Night Live*. "Chi Phi was sort of a jock house. The guys were always on double or triple probation for drinking or hazing violations. Not exactly a bunch of sensitive intellectuals."

"Did anything happen—anything involving the sorority—that might cause someone to want to kill Vicky all these years later?" Carnes' eyes bore into Bardash like drill bits.

"Not that I know of." Bardash shook his head as though totally mystified. "I mean, it's hard to imagine. What could happen that someone would hold a grudge that long?"

Carnes gazed at Rodriguez, then back to Bardash. "If we knew the answer, we wouldn't be asking you."

"It's just too bizarre. Why? I can't even think of someone she dumped who seemed particularly upset."

"Who did she dump?" Carnes asked.

"Well, I guess 'dump' was the wrong word. Vicky was a nice girl—sweet, sensitive. She never really dumped anyone. Her way was to move you graciously into a 'friend' category or phase you out." He smiled wryly.

"You should know," said Carnes.

Bardash looked stung. He shrugged. "Yeah. I guess I should know."

"Was anyone particularly bitter about being 'phased out'?" Rodriguez asked.

"Not that I know of. Sad, maybe. Mad? I don't think so." Bardash pushed against his eyes. Carnes wondered if the pressure he was relieving was in his sinuses.

"How did you feel?" Carnes asked.

"Rotten. These sinuses—"

"No. I mean about the way Vicky phased you out."

"I thought we discussed this before."

"We're just trying to understand what you meant," Rodriguez said softly.

"It left me sort of empty. Down on myself. Don't get me wrong. We were never 'an item.' But you could say that I hoped for more out of the relationship. Being her buddy—well, it wasn't all I had in mind. She didn't agree."

"Can you think of anything that might have made someone unhappy with other girls in the house?" Rodriguez asked.

"Other girls?" Bardash raised his eyebrows. "Are you saying someone else got killed?" He was either truly surprised or a great actor.

"We're not saying anything." Carnes' tone allowed for no argument. "We're asking."

"Now wait—"

Carnes glared at Bardash.

"OK. Other girls? God. I can't think of anything. I mean, what could make you mad at a whole group of girls?"

"You never heard anything? Someone threatening or maybe just blowing off steam about the sorority?" Rodriguez asked.

Bardash shook his head. He grimaced. "Ouch. Shouldn't do that. Damn sinuses." He focused on Rodriguez. "No, never. Nothing like that. Seems bizarre."

"Ever been in trouble with the law?" Carnes went to the curveball.

Bardash shifted nervously in his chair. His breathing seemed a little faster and more labored. Carnes thought he detected a bit of sweat breaking out on Bardash's forehead. Bardash took off his glasses and rubbed his eyes. "Why," he took a couple of deep breaths, "why d'you ask?"

"How about answering the question," Carnes said.

"It's always better to be straight with us," Rodriguez said softly.

"Well, I can't see that it really has anything to do—"

"You can't?" Carnes' voice was heavy with sarcasm. "You can't see why we would want to know you have a sex offense—"

"I just looked through a damn window—"

"When we're investigating the sex killing of your former girlfriend?"

"She wasn't my former girlfriend. Not really, anyway."

"Just answer the question," Carnes said. Bardash gave them a plaintive look. "Besides, it was a stupid little thing. I mean, most of the guys I know would have done the same thing."

"Maybe." Carnes drew out the word to show skepticism.

"I thought they expunged that from my record."

"I don't know the details of Maryland law," Carnes said, "but it's still in the computer. Maybe they can't use it against you and it isn't available to the general public, but we found it."

"Tell us what happened." Rodriguez used a gentle, encouraging tone of voice.

"Well," Bardash cleared his throat with a long rasp. "It was a stupid little thing. I was just a horny college student. Maybe it was because I didn't have much of a sex life. I knew there were all these cute girls in my apartment complex. Some of them left their curtains or blinds open. I'd swear, some of them got a kick out of doing that. I didn't really think I was doing anyone any harm." He stared at Carnes. "I mean, wouldn't you have done the same thing in my place?"

Carnes decided not to share his answer to that one.

Carnes opened the door to their car. "You buy it?"

"Don't know," said Rodriguez. He glanced back at the house. "Bardash is a little too good. Sure lives nice." He swept his eyes around the yard. "Must have a gardener. Lookit all the flowers. And the house. Gotta be nearly four thousand square feet. Three-car garage—"

"Garage?" Carnes was halfway into the car. He looked over the car roof at Rodriguez. "Heat must be getting to me. The guy owns a '94 Lexus and—"

"You wanna see if he has a Maryland sticker in his back window?"

"You got it." Carnes led Rodriguez across the circular drive toward the garage. He wondered if Bardash was watching them from the window. He fought an urge to look. Let the guy stew. The rust-colored doors to the garage were in the sun. They radiated heat. Carnes and Rodriguez gingerly peered in through the windows, cupping their hands on either side of their eyes.

"There it is," said Carnes. "And if I'm not hallucinating from the heat—"

Rodriguez pressed in beside him. "That's a Maryland sticker in the rear window."

"Yeah. Should we go back in there?" Carnes nodded toward the house.

"The guy's a Maryland grad. You wanna ask him why he's got a Maryland sticker on his car?"

"No. About Anna Durant."

"You really expect he'd tell you anything if he were the killer?"

"No."

"Then let's sit on it a while."

They walked back to the car.

"Think he's watching?" asked Rodriguez.

"Absolutely," Carnes said.

Rodriguez reached into the car and pulled out his notebook. He began scribbling furiously.

"What're you writing?"

"Nothing."

"Nothing?"

"Just giving our friend something to think about."

4

Carnes drove with the window down, arm resting on the door, the warm breeze rippling his shirtsleeve and tickling his armpit. Although it was still early, the temperature was creeping over eighty, promising another day of oppressive heat and humidity. Carnes knew what that meant: people out on the streets, tempers rising, bullets flying, people dying. The D.C. rap.

"So what do you think, partner?" Carnes asked Rodriguez, who was staring blankly ahead of them.

"Huh?"

"What do you think?"

"About what?"

"Well, I wasn't raising any cosmic issues, like whether you think some superior, unknown race of superbeings is the driving force in the universe." Carnes smiled. "You looked like you were deep in thought and I wanted to know where that devious mind was." Rodriguez was the least devious person he knew.

"Actually, I was thinking about fishing. I'm planning a bluefish run down the Chesapeake later this week." Rodriguez' face lit up. "You ever gone bluefishing?"

"No," said Carnes. "Fishing always struck me as boring."

"Then you haven't been out for blues." Rodriguez' eyes had an evangelistic glint. "You should come with us. We charter a boat, bring plenty of beer and food, hit the water early in the morning." He stared out the window. "Nothing fights you like a blue. When you get him hooked, he'll pull on that line until the rod is bent over in half and your forearms ache like sons of guns. Boy are they fighters! You gotta reel the suckers in real slow, let them tire themselves out. They'll flop and fight. Just when you think they've quit, they flop and fight some more. I've seen blues snap line—hell, I've seen them snap the pole right in half." Rodriguez chuckled deep in his throat. "By the time you get one of those suckers on board, you feel like you've fought a war—and won." He smiled. "Then it's 'Miller Time.'"

"The old man and the sea."

"Huh?"

"You're the department's Ernest—no, make that 'Ernesto' Hemingway."

Rodriguez smiled. "It's one of those things you've gotta try."

"I don't know," Carnes said. "Guess I'm not into hunting and fishing. I don't want to sound like some crazy animal activist, but you know—it's different if you're gonna eat them."

"What do you think we do with 'em? Take them to the policemen's ball? 'You know my date, Senora Blue?'" Rodriguez mimicked. "For a smart college kid you're real ignorant. Course you eat them. When you catch them, you put them on ice. Usually, there's some guy on the dock who'll fillet them for a few bucks. I've got a great recipe for bluefish in a beer batter." Rodriguez smacked his lips against his fingertips. "You gotta try it. I tried it out on Ellen—"

"Ellen?"

Rodriguez ignored him. "And she loved it. One bite and I guarantee you'll be hooked."

"Or my money back? I'll think about it," Carnes said. "So you're already cooking for this woman?"

"She likes bluefish."

"Right."

Rodriguez stared into the distance. "A couple more of these cases and I'm going to take my retirement and fish full-time. Maybe I'll buy a boat and run charters for you poor suckers every once in a while." He smiled mischievously. "Heck, I might even give you a small discount for old times."

"You're full of shit." Carnes smiled with real affection. "Last time it was a log cabin in West Virginia. You wouldn't know what to do with yourself if you retired." He snorted. "I give you a week, two weeks tops. You'd be hanging around the bull pen with big hangdog eyes. Of course, that's what you look like anyway."

They drove in silence for a couple of minutes.

"So, what about our friend Bardash?" Rodriguez jerked his thumb back over his shoulder.

"No idea," Carnes replied. "On the one hand, could be what he claims—a frustrated, oversexed kid who did something foolish. On the other, he may be one of the coldest-blooded murderers I've ever met."

"That covers a lot of territory."

"All I know is this killer's someone like him, someone who seems to function normally but is bent."

"Bardash is clean." Rodriguez spoke with absolute certainty.

"Why?"

"Well," Rodriguez held up a finger, "one, his story sounded true. He seemed really embarrassed by it all. Two," he raised a second finger, "I get the wrong vibes—"

"Now you're getting vibes?"

"Well, call it what you want. Intuition?"

"You aren't getting mystic on me."

"Don't give me that," Rodriguez said. "You of all people know exactly what I mean. Cop's intuition."

"Cop's intuition, huh?" Carnes peered at Rodriguez out of the corner of his eye. "I read somewhere—I think it was in *Psychology Today*—that intuition is just the subconscious processing of non-verbal cues." Carnes ignored Rodriguez' derisive snort. "For example, you see his body language, hear his tone, and put all that together to form an impression without even knowing you did it."

"Whatever you say, professor," Rodriguez said. "But whatever it is, I got the feeling." He held up the third finger. "And third, you can't deny that Fitz Pardo hasn't been acting right."

"But—"

"Hold on a sec." Rodriguez raised a hand to Carnes' protest. "Let's try looking at this as a straight domestic murder. Pardo gets carried away with the girl and kills her. You know how easily love turns to hate. He knows he's a suspect so he decides to make us think it's some crazed serial killer. He picks out this Durant girl. Maybe he didn't like her looks. He more or less duplicates the murder of his dear Vicky. Low and behold, it works. He's got us running around like idiots searching for some crazed sorority-hating serial killer."

"It's a theory—a little crazy, but a theory." Carnes peered at Rodriguez. "How do you explain the tip Del got about the guy in a Maryland car? What about the girl killed at the beach?"

"Coincidence. You know how many times we get messed up because some bit of information seems to fit a pattern, but it's just a coincidence. Chances are Del's tipster was only trying to score a few bucks with a story. But even if he was legit, it could've been some guy playing hockey at the Fort Dupont arena or driving through the area to Route 295. The girl could've been a coincidence too. She just met some guy in the bar who got a little carried away."

"Geez," Carnes said. "You're really stretching."

"Got a better theory?" Rodriguez demanded.

"A few. The obvious possibility is that it is Pardo."

"That's what I said—"

"But that he killed the girls because he likes to. It gives him some sense of power." Carnes felt a chill despite the heat. "There's something of the wounded animal in him. I feel the same thing in Bardash. Of course, it still could be someone we don't even know about, some other sick puppy who chose that sorority as his victim. God knows why."

"Great. So you're saying we still don't know jack shit?" Rodriguez raised an eyebrow at his own vehemence.

Carnes laughed. "Or Fred Shit."

5

He'd tossed about the bed, his body gripped by the same dream. Or was it a dream? The images were real—nerve impulses stored in his memory tapes, replayed in his head night after night, terrorizing his sleep. When did the dreams begin again? It was always the same. Lights dimmed. Anxiety gripped his insides like a clenching hand. The smells overwhelmed him: sweat, musk, aftershave, and beer. Glasses clinked, a female voice laughed shrilly, voices whispered in muffled excitement. His heart thumped hollowly like a tribal drum.

"And now, the moment you've all been waiting for." Kevin Cranston's voice. Cranston, a horse-faced, cackling sadist, was the senior responsible for this year's pledge class. "Cranston Productions in association with Chi Phi fraternity and our sisters at Alpha Omega present the Chi Phi Follies." In the darkness, someone turned on the music—a burlesque number with blaring horns and insistent drumbeat. Suddenly, a light blinded him, freezing his half-naked body on the makeshift stage.

"Dance, you bitches," roared out a hoarse male voice. A chorus of hoots and laughter. Moving to the music, trying to find some semblance of rhythm. Right, now bend, up and left, and kick. They'd practiced in regular clothes, not these dresses. He danced, cold and exposed, face and neck hot with humiliation. Beyond the glare they hooted and giggled. A cold shock as a spray of liquid slapped across his chest. Beer. Try to duck. "Dance, you bitches." More beer, then popcorn cascaded down over them. It crunched beneath his feet. Concentrate on the music. Keep pace with the music.

His feet slipped on the splattered stage and he went down hard. The room roared with beery amusement.

"Take it off, take it all off," demanded shrill feminine voices. "Yeah!" A chorus

238

of male and female voices. "C'mon, you bitches." He tried to place the voice. He'd kill her. Another spray of beer. "C'mon, pledges." Cranston's voice this time. "Take it all off."

He was a circus cat cornered in a cage. He roared mutely in frustrated agony. Nothing to do but perform. He began pulling off the costume, ears pounding with the whistles and catcalls. Female and male voices yelled, "Yeah!" More beer. "Take it off, baby!" "Show us what you're made of!" "More skin!"

To either side his fellow pledges discarded their costumes in time to the thunka thunka of the music. He was down to his jock. What was going on? Hooting, laughter. "Take it off." He pulled at his jock. "All right!" a girl yelled. "Look. He did it!" A shriller voice this time. He heard giggles and harsh laughter.

He looked around. The others had stopped dancing. Several were laughing. None of them was totally naked. He was the only one. He tried to run off the stage, but a stinging spray of beer, rough hands, and shouts of derision forced him back. "C'mon, pussy, show us what you've got," growled a voice. "Not much!" yelled a female voice. "Anyone got a magnifying glass?" A chorus of laughter. "Hell, you'd need a microscope," shrilled another. More laughter. He grabbed at some discarded clothes and ran.

Del Clinton sat outside the Hornbake Library with the librarian, Meredith Simon. She sat cross-legged on the bench in a loose-fitting, sleeveless shift. She seemed cool and comfortable despite the hot sun. He longed to take off his suit coat, but he was wearing his Glock semi-automatic. The sweat dripped down his side and spine. Undergraduates in shirts and shorts walked by slowly as though they were enjoying the sun. He returned his gaze to the librarian.

"I really can't think of anything, Detective."

Meredith was twenty-six. She had stylish, dirty-blond hair, an expressive squarish face, and lively hazel eyes. She wore only eye makeup. Her perfect skin was tanned a golden hue. Her lips were thick and sensuous; her nose looked a bit too perfect. When they'd walked out, he'd guessed she was five foot ten or so.

A slight breeze brought no relief. Del decided to remove his coat, Glock or no Glock. He stood up and took it off, folded it carefully, and laid it down next to him. She stared at the semiautomatic in its leather holster. "Sorry, it's hot." He wondered why he felt the need to apologize.

She nodded and pushed a wisp of hair back behind her ear. Something about her gesture conveyed a sense of vulnerability. What a silly thing to think. He just couldn't read all the nuances in white people like he could in blacks. Still, it was hard to reconcile this big, friendly girl with his image of the Alpha Omega girl. He'd been thinking they were all cold, overdressed bitch princesses.

Del asked the usual questions: how well did she know the victims? When had she seen them last? Who were their friends and enemies? Would anyone have a grudge? Anyone who might want them dead? It was all completely unilluminating. Although she had lived in the same galaxy, she apparently orbited around a different sun. He forged on.

"Did anything happen when you were an Alpha Omega that might have made someone—particularly a man—dislike the sorority? Anything that made you uncomfortable?"

"Well," she smiled thoughtfully, "I guess there was plenty that made me uncomfortable. This is a good school, but it's also a party school. I saw lots of people getting drunk and acting sloppy. Sometimes it wasn't pretty." She wrinkled her nose. "And the promiscuity! I think some of my sisters never dated the same guy twice and they slept with all of them." She made a wry face. "It's not that I'm a a prude or anything. It was more a question of scale. Of course, we didn't worry as much about AIDS then. Still, everyone knew about herpes and all sorts of other things."

Del nodded. "Yeah, I know what you mean. But did anybody or any event really stand out in your mind?"

"You mean, like the lowest of the low?" Meredith asked.

Del nodded.

"Well, for me, the lowest of the low was the show that Chi Phi put on for us my sophomore year. It was hell week. Our beloved brother fraternity took all the guys who were pledging and put them in dresses, bras, and panties and had them dance and lip-synch some numbers for us. You know, sort of like the Rockettes." She made a tight face of disgust. "That was the nadir. I felt bad for the guys. Some probably got a kick out of it, but some were humiliated. I left when they were stripping. I heard they stripped down to their jocks. One even took off his jock! Maybe I didn't drink enough first. It was just too crass."

Del felt his antenna quiver. "Were any of the guys really upset? I mean, did any of the guys flip out or anything?"

"Not that I know of. I know some didn't join the frat, but that's always true. Some guys won't put up with the hazing."

"Could you give me a list of the guys who took part in the show?"

"Well, I knew a few of them." She rattled off several partial and complete names and Del scribbled in his notebook. "That's probably all I can remember."

"Well, if you look through any old pictures or yearbooks and come up with any more names, give me a call." Del handed her his card. He didn't think twice about it.

When Carnes got home, Duke greeted him eagerly at the door, whining and dancing from side to side as usual. Carnes had spent a frustrating day calling sorority sisters. He'd learned nothing. He told the dog, "Just a few minutes, boy," then he went upstairs. Avery lay on her side, the covers twisted around her legs. When Carnes kissed her, he smelled soap and Petite Nate perfume. He adjusted the covers around her and Ro Ro.

He changed and went downstairs for Duke's leash. The shepherd jumped in excitement, tongue lolling from side to side. Carnes slipped the chain around the dog's neck and they went out the door for a jog.

He wondered what it would be like adding someone to their family mix. He tried to imagine coming home to Avery and Becky. No—for all his feelings toward Becky, he couldn't really picture it. He jogged past the new town houses. When he'd grown up, Bethesda was the wilderness. Now, even Germantown was filling up. Where did all the people come from?

Carnes had called Becky from the coffee shop. She was locked safely in her apartment. A team had Pardo under surveillance. He watched the dog sniff and mark his turf at a tree. The moon was full. Its ethereal light shimmered through the glowing haze. Not usually a good sign. Over his years in the department, Carnes became convinced that the full moon really did make people act crazy. However, he felt at peace. The werewolves are staying home tonight, he decided.

6

He'd watched her long enough. It was her turn to die. Like the others, she had laughed at him. Her betrayal was a live wire against his skin. She spent too much time with that cop. He wasn't here to protect her now. From the moment he'd seen her, the moment he knew, the anger had built up as though he were a pressure cooker without a relief valve. He had to do something to relieve the pressure or he would burst. He knew how to do that.

He'd watched over her for so long, taken care of her. He could've finished her long ago. He'd hoped she was different—that she wasn't really one of them. He'd been wrong. His body quivered with rage. How much did she know, suspect, and tell? He should've taken her out long ago. The more time she spent with the cop, the greater the risk.

What if she hadn't put it all together? No, he couldn't take a chance. The top of his head would blow off from the pressure. He couldn't wait. This way, he would have peace. He smiled. He'd know soon. It wouldn't take him long. The cops were so stupid. He could turn invisible. This would be easy.

She'd let him in. She'd be happy to see him again. Maybe give him something to drink. She wouldn't suspect a thing. Then he'd pounce. She'd know, but it would be too late.

He felt the throbbing in his head ease a little. She would beg him to stop. He could see her, tied up, eyes bulging with terror as he ran the tip of a knife over her skin. She would tell him everything he wanted to hear. Oh, yes. And she would beg. She'd beg for him to stop the pain. Just like the rest.

He looked at the light in her apartment window. The cop had made a bad mistake, leaving her alone.

* * *

Del Clinton hated working the 3-to-11 shift during a full moon. As usual, the calls came fast and furious: a domestic killing, a police-involved shooting, and two different drug-related street killings. His squad hopped from scene to scene. By the end of his shift his body sagged with exhaustion. As he drove home, he fantasized about slipping between the sheets beside Frances.

When Del opened the door, uneasiness overwhelmed him. He was used to coming home to a dark place, but tonight it was lit like a department store. An overpowering aroma hung in the air. Something with garlic and wine. His salivary glands burst painfully into action and his stomach twisted, reminding him he'd skipped dinner again.

"You look like hell." Frances stood in the doorway to the kitchen.

"What're you doing up?" Del asked. She wore one of her nicest dresses, the low-cut green one she'd worn for Katy's wedding. "What gives?"

She put her arms around his neck and gave him a long, sensuous kiss. "We're celebrating."

"Celebrating?" Del gave her a goofy look. "Celebrating what?"

"The baby." She showed her teeth in the smile that captured his heart when they met at Dynamo Jim's party.

"The baby? What baby?"

"Our baby." She grinned.

Comprehension sank in slowly. His face metamorphosed from a look of puzzlement into a broad grin. "A baby? *Our* baby?"

She nodded.

"When?"

"I think the other night. I had this strange feeling this morning. Actually, it was more like an urge to throw up. I bought one of those test kits at lunch. Took the test this evening and—"

He threw his arms around her, picked her up off the floor, and swung her around until they both fell apart dizzy, laughing like crazed children. "God! I can't believe it! I'm going to be a daddy!"

Frances put her hands on her hips and gave him a sharp look. "Don't forget me."

Del grabbed for her again, and she dodged backward. "Us," he laughed. "We're going to be"—he mulled the word over in his mind—"parents." It sounded fine.

"I still can't believe it," Del muttered. He lay on his back in bed. Frances was on her side next to him, her cheek resting on his shoulder, a leg thrown across his thighs. "When I was a kid, I dreamed this kind of thing. A detective, with a beautiful wife"—he gave Frances a squeeze and she giggled—"living in a nice place, bringing up kids. Maybe I wasn't crazy."

"I wouldn't say that," said Frances sleepily.

7

"Hello." Carnes was thick tongued with sleep.

"Carnes?"

"Yeah?"

"Bryant."

Carnes sat up fully awake. "Yeah, Sarge?"

"Another dead girl."

"Shit." Carnes felt the tight hand of anxiety grip his throat.

"Yeah. Just got the call. They want you at the scene."

The clock read 2:23.

"Where?" Carnes said a silent prayer.

"Gramercy Oaks. Off Kenilworth Avenue near College Park. I got a call from Detective Harrison, PG County. Sounds like your guy."

"Do you have a name for the victim?" Carnes held his breath.

"Meredith Simon."

Carnes sighed. "Give me directions."

Four phone calls and five minutes later, Carnes was roaring over to College Park. He had called Clinton and Rodriguez before contacting the surveillance team watching Pardo. The team reported they'd followed Pardo home from work and sat outside his house ever since. From their vantage point up the street, they had a good view of the front of his house and his garage. His lights went out around 9:30 P.M. Carnes wondered if Pardo really went to sleep at 9:30. Seemed too early. Could he have slipped out the back? Pardo had already given them the slip once.

Carnes looked up Pardo's number in the book and dialed. The phone rang four times, then a voice that sounded like Humphrey Bogart's said, "Of all the answering machines in the world, you gotta call mine," while the music from *Casablanca* played in the background. "Leave a message at the tone sweetheart and I'll get back to you." Carnes hung up. Shit! *Casablanca* had been one of his favorite movies.

The usual cluster of police vehicles filled the parking lot at Gramercy Oaks. Del Clinton and Rodriguez stood near the apartment entrance, talking with a tall, thin white man and a shorter black man both in wrinkled sport coats. The Gramercy Oaks was a cluster of tan town houses with balconies. Trees and neat hedges adorned the front. Pathways ran from the parking lot to the entrances of each building, crisscrossing in the middle.

The tall man stuck out his hand. "Harrison, PG County homicide—Hyattsville." He gestured at the smaller man. "This is Harry Mead. You Carnes?"

"Yeah."

"Crime-lab guys are upstairs. ME's crew is waiting to take her to Baltimore. She's been dead a few hours. Perp left the apartment door open. One of the neighbors came in around one with his girlfriend. Saw the door open and was concerned about burglars. Went in. Got sick on the floor in the hall. Called 911."

"What do we know about the girl?" Carnes asked.

"Meredith Simon's the librarian I talked to earlier today," said Del.

Carnes whistled. "A member of the sorority?"

"Yeah. I talk to her and she's dead a few hours later. A very uncomfortable coincidence."

"May have nothing to do with you," Carnes said. "Our killer may have a list of sorority girls he wants to knock off. Maybe he's working his way through them alphabetically: Benton, Durant, Simon."

"Yeah, but what about the Lynch girl? Wasn't she the first?" Del asked.

"The killer saw her in Ocean City. Something triggered him. He kills her and decides to start on the list."

"Seems to me there were a lot of names between Durant and Simon," Rodriguez said.

"True." Carnes considered this. "Maybe he didn't hate the whole sorority, only a part."

"It's possible," said Rodriguez. "But it seems too much of a coincidence. She turns up dead right after Del talked to her. What are the odds?" He turned to Del. "What do you think?"

"We talked out front of Hornbake, the undergraduate library where she worked. We were out in the open. Anyone could have seen us. I think we have to assume this is no coincidence."

Carnes and Rodriguez agreed.

"So what are the possibilities?" asked Carnes.

Clinton shrugged. "He could have been following her."

"Or just happened by," said Rodriguez.

"Or he was following me," Clinton finished.

"He might work or go to school there," guessed Carnes.

"Or he's keeping tabs on our investigation," Clinton said.

Rodriguez nodded. "But there're other possible explanations."

"I was afraid you'd say that," Carnes replied.

"She might have known him. Say, she didn't know he was the killer—"

"I'm pretty sure she didn't," said Clinton.

"OK, then. She knew him as a friend and told him about your conversation."

"Could be," said Clinton.

"Did she give you anything?" Carnes asked.

"Nothing concrete."

"Why would he silence her then?"

"Well, she told me some stories about the sorority and their brother fraternity. I'd asked her to identify some of the brothers," Clinton said.

"So it could be one of the brothers?" asked Carnes.

Mead had been listening. "Let me get this straight. Either he saw you talking to her or it's someone she knew and she told the guy, quite innocently, and 'boom' that was it." Mead rubbed his bristle-topped head.

Rodriguez nodded. "It's gotta be one or the other."

"Unless there was an intermediary." Carnes saw the looks of puzzlement and held up his hand. "Say she called a friend who told our killer. There might be someone else—maybe innocent—who was in between."

"Well," said Harrison, "we'll try to track down everyone she talked to in the last twenty-four hours." He turned to Clinton. "Do I have the timing right?"

"Since early afternoon yesterday. Yeah."

A crime-scene technician carrying an oversized sample case came out. "We're pretty much done up there. You guys can go back in if you want."

* * *

Carnes experienced a weird feeling of déjà vu. It wasn't that Mere
dith Simon's apartment looked anything like Vicky Benton's. The apartment had one bedroom. A long bookshelf constructed from boards and
bricks ran the length of the living room. Although Carnes read serious
fiction, his taste ran more to espionage thrillers and science fiction.
Carnes perused the titles on the shelf. Classics, references, literary jour-
nals. This was not a woman who read romance novels. On the other
hand, he noted a large collection of CDs, mostly rock groups he'd
scarcely heard of. This place felt different than Vicky Benton's apartment.
There was nothing particularly frivolous about it. Still, the sense that he'd
been here before stayed with him.

The bedroom was small. A full-sized bed with an antique wooden headboard with pineapples at the top of the finials filled most of the room.
Meredith Simon's body stretched across the bed. Someone had pulled
her arms and legs toward the finials. Blood was everywhere.

Carnes dragged his eyes from the carnage. Look for the big picture.
A small dresser and a tall wood veneer bookshelf—the kind you bought
cheap and assembled yourself—had been shoehorned into the room.
The shelf bulged with books. In contrast to the classics in the living room,
her bedroom seemed to house a good selection of best-sellers. "You think
she shelved all the books by their call numbers?"

"Yeah." Harrison chuckled.

Carnes looked back at the body. "How do you read it?"

"God. I hate puns." Harrison shook his head in feigned disgust. "Especially at this hour."

"I have to put up with this *all* the time," said Rodriguez.

Carnes feigned hurt. "Who gets the worst of that deal?"

Rodriguez turned to Harrison. "So what do you think?"

"Best guess—he stunned her or knocked her out in the living room,
then dragged her in here. Tied her to the headboard with clothing."

Carefully avoiding the worst of the blood, they eased forward. Harrison pointed at her face. "Looks like socks stuffed in her mouth." A great
deal of blood had darkened the sheets next to her face. Strips of a cot-
ton dressing gown hung from her shoulders, exposing pale skin violated
by scores of lacerations. Pantyhose cut into her throat. Her eyes bulged
slightly. A dark stain of dried blood ran from her nose down her cheek,
joining the blood pooled beside her face.

"Any more thoughts?" Carnes asked Harrison.

"Probably strangled with the pantyhose. But with all these cuts she might have died of shock or from one of the stab wounds. Medical examiner's call." Harrison shook his head from side to side. "I haven't seen anything this nasty in twenty years with the department. What do you make of the cuts?"

"Trying to get information," said Clinton.

"Maybe." Harrison shrugged. "Or maybe he was just having fun." He shrugged "See her nipples? Bit the hell out of her. Almost chewed through one."

"That's consistent with our other cases," said Rodriguez. "What do you think, John?"

"Any signs of sexual assault?" Carnes asked.

"It's a good bet," said Mead.

"What's all the blood near her face from?" asked Clinton.

Harrison stared. "Don't know." He reached into his pocket and pulled on surgical gloves. He studied the girl's face, then carefully pulled the wadded socks out of her mouth. "Shit!"

Carnes moved closer. "What is it?"

Harrison pointed. "He cut out part of her tongue."

"Motherfucker," Clinton said.

"Why would he cut out her tongue?" asked Mead.

"She talked to Del," said Carnes.

"But what'd he do with her tongue?" asked Harrison.

Carnes stared at the body. Amongst the carnage that had been Meredith Simon, he could make out a small trail of blood droplets leading down her chest, over her stomach. "I think I know." He pointed at the fringe of hair between her legs.

"Damn," said Mead.

"I think John's right," said Rodriguez. "The medical examiner should get a little surprise."

Harrison shook his head. "Thought I'd seen everything."

Del Clinton stood aside from the others, a grim look on his face.

"It's not your fault, Del." Carnes put a hand on Clinton's arm. "You had no way of knowing."

Rodriguez turned to Mead. "How'd he get in?"

"No sign of forced entry," said Mead. "So we assume she knew him well enough to let him in. Either that or he had one hell of a good con going."

"You find the panties she was wearing?" Carnes asked.

"I didn't see them anywhere," said Harrison. "Did you?"

Mead shook his head. "It's possible they're in the bedding or something. We'll look."

Carnes glanced around the room. Fingerprint dust residue coated virtually every available surface. He wondered if they'd find any prints on the body. "Can we look around now?"

"Sure," said Harrison. "But I can already tell you the only weird thing you'll find."

"What's that?" asked Rodriguez.

"In the bathroom," said Harrison.

On the bathroom mirror, the killer had left his message in dark red lipstick: a horseshoe-shaped omega and the words *ex libris.*

"Your killer is quite the joker," said Mead.

"What do you mean?" asked Rodriguez.

"Ex libris. It's sort of a play on words. I went to Catholic school as a kid. Learned some Latin. Ex libris means 'from the library of.' She was a librarian, wasn't she?"

Clinton nodded. "An ex-librarian."

"From the library of Alpha Omega," said Carnes. "All the victims we know about were Alpha Omegas."

"Makes sense, in a sick kind of way," said Harrison. "Ex-librarian. From the library of Alpha Omega." He looked at the three grim D.C. homicide detectives. "We're not dealing with a dummy, are we?"

"No," said Carnes. "Whatever else he may be, he isn't stupid. One of our chief suspects is a lawyer who used to go out with one of the victims."

"A lawyer. He'd know some Latin," said Mead.

"And he may have given us the slip tonight," Carnes said. "I called his number before I came. Got his answering machine."

"Doesn't prove he wasn't there," Harrison noted. "Lots of folks, particularly rich folks, can't be bothered to answer their phones, especially at two in the morning."

"Well, whether it's Pardo, Bardash, or someone else, this guy is shoving it in our faces," said Clinton. "He's telling us he's much smarter than we are."

"So far, he's right," said Carnes.

8

"If you were a crazed, woman-hating killer with a thing about a sorority, who would you be?" Carnes asked.

Dr. Crenshaw smiled slightly. "Our killer enjoys his work. He is compulsively careful. He doesn't seem to leave fingerprints or other evidence, just his mark. Highly intelligent. Seems to know police procedures.

"It could be your lawyer. But serial killers often are interested in what the police do. They study the police. Sometimes they follow their own crimes in the press, keeping clippings or videotapes of stories. Some come back to the scene. Others offer assistance to the press or police. This is all an ego-related thing. The power excites them. That's why some collect trophies. Your killer has collected the victims' panties and hair?"

"Yeah."

"And he leaves a signature. This Simon killing is a little different. The way he used the knife—well, it seems more methodical, like torture. I'd say he questioned her to find out what she told your Detective Clinton. But he went beyond that. He got a kick out of it. It's like he's prolonging the act. More mutilation. More pain. Of course we won't know for sure until his next victim. Sometimes the ritual evolves."

"Let's hope this is his last victim."

Crenshaw nodded. "Of course. Anyway, it's different from his ritual in the other killings. As I said, let's assume he tortured her. Then, when he was done, he completed his normal—maybe normal isn't the right word—ritual. The part with the tongue bothers me though."

"Why?"

"It's too obvious. He's virtually telling you he saw her talking to Detective Clinton."

"It makes sense." Carnes sighed. "He knew her. Or he saw them talking. It made him feel vulnerable. Maybe he thought she knew something."

"Right." Crenshaw tepeed his hands before him. "Your killer is getting more stressed. You're putting pressure on him. He feels the stress, but he also enjoys jerking you around. Maybe he's losing control a little. Getting careless. He's given you a clue. There's a chance he'll just disintegrate." Crenshaw threw his fingers apart, pantomiming an explosion. "Of course, there are other possibilities. I've seen cases where the serial killer moved somewhere else when the pressure increased. Gives the police a devil of a time. He settles down somewhere new and starts over again. Sometimes, it takes a long time before the police know they're dealing with a serial killer. They may never see the link to his actions in another city. Remember the Green River killer?"

"Sure."

"That's why the FBI started their database on such killers."

"So what's your guess? Is he going to take off?"

"I don't think so. He has a mission. As long as there are sorority sisters he wants to kill, he'll stay around and finish the job. I think he's getting more vicious, more out of control. He'll make more mistakes."

"Well, if he knew Simon, he may've already made a big one."

"True." Crenshaw drew in a deep breath. "But I must caution you, Detective. There are no guarantees in this business. He could go anywhere he'd find the sorority girls. Might even branch out to the rest of the female population."

"That's a nice thought."

"I know. Is the largest concentration of sorority members here?" asked Crenshaw.

"Yeah, although there are plenty in New Jersey and New York."

"Well, if I were you, I'd keep the pressure on. There's some risk, but it's possible the pressure will get to him and he'll do something stupid. Remember that shotgun killer? After months of nighttime killings he finally went out in daylight, streets full of cops, and began shooting. That was all it took."

"I remember."

"That's an example of what I mean—the stress gets to be too much. The killer's compulsion finally overrides all his controls. Maybe the mask of normality he shows the rest of the world will begin to crack.

"There are probably two schools of thought on what happens. Some think as the pressure mounts the killer needs the quick good feeling he gets from killing more and more. The other view is that, maybe at some subconscious level, the killer wants to get caught. Just remember, this is a compulsive thing and the killer doesn't fully control it."

Carnes nodded. He understood compulsions. He tried to imagine himself as the killer, drawn by his compulsion to torment and kill. Was the killer in conflict too? Or had he totally given himself over to his impulses? Were his controls functioning at all? Did he want to stop?

Carnes realized Crenshaw was speaking. "But I'd guess—and you have to understand this is only a guess—that our man needs to kill more. Part of it is some sort of revenge fantasy. He's singled out this sorority as his target.

"But there's more. He needs the feeling of power he gets from instilling fear and pain, controlling their lives. Killing is like a drug for him. He craves it as desperately as the lowest heroin addict craves a fix. Makes him feel stronger, in control of his life. He lives for that feeling of control, of power."

Carnes nodded. "So you're saying the stress of our getting closer to him may drive him to be more active?"

"I'm afraid so." Crenshaw sighed. "I wouldn't want to be an Alpha Omega."

9

Maria Martinez greeted Rodriguez with a warm hug. Entering her brightly decorated little apartment always lifted Rodriguez' spirits. He'd met Maria at a Columbia Road street festival several years ago. Her broad face was pleasant although not beautiful; she was brightly dressed and had laughing eyes and a buoyant spirit. She immediately captured his attention. In the wake of his divorce, Rodriguez had tried to woo her.

She was fiercely independent though and not ready to be a policeman's woman. Over time, their relationship metamorphosed into a comfortable friendship. He could talk to her about his family, church activities, his work. Maria was active in many of the city's Hispanic organizations. She became the hub of his information network within the Hispanic community.

"You seem well," Maria said. She looked him over with an appraiser's eye. "There is something different, my friend. If I were to guess, I'd say there is a woman in your life."

Rodriguez looked sheepish. "I *am* dating someone."

"Bueno!" She hugged him again. "I have something else to make you happy. I found you someone who used to work at Chi Phi." She spoke in the rapid cadence common in Chile. "This is Rosa Suarez."

Rosa was a small woman. Although she might be only in her late twenties, she looked as worn as an old piece of leather furniture. She cast her eyes downward with the shyness of long habit. Rodriguez knew many South American women who were uncertain about speaking English and worked at menial jobs. They learned not to offend. They were used to being invisible. Rosa had that look. He took her hand warmly in greeting. Her hand felt strong but rough from years of manual labor and exposure to detergents.

He spoke in his slightly accented Spanish. "It is a pleasure to make your acquaintance. Tell me what you have told Maria."

She transformed before his eyes, standing straighter and smiling broadly. Maybe she hadn't expected a policeman to speak in Spanish. "It was several years ago." She ticked off the years on her fingers. "Five, maybe six years, I think. I worked cleaning the fraternity house and serving meals. It was before the university cracked down on—" She used a phrase that roughly translated as "hazing."

"These fraternity boys were rough. Many football players and athletes, I think. They liked to make new boys do things. Make them look foolish. Once, they took a boy to Ocean City and left him on the beach with no clothes or money and told him he had one day to get back. They hit new boys on their bare bottoms with paddles they made. They'd send new boys on scavenger hunts to steal girls' panties, diaphragms. Loco.

"The boys were really proud of these silly things. They told stories about them all the time. I don't think they knew how much English I understood. I was shy and spoke few words." She smiled proudly and switched into English. "Now, I speak good English to work in clothing store." She spoke slowly, carefully enunciating each word.

Rodriguez smiled encouragingly. "What about Alpha Omega?"

"*Si.*" Rosa returned to Spanish. "I was helping at breakfast one Sunday. Before church," she added with a guilty look. "The boys were laughing and talking about their latest trick. They took their new boys who wanted to be in the fraternity—"

"Pledges?" asked Rodriguez.

"*Si,* pledges." She repeated the word in English, and Rodriguez liked the way the word rolled off her tongue. "They took them to that sorority. They made them dress up in girls' clothes, do a song and dance, and strip to their—I think they call them jocks. The boys thought it was very funny. I think they say"—she switched to English—"a hoot." She went back to Spanish. "They started making all kinds of jokes about it. But some of what they said did not sound very funny."

Rodriguez nodded.

"They teased the new boys about their dancing and singing. Wanted them to act more sexy. They laughed about one boy who went loco—they say 'freaked out'—after the show. This boy, he ran out of the house. Very upset. Very crazy. They thought this was very, very funny. Big joke."

Rodriguez realized he was clenching his jaw muscles. "What happened to the boy?"

"I don't think he ever came back," Rosa said. "I heard the story many times later when they drink beers and party."

"Do you know the boy's name?"

"No."

"Do you know what he looked like?"

"There were many boys who came around the house before it happened, those 'pledges.' It must have been one of them. But I don't think I'd know them now."

Rodriguez sighed. "If I could get some photos of boys from the school, from that time period, would you come in and look at them?" He thought about how many hundreds—it might even be thousands—of boys that might include.

Rosa's face was tense. She turned to Maria, a question in her eyes.

"Rosa is waiting for her visa status to be"—Maria paused while she searched for the right word—"clarified. Would there be any, uh, negative outcome if she came in to look at pictures?" Maria asked.

Rodriguez knew hundreds of illegals who either entered the United States after the amnesty program, or hadn't known what to do during the program. His church guided these people through the bureaucratic maze that led to legalization. "No, of course not. This is between us. We can do it here if you like."

"*Si,*" Rosa said. "Thank you. I look at pictures."

10

The department brass was there—everyone short of the chief of police anyway. Carnes figured the chief must have an important golf game with some politician or he'd be here too. Malcolm Randolph, the chief of the Criminal Investigations Unit, had greeted them when they came in and was now ensconced behind his desk. Despite the poorly functioning air-conditioning, Randolph looked cool and collected. He seemed ready for an inspection. His black shoes shone, his jacket fit him perfectly, and his thinning hair was precisely slicked down. Even his thick eyebrows seemed manicured. No hair dared be out of position.

Captain Fletcher buzzed around Randolph like a waiter in a fine restaurant. He had just brought Randolph a Coke—Carnes noticed he didn't ask anyone else if they wanted something to drink—and hovered nearby as though ready to swoop in and top off Randolph's glass every time he took a sip. Lieutenant Rogers and Sergeant Bryant watched the spectacle uncomfortably.

"Sit down." Randolph sounded like a parent speaking to a particularly exasperating child.

"Yes, sir." Fletcher scurried over to a seat. Carnes caught the amusement in Rodriguez' and Clinton's eyes.

"Detective Carnes, you are the primary on this one?" Randolph asked.

"Yes, sir, on the Benton case. Del is primary on Durant."

Carnes knew that Randolph liked the formalities. Randolph was old school. He had trained in the army's elite Criminal Investigations Division and served in Korea before joining the force. He had distinguished himself as a detective and worked his way up through the chain of command. The rumor mill said Randolph possessed a photographic memory. Everything Carnes had seen supported that claim.

Randolph had advanced on pure competence and hard work, not political acumen. He was a no-nonsense boss who demanded proper decorum, loyalty, and discipline, but he showed loyalty to his men in return. These characteristics made him an endangered species in the department.

"I've been getting regular reports"—Randolph nodded at Fletcher—"so I won't ask you to go over the whole thing. But I want an update on this new killing and I want to hear what your game plan is."

Randolph liked a tight, direct briefing, so Carnes gave him a concise account of what they knew and what they suspected about the death of Meredith Simon.

"So you think this one's a little different," Randolph said. "Like the killer wanted to know what Simon told Clinton."

"That's our best guess. The PG folks are checking out all of her friends, acquaintances, et cetera," said Carnes.

"What about the two investigators, Harrison and Mead?"

"They seem competent, sir. Very cooperative. They've worked with MPD homicide before and understand we need to work together on this one."

"I've had two press inquiries about the possible link to the other killings. One from Eyewitness News, one from the *Post*. The chief wants me to respond." Randolph smiled. As long as the crime was unsolved, the lower echelon would respond to the press. When the case was solved, the chief would be holding press conferences and interviews until he was hoarse. "Will it give you heartburn if I confirm it?"

Carnes studied their faces. Rodriguez raised an eyebrow. Clinton shrugged. Randolph knew they were already under pressure; the press tie-in would torque it up a notch. On the other hand, media attention might bring out a witness who knew something. Besides, Crenshaw had suggested ratcheting up the pressure on the killer. A little press would certainly have that effect. "I guess not," said Carnes. "Maybe some publicity on the link would get someone out there thinking. We might even put this on *Crimesolvers*."

Randolph nodded. "I was thinking the same thing." He turned to Fletcher. "Have these men prepare bulletins I can use. I want enough facts to get the media's interest and to get possible witnesses thinking. Hold back enough so we can tell the real tipsters from the crazies."

"How many men do you have working on this?"

Fletcher squirmed uncomfortably. "Just these men on the direct investigation, sir. We've used others for surveillance, lab work, and canvasing, of course."

Sergeant Bryant cleared his throat.

"Sergeant?" Randolph asked.

"I've been using the rest of the men from the squad to help out as needed, sir. But you know how these cases can get balled up if you have too many people tripping all over each other."

"True." Randolph nodded. "But I want other detectives to help out screening calls, checking out the stories. I want these men free to follow their primary leads." He turned to Carnes. "You satisfied with the surveillance on your suspect?"

"Uhm—no, sir." Carnes explained their concerns that Pardo could have slipped out the back door the night Meredith Simon was killed.

Randolph nodded. "I'll see that you get a full surveillance team. Any other suspects we should have under surveillance? This Bardash fellow?"

Carnes looked at Rodriguez and Clinton. Each shook his head yes.

"All right." Randolph checked his watch. "I'm going to ask the sex squad to put a couple of people on this." He held up his hand. "I know you already pulled files. I'll send them over to the FBI's behavioral sciences unit at Quantico if necessary. Humor me on this. Walk over and give them an update."

"Yes, sir," Carnes said.

"Have you spoken to the Bureau's profilers?"

"I've been working with Dr. Crenshaw," Carnes replied. "We also have a request in to Quantico for possible matches. So far, our killer doesn't fit the pattern of any known serial killer."

"Crenshaw." Randolph raised a bushy eyebrow and smiled. "I've used him myself. Good man—a bit eccentric, but he knows his stuff. As good as anyone at the Bureau."

Randolph stood up and looked at Fletcher. "I want daily updates, twice daily if anything breaks. You need any help, call me."

"Yes, sir."

"Anything else?" Randolph glanced at his watch.

"No, sir," they chorused.

"Would you like more Coke, sir? Can I clean your boots, sir?" Rodriguez snorted. "If Fletcher kissed up to him any more, I would have puked." He shook his head. "Retirement looks better all the time. Won't be long before the Fletchers are running the whole department."

"I think Randolph feels the same way," said Clinton.

Carnes studied the pad where he'd been making a list of things to do. "This all keeps coming back to the University of Maryland." Carnes tapped the eraser of his pencil on the desk. "There's got to be another angle, something to check there."

"Well, Harrison's collecting all the pictures he can get to show my witness—yearbooks, fraternity pictures. He'll call me and I'll stop by to pick them up. Maybe he'll have some ideas," said Rodriguez.

"What about the car my source reported?" Del asked. "We got a printout about three inches thick of Japanese economy cars, thousands of names."

"How about if we limit it to College Park, Hyattsville, and the bordering towns?" asked Carnes.

"Heck, it's still going to be a zillion names," said Rodriguez.

"Well, maybe we'll find a name we know," said Del.

Carnes slapped his hand on the desk. "God, I'm stupid! The guy had a Maryland sticker, right?"

Clinton nodded.

"What about University of Maryland parking permits? They must have a list and descriptions of the cars that have permits."

"Makes sense," said Rodriguez. "But it's going to be thousands more names."

"Well, say we check out the last two years. It's still gotta be less than we get from Maryland DMV. Who knows? Maybe they have some computer jock who can search for a specific type of car."

"How certain was your informant about what he saw?" asked Rodriguez.

"Pretty certain, but remember, this is secondhand." Del shrugged. "Hell, I know it's a long shot, but what do we have to lose?"

11

Becky Granite stared at her phone. She'd called Carnes twice now and been told, "He's out on the street." She hadn't left a message. Was he trying to duck her? She hadn't handled things well the other night. She'd felt hurt when he turned her down. How stupid could she be? He'd paid her the ultimate compliment. He'd told her he wanted to develop a real relationship with her before they had sex. Isn't that what she wanted?

Did he mean it, or was this his way of backing away from her? She reviewed the evening. Had she done anything to scare him off? She didn't think so. Maybe she'd pushed too hard, asked too many questions, made him reveal too much. Most guys seemed to get antsy about that.

Becky tried to focus on her work, but her mind kept wandering. In elementary school, her science teacher used a demonstration to teach the class about electricity. The class stood in a big circle around an old hand-cranked generator, holding hands except for Becky and the boy next to her. After the teacher cranked for a moment he said, "Now!" and they reached out to hold hands. A jolt of electricity made them pull back and drop their hands. Maybe that's all that happened last night.

The phone rang. Carol Bromley. Carol spoke in the breathy whisper she used when she called from her desk and didn't want to be overheard. "We going to Barnstormers tonight?"

"I don't think I'm really up to it."

"Oh, come on. Don't be an old poop."

"No, I'm really not in the mood."

"Something wrong?"

"I can't talk now."

"OK, then Barnstormers after work." Carol giggled.

Becky sighed. "Good-bye, Carol." She hung up.

"Where do I have to go to get the list?" Carnes asked.

Jim Grayson sucked in his lip. "Hmm . . . sounds like a tough job. There're probably hundreds of employees and maybe thousands of students with cars meeting that description. You have anything else to go on, like out-of-town plates or something?"

Carnes shook his head.

"Then what are you gonna do, question everyone on the printout?"

"I don't know. Maybe somebody will have a record or an obvious connection to the victim. We'll have to see what we get."

"Sounds pretty tough. Any way I can help?" Grayson asked enthusiastically.

"You've been a big help already," Carnes said. "Maybe I'll think of something later. For right now, just tell me who to see."

Grayson pulled open his desk drawer and placed a directory on his desk. He flipped the pages. "This is it." He pulled a page off a notepad on his desk, wrote something down, and handed the paper to Carnes. "Parking office is across Route 1." He gave directions. "Opposite the Ag building—you know, where they sell the ice cream? Ask for Ms. Moriarity. She'll tell you what they can do."

"Thanks. As usual you've been a big help." Carnes extended his hand to Grayson, who gripped it firmly.

"My pleasure."

Madeleine Moriarity was a short, chunky woman in her late thirties or early forties. She wore her hair in a short cut that emphasized her round moon of a face. Other than some mascara, she didn't appear to be wearing any makeup, but a floral perfume made Carnes take shallow breaths. Carnes believed that clothing should accentuate the positive and hide the negative. Apparently, she either did not agree or she'd grown recently and hadn't updated her wardrobe. Her maroon blouse bulged open at the buttons, and the tight yellow skirt showed several inches of beefy thigh.

Moriarity studied Carnes' credentials with bored bureaucratic eyes, then looked up. "Out of your jurisdiction, aren't you?" Her voice sounded like a nail on a chalkboard.

"New York?" he asked.

"Long Island," she corrected.

Carnes tried his most charming smile. "Suffolk County?"

"Nassau." A look of triumph crossed her face. "And you still haven't answered my question."

"Yes, I'm from D.C., but we're working with the PG County police who're investigating the death of that library employee." She studied him as though he were an insect and she was deciding whether to smack him with a flyswatter or spray him with Raid.

"You can check with Detectives Harrison or Mead. They're the primary investigating officers," Carnes offered.

"The number?"

Carnes paged through his notebook and read off the number. She flipped over a white document on the counter titled "Parking Application" and wrote down the number, her pen making scratching sounds. "Wait here," she commanded, then walked back to a desk in the corner.

Carnes watched from the other side of the pockmarked counter while she sat and dialed the number. She glared at him, then turned so she faced away toward the wall. She talked on the phone for several minutes, occasionally glancing back at him as though checking to see if he'd climbed over the counter and was ransacking her desk. He caught only a few words: "D.C.," "he claims," "I'm busy." Finally, she put down the phone and walked back over. She smiled a frozen little bureaucratic smile.

"All right. They said I should cooperate with you. Whattayawant?"

Carnes explained.

She stood, hands on her hips, glaring at him. "D'you see fifteen people working here? I don't have the time to do stuff like this—"

"It's very important," Carnes said.

"Yeah." She sighed. "Everything's so important. Always is. You know, nobody's ever stepped up to that counter and told me that their problem was so trivial it hardly merited my attention." She snorted. "Now that'd be the day. You'd have to pick me up off the floor."

"Look—"

She held up a hand. "Don't 'look' me. I don't like your tone of voice or your attitude. I've taken shit from the best and worst of them. Nobody intimidates me."

"Intimidate you?" Carnes breathed slowly. "All I was trying to say is—your assistance might help us break this case. We want to get this guy before he kills again."

"Yeah, yeah."

"You could save a life." Carnes wondered if she would care.

"Yeah, sure. I'll get a medal from the president or a Nobel Prize." She sighed. "OK. I've got a student assistant coming in later in the day. *If* it's not a zoo, and *if* my boss agrees, I'll have her run your printout."

Carnes gritted his teeth into what he hoped was a charming smile. "Thank you."

"Leave your number. I'll have her call you when it's ready." She stuck out her hand. Carnes retrieved a card from his jacket pocket like a magician performing sleight of hand and placed it in her palm. She didn't crack a smile, just glared at it for a second and returned to her desk. She glanced back as though to say, you still there?

"Thanks," Carnes said. *It's been a pleasure.*

12

Carnes leaned forward and let the hot air blow across his sweaty back. No air-conditioning again. The radio reported the temperature was in the nineties and the humidity was nearly as high. According to the weatherman, another inversion was raising the misery index in the nation's capital. Typical summer weather. These hot summer days were busy ones for homicide because when the citizenry of the District got hot and uncomfortable, they liked to shoot each other.

When Carnes was younger, people got hot in the summer and their patience melted away, or they might punch somebody who annoyed them enough. Now, everyone carried artillery. Shooting somebody terminated their annoying behavior very effectively. Besides, pulling a trigger took very little energy. No sense getting hotter in a fistfight when you could pull a trigger.

The radio squawked, dispatching some scout cars to an armed robbery. Carnes couldn't imagine where a robber got the energy on a day like this. The miracles of modern street drugs. He turned off Massachusetts and down Fifth Street and cruised through Chinatown. He drove past the old Superior Court buildings and the FOP club to Indiana, turned left, and angled into a space across from headquarters. He picked up a cold can of Coke on the way to the office. By the time he reached his desk, condensation poured off the sides of the can.

Clinton and Wiley sat at their cluttered desks poring over large chunks of a computer printout. Rodriguez was on the phone. A D.C. metropolitan-area map was pinned to the wall. Carnes peered over Rodriguez' shoulder and saw black check marks in the left margin beside some of the entries. Carnes plopped into his chair. "What a miserable day."

"Hell, at least you ain't been riding a desk chair all morning." Wiley slapped at his rump.

"Yeah, you could've been listening to Wes grumble," Clinton said.

"Fuck you."

"I'm man enough if you're—"

"Time out." Carnes held up his hand. "It's too hot."

He pulled up the flip tab and listened to the cool hiss. He sipped the Coke. Almost instantly, his energy level rose.

Rodriguez hung up. "What?" He looked toward Carnes like an eager kid.

"Nothing yet," said Carnes. He described his encounter with Madeleine Moriarity. "Lady makes Wes look like a pussycat."

"The bitch probably needs a good fuckin'," commented Wiley.

"You haven't seen her yet," Carnes said.

"He'd do anything to get out of going through that printout," Clinton joked.

"Maybe Wes would like her." Carnes described Moriarity. "It would be like the mating of killer whales."

"Fuck you!"

Carnes turned to Clinton. "Anything?"

"Not yet. We're just trying to pin down the ones within a ten-mile radius of College Park. Heck, it looks like half the state of Maryland. We haven't even begun to hit the District yet. This could take a week or more." He reached over to the printout. "You want a couple of pages?"

Carnes shook his head. "Randolph'll get us help with this. Ask the sergeant. I've gotta go over to sex crimes and meet with Len Dailey. We're running through more old files. Maybe we can find names to cross-check against your list."

"Knock yourself out," Wiley grunted.

Carnes turned back to Rodriguez. "What about this cleaning woman of yours? Has she looked at pictures yet?"

"No. Harrison should have some yearbooks this afternoon, though. I'm going to run by Maria's with them tonight."

"Let me know what you learn."

13

Lenore Dailey was slim but she had curves in all the right places. Her long black hair framed a model's delicate features in a face the color of rich cocoa. Her dark eyes conveyed a determined intelligence. A picture of her husband, a captain in the Third District, and their two angelic kids graced the wall next to the plaque commending her for "extraordinary performance" of her duties.

Carnes had known Len Dailey for a long time. During his early years on the force, he worked a brief rotation in vice. When he wasn't cruising for hookers or acting as a decoy in the male cruising zones, he'd backed up Len. She was single then and went by her maiden name, Barnwell. Len would stand around in prostitution areas waiting for johns to offer her money for her favors. Once the offer was made, she'd give a prearranged signal and Carnes would swoop in to make the arrest.

Lenore's looks made her a very successful decoy. In fact, one commissioner refused to find johns guilty when she was the decoy. To the astonishment of everyone in court, he said it was unfair to use a woman with her looks as a decoy because no man could resist. Certainly, Carnes hadn't. But their relationship—could he even call it that?—was like a fireworks display: explosive, entertaining, and short lived. Eventually, she had married a rising lieutenant named Kenneth Dailey.

"I've pulled together some files for you to look at—everything with any elements that seem to fit your guy."

Carnes looked at her blankly.

Len gave Carnes the look a teacher might give a student whose mind was obviously wandering. "What did I say?"

"Hmmmn." Carnes tried to look contrite. "Sorry."

"Did you hear a word I said?"

"Sure. I guess I was just reminiscing."

"Shouldn't take more than a fraction of a second."

Carnes held up his hand and smiled. "But it *was* a pleasant fraction of a second."

"You must have Alzheimer's."

"How's married life treating you?"

"Can't complain. How's Avery?"

"Great."

"Ever gonna settle down?"

"I'm working on it."

"I'll believe that when I see it." She smiled. "Like teaching an old dog new tricks."

"I'm good at tricks." Carnes grinned. "But I'm working on the dog part."

"Do tell."

"Well, I'm sort of seeing someone."

"One someone?"

"Yeah."

"Well, that's a step in the right direction. You find Jesus?"

"I didn't know he was lost."

"You know, if you found Jesus you might find yourself."

"You joined the clergy and didn't tell me?"

"No. You can't work in sex crimes without thinking about God. Don't you ever wonder about why things happen?"

"I used to. I decided that God was on extended vacation. He's found some nice tropical island and he's drinking a piña colada and laughing at us right now."

"I can't accept that."

"Different strokes."

"You're hopeless." Dailey shrugged her surrender. "You want to see these files?"

"Sure."

"We had to dig deep for these." She held up a file. "This creep was in for a second-degree sex offense. Worked as a custodian at the University of Maryland and got canned for bothering the coeds. Didn't learn; just moved on to UDC. We had him on a couple of rapes there, but the victims didn't want to testify. I guess I understand it. They're just college kids. So the prosecutor took the plea to the lesser included offense." She slapped the file down on the desk.

"This one used to hang with hookers. Liked to tie them up and gag them. Couple of times he got a bit carried away. Burned them with cigarettes, choked them a little, came in their faces, then split, leaving them tied up. Did three or four that we know about. Some pimp didn't like it and beat him real bad. A little street justice. We arrested him on various assault-related charges. All the hookers disappeared before the trial. No witnesses, no case. We gave him a lecture about not tying anyone up and released him. By the way, he's a local boy. Quite an athlete. Went to the University of Maryland and played on their football team. Never amassed enough credits to graduate. Last thing in the file, he was working sporadically as a day laborer."

Len held up another file. "Now this one's a real gem. Lives in the District. Ex-GI. Did ROTC at Maryland. Likes to dress up in his uniform and go to bars—94th Aerosquadron by the College Park airport was one of his favorites. Picked up girls, got them high, and usually went back to their places. Engaged in a full range of sexual activity, sodomy included. When they weren't cooperative enough, he roughed them up. He finally got really carried away one night. Picked up a young secretary at a bar in the District. She was barely out of high school and pretty straight. Apparently, she expected to find romance. She realized that wasn't happening and got cold feet real fast. He tied her to the bed, then raped and sodomized her for a day or two. Left her tied and gagged.

"Her parents got worried when they didn't hear from her after a few days. Had the keys to her place and went over and found her. She was totally out of it. Spent a few weeks in inpatient psychiatric. Been in counseling ever since. The guy left fingerprints all over her place.

"It was one of my first cases up here. They sent me to the hospital to sit through the medical examinations and interview the girl. Talk about a lost child. She had an anxiety attack whenever any man came near her. They had her on some antipsychotic. Took me days to get all the information we needed to put together charges. They gave him twenty years, but with Lorton overcrowded he's been out in halfway houses for the last year." Len sighed. "Can you believe it?"

"Unfortunately, yeah."

"It's a real kick in the ass."

She gave a capsule narrative of each of the remaining files, placing them on the desk in turn. "These are the most likely in this round. Knock yourself out. Any questions, you know where to find me." She headed for the door, then stopped and turned. "Let me know what you hear. I've got an application in for homicide. I figure dealing with dead people and stone-cold killers has gotta be a step up from sex crimes."

Carnes had brought the stack of files back from sex crimes. He was paging through the one for the University of Maryland custodian who'd moved to the University of the District of Columbia when the phone rang. "Homicide, Carnes here."

"Detective Carnes." The voice was uncertain and female. "I work in the parking office at the University of Maryland. Ms. Moriarity asked me to call and tell you the printout is ready."

"Great." Carnes looked at his watch: 4:35. "I'll be right out."

"We're already closed, but I work until six o'clock. Can you make it before then?"

"I'm on my way."

Carnes started for the door, then remembered he hadn't returned Becky's calls yet. *I gotta be getting Alzheimer's.* He dialed Becky's number. After three rings, a familiar voice came on the line. "This is Becky Granite. I'm away from my desk at the moment. If you wish to leave a message on my voice mail, please record your message after the tone."

"Hi, Becky. John Carnes. Sorry I missed you. Running over to the university. I'll try to reach you later at home." He dialed her home number and left a similar message on her machine.

He made another quick call home. Avery answered.

"Hi, sweetie."

"Hi, Daddy."

"How was school?"

"OK. Christy and Anna got into a big argument, though." Avery prattled on and Carnes tried to follow the disjointed narrative.

When she paused, he said, "Listen, sweetie. I've got to work late tonight. I'll try to come in by bedtime. Tell Carmella, OK?"

"OK, Daddy. I love you."

"Love you too, sweetheart."

In the summer heat, Barnstormers exercised hypnotic powers, drawing people off the street to its air-conditioning, frosty mugs of beer, and other cold drinks. The clink of glassware, ripples of laughter, and scraping of furniture across the wood floors punctuated the constant rumble of voices.

"There you are!" Carol's voice pierced the din. Becky forced a half-hearted smile. *I really shouldn't have come.*

Carol dropped into the chair across the table. "I never expected to find you in the nonsmoking section."

"I don't smoke."

Carol did, and usually they sat at the bar or in the smoking section. "Besides, I couldn't find anything—"

"No problem." Carol smiled. "I've been thinking about quitting."

"If I collected a dollar every time you said that—"

"Yeah, I know," Carol said. "Time hasn't been right yet."

Becky wondered what it would take. Her mom didn't quit until after her aunt developed cancer. She had growled like a grizzly for weeks. Becky realized that Carol was staring at her expectantly.

"I'm sorry, did you say something?"

"Girl, you are one sorry space cadet." Carol laughed. "If you were any farther away I'd need a telescope just to see you."

"Sorry, this was a bad idea." Becky started to stand up.

Carol reached out and grabbed her wrist. "Now, let's not have that. No pity parties. I'm gonna cheer you up whether you like it or not."

For a moment, Becky regarded Carol as though she were a slightly dangerous new life form. Then she settled back in her seat.

Carol held up her hands beside her head, pointing her fingers at Becky, moving them in a rippling fashion. "You are under my power. You will have fun. You will have fun. You will have—"

"What would you ladies like to drink?"

"Anything you want to offer, Bart." Carol batted her eyes and laughed. When Bart started at Barnstormers, Carol prattled on and on to Becky about his "great ass," how he "moves like a leopard," and how "with my luck he's married and has twins or he's gay." The latter seemed to be a strong possibility. Despite her efforts, Carol hadn't managed to extract more than a tolerant smile.

Bart took their order and headed to the bar. Carol watched Bart walk away with a wistful expression. She sighed. "All right." She became fiercely attentive now. "I know you. All these dour looks. It's gotta be the guy. What's going on already? What did he do?"

"He didn't do anything." Becky said.

"Didn't forget your birthday? Forget to hold the car door?"

Becky shook her head.

"OK, he said something nasty about whatever you were wearing."

"No. He didn't do anything."

"You said that already."

Bart arrived with the drinks. "The nachos will be a few more minutes."

"So what didn't he do?" Carol raised an eyebrow. "Oh, I get it. He didn't do the big anything. The old limp noodle routine."

"No." Becky shook her head. "It never got to that point."

"But you think it should have?"

Becky shrugged.

"What a revolting development this is!"

Becky couldn't help herself. Her laughter escaped like a wild thing that refused to be caged. "You know, you really are incorrigible." Becky realized she'd said almost the same thing to John last time they were together. Carol and John were both so glib and funny on the outside, but quite different beneath it all. Pain lurked under the surface. They both needed to be held, to be loved.

"Earth to Rebecca, come in please."

"Sorry. I did it again. Did you say something?"

"It hardly deserves to be repeated. You said I was incorrigible. I agreed and said, 'Ask any of the guys I've dated. It's my best quality.' No, make that my second best quality."

Becky managed a weak smile. "Sorry I didn't miss it the second time."

"No sarcasm." Carol laughed. Several people at nearby tables turned in their direction. "You're just not yourself tonight. I've known corpses who were more fun."

"You have?"

"Hey, I was desperate." Carol shrugged. "Speaking of corpses, did I tell you about my date the other night?"

Before Becky could reply, Carol was off on her monologue. Despite herself, Becky was soon laughing out loud; by the end of Carol's story, her eyes were full of tears.

"Stop, please stop," Becky begged. "I'm going to pee in my pants."

"Please don't do that, miss." Bart stood beside Becky holding a tray. "Your nachos *especiales*."

14

"This one. He look familiar too."

Rodriguez flashed a look of controlled exasperation at Maria, who stood on the other side of Rosa. Rosa concentrated on each picture as though she was going to paint a portrait from memory. Maria gave him a twisted smile and made soothing motions with her hands. Rodriguez sighed, then noted the name and page number in his notepad.

"Bueno," he said.

So far, Rosa had identified six boys she thought were in the fraternity and another fifteen she thought looked "familiar." They were still only halfway through the first book. He checked his watch. He was supposed to meet Ellen Ashburton for dinner at the Bennigans on Greenbelt Road. He'd have to call to let her know he was running late. Rodriguez sighed again. If Ellen couldn't stomach a policeman's schedule, he might as well find out now.

Carnes picked up the printout from a pimply faced, ponytailed coed with almost no chest. She wore faded jeans and a Maryland T-shirt. The printout listed permit holders alphabetically, giving the license number, make and model of the car, a home address, and the number of the lot each person was assigned to. He flipped through the printout quickly, trying to determine how many names and cars were listed.

"What does this mean?" He pointed to a letter.

The girl squinted at the list. "That's a letter lot. Faculty and other staff are assigned letter lots. Usually, they get a lot near their classrooms and offices. For example, this person"—she pointed at a name in the left-hand column—"works over in Agriculture. So he parks in a lot that's not far from there."

Carnes looked at the name: "Granderson, Raymond." He scanned down the column quickly. A name almost leaped off the page at him. "Grayson, Jim." He scanned across the page. Grayson drove a blue 1983 Toyota Corolla. Coincidence?

"Something wrong?"

Carnes shook his head. "No, nothing. Do you have a map of the campus showing where this lot is?"

"Sure." She pulled out a booklet titled "Campus Parking" and flipped to a map. "Here's where the north administration building is; there's the armory and chapel." Her finger settled on the map. "Here's the lot."

Carnes' watch read 5:09. "Any chance they'd still be over there?"

"Could be. They work odd hours in the summer."

"Thanks." Carnes headed for the door.

The wooden arm that served as a barricade for the lot was up. Carnes cruised in. He drove slowly, studying the few cars left in the first aisle. All had parking tags with the lot designation hanging from the rearview mirrors. At least five little econoboxes. Maryland stickers in the back window of three. No blue Toyota Corollas. Carnes turned into the second row. Domestic cars, sporty foreign cars with vanity plates, a student car. About halfway down, on his right, he saw a blue Toyota Corolla. A crimson-lettered University of Maryland sticker spanned the rear window. He checked the license number. Grayson's. He pulled in behind the Corolla and climbed out of his car.

Carnes walked around the Toyota. The bumper displayed the remains of some old student stickers: lot number one. Unlike the other cars in the lot, this one did not have a tag hanging from the rearview mirror. He cupped his hands around his eyes and against the window. Some audiotapes sat in a case on the floor, papers lay on the backseat, an umbrella stuck out from under the seat. No dead bodies.

Carnes climbed back into his car and drove over to the adminis tration building. By now, he knew his way to the registrar's office. A pleasant-looking, oval-faced coed with a punk haircut—short and dark on the sides, reddish bangs in front—sat behind the counter. The henna hair could only have come out of a bottle. She wore two hoop earrings in her right ear and a post in the left. Her nipples pressed against a T-shirt that read "Cancun Yacht Club." She had a friendly smile.

"Can I help you?" She stood, bouncing in a way that confirmed she was not wearing a bra. A tight denim skirt revealed firm, muscular legs to midthigh. Carnes breathed slowly and said a silent prayer for control. One trip to a twelve-step program hadn't changed his instinctive reactions.

"Can I help you?" She repeated. She pushed back her bangs with her right hand.

"Yes, I'm looking for Mr. Grayson."

"Jim? He left at four-thirty."

"You sure? I saw his car out in the lot."

"The Toyota?" She laughed. "That old clunker hasn't gone anywhere for a couple of weeks. You know, his battery died or something. He's waiting for a friend to tow it. It's been a while."

"How's he getting around then?"

She stared at him suspiciously. "I don't mean to be rude, but you haven't even said who you are. You're asking a lot of funky questions."

"You're right. I'm sorry." Carnes tried a disarming smile and pulled out his ID. "John Carnes, D.C. homicide."

"Uhmm." She looked over his ID as though hoping to detect a forgery, then returned wary eyes to him. "Jan Reese." She pushed back her bangs again but did not offer her hand. "Can you tell me why you're, you know, looking for Jim?"

"Jim's been helping me in a homicide investigation. He's really been great." Carnes smiled even though his belly was tight with tension.

"Oh." She knitted her eyebrows, then, a bit uncertainly, returned his smile.

"You were going to tell me about his car."

"He's driving his mom's car." She grimaced when she said "mom's."

"What?" Carnes asked.

"Mother's car."

"No, that's not what I meant. You made a funny face about the car."

"Oh." She laughed nervously. "Guess I must be pretty transparent, huh? It's not the car. His mother died. It was, you know, very sad. He was really very close to her."

"How long ago was that?"

"Hmm." She looked at the ceiling. "A while. I think sometime last summer. Yes. After the Fourth."

"Oh." He felt slightly nauseous. Pieces of the puzzle were falling into place. The mother dies, then Francine Lynch. Who told him about

Lynch's death? Grayson. But the Ocean City police said they'd kept the lid on. There'd been no story about her death. He should've thought of that before! Crenshaw had told him what to look for. Grayson had been too helpful. Del talked to Simon and Simon got killed that day. Grayson must've seen them talking. It all fit.

"What'd she die of?"

"Cancer."

"You sure?"

She gave him a suspicious look. "Of course. I went to the funeral. She'd been fighting it for years. A mastectomy. Chemo. She went through it all. They caught it too late. Her death was a blessing. Course, it ate Jim up watching her die that way. He was, you know, real close to his mom. Spent a lot of time nursing her."

"How long've you been working here?"

"Two and a half years."

"You and Jim close?"

"Friends. We're not *involved* if that's what you mean. My boyfriend goes to school here. He wouldn't approve." She giggled nervously. "Besides, when I started working here, Jim was going with some girl who worked in the Book Exchange. Over on Route 1."

"Oh? He hasn't mentioned her."

"I'm not surprised. They broke up around the time his mother died." Her face clouded. "Real downer. Jim went through a very tough time."

"Sounds like it." Carnes tried a grim, sympathetic look. "You remember when he went to Ocean City, after his mother died?"

"Sure. I was the one who told him—well, we all pushed him—to go. He was, you know, moping around. Depressed. Lethargic. He had the time coming, and the fall registration crunch hadn't started. I think he went for almost a week. Seemed better after he came back. At least, for a while."

Jan brushed back her bangs and studied Carnes. The wary look re appeared in her eyes. "Did he tell you about his trip?"

"No," Carnes said. "Someone else did."

Her face darkened. "What's this really about?"

"I told you. He's been helping me with an investigation. Four former Maryland coeds have been murdered." Carnes didn't think he sounded too convincing. "I need some records he was getting me. Do you know what his mom's car looks like?"

Jan brushed back her bangs and glared at Carnes. "I think you're full of shit." She put her hands on her hips. "You're asking too many questions. I'm not stupid. Is Jim in some sort of trouble?"

Carnes saw something, a flicker of uncertainty, of fear maybe, behind the hostility in her eyes.

"Why do you ask?"

Her tone was sarcastic. "Well, when a homicide detective appears asking all sorts of questions—"

"Nothing else?" asked Carnes.

"No." Her response was adamant but she didn't meet his eyes.

"Nothing?" Carnes asked.

"I said no." She clenched her fists at her sides. Her lips trembled.

"But the way you said it. You want me to believe it. I think you want to believe it. You really don't, do you?"

"That's not true!" Her clenched fists were pale. A tear trickled down her cheek.

Carnes spoke softly. "I need your help. You'll feel better. Tell me everything."

She shook her head. Her lower lip thrust out in a pout.

"You know something. You feel something. Something you saw or heard? You can't hide it."

"No!" The tears ran down her face. "He's a nice . . ." her voice trailed off.

Carnes switched tactics. "Damnit." He smacked his hand down on the counter. She jumped. "This isn't about friendship. Four girls've died. One worked here in the library. You want someone's death on your conscience?"

"No."

"Help me."

"I can't."

"You can! You have to. Four girls. Brutally murdered. They were tortured. Humiliated. They died in agony. They were coeds here just like you. A few years' difference and they could've been your friends."

"I knew Meredith." She sobbed into both hands, her body quaking.

Carnes fought the urge to physically comfort her. He softened his tone. "He's sick. He needs help. Protecting him means being honest. He needs the right kind of help. Tell me. It's the right thing to do—what a friend would do."

Jan spoke through the sobs that shook her body. "It can't be. I mean, there's really nothing—I don't know anything. It doesn't make sense."

Carnes pulled a handkerchief from his pocket and held it out. "You know in your heart. I can see. Tell me."

Jan turned away and sobbed, sucking in gulps of air. She pulled a handful of tissues from her desk, dabbed at her eyes, and blew her nose.

"I need to know what you know. This sounds melodramatic, but lives depend on it. He's not going to stop on his own. He'll keep on killing."

Jan's shoulders sagged and she looked down at her feet. "There are things—little things. Your questions—they're making me, you know, put things together. But it doesn't seem like Jim. He's a nice guy. He's always been nice to me."

"I know this is hard."

Jan took a deep breath and pushed back her hair. "I guess it's lots of little things. He's been really moody lately. Real up one day, then down another. He's been reading all the papers. Even the *Washington Times!* He barely even read the *Post*—except the sports page—until recently." Her eyes pleaded with Carnes.

"What else?" He couldn't let her stop.

"I didn't make anything of it at the time. But he talked a lot about the killings." Eagerly, she added, "Of course, there's been a lot of talk on campus about them."

"But something strikes you about these conversations?"

"I don't know." She shrugged in a gesture of frustration. "Well, a couple of times he made comments about how the killer must feel. Talked about how he was running the police around in circles. It was, you know, a little weird. Almost as though he were gloating about the killer, making fools of the cops." Her eyes widened. "Sorry."

"Anything else?"

"Well, his mood swings. I guess it hadn't dawned on me. But he was up—almost manic—it could've been immediately after each of the killings. Then he'd get tense but sort of disinterested in what was going on here. Recently, he's taken a lot of sick leave. It's just not like him. I thought he might still be depressed about his mother."

"But now?"

"I don't know." A tear ran down her cheek. "I just don't know. I guess what really makes me think—" Her voice choked off.

"What?" Carnes asked gently.

She blew her nose again and took a deep breath. "The other day, the day Meredith was killed, Jim went over to the Stamp building to get lunch. It's up past the library. He came back in a foul temper, talking to himself, cursing under his breath. Wouldn't talk to me about what was bothering him. He said he felt sick. Went home early. He didn't look well. The next day he was cheerful again. On top of the world."

Carnes fought down his excitement. "Well, it may not mean anything. He may be wound up over his mother, as you said." His words sounded flat. "What does the car look like—his mother's car?"

"Fairly new, a big one, Olds 88 I think. One of those metallic blues, almost silver."

"Thanks. Please keep this conversation between us."

"Sure."

Carnes handed her a card. "Call me if he comes in. Be careful."

15

"I thought I was going to die," Becky said.

Carol grinned as she took another sip of her drink. "Yeah. I almost fell on the floor. Bart was so cool. She did a deep voice: 'Please don't do that, miss.'"

Forty-five minutes and another drink had reawakened Becky's sense of humor. Their conversation veered from silly to serious and back again as the nachos and drinks disappeared. Although one or two guys came by, Carol and Becky sent them away, explaining it was "girl talk" time.

"Don't look now, but I think you have an admirer," Carol said.

"Where?"

"Over by the door."

"Anyone we know?"

"I've seen him here before." Carol put her finger to her chin and seemed thoughtful. "I think it's Mr. Shy."

Becky turned slowly. The door was closing.

"He did it again."

"What?"

"He just left," said Carol.

"I guess it's not my day."

Grayson's house was a small weathered block of red brick with a beige porch. Aged paint curled away from window frames and trim. A jungle of weeds battled azaleas for space in the garden. Carnes, Rodriguez, Clinton, Harrison, and Mead crouched behind Mead's nondescript Chrysler a couple of blocks away, sweating profusely in their Kevlar vests. A police van full of technicians waited up the block. Carnes nudged Rodriguez and pointed. SWAT officers from the PG County tactical unit were moving into position around the house.

Harrison turned to Carnes, Clinton, and Rodriguez. "You guys join the TAC unit covering the garage. Mead and I'll follow the ram in the front."

Carnes wanted to go in the front, but he bit off his protest. This was not his turf. Rodriguez nodded slightly. Clinton shrugged. "OK," Carnes agreed.

Harrison thumbed the button on his walkie-talkie. "TAC one. Let me know when your men are in position."

"Roger. About two minutes."

After Carnes left Grayson's office he had been busy. A call to Rodriguez confirmed that Grayson "looked familiar" to Rosa. She agreed he could have been one of the pledges at the house. Then he tracked down Detective Harrison. Harrison and Mead had already interviewed several former members of the fraternity and compiled a partial list of pledges. The name "Jim Gray, or something like that" was on their list.

In barely an hour, Harrison and Mead had assembled their team and obtained a signature from the duty judge on a search warrant. Carnes, Clinton, and Rodriguez had met the others at the scene.

The radio crackled. "TAC one ready."

"OK, guys," said Harrison. "Let's do it."

Carnes' heart pounded as they trotted up the street. He pointed to a place on the other side of the garage. Rodriguez nodded. They drew their Glock semiautomatics and took up positions along the garage wall.

Carnes slid to the side of the door and quickly peered in through the garage window. No car.

"What'd you see?" Clinton whispered.

"Nothing."

"The car?" asked Rodriguez.

"The garage is empty."

Carnes looked in again. In the dim evening light, he could make out the faint ghosts of tools on the walls, a lawnmower, a door to the house. Rodriguez and Clinton joined him.

"Shit," Clinton said. "I got a bad feeling about this." Mead and Harrison were on the front steps along with two uniformed officers carrying the ram. Carnes tried to calculate how quickly they could check out the house for occupants, how soon Grayson—if he were home—would come flying out into the garage.

Harrison spoke into his walkie-talkie. He pushed the doorbell and yelled, "Police! We have a warrant! Open up!" After a moment he motioned to the officers with the ram. They surged forward, splintering the door with a loud crack.

Carnes watched as the officers rushed into the house, then concentrated his attention on the door from the house to the garage. He took deep breaths and counted to himself in thousands. One, one thousand, two, one thousand . . .

16

They could do nothing. It was his game. He made up the rules. He'd waited a long time. They didn't understand. They couldn't even begin to. He called the shots now. He wrote the script. He chuckled.

They thought him insane. No, he was in control. They were puny, simple, almost unworthy of his revenge. He remembered their looks of terror. Fran Lynch, pleading for mercy, offering to do anything. He'd let her, then killed her anyway. Vicky Benton, her eyes ready to pop out of her head. Anna Durant, sweating like a putrid pig, a fat, castrating pig. Only Meredith Simon even made a pass at dignity. He almost regretted having to kill her. She'd been decent until that cop came along.

They had it coming. They'd humiliated him. Now it was his turn. He gave them what they deserved. There was nothing the police could do to stop him. The police were stupid children. He was the pied piper, leading them on. He looked at his watch. The excitement rose in his loins. She'd come out soon. He'd waited too long already. She'd been lucky before. Not this time.

"One thousand fifty-nine." Carnes caught a movement out of the corner of his eye. Mead appeared on the porch and waved them over.

"Well?" Carnes asked.

"Not here."

"Shit," said Clinton and Carnes. They laughed in unison, bodies sagging slightly with the release of tension.

"What happened?" asked Carnes.

"Don't know. Nobody here," Mead said. "We've secured the place. C'mon in. You can help with the search. You know the drill. Try not to touch anything. Point out to the techs stuff you think we should collect or analyze." Mead pressed the button on his portable radio and summoned the technicians. In about twenty seconds the van pulled up in front of the house and technicians began unloading the kind of oversized sample cases salesmen carry.

Clinton watched with a sardonic expression. "You guys need to learn to travel light."

Carnes smiled. "Just like my ex. Took two suitcases to go away for a weekend."

"Mine did the same," said Rodriguez. "Never came back either."

The technicians, a slightly chunky, short-haired brunette woman with glasses and a tall man with wavy black hair, smiled politely as though they hadn't heard the jokes at least a hundred times. They continued to unload their equipment.

Mead led the way in. The front door opened into an L-shaped living room-dining area. A half wall separated the living room from the kitchen. To the left, a short corridor led to four doors. From their vantage point, the rooms appeared to be a bathroom and three small bedrooms. Carnes, Clinton, and Rodriguez headed toward the bedrooms while the others fanned out through the living room and kitchen.

A four-poster queen-size bed, unmade and uninviting, dominated the largest bedroom. Dark wood furniture and dark drapery seemed to suck the light out of the room. The air was heavy with the odors of mildew, dust, and decay. Sections of the *Washington Post* fanned along one side of the bed. A little night table sat beside the bed. Atop the table Carnes could see a cream-colored clock-radio-telephone, a crystal lamp with an age-stained shade, chrome-plated scissors, a pile of newspaper clippings, and a mug containing a small amount of dark brown fluid. A brighter patch of wall over the bed showed where a picture must have hung.

"See anything?" asked Carnes.

Rodriguez straightened up from where he'd been leaning over the night table. "Just these papers. You think he's starting a clipping service?"

"Yeah." Carnes grimaced. "A regular news hound." He could see that some of the articles were about the police investigation of Meredith Simon's murder. They looked around for several minutes, finding only clothes and some men's jewelry.

They walked into the second bedroom. "Looks like the guest room," Rodriguez said.

"Yeah," Carnes agreed. In front of them, a full-size bed sat against the wall, a chair faced the bed from the corner to their right, and a chest of drawers filled the wall to their left. Photographs, many yellowed and ancient, decorated the wall. The air in the room was heavy with dust. "The museum room," Carnes said. "I think Vincent Price musta been his decorator."

Rodriguez chuckled.

Carnes pointed to a book on the chest of drawers. "A Gideon's Bible. Think we could bust him for stealing it from some hotel?"

Rodriguez snorted. "Heck. His counsel will tell the jury what a wonderful, religious fellow he is."

"Goes to church on Sunday. Prays for forgiveness for each girl he tortures. What a guy!" Carnes agreed.

The third bedroom must have been designed as a nursery. It was small and cramped. Aging wallpaper depicting toys and teddy bears peeled away from the walls at several seams. Something dark grew on the ceiling in one corner. A cheap assemble-it-yourself oak-veneer desk sat in front of the single window. A wobbly veneer bookcase stood beside it.

"Matching furniture," Carnes said.

"Very classy," Clinton agreed.

The bookcase seemed ready to spew books like a waterfall. Carnes walked past the bookcase on tiptoe. A clutter of papers and folders and a Commodore 64 computer filled almost every available inch of desk space. A computer printer balanced precariously atop the bookcase beside the desk.

Carnes stood by the desk. "Genuine wood laminate."

"Almost as nice as ours," Clinton said.

Carnes exhaled as though he were bored, but his neck and shoulders were tight with tension. "This looks like a good place to start," Carnes said. Rodriguez and Clinton nodded.

Carnes picked up one of the folders from the desk and, holding it by the edges so he wouldn't disturb any fingerprints, opened it. "Shit. Look at this."

17

"Oh, come on," said Carol. "One more."

"What're you trying to do? Get me drunk?" Becky laughed. She already felt light-headed and wanted to be in decent shape before she drove home. She placed her hand over her glass and smiled at Bart. "How about a cup of coffee?"

"Yeah," said Carol, "a Kahlua coffee."

"Not for me," said Becky. "Plain coffee."

"She likes her coffee like her men, strong and dark," Carol said.

Bart shook his head slightly and went for their coffees.

Becky reached out and touched Carol's hand. "You know, I hate to admit it, but you were right. Having a couple of drinks and talking about it sure beats sitting around at home being miserable. Thanks for dragging me out."

Carol smiled. "Hey, what are friends for? You've done the same for me a dozen times."

Becky couldn't remember ever having to drag Carol out. Carol always seemed to be up. No problem was so troublesome that she couldn't go out, have a few drinks, meet a new guy. Becky wondered at Carol's resilience. Things that would have sent her to the shower for a good cry seemed to be nothing more than comic material to Carol. She appeared to bounce over life's obstacles as though her spirit was made of rubber. She seemed to be a blind optimist who never saw trouble coming. Once it was past, she was already looking forward to the future. All those times Becky had listened to Carol's stories and laughed at her latest mishap, it had never occurred to her that Carol needed the audience. It was interesting how you get insights into people.

He gritted his teeth with frustration. How long were the bitches going to sit in there yakking away? God's joke on Adam was giving Eve the power of speech. Women hadn't stopped talking ever since. He glanced at his watch. They'd been in there for hours. He'd even gone in to check what they were doing, half expecting to find them with some guys. No. Just sitting there beating their gums. His mother had been the same way. Never say in a minute what you could say for an hour. Only death had silenced her. Of course, now he missed her lectures, her insistence that she knew better.

He checked his watch again, impatience gnawing at him. Usually, he enjoyed waiting. He'd think about what he would do to them. But something was wrong tonight. He didn't want to wait. Couldn't wait. His body tingled with the excitement of anticipation, but there was a nervous edge to it. Anticipation was changing into a feeling of almost dread. He tried to shake it off. Just imagine her lying there, helpless, begging "please don't hurt me." Yeah. Begging. He savored the image. She would beg.

18

Clinton and Rodriguez peered over Carnes' shoulder. A pile of news clippings sat in the folder. The headline on top of the pile read "Serial Killer Strikes Again." It was a story about Anna Durant's death. Carnes carefully picked up story after story. He shivered. They were all here. Articles about the killings of Vicky Benton, Anna Durant, and Meredith Simon.

"It fits," said Clinton.

"He's been helping us, but he's also been leading us around. He's on some sort of power trip, knowing what we're doing, playing a part, all the time laughing behind our backs." Carnes shook his head angrily. "And I've been playing along with him. Jesus."

"You had no way to know," Rodriguez said.

"Yes, I did. I should've. Shit! Should've recognized the signs. He was so willing to help—"

Clinton tried for levity. "You're just not used to being helped."

Rodriguez put a hand on Carnes' shoulder. "Stop beating yourself. You're the one who read this thing from the beginning. We hoped you were wrong. But you were right. You put it together."

"More like I tripped over it."

"Cut it out." Rodriguez' tone was sharp. "You know as well as I do, that's what this job is all about. Working hard, beating the bushes, following your instincts, dogging the leads. The answers rarely come in some great burst of revelation. Usually, it's hard work."

Carnes smiled. "OK, OK. Message received. Thanks."

Carnes still wondered if he could have figured it out in time to save Meredith Simon. He imagined Grayson walking across the campus and spotting Meredith Simon talking to Del Clinton. Grayson flying into a private rage. Grayson hovering over her with a knife, eyes alight, body trembling, feeling his power, something sexual and alive driving him. Carnes shook his head and took several deep breaths.

Rodriguez opened the cover of a University of Maryland yearbook. "Holy shit!"

"I gotta get going," Becky said. "I promised to do brownies for the party tomorrow."

"Damn," said Carol. "Forgot all about that." She made a face. "I promised to bring cookies." She brightened. "Guess I can always hit a bakery in the morning." She scanned the room. A tall, dark-haired man with a strong chin—about thirty, she guessed—sat alone at the bar. She liked strong chins.

"If I don't get home and do some baking, I'll be up all night." Becky followed Carol's eyes. "You coming?"

"Huh?"

"I asked if you were coming," Becky said. "But I can see that the answer is no."

Carol smiled shyly. "Am I that obvious?"

"Only to those who know you." Becky reached out and touched Carol on the shoulder. "Thanks."

"Hey, what are friends for?"

A rush of hot, humid air enveloped her as she went out the door, banishing the goose bumps caused by the air-conditioning. For a moment, the filth, the traffic noise, the large buildings all disappeared. She was a girl again, out behind her house, feeling the summer breeze wrap around her like a blanket.

Carol popped out the door behind her. "Walking over to the Metro?"

"Let me guess, his girlfriend was just in the bathroom."

Carol managed a pout. "Now, what would make you say that?"

"Experience."

Carol smiled. "Well, for your information, Ms. Smarty-pants, there was no girlfriend."

"A boyfriend?" Becky asked.

Carol punched her in the arm. "No! I just decided I'd bake cookies."

"Sure."

"Really!"

"This may be a first." Becky linked her arm with Carol's.

"So, you taking the Metro?"

"No. I drove in today."

"Oh, OK." Carol scouted the street ahead. "Guess there isn't a mugger in sight. See you in the morning." They hugged.

They were leaving Barnstormers. His breath escaped his lips with a sound like steam escaping an airtight seal. Finally! She hugged her friend for a moment and then walked over to the garage. He chuckled. "Come to Daddy." He started his car. Heavy metal music blared. He turned it down low. Thump, thump, thump. Like a heartbeat.

He remembered. The girls laughing. The panic rising inside him. For a moment, the memory sapped him of his resolve. He was a frightened boy again. That's what happened that night in Ocean City. She laughed at him. He couldn't take that. Don't be depressed. Be mad. They shouldn't have laughed at him. They would have to be punished.

Her car emerged from the ramp and he snapped back to the present. She paused too long at the street before pulling out. She drove too carefully—the way people do when they've had a few drinks. It would be easy.

That's right, look both ways. Drive defensively. Just like they taught you in driver's ed. Aim high in steering. He chuckled.

She turned right and drove off, taillights a silly face mocking him. He followed at a discreet distance. She turned up Massachusetts Avenue, and he allowed another car between them. After all this time, he knew her routine. She was headed for home.

At Dupont Circle he swung out and passed her. The V-8 roared like a lion. He could see her passing Kramerbooks through his rearview mirror. His heart raced with excitement. The hunt. He hummed to himself, a simple tuneless sound that meandered up and down the scales. He fed the gas. He was the lion, she the gazelle. He glanced around for cops, fed more gas. Get there fast. Lie in wait for the gazelle. Be ready to spring.

"What is it?" Carnes asked.

Rodriguez held open the yearbook. A photograph of the Alpha Omega sorority lay inside the cover of the book. Rodriguez held the photo so Carnes and Clinton could see it. Several faces were X-ed out with black ink. Carnes carefully lifted the photo by the edges and turned it over. A chill started at the nape of his neck and radiated down his body. On the back of the photo was a list of names in alphabetical order with addresses. Carnes ran his eyes down the list. Benton—crossed out. Colwin—nothing. Durant—crossed out. Other names. Epstein. French. Granite. Lynch—crossed out. Many other names. Simon—crossed out.

"Shit," said Clinton.

"In case there was any doubt—" Carnes said.

"There isn't now," Rodrigeuz finished. "We better get Harrison and Mead."

Carnes, Clinton, and Rodrigeuz stood near the door to the small room. They watched while Harrison and the female technician collected and catalogued the evidence. In a desk drawer, they found a picture of a smiling girl in her twenties.

"Look at this." Harrison held it up by the corners. Someone had scratched the word *bitch* across the picture.

Another drawer held several pairs of panties and one Alpha Omega T-shirt as well as an ashtray and several other odds and ends. "A collector," said Harrison.

"A rather eclectic collection." Rodriguez sounded like a Spanish Alistair Cooke.

"Where'd you pick up 'eclectic'?" Carnes asked.

"He's been reading one of those vocabulary-builder books," said Clinton.

The search continued. Harrison held up each item for them to see. Copies of directories, a computer printout, and other papers.

"Well, we know how Grayson assembled his victim list," Mead muttered. A folder of maps and papers gave some clues as to how he followed and tracked his victims.

"Now, if we could only find something that told us where he is," commented Harrison.

"If he knew we were coming he could be miles away by now," Rodriguez said.

"How would he know?" asked Harrison. "The girl in his office?"

"No. She was shook. She wouldn't tip him," Carnes said. *I hope.*

"Well, I put out a description of him and the mother's car. Every scout car in the county's looking for him," said Mead.

"If he's still in the county." Carnes felt cold. "Maybe he wasn't here because he's stalking another victim." Carnes felt it somewhere deep inside. He was certain. Grayson was hunting. How did he know? He couldn't explain what he didn't understand. All he knew was he could feel it. Stalking. Killing. It was what Grayson did. The question: who? Becky? He felt a cold stab of panic. No. He'd made that mistake before. It could be anyone.

Rodriguez looked at Carnes curiously. "It's possible, I guess—"

"But where?" asked Harrison.

"Let me see the picture again," Carnes said.

Harrison turned to the technician. "You have it?"

"Yeah." She handed over a manila envelope and grimaced slightly. "Be careful—prints."

Carnes slid out the picture and held it by the edges as he stared at the faces. Which of these girls was next? He knit his brows with fierce concentration and tried to open his mind to the information. "C'mon, talk to me," he said.

"There he goes, getting mystical again," Rodriguez joked.

"No," Carnes said softly. He stared at the photo for a moment more, then flipped it over. He examined the names. There didn't seem to be any order. Switch left brain to right brain, back again. Feel it. Victim name, skip, skip. Name, skip. His eyes scanned the addresses. Suddenly, Carnes' body tensed and his eyes widened.

"What?" asked Clinton.

"Leave off Meredith Simon and Fran Lynch and what do you see?" Carnes thrust the photo at Rodriguez.

Rodriguez studied the photo while Carnes shifted around as though he had ants in his pants. "Nothing. I mean it's not in alphabetical order or anything."

"That's exactly what it is!" Carnes felt as though his body was going into nuclear meltdown. "Look at the names *and* the addresses." Carnes pointed at several. "He's hitting all the D.C. area girls in order. Assume that Fran Lynch was the first one. He ran into her in Ocean City. Something triggered him. It was random. Then—boom—the pattern starts."

"But Meredith Simon—" Rodriguez said.

"He saw her with Del. Unplanned, but necessary. Then we have—"

Rodriguez nodded. "OK, I see." He ran his finger down the list. "Benton, D.C.; Durant, Rockville." His eyes got wide. "Granite. Isn't that the girl you've been seeing?"

"Yeah. I was right the other night. I felt it." Carnes slapped the picture down on the desk. "I am so fucking stupid! It was there all the time. I felt it, but I couldn't pin it down. I kept telling myself I was reacting emotionally, not rationally."

"But you thought it was Pardo," said Rodriguez.

Carnes looked sheepish. "Right feeling. Wrong guy."

Clinton said, "It's possible, but—"

"I'm not taking any chances. I'm going over to her place." Carnes checked his watch. It would take him at least fifteen minutes. Too long if Grayson was there. He found a phone on the desk. He pulled out his pad and furiously flipped the pages. Her number. He punched it in. Ring, ring, ring, ring. Rodriguez and the others watched in silence. The air crackled with tension.

"I'm sorry I can't come to the phone right now—"

"Shit!" Carnes pounded a rhythm of frustration on the desk.

"Your call is important to me—"

"Fuck! I got her machine."

"—at the tone. Beep."

"Becky. Don't let anyone in. I'll be there in a heartbeat." Carnes slammed down the phone. "Christ!"

"She's probably not home yet," Rodriguez said in a calming voice.

"Maybe." Carnes started for the door. He stopped and turned quickly in the doorway. "Listen, call it in. Send scout cars by her office. Marketing firm: Greystone and Martin. Try Barnstormers. Shit, I'm not sure where she does karate or aerobics. Find her. Give her an escort home."

Rodriguez scribbled.

"Put out an APB on Grayson's car. Grab him on sight. No waiting. No chances. I'm heading for her place." Carnes was out the door before they replied.

19

Becky turned off Connecticut Avenue into a street with low-rise apartment buildings. Her apartment was a half block down. She cruised along slowly, searching for a parking space. It was twilight and there were still several. She passed a light-colored Oldsmobile with a raised hood. A man stood in front of the car, bent over at the waist, head under the hood.

She pulled into a spot two cars in front of the Oldsmobile. When she came to D.C. she couldn't parallel park to save her life, but after a month or so, she had mastered the art. She was still proud of her prowess. As she got out of the car, she noted with satisfaction that her car was only about four inches from the curb, virtually equidistant from the cars in front and behind.

"Becky. Becky Granite, is that you?"

Becky swung around to see a tall young man with curly dark hair and a mustache standing by the upraised hood, smiling broadly. He looked familiar.

"Jim Grayson." He checked his hand as though he were making sure it was clean and then offered it. "We were at Maryland together, remember?" His hand was damp with perspiration.

She still couldn't place the name, but nodded. "Of course."

"What luck," he said. "Darn starter won't turn over. I've done everything I know how to do—I'm not much of a mechanic—and I was about to hike over to Connecticut to look for a phone to call the auto club. Didn't expect to run into someone I knew. Small world."

Becky studied him carefully. For a fleeting moment she felt a chill. *Could this be the guy?* What would a crazed killer look like? She pictured a drooling, twitching psychopath. This guy was as friendly as a lapdog. His face glistened with sweat, and wet patches were visible at his chest and armpits. He seemed pathetic, not terrifying. Besides, she was safe in the street. "Can I give you a jump or something?" Becky asked.

"No," Grayson said. "It's really nice of you to offer, but the battery seems fine. Seems to be the starter." He wiped his forehead with the back of his hand. "Boy, it's hot. When I was in school, I'd always try to get out of town during the summer. Now I work at the university. Have to work most of the summer."

"College Park?"

"Yeah. Started in the registrar's office as a student, then stayed on after I graduated. I like the academic atmosphere."

That was probably where she'd seen him, the registrar's office. She remembered standing in line for hours to work out glitches in her schedule. Maryland was the most disorganized, poorly managed—

"So you decided to stay in the D.C. area too, despite this lovely weather?" he asked.

"Yes. I work for a marketing firm downtown. Greystone and Martin."

"Think I've heard of that. Sounds interesting." He pulled a handkerchief out of his pocket and wiped his forehead. "I was an English major," he smiled. "Not many jobs in English."

"I guess not." Becky was starting to relax. "You could teach or something."

"I've been thinking about it. Maybe go back and get my teaching certificate and a master's. Well," he seemed to contemplate his prospects, "I'm gonna have to save up some bucks before I can do that."

The heat and humidity were beginning to smother Becky. "Look, is there anyone I can call?"

"That would be great." Grayson smiled. "I was hoping I wouldn't have to walk. I've been dying of thirst. A little light-headed. Would you mind calling the auto club for me?" He reached into his pocket. Becky felt a rush of adrenaline and began to back away. He pulled out his wallet and began shuffling through the papers. "Ah, here it is." He held out his auto club card. Now Becky felt stupid.

"Sure, no problem." Becky stepped closer and took the card. The name on the card was Jim Grayson. Well, that was a good sign.

"Thanks, I really appreciate it. Let me know how long it'll be. Sometimes, they take an hour or two." Grayson leaned weakly against the car and wiped his sweaty face with the handkerchief again. He looked pale in the streetlight. "Could you—if it's not a big problem—bring me a glass of water or something? You'd probably be saving my life." His smile was disarming.

Becky felt guilty. Two hours sweating in this steam room heat? She couldn't imagine it. She stood with hands on hips for a moment and stared at him. He certainly looked familiar, and his AAA card confirmed his name. Moreover, all he'd asked her to do was make a phone call while he waited outside. If he were a crazed killer, wouldn't he at least be trying to get himself invited in? Her imagination must be getting the best of her. Still . . .

"I'll be right back," she said.

He pulled uncomfortably at his collar and grinned a lopsided, puppy-dog grin. "Thanks."

Becky half turned toward her apartment. This wasn't the way her parents taught her to treat people. Leaving this guy dying in the heat was just the wrong thing to do. She was being ridiculous. Becky turned back to Grayson and smiled. "Why don't you come in and call triple A yourself? I could get something cold for you to drink. Got lemonade in the fridge."

"I don't want to be any trouble." He wiped his face and sagged a bit. "If it's really OK?"

She nodded. "Sure."

"Thanks. I 'preciate it." He smiled shyly and wiped his forehead again.

"Oh, it's no problem, really," she said. "We Marylanders have to stick together."

Carnes jumped in the car and fumbled with the ignition. *Damnit. Take a coupla deep breaths.* He tried to will his hands to stop shaking, his heart to stop thumping. It didn't work. On the second try, he started the car. He fed it gas and screeched out of his parking space. He raced along until he reached the light at Route 1. *Red, naturally.* His heart thumped like a steel-drum band as he waited for the light to change or for a break in the traffic. "C'mon, c'mon!" He pounded the steering wheel in frustration. When the light changed, he floored the accelerator.

He whipped past the university and prayed there wouldn't be any drunken students crossing Route 1. The fast-food joints, gas stations, car dealerships, and motels flashed by until he reached the ramp onto the Beltway. He took the ramp way too fast, and his rear wheels started to skid. He stomped the brake and countersteered, and the tires grabbed the road. Thank God for the heavy-duty suspension package. He shot out into Beltway traffic, flashing past slower vehicles. A truck drifted into his lane and he stomped the brake. "Asshole motherfucker!"

Carnes took deep breaths to counter the adrenaline rush. This was probably another wild-goose chase. Becky would think he'd flipped out. Well, he could pretend he was looking for an excuse to see her. Maybe he was overreacting. But he couldn't blot out the feeling she was in danger. He sped past the I-95 interchange and New Hampshire Avenue.

How could I be so fucking stupid? Grayson played me like a violin. He reached over and turned up the police radio. He swerved to avoid a car that had braked suddenly. *I'll kill myself before I get there if I'm not more careful.* Mumbles and static from the radio. Shooting in Georgetown. That would draw half the department.

His mind raced. Where was Becky? She could've been at karate or aerobics. Was this karate night? Aerobics? By now, she could be home safe. His message might scare her. Then his mind turned to a darker possibility. Grayson might already have her. He pictured her tied up and helpless on her bed. Maybe she was already dead. "Shit!" Pain ripped into his gut. *No.* He couldn't think like that. He fought the panic. Think good thoughts. A policeman was probably escorting her home now. Besides, he'd be at her place in a few minutes.

20

He watched her climb the steps to the apartment. Firm ass, nice legs, good muscle tone. He smiled. She might be the best of the group. He'd wait until she was totally unsuspecting. Then he'd pounce. He visualized her surprise, her terror. His chest pounded. He couldn't catch his breath. The excitement swept through his body, warming his groin. He felt like Atlas—he could hold up the world with one hand.

She unlocked the door and stood aside while he entered. He fought a strong urge to grab her right there. No. The door was open. Noise would carry. Who cares? Hold on. Plenty of time. He smiled his most winning smile as he walked by her. It would take only a minute for her to get the glass of lemonade. Then she'd be his. This was going to be easy.

Carnes hazarded a quick glance at the speedometer. Seventy-five. He tried to concentrate on his driving as he wove through traffic, past the University Boulevard and Colesville Road exits. In front of him hovered the Mormon Tabernacle, a gleaming white fairy-tale castle.

How long since he'd been in church? Too long. He remembered St. Stevens, his first communion. His small boy's body trembled with fear, his ears pounded, and the organ music seemed far away. The fragrance of candles and incense threatened to engulf him as he made his way on spaghetti legs toward the communion altar.

The red-faced priest loomed before him in robe and vestment. Carnes forced open his mouth, which felt as dry as sandpaper. "Body of Christ." The priest put the wafer on his tongue. For a minute he felt he might choke. No saliva. What would he do with this thing? Could he slip it out of his mouth? He bit his tongue trying to stimulate his salivary glands. They wouldn't give him a sip of the wine.

Carnes hit the brake and swerved, narrowly missing a Honda that had drifted into his lane. "Dumb fucker! Don't you look?" The Honda's driver, a teenage girl, appeared terrified in the pale light. *Shit! Get a grip on yourself.*

He passed Holy Cross Hospital and the Georgia Avenue exit. Connecticut Avenue was next. He remembered with regret what he'd said about God sipping his piña colada on the beach. *God, get me there on time. I'll owe you one.*

Becky reached into the refrigerator and poured lemonade from the plastic pitcher into the glasses. The light blinked on the answering machine. She took a step toward the machine, then glanced at Grayson. Should she check her messages? No. Maybe Carnes had called. If so, she didn't want a stranger listening in on something personal. She pulled open the freezer door and reached into the plastic container for ice. The cold hurt and the cubes clung to her fingers. She dropped the cubes into the lemonade and blew on her fingers to warm them. She glanced at the answering machine again. Its light blinked insistently.

"Interesting," said Grayson.

She stepped out of the kitchen, past the front door, and into the living room. Grayson stood at the other end of the room, admiring the Picasso print she'd purchased at the East Wing of the National Gallery. She walked over and handed him the glass. "Thanks," he said.

"Mind if I sit down?" He looked at his sweat-stained shirt and khaki pants and then at her white couch. "I know I'm a bit sweaty."

Had he forgotten why he was here? "Sure, but didn't you want to call the auto club?"

"Sure. I guess I really am light-headed." He sipped some lemonade. "The heat must really have gotten to me."

Becky showed him the phone in the kitchen and watched from the living room while he dialed. Was it her imagination or was he holding in the button while he dialed?

"Hello. Triple A?"

Did they answer too fast? Last year, when her car conked out, it took her forever to get through to an operator. He began describing his car, where it was, and what he thought was wrong.

"An hour? Can't make it faster?" he asked. "OK. Well, I'll be at—" He glanced at Becky and whispered, "What's the number?"

She told him and listened while he repeated it. Tension built up in her neck and shoulders. Probably being silly, but she couldn't shake this feeling—what Carol called "bad vibes." Maybe it was the way he watched her out of the corner of his eye as he talked, flashing her icy little smiles every few seconds. *Don't be silly. He's probably just nervous.* She wasn't convincing herself.

She returned to the living room and tried to control her rising panic. Should she try to get him to leave now? Maybe she should run for it. Of course, if she was wrong, she'd look like a fool running out of her own apartment.

She tried to think. What would John tell her? For a moment, she saw the look of relief on his face the night he came to her apartment. The night he thought Fitz Pardo was after her. This wasn't Pardo. What would Carnes tell her? She heard his voice in her head. *Run.* The fear rose in her throat. She spun toward the door.

Grayson stepped out of the kitchen, blocking her path. "Leave something in your car?" The smile was still frozen on his face. His eyes were cold. *The eyes are the windows to the soul.* She saw his hands clenched at his sides. Nausea seized her stomach.

"Uh, no." She tried to smile. "Uh, I have some baking to do, and I was wondering if you could"—her voice cracked—"wait in your car."

"You think I would be in your way?"

"No. Look. Let me be honest. I—uh—don't feel comfortable having someone I barely know in my apartment at this hour. I mean, the neighbors—"

He moved toward her. "The neighbors don't even know I'm here." The frozen smile again. "Nobody knows I'm here."

Becky tried to fight her panic. "I'm sorry, but if you don't leave, I'm going to scream."

Grayson stepped back. His face contorted into a little boy's pout. "Don't do that. I'm sorry. I didn't mean to make you feel uncomfortable. I'll go."

He started toward the door, his shoulders slumped in a picture of total dejection. *Thank God.* Becky felt a rush of relief. She'd been wrong. He just didn't want to wait in the heat. Maybe he only wanted company. He was only some poor, lonely guy. She felt guilty, but her hands were still trembling. At this point, she could live with a little guilt. She followed him toward the door to lock it behind him.

Grayson reached for the door. In a quick move, he twisted shut the top lock and engaged the security chain. Panic shooting through her, Becky backed away. Grayson pivoted and threw a punch at her head. Years of karate sparring had honed her reactions. She ducked to the side and threw her arm up in a block. His blow glanced off her arm, smacking her cheekbone and ear. The pain was terrible.

She staggered sideways and put out her hand to steady herself against the wall. She shook her head slightly and stepped back, a dizzying roar in her head. If he cleanly landed one of those punches, she'd be dead.

He lunged toward her and she danced sideways, slipping a foot between his legs and pushing him hard below the shoulder blade. He went down, and his head thumped against the wall next to the entrance to the kitchen. He grunted with pain but got up quickly.

"Fucking bitch!" He moved more cautiously now. "You'll pay for that. I'm gonna kill you real slow," he snarled through bared teeth. "I'll tear you apart." He feinted, and she leaped back. "You're going to beg me"— he feinted again—"to put you out of your misery."

She wanted to run. There was nowhere to go. She screamed as loud as she could.

He lunged at her, hands toward her throat. She ducked and pushed him away. Her legs felt as though they might collapse. *Be calm. Think! Four years of karate and jujitsu. Use it!* She backed toward the door.

He grinned. "If you don't fight, I may let you live." He took a step toward her. "I'm bigger and stronger. You don't have a chance, bitch."

She automatically dropped down into her fighting position, one foot behind the other, feet spread apart for balance. God! What was she doing? She needed more room to maneuver. "Watch out! I'm a brown belt in karate," she yelled. Her voice broke.

He laughed heartily. "Yeah, right. Your hands are licensed weapons. And I'm Muhammad Ali."

He lunged toward her with arms outstretched. She landed a quick three-punch combination to his head and ribs, then danced to the side. Her knuckles felt numb. She'd practiced the combination a thousand times but had never actually hit someone with it. It hurt her but didn't seem to faze him.

A look of amusement filled his face. "Ouch." He faked in her direction and laughed as she sprang back into the living room.

Great, she thought. Like hitting a rogue elephant with a flyswatter. As he moved, she tried to stay out of his reach, using the furniture and space to her advantage. At least she knew where everything was, so she could keep her eyes on him. "Damnit! Why are you doing this?" she panted.

Grayson seemed surprised. "You know. You Alpha Omega bitches humiliated me. You laughed at me."

Becky shook her head. "What are you talking about?"

"Nice try."

"No, really. What the hell do you mean?"

Grayson studied her. "Hell week. You made us dance. Strip. Don't deny it."

The image of the night flashed back to her. She'd been embarrassed for the guys and had wanted to leave. "I hated that," she said.

Anger flashed across Grayson's face. "You're just saying that to save yourself. You yelled at me. You laughed at me."

"No!" Becky said. "I was embarrassed. I felt bad for you. Honest!"

A look of uncertainty flickered over Grayson's face. Becky felt a surge of hope. A curtain of suspicion and rage dropped over his features. "You're lying." Grayson lunged at her again; she ducked under his hands and chopped hard at his side. Her hand glanced off his ribs. She didn't seem to be having any effect on him, but she was killing herself.

"I like fighters." Grayson faked in her direction and laughed at her reaction. "Anna Durant tried to fight me. You hear what I did to her?"

He threw a punch that glanced off her arm and caught her in the ribs, knocking the breath out of her. She gasped. He lunged for her throat. She ducked and scrambled away. The pain in her side was excruciating. She wanted to stop, to curl up on the floor.

"Anna fought." He panted slightly. His eyes glared. "I hurt her *real bad.*" He swung at her again. She caught the blow on her forearm. It went numb. Both of her arms felt like lead weights, useless.

Grayson moved to her right. "She begged to die."

He feinted to her right and then, as she reacted, to the left. Becky backed up and managed a deep breath. She fought the nausea. Her knuckles and arms were no longer as numb; they felt as though she'd been breaking cement blocks. She hadn't felt pain like this since she'd broken her arm as a child. Her head throbbed.

He lunged again and she leaped back. Her foot slipped off the edge of the carpet onto the bare wood floor. Oh, God, she thought. He's backing me into the corner.

Carnes didn't slow much coming off the ramp into Connecticut Avenue traffic. He sideswiped a car and sped down the hill past a small cluster of buildings. The car rumbled over some railroad tracks. He wove in and out of traffic, whipping past the Columbia and Chevy Chase country clubs, havens for Washington's rich and powerful. He sideswiped another car whipping around Chevy Chase circle, but he didn't stop.

He was in the District now. He flipped on his flasher as he accelerated down Connecticut. The radio crackled with activity. The Georgetown shooting. Barroom brawl in the Adams Morgan area. He sped along, steering crisply to avoid collisions, blaring his horn at cars in his path, stomping on the brake and then the accelerator as he wove wildly through traffic. He zipped past the Avalon theaters, a drugstore, a cluster of restaurants.

God! I've got to be in time. More stores, corner groceries, and restaurants raced by in his peripheral vision. He strained to hear radio traffic about Grayson. He heard a call. "Sitting on 4200. No sign of this Grayson." *Morons.* They had the wrong address. Becky lived in the 3200 block. They were over by Wisconsin Avenue. She lived off Connecticut. *Fucking idiots!* Carnes' clothes were sodden with sweat. His hands were so slippery he could barely hold the steering wheel. At this point, he was closer than the scout car. Carnes ran the light at Military Road, narrowly avoiding a car in the intersection. Apartment houses flashed by on either side now. A car ahead of him wasn't moving over to the right. "C'mon!" He pounded the horn. "C'mon!"

Grayson smiled. He seemed more confident now. Another few feet and he'd have her cornered. Without any room to maneuver, what chance would she have against his superior size and strength? Her mind raced. What could she do? *Concentrate!*

Grayson lunged at her, and she launched a moon kick at his head with her right foot. He ducked. Her foot caught him a glancing blow to the shoulder. He grabbed her right leg. He had her. She danced on the toes of her left foot, trying to keep her balance as he lifted her leg higher, stretching her muscles to the tearing point.

She fell and kicked at him with her left foot. The weight of her body and the blow allowed her to wrench her other leg loose. She rolled to the side as he leaped for her, then she scrambled to her feet. He had her wrist. She pulled but couldn't break his painful grip. She got off one, two quick front snap kicks. The second one caught him in the middle of the chest, and he let out an "oof" sound and released her wrist. She danced back.

He was sucking air, but upright. Worse, he stood between her and the door. Acid rose in her throat. She'd tried everything. He was too much for her. Her punches barely fazed him. If only she could run.

"Are you ready"—he panted—"to suffer, bitch?"

Karate class. What was the first thing she learned? Run away from a fight. *Yeah, right.* What was the second thing? A plump woman had asked, "What do you do if you're not very fast?"

"Break his leg." The instructor demonstrated a side kick to the side of the knee. "And run like hell."

Becky took a deep breath. If she missed, he'd have her leg again. Her rear foot slid slightly on the wood floor. She had no choice. She sidestepped slightly to get her rear foot onto the carpet. He moved toward her again. *Now or never.* She pushed off her rear leg, launching her entire weight at his knee in a classic side kick. The edge of her front foot landed above his knee.

"Fucking bitch!" he screamed, and he fell on his side with a thump that rattled the furniture.

She found herself on the floor and rolled quickly away from him. She thudded into a piece of furniture. She'd hit him too high! He had her by the left ankle now. She kicked wildly at his face with all her strength. He let go. She rolled away and up onto her feet. *Free!*

She danced on the balls of her feet the way she'd practiced, facing him. To her horror, he pulled himself erect, eyes wide with surprise and pain. "Fucking bitch!" Then he toppled like a newborn foal who hadn't yet learned to walk. *Thank God!*

Grayson lay on the floor moaning. "Fucking whore!" he bellowed, his face a mask of pain and rage. He struggled to get up again. Becky didn't wait to see if he would make it. She ran for the door. Another second and she'd escape.

Oh shit! The chain was on the door. She glanced back. Grayson half hopped, half lurched toward her. She hadn't hurt him as badly as she thought. Her numbed fingers fumbled with the locks for what seemed minutes. She had them. She pulled the door open.

An arm clamped around her neck. "Not so fast, bitch!" She couldn't breathe. She flailed desperately, connecting with hard flesh. No reaction. They fell to the floor. His weight knocked the remaining air out of her. Her chest burned. She saw bright lights. Then everything went dark.

Carnes swung off Connecticut, tires squealing. His light strobed the parked cars and apartment buildings as he raced down the block. There!

An Oldsmobile with Maryland plates. His stomach churned. Grayson was there! Carnes screeched to a halt and threw open the car door. He started to reach for the radio. No! Becky could die while he called for backup. He jumped out. The Glock appeared in his hand. His chest felt tight and he breathed in short gasps. Carnes started toward the door, the semiautomatic's reassuring weight in his hand.

Carnes' heart thumped an adrenaline drumbeat—D.C. street drums. *Am I in time?* He slipped off the safety, took a deep breath, and went through the main door to the apartment building, gun extended in a two-handed grasp. He hoped Grayson would be armed. Carnes wanted to exterminate him. The bureaucrats could take his damn badge. Sweep right. Sweep left. Nothing. He slid over to the steps.

The stairwell was dimly lit. Mugger heaven. The air was heavy with stale cooking odors. Carnes hated apartment living. He eased up the steps on his toes, listening for sounds of movement. A distant scream. It twisted his insides into a bundle of pain.

What's he doing to Becky? He pictured Grayson hovering over her with a knife, mutilating her. Fighting down a wave of nausea, Carnes threw caution aside like an old rag and dashed up the stairs, grabbing at the banister with one hand.

Going around the corner he slipped and banged his knee on the edge of the next step. *Oh shit. Can't put much weight on it.* He limped on, using the stair rail to help him maintain his balance.

The room faded in and out. Becky's arms ached. They were stretched over her head and out to the sides. Something pulled at her feet. She blinked her eyes and moved her head. Her hands were tied with pantyhose to the head of the bed. Grayson yanked roughly at her right leg and struggled to tie it to the foot of the bed. She screamed and kicked. Her leg came free. "Bastard!"

"Cunt!" Grayson jumped up, raised both hands clasped together in a double fist, and chopped down hard on her chest. The pain was crushing. She couldn't breathe.

Grayson worked on her legs again. Becky tried to move. Her legs wouldn't respond. Gasping, she watched in horror as he tied one leg to the bedpost, then the other. She felt completely exposed and totally vulnerable. At least she still had her clothes on.

Grayson stood and examined his handiwork. He started for the kitchen. Then he glanced at the apartment door. He relocked it and slid the chain into place.

Becky had regained some of her breath. "Help!" she cried weakly. Trying to scream hurt.

"Shut up, bitch." Grayson turned toward the dresser. He rummaged through the drawers. In the second drawer, he found a T-shirt. He grinned. "Perfect."

"Someone, help!" Becky's voice was hoarse, not much more than a whisper. "Stay away from me!" she hissed. "Stay away!"

"Keep at it." Grayson approached from her left side. "Open wide and say 'ah.'"

Becky clamped her mouth shut. Grayson slapped her hard. Forehand, backhand, forehand. Pain spread through her jaw. He jammed the wadded shirt against her mouth, smashing it against her lips and teeth. Her lips and gums felt as if he were using sandpaper.

"Like to fight?" Grayson grinned. "Me too." Still pressing the shirt to her lips with his left hand, he punched her hard in the stomach.

"Ooff!" Her mouth opened involuntarily and Grayson shoved in the shirt. She couldn't even bite his fingers. She tried to scream. Only a muffled, mewling noise emerged.

Grayson walked back to the kitchen. A rectangular wooden knife block sat on the counter. He pulled out a long carving knife and appraised it for a moment. His lips twisted perversely. He pushed it back into the block with a thunk. The next knife had a six-inch blade. Grayson balanced it in his hand, then tried it against the back of his fingernails. "Poifect."

Carnes emerged from the stairs into the hall. He saw movement. A silver-haired woman with dark-rimmed glasses stared at him from the doorway of an apartment next to Becky's.

"Police, ma'am," said Carnes.

She stared at his gun for a moment, then ducked back into her apartment and slammed the door. He heard the latch click. He hobbled toward Becky's apartment. No sounds emerged.

He tried to still his panting as he put his ear against the door. Footsteps. A groaning noise. His hand crept to the knob. Locked. *Shit!* He pounded on the metal door.

"Detective Carnes! Open the fucking door, Grayson! Give yourself up!"

"Fuck you!"

"Open the door, Grayson!"

"Sure. I was just about to invite you in."

"Open it. You need help."

"No. Your girlfriend needs help. And I'm going to help her."

"Wait! We can talk!"

"I don't want to talk."

"Give up, Grayson!"

"I'm not a quitter."

"You touch her and I'll rip out your guts with my bare hands."

"Now you're talking. That's what *I'm* gonna do—with her."

"Touch her, Grayson, and you'll regret it—big time!"

"I'm an existentialist. I have no regrets."

Becky heard Carnes at the door. *Thank God!* But Grayson wasn't giving up. He pushed the couch against the door and piled a chair on top. Then he walked toward her, the knife glinting in his hand. Panic seized her again. She fought a sudden urge to pee. He leaned closer to her. "This is gonna be fun. I always wanted an audience." He turned toward the door. "Listen to this, cop!" He pulled the gag from her mouth. He dug the tip of the knife into her throat. "Scream, bitch."

"He has a knife!" she yelled.

She heard a hard thump against the door. Then another. The door had barely moved. *Oh, God!*

"I love secure doors," said Grayson. "The extra lock was a wise move. Don't want to encourage burglars."

Tears pooled in Becky's eyes. "Why me?"

"You laughed at me, bitch. You won't laugh at me again. Ever."

"Huh?"

He grabbed at the front of her blouse and pulled. A button flew off and the blouse parted. She heard the fabic tear at a seam. The pounding continued at the door. *Get him talking. It worked in the movies.* "Laugh at you? I—I don't understand. What do you mean?"

"I love these superbras." Grayson stuck a finger under the fabric that joined the cups and lifted. He let it snap back.

"Stop!" Becky cried. She breathed deeply, trying to regain control. "Why—why are you doing this?" She heard the tremor in her voice.

Grayson slipped the knife under the front of the bra. Becky winced as the tip scratched her skin, drawing blood. He pulled up, severing the material. "I like to." He lifted the cups and pushed them aside. He sighed appreciatively. "Nice tits. Too bad they can't stay that way." He dragged the tip of the knife across her breast.

Becky tried to sink down into the mattress. "No!" she screamed.

"That's more like it!"

"Leave me alone. Please."

Grayson grabbed her left nipple and pinched it hard.

Becky bit her lip. "Please. I've never done anything to you." The pounding on the door increased—loud thumps that vibrated the pictures on the wall.

"That's better. Beg." He twisted her nipple hard.

"That hurts!" Becky cried. "Stop. Please stop."

"Beg!"

"Open up or you're dead, Grayson," Carnes shouted. "You hear me?" The thumping on the door continued.

"She has nice nipples!" Grayson yelled. "You know how I love nipples!"

Carnes' shoulder was numb. He'd thrown his body against the door repeatedly. Grayson was out of control. He had to know he wasn't going to get out of there alive if he harmed Becky. He didn't seem to care. *What is he doing now?* Carnes had to get in there before it was too late.

Carnes pulled out the Glock and took aim at the top lock. He fired. The report was deafening in the narrow hall. He felt a hot, searing pain in his cheek and felt blood dripping down his face. Must have been a metal fragment. The lock seemed virtually undamaged. *Shit.* She'd followed the advice he gave her the night he thought Pardo was after her. She'd had a locksmith put in a high-quality lock. He wondered where the rest of the richochet had gone. No more shooting. He might not damage the lock much but he could harm Becky or a neighbor.

He heard Becky cry out in again. *Think.* There must be another way in. Maybe a window? He pounded on the neighbor's door.

"Go away! I've called the police."

"I *am* the police!"

No response.

"Please! Open up!"

Still no response.

"I'm holding my ID up to the peephole. Please open the door. Look!"

Carnes waited. Nothing. He heard a scream. "Please! He's killing her!" Then he heard it. The sliding of metal on metal. The door opened. *Thank God!*

The woman wouldn't meet his eye. "I was frightened."

Carnes rushed past her. "You have a balcony?"

"Y-yes." She pointed to the sliding door.

Another scream penetrated the wall. He ran to the sliding door.

Grayson had pulled off her skirt. He ran the knife blade under one panty leg and, with a quick upward flick of his wrist, cut the fabric. The knife blade trailed up her leg. He jammed the tip into her hip hard enough to break the skin. "Stop!" she cried. Tears coursed down her cheek. "Please." He cut the other piece of fabric and pulled off her panties, totally exposing her.

"Very nice." Grayson pursed his lips as though to whistle. "But a little too hairy for my taste." He grabbed a handful of hair and pulled hard.

"Uhhh!" Becky's body arched, and her head whipped from side to side.

"That's very good." He seized another handful of hair and pulled it away from her pubic mound. Then he ran the knife through the hair, half cutting, half pulling it out. She moaned.

Grayson sprinkled the hair in her face. He stood back to admire his handiwork. "Much better. Now, we can *really* get started."

Carnes leaned over the balcony. *Oh shit!* He could barely see in Becky's window, and her balcony had to be at least five feet away. He looked down, felt dizzy. He grabbed for the rail. God, he hated heights. What were his choices? Wait for backup? Hope they could take down the door? There wasn't time. He had to act.

If he stood on the edge of this balcony outside the rail, could he reach her balcony? Maybe, if he could reach the rail and get a toehold. Carnes glanced down. *A big mistake!* Everything started to swim around him. He closed his eyes.

Becky screamed again. Carnes holstered his Glock and swung a leg over the railing. He faced the brick wall as he swung the other leg over. He planted his feet firmly on the edge. *Eyes level. Don't look down. Breathe deeply.* He twisted until his body faced the wall. He reached for the rail of Becky's balcony, extending his fingers until every muscle ached. Not quite. He tried reaching out a foot. No. Too far. Only one way. He'd have to jump. If he missed—

He braced his back against the rail, held on, and took a deep breath. Then he launched himself at Becky's balcony. His body hit hard against the rail; his fingers clawed at the top edge. *Got it.* A jolt of pain in his shoulders, fingers scraped raw, legs numb and bruised. He tasted blood—

must have hit his face. Frantically, he sought a purchase with his feet. He found a ridge. The stress on his arms eased.

What if Grayson heard him? He must have sounded like a ton of bricks hitting the rail. Breathing rapidly, he pulled himself up and peered over the edge. Grayson stood by Becky's head holding a hank of hair in one hand, a knife in the other. He seemed lost in his own world.

Feet scraping ineffectually against the side rails of the balcony, Carnes struggled to get a knee up over the top rail. His knee slipped. Weathered metal sliced through his pants, taking skin and flesh with it. The edge cut cruelly into his fingers, but his grip held. He wanted to scream with the pain and frustration.

There! Carnes felt his body weight tipping over the railing. He focused all his effort on getting one leaden leg and then the other over the edge. He looked in.

Grayson ran the knife along Becky's ribs. Through the window Carnes heard her gurgling cry and saw a pinprick of red where the knife had paused. Grayson ran the knife tip slowly across her stomach and toward her chest. Carnes pulled at the sliding door. Locked. He reached into his holster and pulled out the Glock, his eyes frozen on the scene in her bed.

Grayson grabbed Becky's nipple between his thumb and forefinger and pulled it up. He slid the knife up over her breast. *Oh, my God! He's going to cut off her nipple!* Grayson was saying something to Becky, but Carnes couldn't hear. Carnes pressed the Glock against the glass. *Can't risk a head shot. Too easy to miss.* Carnes sighted along the barrel at Grayson's chest. The knife was only an inch from Becky's elongated nipple! Carnes squeezed the trigger. The Glock fired, and a small hole centered a spiderweb of cracks in the glass.

Grayson stared dumbly at the window, a dark stain spreading on his shirt. He staggered back and stuck a hand out against the wall. Then he toppled over, slowly at first, then gaining momentum like a felled tree.

Carnes swung the grip of the Glock against the spiderwebbed glass. It broke in a shower of fragments. He reached through and groped for the latch. It took all the strength in his punished fingers. He slid the door open and fell into the room headfirst.

Carnes rolled and made it to his feet. Becky's body convulsed in sobs. Everything sounded tinny to Carnes. "Twitch, Grayson, and you're history," Carnes said. He sidestepped around the bed, both hands holding the Glock out in front of him. Grayson lay on the floor, facedown, hand extended toward the knife. His body trembled uncontrollably. Shock. A red pool spread out from beneath him. Carnes stepped on Grayson's wrist and picked up the knife. Grayson groaned a stream of obscenities.

Keeping Grayson in his peripheral vision, Carnes sat on the edge of the bed and began cutting loose Becky's arms. She tried to speak through the sobs. Carnes put his arms around her and felt her arms encircle his neck. She held him tight. Something special—something unprecedented in his experience—passed between them.

"Hurts," Becky said.

He didn't realize how hard he'd been squeezing her. He released his grip and smiled. "Me too." Carnes heard the sound of approaching sirens and, moments later, the squeal of brakes. He cut her legs free. "I need to let them in." He took in her nakedness. "You need some clothes." Becky's expression was dazed. "Something to wear."

Finally, she pointed at her closet. "In there."

He got a purple terrycloth robe. While wrapping her in it he took stock of the bruises and lacerations. He saw nothing serious.

Carnes looked down at Grayson, who was trembling, losing lots of blood. "Grayson?"

"Fuck you," Grayson gasped. He moaned like a child.

Carnes felt the anger drain out of him. He expected to hate Grayson; instead he felt pity for him. How could he feel pity? Grayson had viciously tortured and killed his victims. He would've done the same to Becky. Carnes shook his head and went to the door.

Carnes emerged into the summer night. He breathed deeply. His hands and cheek were a patchwork of bandages. His body sagged with weariness. He didn't care. Although the night was still hot and steamy, the air seemed cleaner, more refreshing than any he'd ever breathed. So much better than the medicinal air in the hospital.

A few of the brighter stars and the moon conquered the haze. As he limped toward the car, his legs wobbled.

Rodriguez walked beside him. He had waited patiently at the hospital for Carnes to be released. "How you doing?" Rodriguez asked.

"OK," Carnes said. He shook his head slightly. "Exhausted really. What happened to Grayson?"

"DOA at shock-trauma."

"Hell, no wonder," said Carnes. He rubbed his eyes, trying to put the memory fragments into the right order. "First, the fire department sent a fire truck, no paramedic or anything. That took fifteen minutes. Then, ten, maybe fifteen minutes later the ambulance arrived. Attendant took one look and called for the 'copter. Didn't start an IV or do shit. By the time the chopper got there, Grayson had probably died of boredom."

"Internal bleeding, heart failure—take your pick," Rodriguez said.

"Last time I criticize the D.C. ambulance service," Carnes said sardonically.

"Yeah," Rodriguez agreed. "Becky?"

"They're holding her overnight."

"How is she?"

"A cracked rib or two. Lots of bruises, minor physical damage. Otherwise? We'll cross our fingers." Carnes shrugged. "She'll be sore for a while, but she's pretty tough. Had to convince her to stay in the hospital."

"She had a rough time," Rodriguez said.

"Yeah. But as I said, she's strong. Give her a few weeks, she should be OK."

"And you?" Rodriguez asked.

"It hasn't all sunk in yet." Carnes stopped. "First time I shot anyone."

"Huh?"

"Just a statement of fact."

"How do you feel about it?"

"Dr. Rodriguez now?" Carnes smiled. "Honestly, I'm numb."

"I guess that's normal. The department'll probably want you to take some leave. Review the shooting. Get you in the counseling program."

"I don't know," said Carnes.

Rodriguez put his hand on Carnes' shoulder. "Hey, there's nothing wrong with getting help if you need it."

"Yeah. Well, we'll see." Carnes couldn't even begin to think about what lay ahead for him and Becky, but he had a sense that whatever it was, they would go through it together. He stared back at the hospital. "Maybe I should stay."

"Heck, she's probably already asleep. She'll be all right for the night." Rogriguez snorted. "What's left of it."

"Yeah. Probably. Where's Del?"

"I sent him home."

"Good idea." Carnes rubbed his eyes. His hands hurt like hell; his arms were dead.

"Captain wants to see us in the morning," Rodriguez said. "Pardo's on the warpath about suing us for harassment."

"Bullshit!"

"Yes. Worst comes to worst, I guess they'll let him walk on the drug charges."

They arrived at their cars. "Do me a favor?" asked Carnes.

Rodriguez nodded.

"I gotta go home to my daughter. Not sure I have the strength to drive."

"You want *me* to drive?" said Rodriguez with mock surprise. "Thought you hated the way I drive."

"I love the way you drive."

"I'll remind you of that when you're better." Rodriguez climbed into the driver's seat of his car.

Carnes fell asleep before they left the parking lot.